Mwalgi

Justice

Cover art by Suzanne Helmigh. Copyright © 2015 by Colette Black
Editing by Jen Hendricks

Published in the United States by
Drapukamo Publishing
PO Box 21
Higley, AZ 85236

Noble Ark, winner of the 2014 Howey Award

"The characters in Noble Ark really leap off the page. Particularly in Aline and Lar, Black gives us a classic and complicated story of love and friendship that transcends all odds. She presents complex emotional and ethical themes that should resonant for all ages. Indeed, Black has set the table for a fascinating series, and I for one am eager to see what fate awaits these characters in future volumes."

—Evan Braun, author, The Book of Creation (The Watchers Chronicle)

"The plot kept moving as more details about their world became known. The story moves fluidly from scene to scene. It kept me turning the pages, kept me wanting more. It has excellent pacing, there was never a dull moment in the entire book. I never wanted to skip any page because each scene brings a new discovery and new questions that I was eager to get answered."

—Sporadic Reads

"A refreshing new take on scifi and aliens. The Mwalgi Colette Black has come up with are a unique race of aliens that I find fascinating. ...Another thing I liked about "Noble Ark" was the technology. Instead of using some form of energy weapon like every clichéd scifi out there, the combatants aboard Noble Ark use what they call acid guns. ...There are force fields, and the Gi use a sort of stun gun the humans call a paralyzer to immobilize their prey. (The paralyzers kind of reminded me of the Wraith stunners in the TV show "Stargate Atlantis," and anything that reminds me of "Stargate" is a good thing."

Desolation

"Colette Black weaves a tense story of forbidden love set within the pressure-cooker confines of an alien starship. Her rich characters claw their way into your heart as they struggle to overcome extreme physical and racial obstacles. Bravo on a tale well told. I can't wait for the next installment."

—Scott Eder, author, Knight of the Flame (The Knights Elementalis)

"An exciting read, "Desolation" continues the Mankind's Redemption Series with enough unexpected twists, close calls and breath-holding moments to keep you on the edge of your seat."

—Kaitlynn (on Amazon.com)

Mwalgi Justice

"Mwalgi Justice is an action-packed, character-driven story that brings new meaning to the term 'star-crossed lovers.' Colette Black offers a new and engaging perspective to alien-human interactions."

—Sean Golden, author, Warrior (The War Chronicles series)

Mwalgi Justice

Colette Black

Also by Colette Black

To my Dad,
for always believing
in impossible dreams.

Prologue:

Calianda's last hope appeared in the form of a tall, half-Mwalgi, supposedly the only one in existence. It had to be Larkin Trovgar, the man she'd helped escape from her former ship, the impossible part-human/part-Mwalgi who had called her "Andi."

As Lar exited his sleek hover-car on the far end of the bare expanse surrounding Calianda and her fellow human prisoners, she felt sure of it. That dark, curly hair was unmistakable, even at such a distance. Full-blood Mwalgis' hair was white. Following him was a woman dressed in the same tsefuur slave clothing as Calianda, the hood of the body-encompassing clothing, near-identical to her own, releasing a thin strand of auburn-red hair a couple shades darker than Andi's. That must be Aline. Lar's love. But why would she wear such clothing, marking her as a tsefuur, slave to the Gi for her spinal fluid?

Didn't matter. He was her only hope.

"Lar!" she yelled over the heads of taller prisoners, mostly full-grown women instead of young teens like herself. "Larkin Trovgar!"

Lar turned in her direction as a guard slammed the butt of his gun into Calianda's shoulder, sending her to the dirt. Under the Gi's red-dwarf sun, the cracked soil appeared a dried up scab. No trees, no buildings, and no shade. The entire planet, draped in shades of blood, reminded Calianda of death, of that place religious believers said the wicked go after they die. Hell. But even hell would be preferable to living as a slave on this forsaken world.

She pulled away from the hot earth, cupping her mouth. "Lar! Save me! It's Calianda!" He might not remember that name. "Andi!"

The soldier's gun struck between her shoulder blades, forcing her prostrate across the burning surface. The poly-alum links at her arms and legs brought those prisoners closest to her down as well. The heat cooked at her clothes, the sunbaked planet burning the skin of her left cheek.

The women grumbled.

"Stop your yelling, stupid girl," said the dark-haired one from behind. "You're going to get us all killed."

"I wish they'd kill me," said Calianda into the dirt. She writhed against the pressure of the soldier's gun. "Lar!"

The soldier gripped the back of her neck, lifting her. Then he changed his grip, turning her level with his face. He said something in Mwalgi, his scaled mouth sneering like a dog baring its teeth. Over his shoulder, far in the distance, Aline stepped back into the car. Lar stared straight at Calianda, his circleh doy covering his entire eye socket, appearing black in the distance like some monster from a horror movie. But that didn't make sense. If he'd found Aline, found his wife, his eyes should have turned gold.

"Lar! You found me!" She let herself smile, relaxing in the grip of the soldier.

Void of expression, Larkin entered the vehicle, a dark shell descending over the shiny hovercar like a hinged bowl.

The soldier shook Calianda, yelling more insults, spitting in her face as the protective hood fell back from her bright hair. A line of flesh along her neckline, exposed by the drooping hood from the Gi's jostling, seared in pain. They'd missed applying protective cream that far down and the seal to her skin wasn't holding. Exposed to Lenfay's atmosphere, it stung like a slow-building chemical burn.

Mwalgi Justice

Calianda whimpered, not expecting mercy and not getting any. If she could just die then this whole nightmare would be over. Lar had forsaken her. He had played at being her friend on the ship. He'd convinced her to help him escape, running to his Gi friends, taking the woman he supposedly loved, his Aline, prisoner like his people had taken Calianda. He must have known his fellow Mwalgi would come after their ship. Had Lar known they would kill her father?

She cringed, remembering the thrust of the Gi soldier's extractor, extending from his middle finger into Da's back, taking spinal fluid. Da had already been dead as they'd brutally slaughtered his body, just for fun.

The Gi soldier holding her finally stopped yelling and pulled the hood back over Calianda's head, leaving her to sweat in the confining fabric rather than burn to death.

The hint of a smile creased her features as she remembered the consequences to that murdering Gi who'd taken Da. Within minutes, the Gi had become violently ill. His friends had rushed him back to their ship but he must have died. For the first time, Calianda had been grateful for her father's Chaerlish beetle addiction. It had turned him violent, a husk of the man he'd once been, but because of the high concentration of drug in his body there was one less Gi in the universe.

The soldier at her side dragged her to follow the other women toward a waiting vehicle similar to the hovercar but much larger, some kind of hover-bus.

He yelled at them in Mwalgi, as if they should understand. He pointed to the bus. "Ohfertsoog." Pointing a gun at them, something from an era before lasers, he made it obvious what would happen if they didn't get into the bus-like vehicle he called an ohfertsoog.

The woman in front of her shuffled ahead. When Calianda paused at the open hatch, the dark-haired woman shoved her inside. It smelled of sweat, and urine, and old blood. She pushed away thoughts of what would happen next, seeking the numb

3

calm the other women seemed to have found. For Calianda, her last sliver of hope had driven away in a black hovercar.

The sight of humans in chains, something her people hadn't had to endure since centuries before their arrival on Saeana, made Aline's gut churn. Not only was it illegal by the five-systems' charter, but it was also more proof of Mwalgi barbarism. It continued to baffle her that they could be so technologically advanced and yet so brutal. She leaned her head against Lar's shoulder, willing her stomach to calm.

"Why in desolation is the old Kerger place full of prisoners?" Lar asked as Jeraud's cruiser started down the road again. They'd traveled from the city, to suburbs, to a mixture of suburb, empty land, and farms with barbarous plants similar to cacti in Saeanan's dry regions.

"Not prisoners," Jeraud corrected. "Community tsefuurs. You know Saeanan cerebrospinal fluid providers are essential to our species."

Aline scowled, but Lar responded with much more diplomacy than she would have managed. "Calling them comm-tsefies doesn't change what they are. They're Saeanans forced to live in cramped living spaces, always sick, their spinal fluid repeatedly extracted until their bodies or minds break. That's not a provider, Jeraud; that's a prisoner and a slave."

With a shrug, Jeraud dismissed the bedraggled Saeanans as if they meant nothing more than a herd of cattle pressed into a slaughter chute. "They opened a new camp west of here. For some reason, they load the Saeanans in the outskirts rather than the city. I'm just glad they don't let them get close to Vazber." He shuddered. "I'd hate to have them in our city when they need a bathroom break or something."

Aline opened her mouth again, but Lar placed two fingers over her lips and shook his head. Was this the same man who couldn't hear his mother called livestock without extending a talon? Regardless of how Jeraud had made himself appear full-Mwalgi, something that still didn't make sense to Aline, their mother was Saeanan. Why would Lar let him treat her and the poor slaves on that deserted waste of land like nothing more than shipped commodities?

Fifteen minutes later, a sign marked an invisible line between the "outskirts" and the suburb of Vazber. After a few twists, they turned into a narrow street on the western side. Away from the predominant apartment dwellings, the homes finally had some space between them—the wealthy district. Among almost any species, on any world, in any city, some markers remained constant. The more space someone owned, the more money they had. They stopped in front of a home much bigger than those they'd passed, one of only three on the street with two stories. Light-absorbing, solar windows fronted the entire home and the roof was made of traditional solar panels, sturdy, colored a dark orange by the red sun.

Aline had thought it would take time, at least a few hours before the council would be able to initiate their mandated surveillance of Lar, their supposed criminal, but at least eight guards circled the opulent home.

In part, Aline felt gratitude for Jeraud's sudden appearance at Cloud's court proceedings. Had it only been that morning that Cloud had tried to take possession of Aline as his tsefuur? Actually, he'd succeeded. If Jeraud hadn't shown up, Lar would have been in prison or dead. Jeraud had allowed Aline to talk with Lar, enter the fighting arena with him, and stopped the announcer from giving Lar the electric shocks that were keeping him from his lung medicine. With Aline's accidental confession in the Des-olashon's brig, Peltay and the prosecutors had all they needed to prove that Lar had killed the Mwalgi monsters who had attacked her and her ship Thanks to Jeraud, Lar would be under surveil-lance for a week instead of going straight to jail. Now, however, it seemed Jeraud's good intentions were both finished and regretted.

Face taut, he stepped from the car. For the first time since meet-ing the taciturn lawyer, Aline thought the brothers might have something in common. Though Jeraud seemed to have a longer fuse, his temper flared just like Lar's, his golden eyes flashing trou-ble and talons flicking in and out of their arm sheaths like the agitated twitch of a cat's tail.

"Who is your superior officer?" Jeraud bellowed at the closest soldier.

"Berat Steinren," the soldier snapped, moving to continue his part in the complex parade around the house, but Jeraud's next words stopped him. "Let him know I'll be bringing him up on legal charges and I'm going to make sure all of his men receive formal reprimands."

That stopped the man up short. "We have orders, straight from Council-President Voserhab himself."

Jeraud sneered, his Mwalgi scales bunching in small folds of silver around his nose and mouth. "Councilman Voserhab is on suspension pending a hearing by the council and will likely be brought up on charges by the end of the month. The mandate you received from the council states that you are to 'keep a watch surrounding my property, and vigilant surveillance of the pris-oner.' It does not say you are to surround my home and scare my children into early talon development! The property line is clearly marked by the hedges in the front, a white fence in back. Stay behind it!"

"Look, here." The officer stepped up, puffing out his chest. "No civvie is going to tell the TMP what to do and how to do it. I—"

Jeraud's talons flicked farther from their sheaths. "I'm the man who had Voserhab kicked out of office, the man who arranged for Trovgarkont Militar Politz to watch my brother, and I'm the man who can make sure you're demoted to a brigade officer instead of berat if you don't get these people out of my yard!"

Another man, burlier, swinging his wide arms back and forth like he'd prefer to crush a pile of bricks, stomped across the manicured rocks to join them. "What's the problem here, berat? Why are you chatting with this half-Saeanan civilian instead of making your rounds?"

Aline noted Jeraud's barely contained sneer, but when the hoptberat spit at Jeraud's feet he didn't twitch.

"Are you the hoptberat in charge?" he asked.

"Yes, and we'll carry out our orders without civilian interference, thank you."

"You probably didn't read those orders very carefully," Jeraud's mild tone somehow frightened Aline more than his extended talon. "Regardless of my heritage, I am Jeraud Trovgar, the attorney involved in this case. I've already explained your orders to your berat and what I will do if they're not followed. I suggest you listen to him. You have one hour."

Jeraud stalked up his walkway, a set of dark red stones sculpted so only a few centimeters of the yard's pale pink rocks fit between each one. His scaled feet slapped each paver as if he wished to snap them in half, making his way up granite steps, across a large granite porch, then disappearing through the front doorfield.

The hoptberat's stare turned malevolent as he followed Jeraud's retreating back then turned to Lar, letting his fangs extend. "I can't wait until you try to escape half-breed. I'll cut you in half then have livestock for dessert."

As Aline had expected from Lar when Jeraud had made similar statements, Lar's talons fully extended, their marbled surface a rusty pink and black under the sun's glare. She took hold of his arm before he could do something rash.

The hoptberat laughed and returned to his people.

With a wary eye on the angry patrollers, Lar took Aline's hand.

After so much time on the Mwalgi ship, with Cloud bonded to

her and always touching her hand or stroking her arm, Aline automatically flinched. He frowned, releasing his tenuous grip and gesturing for her to go ahead. Aline almost reached for him, but it was too awkward. She didn't know if she should take Lar's hand, embrace him, or keep her distance.

She'd believed him dead. Cloud had almost convinced Aline to become his wife, and now Lar was back and Cloud was dead, and the whole mess was Aline's fault. She had developed feelings for Cloud, but she'd never stopped missing Lar. Was she a traitor to one or the other, or both? Did she dare even trust her own feelings as she and Lar continued from one dangerous situation to another, saving one another's lives? Maybe it was combat-love, the kind that occurs between two people who become interdependent on one another during times of stress, but when peace comes they realize they're strangers. There were no answers, at least no easy ones.

Passing beneath two large trees, more like a hulking morass of twisting branches, the sun-stained leaves no bigger than orange-brown sunflower seeds, Aline paused at the threshold. She'd faced Mwalgi, fought impossible odds, all without hesitation, but meeting Lar's family terrified her in a way she didn't know how to confront.

She stepped aside. "Go ahead."

Lar glanced at the circling soldiers. "I don't want to leave you out here by yourself."

"I won't wait more than a minute. If any of the soldiers come close, I'll get inside. I just need a moment."

With a last glance at the men and women being called by the hoptberat to the thorn bushes fronting the rock yard, Lar nodded and stepped through the doorfield.

Aline took a few deep breaths. How bad could it be, right? Jeraud seemed colder than she'd expected. Actually, he was horrible, but Lar had grown up around these people; they were his family. He was an amazing man, and he talked so fondly of them, so they couldn't all be like Jeraud...she hoped. Another deep breath and she followed Lar inside.

The situation immediately reminded her of the day she'd taken him to meet the Tanakas aboard the Noble Ark. Children screamed as Aline entered, just like Michiko and Jody had, but Michiko and Jody had been teasing each other and screaming in play. These screams held legitimate fear.

A Mwalgi woman, probably Jeraud's wife, sat on a bright purple couch near the wall. One child gripped her side, head buried against her scaled chest, the child's wide shoulders covering most of the bright yellow beyesh that child-bearing Mwalgi wore. This beyesh appeared as something between a bikini and halter top. The other child, a wide-eyed, screaming baby, sat on her lap. They stared at Aline as they wailed.

Adding to the cacophony of noise, Aline's surroundings were a turbulence of color. The purple couch, bright green cushions, even the lemon-yellow curtains in the adjoining kitchen, screamed a challenge to the red-drenched hues Lenfay's sun continually forced on the planet's inhabitants.

Lar stood in the middle of the room, a Mwalgi woman wrapped around his neck. The room smelled of mint and strawberries, or something similar to strawberries, though Aline wasn't sure if the perfume was part of the house or emanated from the girl. Who in desolation could she be? He'd claimed he'd never felt anything for another woman besides Aline, not even the slightest emotional interest to make him breeyae and start changing the color of his eyes. Yet the girl gripped him pretty tight for someone who wasn't either a family member or something more.

Aline waited, pulling at the neck of the tsefuur jumpsuit Cloud had forced her to wear, its billowing folds covering her from head to toe. Though still warm, the home was a relief from the sweltering heat outside. The biting sensation she'd experienced where her skin had been exposed, like the prickling of thousands of red-hot needles, had disappeared. The breather had stopped its thrumming, suggesting the air in the home was clean, pure, and Aline hoped, fully breathable. She'd love to be rid of the stupid device Cloud had crammed down her throat when she'd stepped from the Trovgarshtodt city transport into Lenfay's atmosphere, but she should probably wait to be sure.

The girl released Lar. Her high cheeks, bright eyes, and girlish demeanor suggested she was near Aline's age, though she wore a beyesh. Aline leaned forward to get a closer look. She hadn't seen that indigo shade of circleh doy ringing a Mwalgi's ice-blue iris since before she and Lar had bonded, turning his eyes gold. This must be his younger sister, Meladise. It didn't make sense, though. This girl appeared full Mwalgi and the way she filled out her blue, bandeau-style beyesh suggested she'd had at least one child. Yet, her eyes weren't gold, so she couldn't be married or bonded or whatever.

Taking in Aline, Meladise clapped her hands together, slapping Lar on the chest in excitement.

Aline relaxed, sharing in the woman's smile.

"I can't believe it." Meladise hugged Lar again. "A tsefuur! Jeraud refuses to let me own one, but now he can't refuse. Nobody at school can harass me and call me livestock if I have a tsefuur. This is beyond orbital!"

Aline's grin froze, melting into a tight grimace.

"No," said Lar, but his sister wasn't listening.

"Bow, tsefuur," said Meladise, raising her chin to look down her narrow nose. "You should be standing behind your master, so now you must bow to me." She giggled and turned to Lar. "I've heard you have to really teach them how to behave, right to begin with, or else they can give you a lot of trouble."

Aline couldn't believe this. First, Jeraud treating the Saeanans like livestock. Now, Meladise thinking Aline had shown up as her personal slave.

Lar stepped between Aline and his sister. "She. Is. Not. A. Tsefuur."

Meladise put her hands on her hips, voice rising to match her brother's. "Look at her. She has to be."

Was the girl being obtuse or just refusing to accept what was obvious. Either way, she had a point. Aline wasn't going to go another minute collared like a Mwalgi slave, even if that collar came in the form of a baggy gray jumpsuit. She released all of the fastening tape and pulled the suit off, careful not to rip the fabric in case she needed it later. Then she reached down her throat, coughing and gagging until she removed the breather Cloud had forced on her before pulled off the strange lenses that had protected her eyes. The air felt clean, as pure as any spaceship. She took a deep breath. From what Lar had told Aline of their planet, Jeraud must own an expensive filter to make the air this comfortable. If their family was as hated as Lar had told her, how could he afford such luxuries?

"How dare you," Meladise hissed. "A tsefuur dressing like a Mwalgi. You have no right."

Aline stepped around Lar. "I'll never be anybody's stinking tsefuur."

Lar gave her a quick glance, the twitch of a grin flickering across his face as he took in her boy-shorts underwear and bra. Aline didn't care. It covered enough, and she was not going to dress like one of their slave-tsefuurs for one more second.

"You have to have noticed my eyes by now." Lar said to Meladise.

"I thought you'd fallen for one of the women soldiers. You will be okay, won't you?"

He took another appreciative glance at Aline. "I hope so."

Jeraud entered the room, his silver-white hair gone, replaced with a dark bristle that covered his entire scalp. His face was now bare, showing a narrower version of Lar's masculine face. His only visible scales were on his neck, hands, and swirled up his arms, an exact replica of Lar.

"What you're refusing to accept, Mela," Jeraud drawled, "is that the Saeanan is his wife."

Meladise' gaze narrowed. Jeraud may as well have pointed out Lar marrying a dog, and maybe to them, it seemed that way. But their mother was Saeanan! Jeraud's reappearance, devoid of all the scales and now showing his bristled hair, proved that. Could they see her like the other Mwalgi did, some subservient beast to be harvested and discarded, but never to think, love, or be loved? Not

Lar's own family.

Meladise spat at Aline, who moved easily to one side, letting the spittle sit on the carpeted floor.

"Meladise!" Jeraud's wife reprimanded.

"I didn't make him bond to me." Aline chuckled, remembering how she'd felt tricked when she'd discovered the golden circleh doy around Lar's sea-blue irises. "I didn't even realize—"

Talons suddenly extended, Meladise jumped around Lar with the grace of a panther as muscles bulged beneath her scales. Lar's sister was going to be every bit as good of a fighter as her big brother.

Aline knew Lar's family might not appreciate him showing up with a wife, especially considering all the complications they were bringing with them, but she hadn't expected an attempted murder. But there was no mistaking the fact that Meladise's talons were aimed to kill.

Under normal circumstances Aline could have stepped out of the way and dealt with the girl, but this day hadn't come close to normal. Exhausted from joining Lar's fight against Tenrick Leutsimmer, and still dehydrated from her time on the Mwalgi collections vessel, Aline was in no position to challenge anything more than Lenfay's increased gravity. And Lar wasn't in much better shape. His time as a prisoner aboard the Saeanan ship had kept him from Aline for so long he'd started another round of severance. His circleh doy was more than half black, he was weak, and he kept experiencing random muscles spasms. Added to that, though his lungs now sounded clear, he was still recovering from the acid darts he'd been shot with during his capture.

But when Meladise struck, Aline didn't have time to think about their disadvantages. Letting Lenfay's excessive gravity help her for once, she dropped to the carpet right on top of Meladise's spit, and rolled to one side. The crack of clashing talons sounded above her head.

As Aline struggled to a crouch, Lar and Meladise were locked, talon to talon. Meladise pushed Lar down, forcing him to one knee, satisfaction glowing in her blue eyes. She shifted her stance, switching her attention to Aline for another attempt. That was her mistake.

Taking advantage of her shift in strength and attention, Lar threw her arm to the side, pounded a clenched fist to her shoulder blade, and swiped his talon across her back. Aline watched in horror as Meladise's scales ripped with the sound of tearing fabric. Jeraud shoved both of his siblings back as the claw did its damage, but Aline still expected to see blood stream from the wound. Instead, Meladise sported only a faint red line along a patch of skin while a few drips of near-clear skalwass leaked like blue-tainted water from her real scales.

Jeraud stood between his siblings, looking from one to the other with a glare that could melt steel. He raised his head, yelling a Mwalgi challenge. Immediately, the tension broke. Here was this big brute of a man, almost as tall as Lar, and his yell didn't sound much better than Aline's—a sick cat compared to Lar's lion of a roar. Aline held back a snicker.

"Don't laugh," whispered Lar, crouching next to her in fighting stance. "He's very sensitive about it."

"Then why does he do it?"

"Because I get angry," Jeraud answered, a hint of a smile peeking from his stern expression before he forced it back and turned on Meladise. "You have insulted our species and our family by your lack of control."

Meladise raised her arms as if she could call down judgment from the skies, talons extending in and out of their sheaths in rhythm with her heavy breathing. "But he bonded to a...to livestock! How can you be okay with that?"

Jeraud's talons peeked up at the edge of his arm sheathes. Glancing at Lar, Aline realized all the siblings' talons pulsed, out of sync and at different rates, but they all shared the same angry twitch.

"I'm okay with that," Jeraud said to Meladise with forced calm.

"Because he is my brother, and I would never attack my own family."

Meladise burst into tears. "It's bad enough that I had to be born some sick half-breed." She began pressing her false scales to her back, but couldn't really see what she was doing. To Aline's surprise, despite the slit, they eventually stuck, though somewhat askew. "Now I have livestock for a sister-in-law."

"You say that word again, and I will cut you," warned Lar. "Sister or not."

Jeraud turned his angry stare to them. "You cut her and I'll turn you out of this house and straight back to that waiting prison cell." He returned his attention to Meladise. "You use that word again in front of your brother and I'll confiscate your electronics, including the ear-bud."

"You can't—!"

"I can and I will. You'll behave yourself or you'll find yourself stuck in your room with nothing to do but mime hand signals to your friends from your window."

Meladise glared at Lar and Aline. "If I even have any friends after this. I'm sure the whole city already knows. Everyone's going to be laughing behind my back."

Jeraud shrugged. "Deal with it. Lar and I had to."

Meladise whistled, a door flap sounded from a small room at the back of the house, and the click-click of nails against tile approached. When Aline saw the thing approaching she had to resist the urge to step back or look for a weapon.

"Come on, Sari." Meladise snapped her fingers, the scales making a sound like the rub of thick paper, then grabbed a harness with an attached leash from a hook by the doorfield. "Let's get out of here."

The dirt-colored animal, a nyarhoond Aline guessed though Lar's description hadn't done it justice, raised and dropped cloven forefeet on the tile in excitement. The oversized ears on its dog-like head stood on end as it wiggled its plated body. While Mwalgi scales were hexagonal and didn't overlap, this beast's scales reminded Aline of a snake, complete with pale underbelly. It had the under bite of all under bites with lower teeth at least four centimeters long practically touching its flared horse-like nostrils.

It hopped over to Meladise on tripod-style hooves, its oversized tail and huge haunches giving it the appearance of a mangled kangaroo. Aline couldn't have imagined anything like this taking the place of a dog, or a pet of any kind. It seemed so strange, and well...repulsive. But she'd never been exceptionally fond of pets, not since she was a small child, so maybe her viewpoint was skewed.

Stomping to the doorfield, the hoond on its leash, Meladise pressed her hand to the panel. A bell pinged and they had a full view of the soldiers walking the outskirts of Jeraud's property, twice as many as had been there before.

"I'm going to Bernad," Meladise said. "Since my dear brother tried to kill me, maybe Bernad can fix my torn fals-skalen."

"Fals-skalen?" asked Lar. "Artificial scales?"

Jeraud gave a curt nod. "It's a new thing."

"Be home for dinner," called Jeraud's wife from where she still holding her open-mouthed children on the couch.

Meladise glanced at Lar and Aline. "I'll be home by curfew." She walked through the doorfield with the hoond and it turned opaque again, hiding the eternal march of the house guards.

Jeraud sighed, running a hand over the bristles of his scalp.

His wife echoed the sigh. "She's getting worse, Jeraud."

He frowned. "I know." Pasting on a smile he turned to Lar. "This is my wife, Velga. And I'd like to introduce you to your niece and nephew, Isole Suzanne and Dacien Lar. I hope you don't mind that we gave him your nickname, Lar. Velga liked the combination with Dad's name."

Lar helped Aline to her feet then took tentative steps forward. "At first, I wondered when you'd adopted them." The children stared, but didn't react as he came close and knelt by the couch. "Then I saw their scale patterns, identical to our own. How, Jeraud? I thought we couldn't have children."

Jeraud glanced at something on the wall, the same way Lar had glanced at the observation devices aboard the Desolashon. Surely, they weren't watched in their own homes.

Shrugging, Jeraud scooped up Isole. "I don't know. I'm just grateful for the miracle."

Aline took a few steps closer, wanting to see the girl's scales, so similar to Lar and Jeraud's but somehow different. The girl spotted her movement and began to whimper. Aline put up her hands, a gesture of surrender, and stepped back.

"She's never seen a Saeanan," said Jeraud. "Her namesake, really her middle name, is after our mother who died before I met Velga. And as Meladise said, I refuse to have anything to do with tsefuurs."

He said it with such bitterness, Aline wondered at the seeming fondness for his late mother, and hatred for her species.

"From what Lar told me, your father only died a few years ago. He didn't go into severance when his wife passed?"

She watched both the brothers' shoulders slump.

"He immediately went into severance," said Jeraud. "But the progress slowed after Velga and I breeyaed for one another. We thought he might survive. After our bonding ceremony though, it took hold again." He shook his head.

Lar held out his hands to Dacien. The boy reached up and gahed at his uncle. "I knew when Dad saw me off for collections training that I wouldn't see him again. He knew Meladise would be cared for, Jeraud and I could make our own way, and he just couldn't live any longer without his wife. It happens." He stared at Aline as if trying to absorb her essence, hold onto her in some kind of last memory. "Mwalgi almost always die of severance if their bonded dies. For the sake of children, if they're young, sometimes a Mwalgi will survive until the children are grown, but otherwise...."

"That's so sad." Aline moved to put a hand on Lar's arm, to lend some comfort, but she didn't make it. She stumbled, exhaustion overwhelming her at last. Lar dropped Dacien back into Velga's arms, going on one knee to catch Aline. She tried to get back on her feet, but Lar scooped her up. She could feel his muscles tremble with the effort. He had to be as weak and tired as she, but he refused to set her down.

"She needs water," he told Jeraud. "And sleep. A lot of both."

Jeraud left the room and came back with a large pouch of cool water, similar to the ration pouches used on the Desolashon. Aline gratefully gulped it down.

"Don't give her too much at once," said Jeraud, taking back the container. "Both of you need to shower. You can get her another pouch after you're both clean. There are clothes in the bathroom. When you want the next pouch, press the refrigerator and request it. Make sure you put the empty pouch in the recycler on the side so it can be sterilized and reused. There's a heavy fine now for disposal of reusable items."

Lar nodded and Jeraud gestured to a room behind a set of stairs. It appeared to be a guest room with an adjoining bathroom.

Upon seeing it, Lar cocked his head in surprise. "It has a Saeanan-style toilet?"

Jeraud shrugged. "I don't know why I did that. It's only in the guest bedroom, but it was something Mother always wanted and we could never afford. She had to use that stupid outhouse Dad built for her and she absolutely hated it."

Lar smiled, a melancholy reminiscence. "I wish she were here."

Jeraud's face turned hard. "No. I'm glad she's not."

He didn't explain himself, just turned on his heel and returned to his wife and children. Lar carried Aline into the spacious bathroom.

Aline struggled from his arms, standing on her own two feet. "You're not showering with me."

He nodded, like some obedient servant. "I understand, but I will stay in the room, turned away, so I can be here if you need me."

She wanted to kick him. Where was the Lar she knew, the man with fire, and sarcasm, and unexpected jokes when she least expected? Had his time on the Future, or his severance, or his family's strange reception kicked it out of him? Or was it something more, something she didn't understand?

She didn't know, but she couldn't deny the fact that keeping her legs under her was becoming a difficult challenge.

As he turned his back, she removed her bra and underwear then stepped into the glass enclosure. To her surprise, it responded just as a Saeanan shower with plenty of water pressure, verbal-command soap, and even a massage mode.

Refreshed, she reached for a towel but found none.

"Tell the shower to do moisture retrieval," offered Lar.

With the command, a sucking wind blew her dry, even her shoulder-length hair and the moisture that had pooled around her feet.

"Our planet is water-poor," Lar reminded her, his back still turned. "It is almost as precious, and expensive, as Saeanan cerebrospinal fluid and cannot be wasted."

"Your oceans are small, but I saw bodies of water before the vetromlift landed. Can't you use what you have?"

"The chemicals in the air are nothing compared to what is in the water. Purifying it is costly and time-consuming."

Too tired to question further, Aline put on the bright blue bikini top Jeraud or Velga had left for her, along with a pair of matching underwear, and some calf-length pants made of such a light material that it felt like a breeze on her legs. Lar guided her to the bedroom, not touching her, but staying close until she lay down.

"I will bring us both some water then I'll shower and find a space on the floor to sleep," he said.

Aline shook her head. "We're both too tired. We can share the bed."

She couldn't tell if he looked relieved or disappointed. Nothing about him, about his family, about the whole stupid planet, made any sense. He nodded, expressionless, and left the room. A moment later, she drank from the water pouch he offered and lay back on the soft bed, used to the Mwalgis' lack of cover-sheets or pillows.

Later, Aline roused enough to sense Lar's weight joining hers on the mattress. She felt his scaled hand run the length of her arm and then he rolled to the other edge of the bed, well clear of her.

She sighed in her sleep, grateful Lar was giving her space. She needed time to think and put herself back together, but what if his behavior meant more. What if this time, his severance had gone too far for her simple presence to fix?

Lar woke with his arms wrapped around Aline, one knee between her thighs. She faced his chest, but she didn't snuggle against him, not like she had when they'd shared the bunk on The Desolashon. And if she found him holding her like this she'd think he was trying to pick up where they'd left off. If only they could.

Aline had declared her love for Cloud as the man took his last breath, and now she was in mourning. Lar didn't blame her. She'd believed Lar dead, and she was Saeanan after all. Their emotions healed, they moved on, and they fell in love with others. She and Cloud had even consummated their bonding, which meant she'd fallen for Cloud even harder and faster than she had for Lar. Though Lar's love for Aline and his knowledge that she didn't return his feelings would plummet him deeper into severance, her feelings for him had never quite blossomed. Not that it mattered. It was best that she hadn't grown too attached. In less than a week, Lar would be in a jail cell. A week after that and his death would be part of his people's Consecration Festival.

With care, he moved his leg and released his arm from beneath her head. Pushing back an errant strand of auburn hair from her face, he watched her sleep for a few minutes, comforted by the steady rise and fall of her chest, before rolling off the bed and making his way to the kitchen. Aline wasn't the only one who'd become dehydrated while aboard the Mwalgi ship. Between the water Lar had given Cloud for her sake, Mistar Peltay's restrictions on Lar's rations, and the number of times he'd been nearly killed trying to reach Aline, Lar needed water almost as much as she did.

He turned on the lights. Though Lar had woken late in the day, today was a dark-day, fifth day of the week—Fendi. It seemed strange to Lar now, having lived on a Saeanan ship where they simulated their days and nights by the intensity of their corridor lighting. Lenfay's rotation was too slow for a day to consist of both sun-brightened hours and moonlit ones. If they'd followed such a cycle their days would be forty to forty-eight hours long. That was impractical, so they had light-days and dark-days.

His scaled feet slapped the tiled floor as he made his way to the state-of-the-art refrigerator, his footsteps echoing in the still house. He gave the door a tap. "Water."

The dispenser door slid up with a whoosh, revealing the water pouch.

"You're up earlier than I expected, considering all that happened yesterday." Lar suppressed the instinct to flex his claws as Jeraud finished his walk down the plush-carpeted stairs and into the kitchen. "Where's the Saeanan?"

"Her name is Aline," said Lar. He guzzled his water, keeping a curious stare fixed on his brother.

"Whatever," said Jeraud. "Just be glad I don't call her livestock. Probably just as well she's still asleep. We need to talk."

Lar wasn't sure what was going on with Jeraud, and he'd keep his temper in check until he figured it out. As much as Lar would have liked to mark Jeraud with a talon, or just shove a fist against his jaw, he didn't dare risk Aline's chances for survival. So Lar watched him, every slightest move.

So far, Jeraud hadn't even twitched a finger. He seemed fine with calling Saeanans livestock even though that word would have gotten their mouths washed out with cleanser when they were younger. They'd been bullied and worse by Mwalgi who'd called them names like that, but it was as if Jeraud had turned himself pure Mwalgi and forgotten their past. This wasn't the brother Lar had known, the man who'd fought for Lar's release from the collections military a few years ago.

Placing the empty water pouch in the recycler attached to the refrigerator, Lar faced his brother. "In a week they'll take me away. At that point, there's nothing you can do to defend me, and I don't want you to try. Just promise me you'll take care of Aline. Get her off planet if you can."

Jeraud gave a dry laugh. "You have less time than that. They counted yesterday as one and they'll pick you up first thing a week from then. But you're right. I think I've paid any brotherly debt just by getting the two of you from Trovgarshtot when they would have immediately thrown you onto the consecration queue. I'll keep the Saeanan, and Mela will finally have her tsefuur. At least you don't have to worry about her dying in your absence since her affections won't last long."

Lar's talons itched within their sheaths, wanting desperately to take a slice at Jeraud. "You can't treat her that way. If you can't get her home, she's to at least be an equal member in this household. Promise me."

"I can't promise you anything, Lar. Your Saeanan doesn't know how to behave. You want to try to keep a woman like that alive in this city, be my guest."

"I'll be gone."

"Just like that?" Aline's restrained anger echoed through the house.

"Great," Jeraud muttered. "There goes the private conversation."

Aline slipped into the kitchen, keeping a wary eye on Jeraud, as she spoke with barely suppressed rage at Lar. "You're just going to give up? Throw your life away out of some twisted sense of honor? I thought you'd figured this out. There will be no more sacrificing yourself to save me. Fighting or dying, we're in this together."

"The authorities will come for me, Aline. There's nothing you or I can do about it."

She smiled, the same smile he'd seen when they'd taken on David and Ari in the hologames. "Well then we'll just have to—"

"Enough!" Jeraud interrupted, sweat erupting across his forehead. "This conversation is stupid and dangerous. Lar, take Aline into the washroom and both of you get cleaned up and ready for breakfast. I'll fetch Velga."

Lar almost told his brother which part of desolation he could throw himself into, but he saw Jeraud's fingers, ring and pinkie pressed to his palm, others pointed out like a small laser pistol. It lasted only a second, a twitch of the hand, but Lar knew the meaning; what Jeraud had said was important. Did he mean stopping the conversation, or getting cleaned up for breakfast? And why the secrecy within his own home? Lar almost scanned the room's corners for cameras then stopped himself.

"Come, Aline." He grabbed her hand, pulling her from the kitchen to the base of the stairs. "Let's get washed."

"Are you serious?" she whispered. "We can't just ignore this. We need to—"

"Hush," said Lar, dragging her after him toward the washroom. She resisted, but not with any determination.

"Did you just shush me? Are we back on The Desolashon, because I don't see any metal walls or...."

She trailed off, eyes darting side to side, searching the room's corners with her peripheral vision. He pulled her into the bathroom and shut the door. Turning on the sink water and the shower, he turned to her, like he had in the corridors on his ship when they'd needed privacy. He didn't dare kiss her like he had then, but he leaned close, whispering in her ear.

"Jeraud gave me a signal, something we did when we were in school and the cameras were always watching. There must be some kind of surveillance in the house."

The silver water retrieval box—the retti—on the far wall clunked as if trying to escape its moorings. Lar shoved Aline behind him.

"Why is the hand dryer shaking?" she asked, sounding more angry than spooked. By the All, he had missed her.

"Maybe the retti senses your eagerness to fight and has come to life for your entertainment."

"Was that a joke?" Aline asked, matching his sarcasm. "So I am with the real Larkin Trovgar, not some clone look-alike. I was beginning to wonder."

The retti went still, clinging to the wall in silence, but before they could leave the room the wall swung open, Jeraud standing on the other side, two fingers over his lips. With a hand, he ushered them to join him in the dim light where he stood on a staircase leading into a dank cellar. Emanating from the dark space, an ell plant's pungent odor mixed with some kind of sulfur, a sickening combination.

To Aline's credit, she didn't make a sound, only gestured to the shower and sink, still running precious water, and gave Jeraud a questioning look. He frowned, but motioned to turn them off. Lar commanded the shower as Aline spoke the command for the sink then they followed Jeraud down. Lar only hoped he could trust his brother.

As soon as the bathroom wall had shut behind them, Jeraud
embraced Aline, giving her the warm smile Lar had expected when
they'd entered his home.

"I'm so sorry," he said.

"Surveillance?" Aline asked. "Inside your homes?"

"That's illegal," said Lar. "They can't—"

Jeraud shook his head, leading them from a landing to steps
carved into the rock beneath the house. "They can now, for anyone with any affiliation to the government, no matter how slight."

"But they don't know about your cellar?"

"They suspect, I'm sure, but they don't have sufficient proof to
warrant a search. Besides, I'm not stupid enough to be doing anything illegal down here. They could only fine me for keeping an
area of my home unregistered and bring up minor charges for the
black-market devices I've installed to keep it hidden. Visual surveillance isn't allowed inside private areas like bathrooms and bed-
rooms, but auditory surveillance is all through the house. I needed
someplace to take clients where their privacy is assured, and it has
given Velga and me a place we can talk."

Lar scanned the room. For the most part it looked like any
household storeroom. Boxes and crates were stacked to each side
of the stairs. Jeraud had a desk against the wall across from the
steps, a monitoring device that projected everything around his

property onto a holotable, and a "corner office" consisting of comfortable chairs, a plant, and a simple computer table.

"Mela won't show up and try to murder me while no one is looking?" Aline asked.

Lar couldn't suppress a growl at the suggestion, but he didn't remark.

Jeraud hung his head. "The government wouldn't care if she did. With the shift in power to the Manifesto Party, the treatment of Saeanans has deteriorated beyond measures I would have ever imagined. They've doubled the collection camps, steadily reduced the approval of private tsefuurs, and are now moving to abolish the practice of owning private tsefuurs."

"Not that I agree with the practice," said Lar, "but some private tsefuurs are coupled with a bonded Mwalgi. For the short time they had me at a collections camp, I saw one of the guards who had been there too long bond with one of the prisoners. To completely abolish their existence would be murder to both."

"You were a guard in a collections camp?" asked Aline with obvious disgust.

"For a short time," Lar emphasized with a smile. "I caused too many problems so they sent me to ground forces to finish my training."

Jeraud grabbed a simple folding chair and sat down. "The Manifesto's propaganda claims that people like those, who bond with camp tsefuurs, are causing the CSF shortage, completely downplaying the Saeanans' invention and efficient use of acid guns. As a part-Saeanan, I'm sure our family would be in danger if I hadn't proven myself useful as an attorney."

"And what about Mela?" asked Lar. "When I left, she was bright and happy. She would have never said the things about Saeanans she did yesterday."

"You've been gone six years, Lar."

"Six?" asked Aline.

"Mwalgi years," Lar reminded her. "Three Saeanan years." He'd become quick at making those conversions while incarcerated on Saeanan ships.

Jeraud continued as if they hadn't interrupted. "Our mother died, you left, and then our father died. Mela and Velga didn't get along well, still don't. They're both headstrong and Velga has no patience with the direction Mela is headed..."

He glanced at Lar then stared at a holograph table, showing an aerial view of the authorities circling his property, their images a heat-sensor red against the black and gray shadows of dark-day.

Lar could tell there was more. "Tell me. Don't try to keep secrets. You know that never ends well."

Jeraud shook his head, somber. "No, it doesn't." He took a deep breath. "All right. It's all because of you."

"Me? How?"

"She idolizes you."

"Her behavior yesterday—"

"She'd become obsessed. The schools near Trovgarshtot have strong governmental influence. You remember how it was, all the indoctrination on the Mwalgi Destiny, always talking about Saeanans as livestock, telling us that becoming a CSF collections officer was the highest honor we could ever aspire to. Well, it's gone beyond even that."

"It was a bunch of pellets," Lar said. "We all knew that. Mela should know that."

"I've tried to influence her," said Jeraud. "To remind her of mother, but with surveillance everywhere, I have to be careful what I say. If I don't appear to fit in, or at least be trying, I could lose everything. Nobody wants a half-Saeanan attorney, no matter how good I am, unless they believe I support the Manifesto Party. I've had no choice, Lar. You understand that, right?"

He didn't. It was one thing for Jeraud to protect his wife, his children, but he didn't have to make such an opulent lifestyle for them, not at the expense of his values. What kind of legacy was he leaving them if they learned to follow whatever whim society thrust upon them for the sake of popularity and wealth? No, Lar didn't understand, but fitting in had always been important to Jeraud. Lar had been the one to pick fights, to defend their mother. Jeraud had been the one to avoid the bullies and pretend he didn't hear their crude words. It wasn't a fault, really, just a different way of coping, but it wasn't something Lar had ever understood.

To Lar's surprise, though, Aline nodded with sympathy. "You can make crazy sacrifices for family."

She turned melancholy and Lar wondered if she reminisced over her father's sacrifice that had saved her as a child.

"Why haven't you brought Mela down here and told her everything you've told me?" asked Lar.

Head hanging, Jeraud released a sorry sigh. "Because it's too late. We've only been here a few months and I don't trust her not to turn on us. She's heavily involved with Lenfay's Youth, and they've been completely indoctrinated that family means nothing compared to their devotion to the Manifesto cause."

"So, she believes it all," Lar stated. "She thought I was out killing Saeanans and enjoying it."

Jeraud nodded. "No matter what I said, she'd go on and on about how you were top of your class in training, an honorable soldier. And when you became a morten-rank officer so quickly, she couldn't talk about you enough. Since joining Lenfay's Youth, she has become more ruthless and more anti-Saeanan each day."

"And then I came home, an accused traitor, with a Saeanan wife."

Jeraud nodded. "I'm not sure what she'll do, Lar, but we can't trust her."

"You're right. Aline's safety will be difficult under such circumstances."

Before Aline could chastise him again, Jeraud snapped back. "Not her safety. I meant we can't trust her with your escape plans. You don't think I'm going to let them take my brother and sacrifice him to the masses do you? I might be a coward, and a good one, but I'm not a traitor to my own flesh and blood."

"You can't," said Lar. "You'll put your family in danger. And if they caught us, what they'd do to Aline is not an option."

Lar should have expected it, but Aline had been so silent he hadn't noticed the flare of anger his words had caused until she smacked his shoulder.

"You need to get this through your thick-scaled brain. You don't get to make decisions for the rest of us. We choose our risks, and we'll be the ones to live by them. I don't want you to sacrifice yourself for me. I told Cloud this in the courtroom, and I'm telling you now, I'd rather die on this planet than have to live on it. If there's a way to get away from this city and off this desolate rock then we're doing it."

"She's not outspoken much, is she?" asked Jeraud.

Lar nodded solemnly. "She has trouble voicing her opinion."

Jeraud smiled, the wide, flat smile of a Mwalgi that had taken Lar so long to unlearn and change to a Saeanan smile, the corners of his mouth lifted.

"She's right though," said Jeraud. "You always played the martyr in school and you're trying to do it now. We want you to live a life with us, not die for us. Mother and Father would expect you to fight for survival."

Lar nodded. If Aline wanted off Lenfay so much, he'd find a way to get her home or die trying. Maybe, in time, she would decide to stay with him. Maybe...

"The children," Lar asked Jeraud. "We're half-breeds. We can't have children. So, how did you get Isole and Dacien?"

"Because of Father," said Jeraud.

Aline took hold of Lar's arm with both hands, leaning toward Jeraud with hope and expectation. She would never admit that her desire for a family could affect her feelings toward Lar, but he knew better.

Lar tried to contain his own hope. He'd been told his whole life, by everyone, that he was sterile, but his voice betrayed him. "I know that our father changed mother on some biological level so we could be born. That was passed down?"

Jeraud dashed their hopes with a single shake of his head. "I don't think so. When Velga and I were married, Father gave us a bottle of Altherivan spring water as a wedding present."

Aline dropped her hands to her sides. Lar longed to embrace her, whisper some platitude that would make it better, but there was nothing to say. With him, a traditional family would be impossible. He couldn't blame her for preferring to keep her distance.

Lar ignored the pain of denied hope and focused on what Jeraud had said.

"Wait," said Lar. "That's an unusual gift from a parent, but I don't see the connection."

"The cap wasn't sealed and it had instructions that we were to both drink from it, along with wishes for a happy family. Afterward, Velga had horrible abdominal cramps for two days and two months later she was pregnant."

"You think father put some kind of biological agent into it? Bio-nanobots maybe?"

"I don't know," said Jeraud. "After Velga became pregnant, government investigators came in and ransacked our home for evidence of biological tampering. But by then we'd already recycled the bottle and there was nothing to be proved. I'm sure they would have killed our little family to keep everything a secret, but a friend of Velga's "leaked" the news, pro-Saeanans took up our cause and Velga's mother helped us maneuver the politics. Thanks to her, I used the opportunity to propel myself higher in the public eye and even made steps toward a decent career."

"Considering how much she hated us, I'm surprised she stepped in."

"Don't worry. She wouldn't do it for me, but she's devoted to Velga, thank the All."

"The authorities," asked Lar. "They didn't suspect Father?"

"Of course they did. And though I tried, there was nothing I could do to protect him. He gave me his research on a data pearl the day before he died. I'm constantly being scanned, but they won't find it. Velga has it in a safe place no one would ever suspect."

"Have you looked at the data?"

"I'm an attorney, Lar. Biology and xenobiology don't mean anything to me. I considered taking it to a biologist friend, but I'm not sure I can trust even him. I'm working on some black market contacts, hoping to get it to an Altherivan lab." Jeraud glanced at

Aline. "But if you think it might help you, maybe you should take it."

Lar appreciated his brother's trust, but put a hand up, shaking his head. "It wouldn't mean much more to me. My focus was electronics and physics."

"But if you found someone who could help you," Aline said, "you'd have the information you need."

The way Aline said it, as if he could get help but it had nothing to do with her, made Lar uneasy. Aline wanted a family, though he still wasn't sure if she'd hoped to have one with him. He could take the data pearl, and maybe that would give her the hope she wanted, but there were risks.

"If you can copy it—"

Jeraud shook his head. "It's damaged. I don't know what happened before Dad got it to me, but though the content are fine and readable, it won't copy and I don't understand it well enough to transcribe any of it."

Lar deliberated, staring at the floor as he fought the urge to give Aline what she wanted, against his better judgment. He raised his head.

"I can't." Lar turned to Aline. "The likelihood of us getting caught or not surviving is higher than I want to admit. If my father found a way to alter Mwalgi-Saeanan biology so we can have healthy children, that information could prove to be powerful and important. We can't risk it getting lost. You understand, don't you?"

Aline blinked and turned away, probably hiding oncoming tears. "So, you'll never be able to have children?"

Lar gave her the honest answer she deserved. "I doubt it."

Aline took a deep breath and turned back to him with a tight smile and a shrug. "Okay then."

She seemed fine aside from her rigid stance and the fact that she'd stepped away from him. It shouldn't matter. Lar probably wouldn't survive long enough for it to be an issue, considering the severity of his severance. He let the problems between him and Aline drop for now, turning back to Jeraud.

"And then Father died soon after your marriage?" Lar asked. "Was it awful for him? He was always unsure of the Offering Festival, but I doubt he was given a choice, especially if the officials suspected him of biological alterations."

A shadow fell across Jeraud's face. "The military board didn't tell you? He was murdered. His ashes were scattered around the trees in our front yard."

Lar gripped a nearby chair. "Murdered?" Without thought, Lar's talons extended. "Those lying leezards. Who did it?"

"I'm sorry to drop it on you like that," Jeraud said. "I thought you knew. They never caught the killer, or should I say assassin. With the TMP's level of surveillance, I doubt it could have been anything else. Someone from the government had to have had a hand in it."

"So you think they killed him because Velga got pregnant? Why?"

"Many considered you, me, and Meladise anomalies, something they need never worry about again. But if we can reproduce, having children without mental challenges and that don't need CSF, it would change everything—the structure of governmental power, the military, and our economy."

"You think it matters that much?"

Jeraud licked his lips, reticent. "I shouldn't tell you this, but in trying to find father's killer I've uncovered other information. I believe there are plans to colonize Saeana."

Lar snarled in disgust. "Aline and I figured out the military intends to take over the planet. Keep it as a sort of over-sized livestock pen."

"No," said Jeraud. "It's worse. I've seen colony ships. I suspect the military is planning to create breeding centers for the Saeanans they deem fit, and put civilians on the rest of the planet."

"They can't," breathed out Aline. "The slave camps are bad enough, but that would practically be speciocide."

"I think they've found a way around the council, at least so none of the worlds will do more than implement temporary sanctions."

"But what does any of this have to do with Father's research?"

Jeraud raised his eyebrows. "Think about it. If the general populace realized there was a way for them to live without the need for CSF, the best case scenario would be increased resistance to the colonization."

"Worst case?" asked Aline.

"Widespread civil war," responded Jeraud.

They all stood silent for a few moments, letting the implications sink in.

Aline's pinkie made a few taps against her thigh. "Well, there's not much point in discussing it further. The only thing Lar and I can do at this point is get off this desolate rock. You have a plan?"

Jeraud shook his head. "Not entirely, but I'm working on resources. We have four days to make it all work."

"But they promised a week," said Aline.

Lar placed a hand on her shoulder, noticing the way her muscles tensed at his touch. "Lenfay's weeks are six days long." He glanced at the projection table. Guards crisscrossed one another's paths like the weaves of a noose waiting for its next victim. "Whatever we come up with, it had better be good."

Hours staring at their guards' bored faces availed them nothing. Shift changes occurred, the men and women took regular breaks, but the tight pattern barely paused and never ceased. As far as Aline could see, the only escape was to fight their way out.

In normal physical condition, she and Lar might stand a slim chance of getting past the guards and out of the city, but the increased gravity on Lenfay took its toll on Aline. It would take time, and a lot of the gravity-compensation strips Lar was having her take every day, before she would adjust. As for Lar, she'd never imagined he could be so sick. He tried to hide it, avoiding her most of the time, but she saw his muscle spasms, leaving appendages temporarily useless and him short of breath. And Aline was responsible. She knew what he needed, knew what might cure the severance, but she didn't know if she could pretend to be in love with him when she was so unsure. Wouldn't that kind of deception be worse in the end?

Moments together like this were rare, but Lar had to spend some time studying the guards' movements if they were to work on a plan. Aline stepped behind his chair. She placed her pale hands on the skin of his shoulders, enjoying the deep contrast in their complexions. The smell of him, human male mixed with desert sage, brought back good memories, but she pushed them away. She couldn't lead him on again.

Pulling her hands away, she looked over his shoulder. "We're going to have to fight our way out."

"Maybe," Lar murmured. "Maybe not. They're very focused on the house. Too focused."

A muscle in his biceps twitched, dropping his hand, limp, at his side. He pretended nothing had happened, but Aline knelt down, massaging the muscle. Lar's gaze shifted from the guards to her upturned face, his expression questioning. Aline knew what came next, what he wanted, and that it might help him more than any amount of massage, kind words, or soft gestures. But when his mouth started to descend, she couldn't go through with it. Gripped with sudden fear, she came to her feet and stepped away, pretending she hadn't noticed the moment, just as he pretended the severance wasn't slowly killing him.

Panic welled in her chest. Cloud had told her Lar's severance was too far gone for her to heal. Was he right, or was Aline killing him by her indecision. The thought paralyzed her.

Flexing his arm, Lar rose from the chair. "It's getting close to dinner. We should go up."

Aline swallowed back her tears, shook her head. "Go without me. I'm not that hungry."

Lar took a step toward her then seemed to rethink his actions, coming to a sudden halt. "You need to get your strength up. No matter how we make our way out of here, it's not going to be easy."

"I know. Please, I'll get something later."

Lar flashed his familiar smirk, but there was a sadness in his eyes that didn't match the playful expression. "Meladise is going to think you're awfully strange, spending so much time in the bathroom and bedroom."

"Seems a lot safer than anywhere within reach of her claws."

Lar's angry frown returned in an instant. "I love my sister, but you know I would never let her hurt you. Never."

"I know," said Aline. "Which makes it harder. I'm the wedge between your happy family, and your brother is risking so much to help us. It could all blow up in his face."

Lar closed the gap between them, placing his scaled hands on her shoulders, something Cloud had always done before demanding a kiss. But had he demanded, or had she willingly given? She still wasn't sure, but the reminder forced her to step away and Lar let his arms fall back to his side, his disappointment obvious.

"I defended Velga once," he said as if nothing had happened. "After her former friends discovered she'd breeyaed for a half-breed and thought they should mark her for her disloyalty to the Mwalgi Manifest. I took some cuts for that, but that's what family does, we take care of each other whenever we can, no matter the consequences. And someday, I hope, Meladise will understand that."

"Go enjoy some time with them, without my presence adding to the tension. I need to be alone for a little while."

Lar finally turned toward the stairs and headed up. Aline sat on the stool he'd vacated, staring at the guards' weaving patrol patterns, but not really seeing them. She didn't know how long she sat that way, tears trailing down her cheeks. It might have been minutes or an hour before Velga cleared her throat from behind Aline. She held a plate of steaming food and two packets of water.

"You okay?" Velga's Vasershtot accent made the Mwalgi consonants harsher than Aline was used to, though Aline knew her own accent softened the words too much.

Aline wiped the tears. "I'll be fine." Inwardly, she cursed at the tremor in her voice.

Velga set the plate and water packets on the table, changing the settings on the projector so the guards' images didn't walk through the food. "This is not an easy situation, but we will find a way to get you out."

"I'm so sorry," Aline said. "Sometimes I wish I'd just died on that ship and then none of this would be happening."

"No," said Velga. "I am grateful."

"But—"

"When Jeraud's father brought me to work in his home, he'd intended me for Larkin. Upon talking with Larkin, I no longer saw the strangeness of his skin, but only his quick wit and intelligent mind. I spent much time with the family after that and when I breeyaed, I honestly wasn't sure which brother I was falling for. I love Larkin more than any man other than my dear Jeraud. He is like the closest brother. It is because I did not fall for him that they were able to conscript him into the collections military, and it is because of him that I met my bonded."

"And now our presence is tearing your family apart," said Aline.

Velga shrugged. "Ripples must happen in all families. And Larkin loves you like he could never love me. He never even breeyaed for me, not the slightest dusting of gold in his eyes. I've been his sister since the day we met. But you, you must be an amazing woman. He says he started to fall for you the moment he saw you."

Aline couldn't suppress a small laugh. "I was horrible to him then." The laugh turned to another round of tears. Was that all she did anymore, cry? "I'm sorry, it's just, the severance is because of me, and he's going to die, and I can't make myself do anything about it."

"You have only to love him. It will take time, but his body should heal."

That's not what Cloud had said, but that was only half the problem. "That's just it. I don't know what I feel, or what I should do. I fell apart when I thought Lar had died, but then I started to care for Cloud. Maybe my emotions were a reaction to the stress we were under. He saved my life so many times, maybe I just think I love him."

"I'm not sure whether you talk of Larkin or this Cloud."

"Exactly! Even though I still missed Lar, I was going to marry Cloud until we came to the planet and I realized I'd rather die than live here. How can I tell Lar I love him when I don't even know my own mind?"

Velga shook her head. "You can't. You must wait to breeyae again."

Aline huffed in exasperation. "I'm not Mwalgi. I won't breeyae. My eyes are the color they are, brown, and that won't ever change."

"Breeyae is more than a change to the eyes, it is a change to the heart. Your heart has been through much, and inside yourself, I believe your eyes are as black as Larkin's. You both need time to heal, to be with one another without expectation, only with patience."

Aline pushed her fork through one of the guards approaching her plate of cold food. "Time is something we don't have."

"You have only to stay together. The rest will take care of itself." Velga pressed Aline's hand so her fork touched the food. "Eat, then sleep. I believe there is much planning to do tomorrow."

Velga kissed Aline's cheek, her rough face scales brushing Aline's damp skin. It was a gesture of close friendship she'd seen among the Mwalgi, but not something she'd ever expected to experience. It seemed strangely intimate; less comforting than a hug, but more dependable. With a smile, Velga left up the stairs, turned up the other set of stairs that seemed to go through the middle of the house, and entered her bedroom.

That night, Aline fell asleep before she and Lar could talk. When she woke the next morning, he was sleeping on a mat on the floor. Aline longed to touch him, to stroke the black curls at his neck, but she couldn't push back the inexplicable fear that followed the thought. So she made her way to the kitchen and a breakfast of small blue eggs she'd never seen before, a type of bright pink juice that reminded her of lemonade, and a gritty toast that tasted like ground cashews.

When Lar entered the room, she didn't have the courage to look at him, but only stared at the half-eaten food that had turned leaden inside her stomach.

"When you are finished," he said, "you should get cleaned up for the day."

Aline understood the meaning. They were to meet in the cellar. Jeraud must have acquired the items Lar had requested, so now they needed a plan to get out.

Meladise entered Lar and his tsefuur's bathroom, where the woman seemed to spend all of her time. It adjoined their bedroom so Meladise suspected that's where she really went. For once, everyone seemed to have disappeared, busy with their own projects. This was Meladise's chance to investigate and hopefully come up with a plan. If she could have managed a moment alone with the Saeanan livestock, she'd have slit the weakling's throat and finished her brother's suffering once and for all. Better he die of severance and be consecrated for the festival than put to trial for crimes he'd been tricked into committing.

That stinking livestock pranced around the house as if one of the family, eating their food, drinking three times as much water as any tsefuur she'd ever heard of, and reeking worse than a nyarhoond in heat. Though Meladise might have been unfortunate enough to have a Saeanan mother, she made sure she never smelled like one.

For as much time as the tsefuur spent near the bathroom, that Saeanan odor should have been much stronger. Meladise sniffed around the room, leaning close to the retti, though careful not to accidentally initiate water-retrieval and alert Velda that Meladise was no longer in her room. Since the livestock had arrived, her sister-in-law had kept an even closer eye on Meladise than usual.

A faint draft near the shower's edge cooled the skin on her

cheek. "I knew it," Meladise whispered to the blank wall, her fingers digging at the crack running the length of the shower. It appeared like nothing more than a shoddy caulking job, but Meladise had suspected something strange about this house since they'd moved in. Hard as she tried, there was no prying the door open.

"The girl has to be getting through here somehow."

Perhaps the door could only be opened from the other side, in which case Meladise didn't have a cracking chance. Instead of pulling, she began to push at the edges, trying to find some give or some type of lever. With a swish of dank air, the retti rattled and the door pivoted inward, hitting the toilet seat. Meladise slipped through the tight opening, barely. How did Lar manage this? Stepping onto a narrow landing, Meladise crouched at the top of rock-hewn stairs going down into a cellar. Another set of stairs went up to the second floor, Jeraud and Velga's bedroom. How nice of them to never bother to tell Meladise about any of this.

Jeraud's voice carried up from below. "Did you hear something?"

"Your soundproof walls keep us from hearing anything going on inside the house doesn't it?" asked Lar.

"Unfortunately, yes. It works both ways."

"I'll check it out," said the tsefuur.

Meladise readied her claws. She'd finally have a chance to be rid of the livestock without her brothers' interference.

"No, I'll deal with it," said Jeraud. "It's probably the bathroom wall. We've been having trouble with the latch mechanism."

The slap of scaled feet on rock stairs approached. With the stealth she'd learned in her military class, Meladise shut the wall so that it nearly closed, climbed the railing on the dark side of the stairs, and slipped over the side, hanging with part of her torso and her legs behind a stack of holiday Neyell crates. She'd wondered how the decorations seemed to appear like magic last year and figured it was one of the many storage spaces in the house. A secret basement half the size of an entire floor had never entered her thoughts.

Jeraud came up the steps, secured the latch on the wall then tripped down the stairs again.

"Sorry," said the tsefuur. The girl was such a clod, always apologizing and scraping yet never even lowering her eyes as a proper tsefuur should. "I thought I'd shut it well."

Jeraud brushed away the pathetic apology. "I should have fixed it a long time ago. So, I was saying, Mela's attack on Aline served a good purpose." Mela cringed at the babyish nickname. "Because of the tear in her fals-skalen, and the fight she got into at school last week, I was able to place a large order with the manufacturer."

"There's a manufacturer? For just the two of you?"

"Four, with the children, but there's a fair demand for them from the regular populace. The fals-skalen work like a Saeanan bandage for inner scale injuries. Less chance of infection and as long as it's replaced often, it gives a Mwalgi a normal life expectancy. Dad was working on it when you left. He signed over the patent for a large sum of money right before he died. I used my portion to buy this place and give my career the boost it needed."

Meladise imagined him gesturing to his house, the only thing that really mattered to him besides his bossy wife and the malformed brats they'd produced.

"People aren't as prejudiced if they think you have money," said Jeraud.

Meladise almost laughed out loud. What her big brother didn't realize is that they were just as prejudiced if not more. The money only made them willing to talk behind his back instead of to his face. That was another reason Meladise hid her skin and claimed she was Velga's niece. What Jeraud didn't understand was that the only way to really make it in this world, was to fit in.

"Mela's portion is in a trust fund. I imagine she'll spend it to boost her military ranking when she joins." Jeraud said that with the disappointment she'd heard in his voice every day for the last year.

Arms starting to quiver, Meladise realized she had to move soon or she'd be making an unwanted grand entrance. She'd waited too long to be able to climb back over the railing. Her arms refused to pull her up. Hooking her feet on the rails along the stone-carved stairs, she climbed closer to the boxes, carefully lowered herself behind them, dropping the half-meter to the floor in perfect silence...then she bumped the box.

Pellets! Meladise went still. If they searched at all, they'd find her without much trouble.

Someone kicked at the box. "I've seen more scurrying sarzen in this basement than we had in that cave when we were kids," said Lar. "The vermin will start nesting in your boxes soon. You really need to set some traps."

"I know," said Jeraud. "But Velga hates it when I do. I don't see the point in wasting them, so I cook them up for dinner, but she hates the taste."

Lar laughed. "I guess she didn't grow up quite as poor as we did."

"No, you know Velga, she was a rich girl and she's used to a different life than we ever had."

More like rich brat, Meladise thought. Though she didn't like eating the fat sarzen either.

"So, did Lar get a portion of this inheritance?" the tsefuur asked. What a money grabber. "Could he somehow pay his way out of this whole mess?" And a dishonest one at that.

"Believe me, there are plenty of officials who can be bribed, but not with as much attention as this case has gained within the council and the military circles. No, your only way out is to escape. I've withdrawn Lar's money on his behalf, put it into a secret account that only he has the code to access, but I can't be seen buying weapons or anything obvious. When you leave, it has to appear that you did so without our help or knowledge."

Meladise couldn't believe this. A murderer, practically a convicted felon, and Jeraud gave Lar full access to his money? Just because he was family? How many times had she asked for just a small portion, and Jeraud had told her she wasn't touching it until she came of age? Both of her brothers were hypocritical, two-faced liars. She almost stormed out to confront him, but Lar's next question made her more eager to listen than rant.

"So, what's this grand plan of yours?" asked Lar.

"It's more like part of a plan. I'm expecting your military expertise to help with the rest. With the extra fals-skalen, we can disguise you and Aline as Mwalgi. I still have the lenses Father developed for Mother. They're both gold, of course, so you'll travel as newlyweds going to see the husband's family. That way, if anyone starts asking questions, Lar knows Lenfay well enough to answer them. Aline, you'll have to pretend to be very shy so Lar can do all the talking. Your Mwalgi is good, but best not to press it."

"Okay," she said. "I can do that."

"This is serious," said Lar. "You can't become angry and decide to show someone a lesson."

The tsefuur barked a laugh, though it sounded nothing like a Mwalgi. Pathetic. "Says the man who can't hear the word livestock without going into a rage."

"Point," he said and Meladise could hear laughter in his voice. "How does she wear the scales and still survive our atmosphere?"

"As protection, the fals-skalen are almost as good as our own. They're not as strong, as you saw from Meladise, but they'll reduce dehydration, protect the skin, and Aline will be able to withstand the sun's electromagnetic rays. She'll need the purifier in her throat, though, which is another reason for her to keep silent."

"I hate that thing," said the ungrateful tsefuur.

"My mother did, also," said Lar. "But if you suffer it for a little while, I think I might have a way to get us off this planet. Jeraud, did you say you have some black market associates?"

"Yes, but I can't bring anything into the house to help you escape. We're being watched too closely for that."

"I understand," said Lar. "Could they get the equipment and hold it for us in Col de Pluurs?"

"I don't know if there's even a town there anymore. The Zomeh season was bad the last couple of years. The cost of avyon grain was out of the system."

"It's probably all the better if there isn't one," said Lar. "It's just a meeting place. You give them half the money up-front, in my name, and I'll give them the rest when we arrive."

Meladise heard the scratching of an old-fashioned carbon pencil to paper, a list that could be burned and never traced. After a moment, she heard the paper rustle as it was folded.

"I hope you know what you're doing, Lar. I don't see how a few spare parts will get you off-planet."

"Remember where we grew up," Lar told him. "Remember how I spent my time there and what we left behind."

A pause, Jeraud's guffaw. "You really think you can make it work?"

"I think it's the only chance we have. There will be DNA scanners anywhere else we go."

"I guess you'd better start praying a bit harder to that All you and Mother believed in, because I think that kind of a plan will take more than a miracle. Speaking of, I have no idea how to get you past those guards."

"Let me take care of that." Lar sounded relaxed, no worry in his voice, which meant he'd thought the plan out already. "I have some ideas, and it won't take anything you don't already have around. And the less you know, the better."

"Just make sure you don't start taking things apart where we can see them. I need plausible deniability here."

"Of course. I may have gotten into a lot of trouble when we were in school, but deniability was one lesson I learned well."

Jeraud laughed. "We both did."

They talked a bit longer, the way brothers always do, and Meladise's sadness and anger escalated. Her brother could have come back a hero, overcome everything their heritage had put on them, like Jeraud, but that flame-haired tsefuur had destroyed his career and his life.

As Jeraud took the stairs to his bedroom, Meladise slid farther into the shadows. She peeked around the box to see Aline sitting close to Lar, studying the movement of the guards outside their house on a projector board."

"What are we going to do?"

"I have an idea, but I want to be sure I can make it work before I say anything."

Meladise wasn't likely to learn more, not yet. It appeared Lar was even keeping his ideas from his precious tsefuur. Meladise needed to speak with Bernad, decide if she should report her family or hope for more information. She wouldn't have minded turning in all of them right now, but without Jeraud and Velga Meladise was too dependent on them until she joined military school.

Silent as the rodents living among the crates, she climbed back up the stairs. This time she snuck into Jeraud and Velga's room, where she wouldn't have to worry about a loose retti giving her away.

She went downstairs and slipped from the house. Velga would assume she'd left for school. In the cool air of a dark-day, she easily made her way among the black and gray shadows that a stupid tsefuur couldn't manage. The bloom of sileyn flowers filled the warm air, calming her nerves and heightening her purpose. She'd find Bernad, assemble the local Youth, and make sure Lar's escape never happened. It would be better if her brother died of severance before the trial, but to let him escape would be even worse. No matter what Jeraud thought he could cover up, such traitorous action would forever ruin their reputation, and her chances at high rank within the military. No, Lar had to be stopped and without a scandal, which meant she had to catch him before he slipped past the guards

As soon as Jeraud stepped into the basement, Lar couldn't help but practically pounce on him. What had taken his brother so long? Aline stopped her pacing, but kept back, as if unsure of her place in the discussion.

"You need to go to All-devotion with Velga and the kids today," said Lar. "And Mela too, or at least get her out of the house for a couple of hours."

"Today?" asked Jeraud. "Why not tomorrow? You'd still have time."

Lar shook his head. "Aline and I must go on a dark-day. The guards focus so much on the shadows around the house, they don't see much else."

"Are you sure? We've had so little time together. After this, we'll never see you again, one way or another."

Lar had to choke back the catch in his throat. "You've done so much for us. I don't want you implicated in this in any way. Lock us in our bedroom before you leave. I'll have to cut the wall to disable the lock, but I'll keep the damage minimal."

Jeraud nodded. "Remember, there's audio in that room and the bathroom, video in the others. Also, I'll have to set the house alarm when we leave. It'll alert the authorities if you go out any of the doorfields."

"Do it. It won't be a problem. There's going to be some destruction to your property. I'll leave some money to cover the damage."

Jeraud waved the issue away, as Lar knew he would. "Don't worry about it. Actually, the more you tear things up, the less it will look like I had anything to do with your leaving. Go ahead and make it look good."

Lar kissed Jeraud's cheeks. "I'm sorry about the circumstances of my coming home, but it's been good to see you one last time. When you are able, tell Mela that I love her, and I'm sorry, about everything."

Tears in his eyes, Jeraud embraced Lar, squeezing him so tight a spasm jerked across the muscles in Lar's shoulders. With care, Jeraud released, making sure Lar was steady on his feet.

"Keep your bonded close," Jeraud said. "I'm sure the severance will pass, given time." He turned to Aline, who brushed away her own shimmer of tears. "Take care of my little brother, okay?"

"I'll do the best I can. I promise."

Jeraud closed the distance and embraced Aline as he'd embraced Lar. "Lar chose well. If I could have hand-picked a sister-in-law, it would have been someone like you. It's easy to see that you're right for each other. I'm not a religious man, not like Lar, but I'll be praying at Devotion for your safe journey and a happy life together."

"Thank you," she whispered, the tears escaping down her cheeks.

Lar gave his brother a gentle shove up the stairs. "Time for our performance."

Jeraud eased up to his bedroom and Lar and Aline made their way into the bathroom. As they slipped toward the hallway, Velga appeared coming down the stairs to the living room, she and the kids dressed in their Deemosh-best. Fals-skalen made the children look full-Mwalgi. Time to initiate the plan.

"You're still a member of the Diseep d'All?" Lar asked her. "How can that be, when you have such antagonism toward the Saeanans?"

By the way Velga jerked to full attentiveness, and her intense stare at Aline and Lar's eyes before she responded, Velga knew something was up. "I don't despise them. I just understand their place in the All's universe."

Lar shook his head in disgust. "Have all the members turned as you have?"

"Some," said Velga. "Not enough."

"I wish to go to Devotion with you. Worship as I should and see if what you say is true."

Velga hesitated and Jeraud shuffled down the stairs just in time, wearing loose dress-trousers and a flowing dress-shirt, the opening at his neck embroidered with the Trovgar pattern. His blue slacks coordinated with Velga's calf-length, yellow-flowered navy skirt and the yellow beyesh she wore, strips of fabric flowing down to cover most of her waist.

Jeraud scooped up Isole, dressed in a skirt matching her mother's, making the toddler giggle. "You're not leaving this house, Larkin."

"The guards could escort us."

"Your presence is enough of an embarrassment to our family. I'm not having you accompany us to Devotion with guards at our sides like we have some part in your atrocities." He paused on the stairs, yelling upward. "Meladise!"

Groggy-eyed, she stuck her head out the door. "What? It's still morning, on a weekend. Nobody in their right mind should be awake yet. Let me sleep in."

"You need to put on your scales and your nicest clothes. We're going to Devotion."

"Since when?"

"Since I want out of this stinking house and I don't dare leave you alone here with the Saeanan."

"I'll stay in my room."

"Like desolation you will! You don't think I know you tried to jimmy the lock on their bathroom? I saw the marks around the doorfield panel. Now get dressed and get down here. We need to leave in ten minutes."

"Fine!" she yelled. "Let me get my scales on."

Jeraud handed Isole to Velga. "I shouldn't be lecturing her when I still need to put on my own scales."

Isole only stayed with her mom a moment before reaching to Lar. He had to choke the emotion from his face as he took the sturdy girl into his arms. She was going to be a beautiful, strong woman someday. Her dark hair, curly like Lar's instead of straight like Jeraud's, framed the Saeanan skin of her face when she didn't have the fals-skalen, and she had her grandmother's blue eyes, like Lar and Mela.

She squirmed down as Jeraud opened a cabinet in the kitchen and started pressing on fals-skalen designed to conform to his face. They fit so well, Lar was amazed anew at his father's bio-engineering prowess. Of course, he already knew the extra scales were there, but having his brother do this while Lar watched would strengthen the idea that Lar put his plan together without Jeraud's knowledge.

Isole padded across the kitchen on her little scaled feet, and reached up to have Jeraud hold her again. As soon as he lifted her, she grabbed at the crease along his jaw line, where the fals-skalen met Jeraud's natural scales.

He laughed, pulling her hand away. "See why we need extra scales," he told Velga. "Between Mela's fights and this little demon, we need back-ups."

"I wish they weren't so expensive," said Velga. "But I can see your point."

This was good. Now the videos would record why Jeraud had needed the extra scales, and it had nothing to do with Lar and Aline.

Mela showed up at the top of the stairs, not in a skirt but wearing nice orange dress-pants, flowing to her ankles, along with a matching top. "All right, I'm ready, but what are you going to do with Lar and his tsefuur? You can't just give them free run of the house."

Aline tensed at his side. Lar's muscles clenched, making his calf spasm. He forced himself to lean against the wall rather than re-act. At least she hadn't called Aline livestock.

"I'll lock the doorfield on their room," said Jeraud. "I increased the intensity setting so they won't get out."

"What?" Lar bellowed, making sure he sounded significantly indignant. "All-devotion lasts past lunch. What are we supposed to do in there for hours on end until you return?"

"You'll survive. You could enjoy your time with your bonded, but, oh right, she didn't bond back did she? You did all of this, put your entire family at risk, so you could humiliate us all and die. I've tried to care, Lar, I really have, but you've brought this on yourself. In two days, you'll be gone, and as sad as it makes me to say this, I'll be glad to be rid of the whole situation."

"You're not my brother," said Lar. "I don't know what has happened to you, but I'll be glad to denounce you as family before they slit my throat."

"Please do," Jeraud spat back.

Lar looked to Mela, expecting a look of triumph and agreement. Instead, she watched their exchange with a mixture of disgust and anger. Why wasn't she happy to see Jeraud's disdain? If he'd had time to think on it, Mela's reaction would have disturbed him more, but her focus had shifted to Aline like a cat eying its prey. From her perch a few steps above, Mela leaped.

Thank the All Aline was better prepared than Lar. She avoided Mela's talons by grabbing the girl's clenched fists. Twisting as they fell, Aline forced Mela to her back. Aline straddled her waist. Lar might be hampered by his muscle spasms, but at least Aline would be combat-ready when they escaped.

"If I had a weapon, I could kill you right now," said Aline, her Mwalgi pronunciation perfect. "Lend me your talon, please," she said to Lar.

Lar's indecision between doing as Aline asked and protecting his sister only lasted a moment. Aline wouldn't really hurt Mela, though she certainly had a right. Leaning forward, he unsheathed.

"You can't—" Jeraud put Isole on the ground, lurching forward to stop them, but his face didn't appear that concerned.

"Mark her for me," said Aline.

The tip barely above the sheath, Lar ran his forearm across the natural scales of Mela's belly. Jeraud yanked Lar's arm away, but the damage was done. Clear fluid—skalwass—leaked from the wound and puddled on the tile floor.

"That's from me," said Aline. "You ever attack me again, and I'll kill you."

"With what?" Mela sneered, but Lar heard surprise and fear in his sister's voice. "Your fingernails?"

Jeraud grabbed Aline by the arm, dragging her to her feet, but Aline slipped a hand to the sheath she kept at her calf and pulled the hunting-style knife Lar had given her aboard the Desolashon.

"This," said Aline. "Down your throat. Either that or I can use a chair leg to bash in your head."

"That's enough!" yelled Jeraud. He threw Aline at Lar. She caught her balance as Lar wrapped an arm around her waist, keeping her from retaliating.

"You two, in that room!" Jeraud pointed to the bedroom. "If you're lucky, I'll let you out for dinner, but you won't see my face before then." He yanked Mela upright so he could yell at her face to face. "You are grounded for a week. No friends, no electronics, nothing! Hand me your ear-bud."

"What? Because I attacked his livestock? That's not fair."

Lar tensed, and this time Aline kept him back, pressing her back to him until he stepped closer to the wall. Did she realize how much that proximity made him want to run his hands along her curves rather than keep them sedately at her waist?

"I warned you the day they came," said Jeraud. Lar returned his focus to the conflict in front of them. "I meant what I said. Hand it over."

"Or what?"

Jeraud unsheathed. "Or I'll take them for good and I'll ban you from this house."

Velga grabbed his arm. "Jeraud, no. That's too much."

Taking deep breaths, Jeraud calmed, looking at his wife and relenting. "Mela, you'll get them back in a week, but I told you what would happen if you attacked her, that you would lose your tech and get grounded. I have to follow through."

Lar feared Mela would rebel, walk out the door and find one of her friends to stay with until she entered the military, but like Jeraud, she took a deep breath and calmed. Pulling the small bud from her ear, she placed it in Jeraud's hand.

He dropped it in his pocket and gestured to Lar and Aline. "You two, in the bedroom."

Without a word, Lar and Aline walked through the open doorway. Jeraud gave them a last look, his eyes expressing the regret and goodbyes he didn't dare say, and then he ordered the doorfield shut and locked. It turned the color of the wall then changed a dark pink, letting them know they'd receive a debilitating shock if they tried to walk through.

"You all right?" Lar asked Aline.

"I'm fine," said Aline. "What now?

Lar eased himself to the bedroom corner, jumped up, and brought down a camouflaged device, no bigger than his thumb, from the wall. Working fast, he popped open the back on the recorder, removed a chip no bigger than the edge of his finger nail, and then flexed his fingers to make his extractor extend from his middle finger.

Nodding to Aline, he motioned her to the extractor. Somehow, she understood. Grabbing a pin, she eased a replacement chip from the hollow tube and handed it to him. He popped it in, replaced the back, and returned the recorder to its space.

Lar smirked, making the corners of Aline's mouth lift, if only for a moment.

"Now," he said. "We leave this place."

"I'm guessing you rigged the surveillance in here so they can't hear us, but what about the rest of the house?" Aline asked, excitement and fear mounting with her realization that the time had come. "They're going to know something is up."

Lar shook his head. "I put in programming that recorded our seconds of silence, and will transmit that recording over and over. All of the surveillance is connected and the other rooms will do the same—normal pictures in places with video, and the audio is only silence. It will be several hours before they figure it out."

His cocky smirk grew wider. Every time Cloud had given her his flat-line attempt at a smile she'd missed Lar's wicked grin. Her heart skipped a beat seeing it now. Again, though, she was in a situation where her survival depended on him. Would her feelings for him remain if it didn't?

"You are truly amazing," she told him.

"Not so much," he said. "Just good with technology."

"Understatement."

Lar took her hand and she let him, not even flinching when his scaled palm slid across hers. "We have much to do. We must put the gleiterres together and attach some motors."

"Gleiterre?"

Lar pulled her along, toward the family basement that was part of the home's official floorplan. "I will show you."

He led her down the steps, past the holomovie room, exercise equipment, and shelves of children's toys. Aline stepped over a plush version of Meladise's nyarhoond and followed Lar into a storage room with a pile of dusty poles and a tarp dominating the closest wall. When he started to pull it out, making her sneeze, Aline realized what they had.

"Hang Gliders?" Aline said in English. "How can we possibly get those assembled without the guards noticing, and where will we take off?"

Lar pointed up, speaking the English his mother had taught him with his harsh, yet adorable, Mwalgi accent. "The roof."

"I've done a bit of hang gliding. The roof of a house isn't long enough for a safe take-off."

"True," said Lar. "Which is why we must attach the motors. We must drag these up to the attic. Will you help me?"

"We're insane," Aline said, but she reveled in the challenge. If this worked, she and Lar would go right over those desolate guards' heads.

She grabbed as many poles as she could carry and started up the stairs toward the attic. It took them four trips, but the gliders were nearly finished when Aline retrieved the fals-skalen from the cupboard in the kitchen, the gold protective lenses that encompassed their entire eye sockets, and the horrible breathing device, with the totally original name which translated from Mwalgi as "breather."

She inserted the lenses and with Lar's help, then covered her face, arms, torso, and legs in fals-skalen. The rubbery covering adhered to her as if a million rubber suction-cups clung through her first layer of skin to the lowest layer of epidermis tissue. It didn't hurt, but sure felt strange.

He held one of the last pieces, looking like a wad of silver cloth with a white bristle-brush attached. He ran a hand through her hair. Part of Aline wanted to move into the touch. The other part wanted to shy away. What had happened to her with Cloud? It was as if she'd returned to the little girl playing soldier aboard her father's ship, the girl Lar had met months ago.

"We must shave your hair," he said, letting her auburn strands slide between the skin and scales of his fingers.

Aline put aside her irrational fear of his touch and took his hand. "I've always wanted to see myself bald. It's a fashion in New London right now. Maybe we'll be lucky and make it home before some other fad takes over."

His eyes grew sadder, making the black coils of his circleh doy seem more prevalent, his words almost prophetic. "Maybe you will. I will try."

"You can't—"

He pressed fingers to her lips. "We have not time to argue."

Holding wads of hair in his hand, he ran the clippers over each section of her scalp, careful to not let any fall to the ground and throwing each section into the incinerator. The clippers tickled and Aline had trouble standing still. When he finished, she let out a laugh, running her hands over the smooth skin from forehead to nape. Lar helped her adjust the fals-skalen and adhere the bristly, white mohawk.

"My clothing will take care of the rest?" she asked him.

Lar shook his head. "You must cover your entire body in fals-skalen and use cream on your orifices. I'll help with the scales, and I will try to keep my touch from becoming uncomfortable."

Lar would never take advantage of her, never touch her in any way that she didn't want. When he'd done therapy to help her recover from acid-dart poisoning, even though he had secretly bonded with her, he had never let his touch grow intimate. But she still couldn't let him do it. She wasn't sure if she was too embarrassed or if it might be something else, but the situation brought on a fear that she wasn't willing to face.

She found a corner behind some storage crates. "I've got the hang of it now. I'll put them on myself."

Aline took care of her private areas, but needed Lar's help with the top of her buttocks and back. As he'd promised, he was as professional as a doctor with a patient.

Lar used the remaining fals-skalen on his skin. As he had for her, she helped him with his back and buttocks. Even with as little concern as Lar showed for modesty, he stayed turned away to finish attaching the scales to his most private areas. She remembered the first time Lar had slept in the same room with her, behind the force field that had kept him a prisoner. She'd wondered how far down the kite-shaped scales across his chest extended. The question struck her anew and piqued her curiosity way more than it should considering Cloud had died only four days ago. If she was so over Cloud, why did getting near Lar frighten her so much?

They put on their Mwalgi clothing; Aline in a black sports-bra-style beyesh that flattened her chest almost to Mwalgi expectations and her boy shorts underwear, Lar in black boxer-shorts. They had more traditional clothing—flowing pants, loose shirts, and jewelry that suggested wealth—in their packs.

As soon as Lar was sure they were entirely covered, that Lenfay's atmosphere would cause no harm, he took a laser-saw and started cutting a hole through the roof. To Aline's surprise it managed a clean cut through the solar roof, not a crack or crunch from the glass-like panels, just the whisper and hum of the saw.

He worked on the roof in intermittent bursts, listening for a reverberating thrum from outside that Aline could barely catch. As the toxic atmosphere entered the attic, Lar's black and gold circleh doy expanded, covering his entire eye socket.

"How do the guards not hear this?" Aline whispered.

"The Vetromlifts, when they travel from orbit to the planet and back, fill the valley with a slight rumble as they brake and take off, very similar to a laser saw. I hope gliders' motors are as silent."

Aline remembered hearing the Vetromlifts as she'd walked to the courthouse with Cloud. She hadn't paid much attention to them amid the sea of unfamiliar sights, sounds, smells, and the possibility of an attacking Mwalgi.

With a nice-sized hole, they pushed the hang glider parts onto the dark roof. Shoving the last piece through the hole, it scraped along the side of a panel. The shuffle of guards around the house stilled. A multitude of lights flashed around the home's perimeter. As the lights angled upward, Lar and Aline flattened themselves to the roof. The sky above them lit up, but left them in shadow.

The beam rested on the edge of a glider.

"What is it?" asked one of the guards.

"Looks like Trovgar has a bent panel brace, half the solar panels appear to be missing."

A pause. "A lot of homes got damaged in the last storm, though I'm surprised the rich mutt hasn't fixed it by now."

The beam turned off. Lar and Aline stayed still until the guards' movements became regular again, and then they still waited another five minutes or so. They finished the wing assembly and attached the propellers in spurts of near-silent activity. Mwalgi had good hearing. If not for the helpful weather, a breeze that felt like heat swelling from an oven, they'd have been caught.

In the darkness, Aline stumbled at the hole in the roof. Despite seeming oblivious of her to that point, Lar jumped to her side. He spun her from the edge then held her close, feet off the roof, for several seconds in absolute silence. No lights beamed up from below, and Lar finally released her, though her heart continued to race and her breathing was anything but shallow.

By the time they'd finished with the assembly, Lenfay's half-lit red moon was drifting below the horizon.

Aline fumbled with the straps, but even with a strip of moonlight, she couldn't make out the buckles.

Lar stepped forward, whispering in her ear as he finished her straps. "It's nearly meenakt, like noon on your planet; it's the darkest part of a dark-day. I'm sure the protective lenses don't help you see well, either."

Aline relented, feeling like a child on her first airship. "Where are we going?"

"We'll go south off the roof, veer to the west, past a park, and we'll make the landing in a little gully just past a line of boulders at the park's farthest end. Just follow me and everything should be fine."

Aline knew better. There was no such thing as a flawless plan.

Lar adjusted the harness, making the near-weightless glider fit snug, but not too tight.

"Don't leave until I clear the house across the street," Lar whispered. "It's smaller, so it shouldn't be a problem, but just in case."

Aline couldn't believe this. "So, you're to be the guinea pig, the experiment? Playing the martyr again?"

"No," he said, but she could tell she'd struck a nerve. "But it makes no sense to have both of us get hurt, and my Mwalgi scales, the real ones, will survive a crash better than your Saeanan skin."

He had a point there, but she knew that wasn't the reason he insisted on taking the greater risk. He still considered himself expendable.

Before she could say anything more, he was gone, strapping himself into the hang glider at her side. As a vetromlift hummed in the distance, he turned on his booster engine, ran the length of the roof along the braces between panels, and disappeared into darkness. If not for the faint glimmer of the glider's dark wings, Aline would have thought he'd disappeared into thin air. The glider bobbed and Aline worried Lar might not clear the next house, but the engine did its job. Moonlight reflected off the poles for less than a second as he lifted into the air and started to bank west.

Aline had spent too much time watching instead of preparing for her turn. A vetromlift hummed, but she wasn't ready. She waited for the next one as she scanned the sky for the faint glimmer of a solar glider, the fabric so obvious during the day yet invisible at night. With the Vetromlift's next hum she started the engine, a stronger one than Lar's.

Flashlights turned on, scanning the area. Before she reached the roof's edge the glider pulled her body into the air. A light beam bobbed beneath her toes as she pulled up her legs. She passed directly over a guard arcing his light into the house windows. She resisted the urge to spit on him, letting the glider carry her over the next house then banking west, as Lar had instructed. Though the sliver of moon brightened the western horizon, she found no glimmer of fabric, reflection off poles, or silver-red scales. Lar was nowhere in sight.

A light breeze brushed Meladise's face and she turned it up to the fading moonlight, enjoying her solitary walk. Her scaled feet slapped softly on the gravel walkway leading home, the perfume of night-blooming flowers sweetening the air.

The season of prontom had just begun, the dark-days still cool. Though some people disliked walking in shadows, she loved days like this above all others. Without the garish brightness of a light-day, she looked like any other Mwalgi. Before the fals-skalen, Meladise had avoided leaving the house on light-days, hating the stares and sneers from random passersby when they noticed the skin on her face and her dark hair. Now, that wasn't a problem, but she still preferred the shadows of dark-days, letting her blend in, making her free.

Almost home, she paused to stare at the moon's pockmarked surface hovering on the horizon. For a brief moment, the red crescent nearly disappeared, passed by a large triangle of deepest black. As the contraption banked to the west, Meladise saw the brief outline of a woman hanging from a glider. She soared out of view, toward Solay Park. Strange. Nobody used gliders in the city, so who...? Lar and Aline. It had to be.

"Bloody fluids!" Meladise cursed.

She connected to her earpiece, but it wasn't there. "Aaah!" she roared at the moon, a better Mwalgi challenge than Jeraud had ever mastered, probably better than Lar, too. Because of one desolate brother, the other had taken all her tech. The park was the only space Meladise could think of that would be open enough for a landing, but she didn't have a chance at stopping them without Bernad and their team. She'd have to find him on the way. Grateful for her military classes, she took off at a fast sprint.

Luck was on her side. A familiar hover board came around the corner. Meladise wheeled around and caught Bernad by the arm. For the first time, she wished he dressed up once in a while. With nothing but scale to grip, unless she wanted to pull his shorts off, she couldn't get a good hold. Her brief yank was enough, though. He hopped off the board running, slowing to a stop as the board circled slowly to his side.

He turned to confront her. "What in...Meladise? What are you all dressed up for? Did you go to All-devotion or something?"

Meladise didn't have time for him to laugh at her while she explained.

"Let me share the board with you. We've got to get to Solay Park, now!"

At his mental command, the board made a slight alteration in direction toward the park. "Okay, sure. What's up?"

"I'll explain on the way," said Meladise. It was tight, getting them both on, but they'd done it before. "Can you call the Youth? Have them meet us there?"

As Bernad talked to the crew via his earpiece, Meladise wrapped her arms tighter around his hard abs, reveling in the feel of the muscles beneath his scales.

"They're on their way." Bernad's arms wrapped over hers and she pressed her body tighter against his back, especially her chest. He liked that. "You know, skin or not, you're the most burning girl in the solar system."

She kissed his shoulder, wishing they were headed to her house instead of trying to head off her stupid brother and his tsefuur.

"So what's going on?" he finally asked.

"Jeraud dragged me off to devotion with him and his family this morning. I figured it was so Lar could make preparations for his attempted escape tomorrow, so I headed home early so I could catch him in the act and get the authorities to take him and his livestock out of our house."

"But something went wrong?"

"Wrong in the worst way. He and the Saeanan found my brothers' old gliders, from when we lived in the wilderness."

"No way!" said Bernad, more impressed than he should be considering what this could mean to her family's reputation. "So they took the gliders off the roof and are headed to the park? Crazy, but kind of smart. I bet the guards never even looked up."

"No, but I did." She gripped his arm. "Think what their escape could do to my reputation. What it would mean to our careers in the military. My family line is already tainted by Saeanan blood, and the Collections Force allowing bonded couples to join up is new. People are going to notice the gold in our eyes soon. What if they won't let us in because of my brother?"

He returned her grip, leaning further into the hover board's speed. "Don't worry. We'll find them. Even your famous brother and his 'salmond' won't stand up against an entire squad."

"Salmond?"

"Hadn't you heard that? Some of the Mwalgi troops nicknamed her 'the salmond.' She's supposed to be slippery in a fight and wicked fast. I think it's all exaggeration."

"She seemed like a wimp to me," Meladise agreed. "I think she's had luck and my brother, but she's just another soft-skinned Saeanan."

Aline hadn't moved particularly fast or been that impressive, at least until that morning. For a moment, Meladise worried she might have underestimated the livestock. No, the girl had surprised Meladise. That was the only reason she'd gotten the better of her, and it wouldn't happen again.

She leaned into the board with Bernad, arriving at the park's edge as a looming dark shadow descended amid a game in progress at the other end of the park. The dust already swirling from the game, puffed up in a giant circle as Aline came to a running stop and the glider's wings folded. People scrambled out of the way, yelling, but the livestock seemed more focused on removing her glider harness than the gathering players. As the dust from the game settled, Aline scanned the park, looking for someone.

"She's lost my brother," said Meladise. "Let's get to her first."

Bernad shook his head. "Not just the two of us. Even if the rumors about her aren't true, she must be somewhat skilled to have gained the reputation. We need to wait for the squad."

Bristling with impatience, Meladise paced while watching Aline. The livestock was getting her bearings. She made her way to the boulders lining one end of the park, peered over one of the smaller ones, then started to climb over.

"The gully!" Meladise slapped Bernad's chest. "It's big enough and flat enough to make a glider landing. Makes a lot more sense for them to go there than dropping into the middle of a park."

"You think she found your brother over there?"

Meladise nodded, just as five members of the local Youth coasted in on their hover boards.

"What's up?" said Safiya, stepping off her board.

As group leader, Bernad took charge. "Meladise's brother is trying to make a break for it. We want to stop him, but try to keep it quiet for Meladise's sake. You can understand why she doesn't want this blowing up into more of a scandal than it's been. You guys in?"

As Meladise had hoped, everyone nodded.

Bernad scanned the group. "Where's Andray?"

Safiya shook her head. "Late, like always."

"Well, this time he gets left behind. We're headed to the gully past the rocks on the other side of the park." Meladise joined him again on the board. "On my mark." He pointed forward. "Move out."

They appeared like nothing more than a bunch of teenagers hanging out at the park on a nice dark-day. Meladise probably stood out in her long pants and the formal beyesh over her breasts, but no one noticed them. They were more focused on the glider abandoned in the middle of the field. They probably hadn't gotten a good look at Aline, but Meladise was still surprised nobody seemed to realize the glider had been landed by a tsefuur.

They reached the boulders, but the hover boards wouldn't make it over. Bernad and others of the squad carried theirs. Some left theirs locked and out of the way.

Meladise's stomach turned when she climbed over the rocks and caught sight of Lar and Aline. Abandoning his glider, Lar ran the twenty meters to his tsefuur, embracing her as if he'd never let go.

Bernad circled his finger in the air. "Surround them. If they try to resist arrest, we fight, to the death if necessary."

"I'm sorry, Bernad," said Safiya. "But I'm not dying for Meladise's reputation. That's taking this a little too far."

A couple of the others mumbled agreement.

"I guess that's your choice. We're not really in the military yet, but we are Lenfay's Youth, the future of our world and our species. And when we are in the military, I know that a squad that sticks together survives and gets quota. The squads that don't have each other's backs, those are the ones where everybody dies."

Wide-eyed, Safiya took a deep breath and nodded. "All right. I'm in, but I hope you know what you're doing. I've heard rumors about Larkin Trovgar and his salmond. If half of what I've heard is true, you're leading us into a death-trap."

"It's all exaggerations," said Meladise, trying to dismiss the knot in her gut. Aline had had a lucky moment, that was all. "Lar is deep in severance and the livestock isn't that tough."

Safiya shrugged and the squad moved out, circling around the two lone figures who'd started collecting their packs near Lar's glider. Of course, he'd taken all the extra weight. Another evidence of the livestock's weakness.

Meladise had hoped it wouldn't come to this kind of physical confrontation. She'd hoped to catch Lar in the act of planning their escape and be able to call in the guards and be done with the whole mess. But now, her brother would fight. His tsefuur didn't want to stay here, and he would defend her to the death. Meladise hated to do it, but watching her brother die with honor would be much better than watching him die of severance, or worse, watching him be executed as a traitor. They would have to kill him, but in the end, this was better than the alternative.

As the others circled, Meladise approached her brother head-on.

He stiffened, pushing the cowardly livestock behind him, and waited.

Meladise stopped about ten meters from him. "Lar, it's over. I'd hoped to catch you before you left the house, but I guess it's too late for that. You need to come with us and turn yourself in."

Lar took a deep breath, shaking his head with a regret that suggested he didn't even consider her a threat. "Don't do this. I don't want to hurt you or your friends."

How dared he dismiss her as if she were a child?

A muscle twitched in his thigh. He stumbled to one knee, but his superior gaze didn't waver.

Meladise extended her talons, the same translucent white marbled with black as Lar's. She gestured for Bernad and the others to join the assault. The least she could do for Lar was to make his death quick.

10

Lar didn't want to kill anyone, but with the severance causing him to stumble, creating a handicap, he didn't know if he could win this fight without some casualties.

Aline trembled beside him, whether from fear, exhaustion, or anticipation, he didn't know. Knowing her, probably anticipation. Before she'd climbed from over the boulders of the park he hadn't been frightened, he'd been terrified. There was no question, severance or not, he loved her as much as before, maybe more.

She took a deep breath at his side, the tremors stopped, and she seemed to relax as she took a fighting stance.

Yes, she'd committed her love to Cloud, but she'd been through more than any woman should have to endure, and she stood again at Lar's side. For now, for as long as it lasted, that would be good enough.

"Kill them if you have to," said Lar.

"But your sister—" she protested.

"We have to defend ourselves and she made a choice. If that's the consequence then it's hers. No one else to blame."

Aline nodded, but he knew it would be hard for her. She missed her own siblings so much she couldn't imagine harming Lar's. It would be better if Lar faced his sister, though he wasn't sure he could carry out his own order.

As the squad of teenage soldier-wannabes circled, the spasm in

Lar's thigh relaxed. Lar stood so he and Aline were back to back, the way they'd ended up the first day they'd met.

Lar noted the approaching gang's irregular spacing, the tense muscles that would cause them to strike too early or lunge too hard. He felt sorry for what was about to happen, but as a twinge in his back made him arc to one side, he knew there was no avoiding it. Not entirely.

"Meladise," said Aline. "You don't have to do this. You can just walk away and nobody will be hurt."

That only seemed to infuriate Mela. With more fluidity than Lar had expected, she swiped at his exposed shoulder. Lar met her talon with his own, swiped her legs out from under her and threw her to one side, knocking down one of her friends as she tumbled.

A Mwalgi howl filled the air as one of the boys, a fair amount of gold in his circleh doy indicating his transition from breeyae to becoming entrenched, attacked. Not wanting to end the boy's budding romance by ending his life, Lar pulled back on his talon, shoving the boy down with his forearm.

"Bernad, you okay?" Mela asked as she came to her feet.

A brief recollection of the name came to Lar. This kid was their group leader and Mela had talked about him quite a bit.

Lar wasn't given time to think about the connection as more attackers rushed forward. He slashed and deflected, keeping them at bay. At one point, Lar grasped the head of a girl at his feet. And he almost did it. How many necks had he snapped while defending Aline aboard the Noble Ark? How many Mwalgi had he killed? But this wasn't the same. A misguided teenager wasn't a hardened veteran guilty of war-crimes. On the road she traveled, she may someday become that, but not yet.

Swiping a finger across her ear, he dislodged the earpiece that could call in the authorities then slammed a fist across her skull, near her military-length bristle of white hair. Her eyes rolled up and she slumped to the ground. She'd survive.

Aline was having better success. Somehow she'd confiscated a hover board. She must have knocked out the owner's earpiece in the process, because the board stayed in her hands like any ordinary piece of plastic. Wielding the board alternately as a club and a two-handed sword, she bashed her attackers to the ground. Lar's quick glance gave him a good view of her signature kick, right to the center of a girl's chest, sending her flying past their packs a few meters away.

Three down, probably still alive, and four to go, including Mela.

A muscle spasm sent Lar to one knee again, but he knew how to fight while debilitated and outnumbered. He'd been doing it since he was a kid.

A thud from behind suggested Aline had taken out another attacker. As much as Lar had wanted to keep Mela as his responsibility, Bernad's abilities were much better than his first attempt had suggested. Lar's severance-sick muscles were beginning to fatigue, the spasms growing more intense and more frequent.

With a Mwalgi challenge, Mela ran at Aline, out of reach from Lar's claws. To Lar's surprise, Aline screamed her own challenge. The breather in her throat made it more guttural, almost as grating as a real Mwalgi.

Lar blocked and sparred with Bernad, but kept an eye on Aline. She was tiring. The board in her hands cleared the dirt by only a few centimeters as she slammed it across Mela's side.

A spasm in Lar's forearm forced him to fold under Bernad's descending claw. The boy's talon sliced through Lar's fals-skalen across his lower ribs. Lar punched Bernad across the jaw.

The resounding crack of Aline's board, splintering into multiple pieces, echoed louder than the damage to Bernad.

Lar glanced at Aline, weaponless against his sister, and without her usual strength. Lar had a choice to make.

Bernad slashed out. Lar leaned back, avoiding the talon and jumping to his feet in one motion. With the boy overextended, it was easy for Lar to bury a claw in Bernad's side. The boy's eyes went wide, taking in the flow of blood and skalwass running between his scales. Rather than make the kid suffer, Lar swiped his other talon across Bernad's neck, a quick and honorable death.

Lar turned, found Aline on her back with Mela standing above, still struggling amid a whirlwind of swirling dust. Mela's claw plunged down. Aline rolled. Mela jumped on top of Aline, straddling her as Aline had done to her earlier that day. Aline was obviously exhausted. Lar could see it by the way her body bucked against Mela, as if in slow motion.

"You're nothing more than livestock," said Mela. "Now, I'll gut you like I would a barnal cow."

Mela raised her talon, her face grim with determination.

"No!" Lar screamed.

He tackled her to the ground. Lar ended up in the dirt, but Mela's back was to him and he still had a firm hold.

Mela tried to plunge a talon into Lar's side.

Lar released his grip and shoved her over.

Always determined, Mela's focus returned to Aline who was getting to her knees, the breather rasping like sand on stone in her throat.

Mela had rolled too far for Lar to grab hold of her, so he wrapped his legs around her torso. Fiery eyes blazed back at him. A spasm twisted down his neck, but Lar raised his body. With Mela gripped between his knees, he yanked her off her feet and slammed her back to the dirt. She "oomphed," then gasped for breath.

It took Mela a moment to get her bearings. Determined as any leezard, she turned her attention again to Aline.

Lar's roar stopped Mela cold, eyes wide. He rushed her, talons fully extended. His talon ripped through scales and flesh across her arm. Backhanding her, he sent her spinning. She tried to fight back, but Lar was on a rampage. He didn't see Mela anymore. He only saw Aline's exhausted body and the Mwalgi who threatened her. Claw to claw, he beat her back. She was good, one of the best in her squad. Lar was better, and despite severance, he slammed her to the ground and had his talon to her neck in seconds.

"Lar, don't!"

Those two words saved his sister's life. The tip of his talon released skalwass from her neck scales, the clear fluid running from her neck to moisten the dry earth below, but there was no blood.

"She was determined to kill you," Lar said. "She would have killed us both."

Aline came behind him, placing a hand on his shoulder. "She's your sister."

"Not anymore," he growled.

For a moment, Aline didn't say anything.

Mela glared at them both. "I'm with him. Whatever you're going to do, do it. I'd rather be dead than be related to a traitor."

"I'd give anything to see my brother or sister again," said Aline. "Even if they'd turned into a creature from another planet, even if they hated me."

Lar shook his head but Aline was right. It would probably cost them, but he couldn't kill Mela now. Not in cold blood.

Aline trotted away, in the direction of the packs. When she returned, she held the blue rope he'd packed. "Can you tie this in a way that she can't cut it?"

Lar grunted, but turned Mela onto her stomach, making sure to slam her face into the dirt. With some quick ties he had her elbows and wrists lashed behind her back. "If we leave her anywhere, she'll use her leg talons to cut through and be gone in minutes."

"We need to talk to her, Lar. It sounded like she knew we were leaving. We need to know what else she overheard."

This whole thing was spinning more and more out of control, and the more they tried to act with honor, the more trouble they created. Lar knew he couldn't just kill all the ignorant teenagers, but it would have been easier.

He pulled Mela to her feet, surprised when her eyes widened and she fell back to her knees. "No! How could you?" she screamed. "You murderer!"

Only then did Lar get a good enough look at her eyes to understand. A sprinkle of gold, so slight it would be difficult to notice without the moonlight, dusted the protective circleh doy.

The one kid Lar had killed was the one Mela had loved.

"I'm so sorry," Lar said. "I didn't want to hurt him, but I didn't have a choice."

She spat into the dirt at Lar's feet. "I'll never forgive you for this. I'll make sure they hunt you down. You're going to boil if it's the last thing I do."

"What makes you think you can find me? I know the Mwalgi wilderness, and you hardly remember it."

"Lar," Aline interrupted. "Her friends are starting to wake up. I don't think I can do this again."

Mela smirked at him, the glint in her gold-specked eye vengeful. "You'd better run away big brother. You have a train to catch."

And then he knew which of their conversations she'd over-heard.

Lar sprinted around the area, picking up communication de-vices and attaching them to his ear. It took a few minutes to get past the firewalls and mentally reprogram the circuitry for himself and then Aline, but by the time the first of Mela's friends started to get to his feet, Lar had hover boards ready. Grabbing Mela's arms, he lifted her onto a board.

"You're not taking me anywhere," she protested, going limp.

Careful to keep her claws pointed away from his face or shoul-der, he slung her over his back.

"You should have let us go," Lar grumbled. "And now you'll have to pay for what you've done, even more than you already have."

Mela slung insults at them, using words Lar hadn't realized she knew, before he stopped and gagged her mouth. They took backroads, alleys, and even managed along rooftops to get out of the city without being seen by surveillance. Aline handled herself well, taking to the hover board as if born to it. She was a natural athlete and Lar couldn't help but admire her form as they traveled.

Leaving the city, they traversed farmland that brought back happy childhood memories. These were the places he and Jeraud had gone to get away from the city. More rundown than he remembered, Lar found cover in the form of a barn. The floor still had dots of steaming metal, leftover from the passage of many slithering feet. The place smelled like overcooked flesh.

"Be careful," he warned Aline. "I'm guessing the barnals are at pasture somewhere, but the barn hasn't been cleaned well."

Aline wrinkled up her nose, taking in the patches of steaming metal with surprise. "Barnals? The things you eat and herd like cattle?"

Lar laughed, understanding her confusion. "Yes, but they look nothing like Saeanan livestock. They have one foot, like a snail but scaled. From that foot they extend multiple sharp diggers deep into the soil to extract water they then store horns that extend from their carapace."

Aline squatted to inspect the metal floor. Small dents were eve-rywhere, some of them encircled by steaming metal. Sporadic larger circles discolored the bright gray metal to a near-white. She reached to touch one.

"Don't touch the white spots," Lar said quickly.

Aline jumped back, still studying the floor with open curiosity.

"That's from their mouths searching for food. They leave a highly acidic residue in the process."

Aline continued to study the barn. "Do they eat grass, like cat-tle, or something else?"

Lar shrugged. "Not much grass on Lenfay, but barnals eat mostly plants, and whatever they happen to find on or around them."

Aline raised her eyebrows at that. "Omnivores?"

"Not by design, and they won't eat anything much bigger than a leezard, even by accident. They have high muscle and fat con-tent, they're stupid, and about the size of a Saeanan dog, so they're manageable livestock compared to other things native to Lenfay."

She shivered. "Sounds similar to lerf."

"Distant cousin," Lar said.

Mela bucked on his shoulder, which was getting sore. Consid-ering the number of muscle spasms that had dumped them both to the ground, she probably didn't feel much better.

"So what do we do with the master spy, there?" Aline asked.

Lar dropped Mela in a dark corner, away from the barnals' path-way. "She knows about the rendezvous point we planned and she knows where we're headed."

Aline sagged, finding another wall to slide down with an area of clean floor. "So we'll have to change our plans."

He reached into their bags, finding the package of bone sup-plement strips she needed to take every day and handed one to her. "More than that. We have to take her with us."

The strip dissolved on Aline's tongue, supposedly tasteless, but she gagged and screwed up her face. "We can't do that. You know she'll give us away. Besides, we don't have enough fals-skalen, not with all the damage we sustained."

Lar took a closer look, at her and at himself. "You're right. It's not too noticeable on a dark-day, but if anyone sees us on a light-day we'll get caught. Besides which, I'm sure we didn't avoid all the cameras on our way out, not the hovering vids. It's only a matter of time until they find the right files and know where we are and exactly what we're doing. We have to change everything."

"Is there enough skin salve that we could take her fals-skalen? Could we make it work?"

"She knows too much," said Lar. "One part of the plan that we can't change is that we have to get that delivery in Col de Pluurs and the only safe place to hide until then is near the dead zone. She overheard all of that." He looked at his sister with sadness, but determination. "We either have to take her with us or kill her."

Aline couldn't believe this. Would he really do it?

"You can't kill her. She's your sister."

Lar clenched his fists, talons peeking form the edge of his sheaths. "She would have killed us, and she's just lost the boy she'd breeyaed for. If she has to die to betray us, she'll do it."

"I know," Aline said. "And she deserves it, but she's your sister."

Lar squatted down on his haunches, thinking, looking from Aline to Mela. "In rare instances, severance can cause temporary insanity. The gold in her eyes will turn black in about a week, but it won't be enough for anyone to believe she suffered a severe level of severance. If we use my lenses, color them part black and put them on Mela, then anyone seeing us would believe the story. If we get another breather, I could reprogram it to alter her speech, make her unintelligible."

Mela shook her head no. She struggled anew against her restraints, screaming behind the rag tied around her mouth.

In an instant, Lar was at her side, talon fully extended near the base of her throat.

A look of fear passed over Aline's features that he hadn't seen directed at him since aboard the Noble Ark. What must she think of him?

He wouldn't have really killed Mela at the moment, but Mela

must have believed him as much as Aline did. Mela went absolutely still, realization of her own mortality dawning in her eyes.

"I will kill you," Lar said, though he hoped against odds it wouldn't come to that. "At the first sign of trouble. You may think it's noble for a soldier to die in the line of duty, but getting killed for being stupid is just that, stupid. A smart soldier waits for their moment. Aline is willing to wager her life that we can keep you from finding that moment. I'm going to concede to her wishes, for now. But one false move, one refusal to do what I ask, and I'll take your life rather than allow this charade to go any further. Understand?"

Mela nodded, obviously angry, but taking his words to heart. She would wait for her moment, and Aline and Lar would have to watch her like leezards stalking prey.

He turned to Aline. "In order for this to work, you'll have to play the part of tsefuur."

Her look of disgust almost undid Lar.

"Cloud tried to make me play obedient tsefuur," said Aline. "Groveling behind him, bowing to everyone like a tamed dog. When you showed up in that courtroom, I was about to attack the council members rather than have to live a life like that."

"I would never let you live a life like that," said Lar. "But if we're going to get off this planet, we'll have to ride the transits, replenish supplies, and be seen. We don't have enough undamaged falsskalen to cover you and Mela. Either we kill her or you'll have to play the tsefuur."

Aline bristled with anger. "I know, and you're right. I kept my temper and survived that horrible Mwalgi ship, I guess I can do this. But if it comes down to death or capture, I won't continue playing the good tsefuur."

Lar couldn't help a small grin. She had survived living aboard the Desolashon, in part, because of the times she hadn't kept her temper. She'd made the Mwalgi troops respect her. This was an entirely different kind of challenge, and he wasn't sure either one of them were up to it.

Even suggesting it probably made her see him as any other

Mwalgi, willing to treat her like a tsefuur to fit in. Maybe this was what Jeraud had faced. Maybe his big brother had had good reason for the choices he'd made.

"Keep your knife accessible," he told Aline while staring down his sister. "Watch her."

"Where are you going?"

"To steal what we need while it's still a dark-day. I think I can avoid the main cameras. I'll have to figure something out for the hovering vids, but I was going to have to do that anyway."

"What if the rancher comes back?" Aline asked.

Lar's shoulders slumped. "I'll try to hurry, but if anyone comes in here, you'll have to subdue or kill them. We have no choice."

For a moment, as Lar stepped through the wide doorfield, the darkness pressed around him, not even a red moon to illuminate the barren landscape. Lar's eyes adjusted, and the doorfield closed, shutting Aline into the cell-like barn. Lar hated leaving her, especially after all they'd gone through on the Desolashon. There, they'd only had a ship full of people to contend with. Now, they had an entire planet.

They traveled through the night; from the end of the dark-day as it turned to a light-day. As far as Aline could tell, Lenfay's dawn happened while the Mwalgi slept. When they woke for a new day, their sun had already been up for three or four hours. Strange.

As the sun hit, they walked the outskirts of the farming community, which looked more like a semiarid desert with all the scrub-brush and succulents placed in neat rows. Though they needed to travel west, they went east, Lar making sure that the occasional surveillance camera caught their picture, torn fals-skalen and all. It only took about twenty minutes of walking, once they reached the edge of the next town, to arrive at Lar's father's home, kept vacant by order of the government.

Aline took in the torn cushions, fluff drifting across a dust-coated floor. Pictures' frames had been smashed, the simple art-work of children and family portraits sliced open. The smell of dirt and rotting fabric was like nothing Aline had ever encountered. Humans had only been on Saeana for just over a millennium and even old homes, at least in the areas where she'd lived, were rarely abandoned. The dusty mangled rooms seemed sad, like an erased memory chip.

Lar urged Aline into a small chamber, activating a filter so she could safely remove her fals-skalen and put on the horrible gray outfit of a tsefuur. Mela balked at the breather Lar crammed down her throat, but one twitch of his claw and she'd gone still.

"Won't they come looking for us here?" Aline asked.

Lar nodded. "Eventually, but I stole a computer while I was out and I need some tools and equipment I had hidden in my old bedroom so I can finish infiltrating the government's systems for our cover story. I also need to update an anti-surveillance device I finished last time I was here."

It took more than a few minutes. While Lar worked silently in a back room, Meladise watched Aline without seeming to blink. Aline kept glancing from her to the home's broken doorfield, expecting Mwalgi enforcers to come pouring in. She spun her knife hilt between her fingers, practiced balancing it for a quick throw, and kept light on her feet.

"Done." Lar's deep voice from behind almost made her drop the knife.

Way to be prepared, she chided herself.

He held up a small metal ball, about the size of his thumb. "I fixed my scrambler. If our situation becomes difficult, I can block surveillance."

Aline hoped their situation didn't become that desperate. If they were having to avoid detection, then the plan had failed.

They left the house without seeing any enforcers, though there seemed to be a lot of them milling around the streets. Lar acted relaxed, as if this was normal, but as a half-breed on this bigoted planet he'd probably learned how to handle himself in sticky situations, though she doubted it had ever been this sticky. One wrong step and they'd be as good as dead.

He walked with Meladise, one arm around her waist as if helping her along, his sheath against her stomach. They looked like a cozy couple who'd been through a difficult time, not a brother and sister prepared to murder one another.

After what seemed like an entire day with Aline sweltering inside the tsefuur outfit, they entered a large building, a shvebon Lar had called it, but other than the Mwalgi population and slight cultural differences it looked like a regular hovertrain station.

Lar whispered to Aline as they entered. "Keep behind us, like you did on the street. Stay on Meladise's other side so people can't hear her if she whispers."

Meladise had figured out that if she whispered then those clos-est to her could understand, despite the breather in her throat. As they passed some kind of hover-bus, Lar kept Meladise separate from the disembarking passengers, but now Aline had to listen to her.

"You've done this well," she said to Lar. "She smells even more like a tsefuur than she did before."

"That's the clothes I borrowed," Lar said back with a loving smile so false Aline wondered why the guards weren't already dragging them away.

"No, she smelled like that back at the house, too. That's how I found the hidden basement, you know. I followed the smell past the wall."

Lar growled. "She smells nice. Like sweet carpace root and fresh water."

"She smells like Sari when she's in heat."

Aline bit back a retort, but it was all she could do not to slam an elbow into Meladise's smug face.

"Careful!" Lar whispered past Meladise, his eyes darting to those around them. "A tsefuur would get reprimanded for the murderous look you just gave her."

With a satisfied smile, Meladise garbled something at Aline. She really did sound crazy with Lar's altered breather. Then she slammed the back of her hand across Aline's face. Scales were smooth, but also hard. Aline would have a bruise across her cheek. If she hadn't turned, Meladise might have broken her nose.

Aline fumed, balling her fists, but she lowered her eyes in sub-mission. There was nothing she could do and Meladise knew it, the filthy sludge.

Lar's talon twitched at Meladise's side, but she taunted him with a laugh that added credence to their story of insanity.

They'd reached the front of the line. Now the real test began. Lar kept a tight hold on Meladise, and though Aline had to keep a few centimeters back, the only Mwalgi likely to get close to a tsefuur were hungry ones. But even a starving Mwalgi wouldn't try to attack someone's property with transport guards everywhere.

In intervals between the red-tinged force field encompassing the boarding area, multiple arches extended to the floor like solid sheets of metal. Aline knew from her time aboard the Desolashon that these were upscale versions of a doorshield. As people presented credentials and were waved through, the metal sheeting beneath the arches seemed to melt away. At both ends of the force field, and a few spots in between, the transport guards sported laser-proof vests, arm guards, and leg guards. Lightweight, breathable helmets with hinged multi-purpose face guards resting on top made the look even more alien and ominous. Aline shivered, despite herself. The barbarity of their culture mixed with such a focus on order; she wasn't sure how they managed it. This was so much worse than even the Desolashon.

Lar approached a black box attached to the front side of an arch.

"Ticket?" came an automated voice.

Releasing Meladise' left hand, Lar held out his index finger. He didn't seem to even need to hold it under the box for the scanner.

"Fals-skalen detected," said the bland voice. "Authorized under 'injuries incurred during military service.' Submit your identification to the scanners."

At this point, he placed his finger under the box.

"Identification verified," said the voice. "Admission for two passengers, Steren Klein-Treyt and Baynees Klein-Treyt, to Bayrbon, Kermainde district, approved."

Lar's grip on Meladise tightened, but his voice remained relaxed. "Requesting an additional ticket for our recently acquired tsefuur, please."

"I show no record of a tsefuur registration under your name, sir."

"Purchase number 2596 dash 4TRZ. The registration is under review."

Aline caught a bead of sweat at his temple and knew this was the part that had Lar most worried. He wasn't sure if his computer hack had worked.

Other than a low-frequency purr, the ticket scanner remained quiet. Lar and Meladise's sheaths twitched with tense anticipation.

"I have no record of a tsefuur purchase with that confirmation number."

Meladise raised her face, finding the guards standing at each end of the entrance gates. Angling away from Lar, she took a step toward the closest pair.

"Don't fret, dear," Lar said, yanking her back. "We won't leave your pet behind."

Aline understood why he said it, and why he's said it so loud, but it still made her fume inside. She kept a calm demeanor, but if she had the means she would have liked to mark the entire race for their twisted view of humanity.

He raised his voice, as if that might make some difference to the scanner. "It will be in the family transfer files. My brother-in-law gave us a significant discount and we paid the fees."

Another moment of whirring and the guards walking their way veered back to their watch-posts.

"You have access," stated the scanner as the doorfield flickered then disappeared. "The tsefuur's registration must be complete within one week, by Merkdi, Prontom seventeenth, nine-thirty swah, in order to access more tickets. You have three tickets available for the rest of this Mwalgi year, 1034 psf, with a maximum travel distance of 150 kilometers."

Lar nodded and they entered. Most of the words they'd used made no sense to Aline, but she didn't dare ask. Meladise was their prisoner, but Aline might as well have been the one trussed up and gagged.

Lar accessed the train schedules via his stolen earbud, leading them to platform 9.

As they waited, Meladise continued her whispers to Aline.

"Eventually, someone will figure out who you are. When they do, I'll stand back and watch them gut you like a Vulfbaeor."

Not responding to her constant threats and insults was more torturous than having to play the demure tsefuur.

"Leave her alone," said Lar. "She's the only person keeping you alive."

As people crowded onto the platform, Lar had to concentrate more on keeping Meladise distant from the passengers, less on what she whispered to Aline.

"So, what did you do to trick him into killing himself over you? Go naked in front of him until he bonded? Are you laughing now, watching him slowly die?"

And Aline could say nothing. She bit her lip, keeping back the retort she would have liked to make. Neither she nor Lar had intended to develop a relationship. Aline had hated the Mwalgi, all Mwalgi, until Lar.

And that former hatred was starting to resurface as Meladise continued to talk, mock, and accuse. Aline was past the want-to-strangle-this-girl phase and moving nearer an intent to murder, Lar's sister or not. The Mwalgi threat of ripping out an opponent's intestines, in that moment, was something she considered reasonable.

Lip bleeding, Aline continued the stifling pressure from her teeth, forcing herself to remain quiet and obscure.

She didn't notice anything but Meladise as the train stopped and they boarded, finding seats away from the other passengers. She gave no more than a cursory glance to the scraggly man who followed in their wake, head down, eyes lidded. Had she seen a touch of red?

"There's no way this plan of yours will work," said Meladise. "I'll make sure of that."

Aline's attention was drawn back to Lar's sister.

The man followed them off the hovertrain to their next connection. Aline noticed, but was too busy watching Meladise to focus on his behavior. A lot of people followed them off and about a quarter of the group continued to the last platform with them. If he followed a little close, the station was crowded. A lot of the Mwalgi didn't have much choice but to get near the sweating tsefuur.

Meladise was right. Aline stank. After a few hours in the strange suit Lar had shown her a drinking tube attached to the hood where she could regain some of her lost water with recycled sweat. Somehow, rather than alleviate the smell, the recycling process in the outfit seemed to exacerbate the problem. She smelled worse than an old spacewalk boot.

Waiting with Lar and Meladise, trying to ignore the girl's whispered insults, Aline smelled the man over her own stench before she realized how close he'd come. He reeked of desiccated flesh and stale urine. Aline scooted to Meladise's side, gaining a few disgusted looks from other passengers.

Lar must have noticed more than he let on. As the train pulled near the platform, he turned to the man, letting his fangs descend between his lips, growling deep. The man backed away, eyes downcast, talons twitching at the edge of their sheaths.

Aline watched the man shuffle away, and sure enough, when he raised his head she saw the red circleh doy encompassing the sockets. On instinct, Aline reached for the knife in her boot, stopped, took a deep breath, and stood upright. She didn't dare defend herself in the middle of a train station full of Mwalgi. She had to keep her cool, no matter what.

Lar shook his head. "The man's been cut from his government allotment of CSF, rotting from the inside out. Keep an eye on him. He's desperate."

Nobody knew how the Mwalgi had developed a need for human CSF, but Aline could no longer assume it was a type of drug addiction. His people really did die if they went too long without it—a very strange and unnatural adaptation.

As they stepped onto the westbound train, Aline watched the crazed Mwalgi. The man took a seat and kept his distance, but only just. There was no question he was waiting for an opportunity. Lar, Aline and Meladise remained standing, holding to the train's long metal bars for support when necessary. The doors swished closed and the train accelerated from the station.

In her efforts to watch her back, Aline almost missed Meladise's whispers. "There's not enough CSF to go around. That's why there are people like that. When I get into the collections military, I'm going to focus on making higher quotas so men like that won't have to suffer."

In that moment, Aline saw Meladise as a Mwalgi soldier, not Lar's troublesome little sister. She would become like Betette, a blood-thirsty, immoral parasite—only Meladise would perform her atrocities with a sense of national pride, not hunger.

The train lurched forward and Meladise continued her description of the kind of soldier she would become, the pride of Lenfay. She would slaughter and capture humans for the sake of people like the man stalking Aline. If Lar heard any of it, he didn't acknowledge, but he was focused on the crowd, the cameras, and staying alert to floating surveillance.

"It's ridiculous," said Meladise, "to take time torturing or feeding on Saeanans, though I've heard there's nothing like it during the heat of a collection raid. But that's not the point. We have to think about our planet, our people. Every Saeanan from which CSF is collected could save another Mwalgi."

In her mind, Aline saw Betette during the final attack on the Noble Ark, straddling Aline's belly, relishing the blood seeping from Aline's sliced middle finger. Glancing down, Aline wiggled her tight tsefuur-gloves that attached to the cumbersome jumpsuit. The middle finger on her left hand flopped a bit, all three fingers the same length inside the gloves.

As much as Meladise had tried to goad Aline before, the stupid girl didn't realize she was finally succeeding. "The trick," she went on, "is to get in, get all the CSF, and get out. And you can't try to show mercy to the children. I mean, what are you really saving them from? Saeanans are horrible to orphans, locking them in big pens and treating them like they're infected with disease. It's better to make their CSF useful than let them be subjected to that."

Aline had been made "one of those orphans," treated with well-meant concern and pity. All of the psych evals, the special training, the pills to "manage grief and aggression," had been horrible, but it had also helped her survive after she'd watched her entire family murdered before her eyes. Meladise would have killed her in order to "spare" her.

Aline clenched her fists. "Shut up."

"I guess some of the Saeanan children try to hide," said Meladise.

Aline's body grew hot. Different than Lenfay's heat, this came from inside. Her shoulders tensed, hands clenched so tight the muscles in her arms quivered.

Meladise continued. "I've become particularly good at smelling out the little beasties, which is how I realized you were in the cellar at my brother's house. In their special closets..." Where the Tanaka family would have been found. "...in foot lockers with false backs..." Aline's brother, sister, and mother, were pulled from their locker by the crazed Mwalgi who'd slaughtered them, along with her father, while Aline had watched. "...and I've heard some of the smaller children can even get into the air vents. That one should be easy."

Aline had been pulled from the air vent, forced to wallow in her family's blood as the renegot soldier, gone crazy with his need for CSF, had smeared their blood on her arms, hair, and face.

Aline's clenched jaw released in a harsh whisper. "You're just like them. You'll be worse than Betette."

The heat inside rose like a volcano, refusing to be quenched with reason. Aline reached into her boot, retrieving the thick-handled knife Lar had given to her. She dug the knife into the girl's back, away from the scales running down her spine. The tip caught on one of the swirling sections that extended like tiger stripes toward Meladise's side. It slid then gratified Aline by slicing into the fals-skalen at an angle, landing in flesh. Meladise cried out in pain and surprise. Red liquid embraced the blade.

A woman caught sight of the blade and screamed. Others followed. The train car erupted as people rushed for the exits to the attached cars.

Meladise brought her talon-ready arm back, missing Aline's fingers by a centimeter but catching the blade. She tore it from Aline's hands.

Some do-gooder who must have thought he needed to play the hero lunged toward Aline, talons extended. Sensing him, Aline ducked.

Talon clanked against talon. Aline looked up to see Meladise and the man's talons locked. She must have been forced to defend herself.

Aline searched for her knife while Lar fended off another interfering do-gooder, a female with obvious military experience. Her beyesh suggested she had children.

There was the knife, between Aline and Lar. She dove for it.

A whistle and a whoosh of air sounded above her shoulder. Aline grabbed the knife and rolled to her back. The man had tried for her again, missed, and Meladise appeared to have to again defend herself from his clumsy attempts.

Knife up, Aline jumped to her feet, back to the seats lining the car's edge, expecting another attack.

She watched as Lar swept his talon to the woman's neck. He

had killed to save Aline before, but a woman with children? He nicked her throat then kicked the woman backward, through the doorfield into another car.

"Security will be coming," he said, backhanding the man unlocking his talon from Meladise.

The man staggered. His eyes darted from Lar to Meladise. "Let the livestock kill you then." He joined the others who had run into the adjoining car.

By the five systems, what had Aline done? She thought she'd learned more control than this. Tears threatened at the corners of her eyes, but now was not the time. She swallowed down the emotions, like she had during Mwalgi attacks, and focused on the moment.

"Is there a way to get off?" she asked Lar.

"Maybe."

He tore his talon through the circuitry of the loading doors where they had entered then pried the heavy panels apart. A red doorshield waited behind it, the blurry terrain passing in the background.

"Oh, for all the water...," He banged his fist against the wall, sending an eerie screech through the car. "You touch her," he told Meladise, "and I'll kill you. Step to the other end, away from both of us."

With a smile, Meladise did as he ordered.

Lar moved to the doorfield he'd sent the woman through, fiddling with the wiring in a box at the side.

From the corner of her eye, Aline saw a flash of movement. The red-eyed Mwalgi who'd followed her since they'd arrived at the station sprang at Aline from between a row of chairs. Fangs protruded between hungry lips.

Aline swung with her knife. The handle connected with his skull, bringing him down. He gripped her clothing and Aline lost her balance. He fell on top of her, eyes gleaming like the crazed soldier who'd killed her family. She swung the knife again, but too late.

Through the bulky tsefuur jumpsuit, his narrow fangs pierced the weave and found flesh. Mwalgi toxin released into her bloodstream. Her ribs numbed as the knife slammed into his skull a last time. A resounding crack echoed through the car. The body pinning her to the floor went limp, fangs still buried deep in her side. It didn't matter. He'd already done his damage; the paralyzing sensation spread. Aline found it hard to breathe. Eyes frozen forward, she watched Meladise, by the doorfield leading to the next car, her expectant smile turning to disappointment.

Impotent anger surged within Aline. The girl had seen the crazed Mwalgi and hoped to watch Aline die. With a shrug, Meladise turned toward her escape, the car through which the male passenger had run. She almost leaned into the doorfield before she realized it had turned red. The entrance doorfield at Aline's feet, leading to the passing landscape, hummed a little higher, a different frequency. If Aline could have smiled, she would have given Meladise a wicked grin.

The girl stalked to the entrance door where Lar had joined Aline. "You're cracked if you think I'm jumping off a hovertrain." She kicked Aline's shoulder, but Aline felt nothing. "This was all your livestock's fault."

"I don't know what you said, but I'm sure the attack was deserved. And if you think she has a temper, little sister, you don't remember mine."

With that, he hit her, a sudden punch to the sternum that Aline had taught him. Breath knocked out of Meladise so she couldn't even scream, but flew from the compartment into the open air.

"Remember to tuck and roll," he yelled after her.

A thud sounded followed by a distant scream, more angry than hurt.

The doorfields leading to the adjoining cars turned blue. Several security guards carrying guns like Aline had never seen before, brought them to bear and entered. Lar had his back to them. Aline wanted to scream, to warn him, but that crazy Mwalgi had paralyzed her. She couldn't make a sound, couldn't even give a twitch of the eye.

Lar must have heard them. He gave a panicked glance at the

passing terrain. If that doorfield turned red, Lar would be seriously hurt by going through. Such a shock would kill Aline—instant heart attack. He could jump now or risk them both.

Go! Aline yelled, though her mouth refused to form the words.

He kicked the dead Mwalgi from Aline, but his calf twitched with severance, sending him to one knee. Without losing momentum, he wrapped an arm around Aline's stomach. She had stiffened from the Mwalgi venom, but somehow he forced her legs into a tuck position on his lap. And then, like a swimmer doing a back-dive, Lar used his one good leg to thrust them both over backward. The doorfield turned red as they spun clear.

They somersaulted high, but at an awkward angle. Extending one arm as they landed, Lar held her tight. Bone cracked, the sound an angrier version of their crash through brittle foliage. Aline sensed Lar's pain through the muscular ripple where his chest touched her back. He cried out yet wrapped the broken arm around her head, creating a protective cage despite the ongoing abuse.

They tumbled over and over, crashing through more bushes, thorns grasping at Aline's clothing, tearing gaping holes that allowed the next branches to bite into flesh. The toxic air hit her skin, making the cuts an ever hotter fire. She whimpered without sound.

After a few more turns and another bush, they came to a stop.

"Bloody fluids!" screamed Lar, setting Aline carefully to one side. "I'll kill her."

He left Aline in the dirt, still paralyzed. She stared at Lenfay's giant red sun as it blazed down, a magnified spotlight, sizzling her like bacon in a frying pan. His footsteps disappeared into the distance then Aline heard an "oomph," a scream, the ting of talon hitting talon.

Lar roared in sudden pain. "Bloody All!"

Aline had never heard him curse by the name of his God. What if Meladise got the better of him? It didn't seem possible, not Lar, but he was wounded, and his severance wasn't healing. Suddenly, Aline didn't care about the hot dirt competing with the toxic air to burn her alive. She needed to get up. She needed to help Lar.

As she struggled for bodily control, her rasping grew more pronounced but she accomplished nothing. The grunts and scuffles between Lar and Meladise stopped. Heavy steps approached. Aline stilled. It could be Lar, come to help her, or Meladise, come to finish her off.

Meladise's short-cropped dark hair, almost as short as Aline's, came into view first, but the angle was all wrong. The girl wasn't walking. Her face hung, limp.

Lar plopped his sister down like a pile of rags, and maybe to him, in that moment, that's all she was, because he used his left hand to rip off what was left of her clothing. Gritting his teeth against the pain of using his right arm, Lar bundled Aline's jumpsuit together using the remnants of Meladise's. The smaller holes fused together on their own as he tied off the larger ones. The outfit finally had some form instead of feeling like an oversized bag, but she suspected she could pass as a large bundle of cleaning rags. The tingling burn on her skin had lessened. At least the atmosphere seemed to have stopped seeping in.

Lar left her line of sight again, returning a few seconds later with one of their backpacks. The other still sat in the train car where Meladise had left it.

"This is going to burn," he said.

What was he saying? The burning inside her suit had just become manageable.

Lar connected the can in his hand to a valve in the neck of her clothing then pushed the lever. The can hissed. Every inch of skin felt like it was being peeled from her body by a shard of ice. If she could have moved, she would have writhed and screamed. She managed to finally whimper. Tears leaked from her unblinking eyes.

"I nullified the atmosphere still trapped inside the clothing," he said. "The spray's residue will serve as temporary protection until we can get something better, but it stings some. I'm sorry."

Beside Aline, the still unconscious Meladise started to writhe, expressing Aline's pain in a way she couldn't.

Lar took what was left of Meladise's clothing to tie her arms together. "I should leave her. Let her die here as she would have left you."

She was his sister; Aline understood if he couldn't do it, and part of her didn't want him to. But with everything that had just happened, she'd also understand if he did. The paralysis had finally lessened enough for Aline to almost shrug, a small movement, but Lar caught it. It was up to him.

With a sigh, he nodded. "I am Diseep d'All. I take not life without immediate reason or just cause. I have just cause, but she will live, for now."

He reached inside the pack, removing a tube of skin cream. He treated Aline's face and neck first, where the tsefuur jumpsuit didn't cover. She finally relaxed, her muscles unclenching.

Lar rubbed cream on his arms, legs and torso, where the falsskalen had torn. By the time he ministered to Meladise, she was screaming at him. Aline was grateful for the device in the girl's throat, turning her loud profanities to moderate gibberish.

As the muscles in Aline's neck started to loosen, she scanned the horizon. On Saeana, after the kind of struggle they'd had on that train, their time would be limited before a police force would show up. It had to be worse on a government-heavy planet like Lenfay.

"Good," Lar said to Aline. "You're starting to move. I'm using my scrambler to frustrate all signals within twenty kilometers, but it won't be long until enforcers arrive. We have to hide."

Aline scanned the area again. Other than some far distant mountains, there was nothing but dirt and the occasional scrub brush within a day's walk in any direction.

Wetting her dry throat, she managed to form a single word. "Where?"

"Not where," said Lar. "How."

Securing their backpack, he waited for a spasm in his rib to pass as if it was nothing more than a minor inconvenience. It bothered Aline that he didn't even seem to notice the pain anymore. Had he grown accustomed to it, or was he so sick he didn't care? Aline struggled onto her side, hoping she'd be able to walk, but Lar shook his head, throwing her over his left shoulder. With his other hand, he shoved Meladise in front of them.

"Walk. You put out your talons, and I slit your throat. I can hide a dead body much easier than a live one." Lar took them deeper into the sun-stained desert.

Though they didn't walk for long, it didn't seem possible that they could evade the authorities. They would know exactly where to look for their ragtag group, and even if they did somehow get away, Aline didn't imagine she'd survive long in a Mwalgi desert. How could she have been so stupid?

Aline couldn't breathe. She had willingly laid down in the shallow dip Lar and an unwilling Meladise had created, had even kept her cool when the brown tarp was placed over them. But when the first pile of dirt hit the tarp and Meladise grunted through the gag in her mouth, Aline had wanted to scream. She'd known the enclosed space would be difficult, but she'd told herself she could do this, that she could trust Lar and everything would be fine.

He'd slipped under the tarp between her and Meladise, making the cramped space tighter. The thick roots of a huge thorn bush cut through the tarp and dirt, right between Lar's knees. His outstretched leg pressed Aline tight against the shallow hole's side. The root he held at her shoulder, giving the appearance of another growing plant, pressed on her. He'd made her more immobile than getting buried alive in a casket. She couldn't move and it was getting harder and harder to breathe, especially with the stupid breather crammed down her throat.

It wasn't only the lack of oxygen that threatened. The Mwalgi searched for them. She could hear their scaled feet slapping the hard earth, shuffling through the rocks and dust, the vibrations thrumming through her body. She remembered how the air unit on the merchant space vessel had thrummed when she'd played hide and seek with her siblings so many years before. While she'd curled up in the cramped vent, the crazed Mwalgi soldier had found her family, his feet slapping against the hard ship-deck the same way these men's feet slapped against the dirt, coming ever closer, smelling her, reaching for her.

Aline clenched her eyes tight, holding back the scream. She couldn't breathe. They were coming, but she had nowhere to go. She had to get out. Had to breathe.

The faint whistle of Aline's breathing device let Lar know she was still alive, and still close to hyperventilating. He could only hope that the tarp and dirt covering them would mask the faint sound...and that she could keep a grip on her sanity.

Mela lay still as death on his other side, his claw sheath resting lightly on her collarbone, the position beyond painful to his broken arm. The men, whether local authorities or government enforcers, continued to comb the area around them. Lar had chosen a location with multiple laypin holes. The fresh-turned dirt between bushes would look like nothing more than another nest.

He'd uprooted the bush in his left hand as soon as Aline had been able to walk, so there were no uprooted plants giving them away, and the larger bush kept those investigating from actually getting close enough to step on anyone. No, what kept them looking was their scanners. Lar had scrambled their equipment enough that despite knowing there were heat signatures nearby, they could be anywhere in a twenty kilometer radius. These men were flummoxed, but refused to go home.

The faint whistling stopped. Aline?

Lar didn't dare release the bush, but he stretched out a finger. Touched her shoulder. She gasped. A quiet one, thank the All, and shuddered away from his touch.

She'd always had trouble being touched, but aboard the Noble Ark she'd gotten over it, at least with Lar. Now it was back. He revolted her all over again. Maybe not as much as at the beginning, but enough that she may never again want to be close with him.

The faint whistle stopped again, but Lar didn't dare touch or console Aline. He'd made sure there were small holes in their camouflage, enough to let in air, but maybe her breather was malfunctioning. She could be dying right next to him and he wouldn't know it.

Aline tensed, her muscles like rock at his side. Sounds of opening containers, equipment being placed within, a few swear words, and the order to "Wrap it up. We're done here."

All tension at his side disappeared. Aline went limp. Dead? Suffocated? If so, then this was all for nothing. He might as well jump out of the shallow hole, kill the men, and kill...no, he wouldn't kill his sister. There would be no point. Not if Aline was gone.

It wasn't the enforcers' faults either. They were doing their jobs. There would be no killing. He was overreacting. He relaxed inside the hole, closing his eyes.

A brown-scaled leezard slipped into the hole between his and Mela's feet. This was what Lar had worried about most; with them prostrate and vulnerable, any number of creatures might come calling. The leezard scurried forward on its eight claws, its fat tail testifying of a recent meal. Like most desert creatures, the leezards were rarely sated, and it turned to Mela's bare leg. She whimpered, but if Lar did anything to dissuade the creature, they'd be found out. Aline was still alive. She had to be, so they couldn't move. He extended a talon, letting the tip rest on Mela's neck.

The creature opened its wide mouth, the edge of its gums sliding over one of Mela's scales until it encompassed the rim. Mela tensed. Lar sensed her pain as the leezard injected its needle-like teeth into the crevice. Her scales swelled, a natural response to stop the intrusion, but too late.

As soon as the footsteps receded and their vehicle engines fired up, Lar released the bush. He shook Aline's shoulder. No response. If he jumped up from the hole now, he'd still be seen. Mela moaned in earnest now. He didn't stop her, and removed his threatening claw from her neck. She could scream. No one would hear her over the rising whine of the engines.

He reached down, placing a hand across Aline's rising and falling chest. She was breathing, but non-reactive. He listened to the receding vehicle, counted another sixty seconds while Mela howled against her gag, then threw back the tarp.

Hot sand and dirt scattered, the sun illuminating Aline's face from the western sky. She gasped, her sudden scream joining Mela's muffled hysterics, eyes darting side to side while Lar stroked her salve-covered face.

"Thank the All you're alive," he said. "I began to worry."

She calmed, took a look at Mela, then batted his hand away and screamed anew. "What in desolation is that?"

Lar took a deep breath. "A leezard. But we can do nothing about it until the vehicles are a little farther away. Even with my scrambler, they would notice a fire."

"That's a lizard?" Aline said. "I mean, it has scales, almost everything here has scales of some kind, but that thing has claws instead of feet. Eight of them! Except for the tail, it looks more like a spider."

"The names are similar, but yes, the leezard appears nothing like the lizards that live in the warmer parts of Saeana." He stared in the direction the vehicles had gone. "I think we may risk a fire now."

Extending both arm talons, he struck them together, gritting his teeth against the pain in his arm. A spark finally flew, caught the uprooted bush Lar had held in his hand, and burst into flame. He pushed the bush as close to the leezard as he dared without charring Mela's leg, though she would have deserved it.

"Why can't you just kill it?" Aline asked as the leezard writhed, trying to retract its teeth from between Mela's tightened scales.

"If I kill it, the teeth will release from the leezard's mouth, remaining in its victim. If I make the creature uncomfortable, it will take its teeth and go."

As predicted, the leezard finally pulled its teeth free and scurried from the flame. Mela didn't let it get far. As it clambered up their narrow ditch she extended a leg talon, pushed herself downward with sudden ferocity, and pierced the creature through the back.

She watched the dying creature with satisfaction.

Lar chuckled. "You have good mastery of your claws, little sister."

He untied the gag around her mouth and put out a hand. She coughed and spat, but couldn't expel the remastered breather.

Lar reached his fingers into her mouth. "Do not bite me."

Of course, she did, but not until he'd removed the device from her throat. He dropped it on her tongue, pulling his hand back with a curse.

Mela spat the breather into the dirt. "You're a—"

Aline slapped her. Like Lar, Mela may have had scales on other parts of her body, but her face was regular human skin. Aline's rough gloves scratched Mela's cheek, leaving thin red lines. It must have hurt, because Mela winced.

"My opportunity will come, Saeanan tsefuur," she said. "And when it does—"

"I'll kill you," said Lar, the resignation in his voice heavy. "Don't pretend that it was Aline's actions that took us here. You goaded her too far. I'm sure if I had heard more, I might have reacted with more violence, and much sooner."

"So, it's my fault you threw us out of a moving train, nearly killing us all?"

"Yes."

"No," said Aline. "It's her fault she purposefully goaded me, my fault I let it get to me, and your only fault, Lar, lies in keeping us alive." She paused, the corners of her lips turning up. "And I don't consider that a fault."

For that small smile, Lar thought he might go through it all again. He wanted to scoop her up, kiss her until she couldn't breathe, but he thought of the way she reacted to his touch, remembered her words to Cloud, and kept restraint.

"You're both making me sick," said Mela. Can I have some cream for the stupid tsefuur's claw marks before it stings any worse?"

Lar pulled his eyes from Aline and rummaged through the pack. After applying the cream, he picked up the dead leezard lying at her feet.

"Hey, that's mine," said Mela. "I killed it."

Lar shook his head. "We will share the meat. Aline needs its water."

Turning it over in his hand so the creature lay on its back, Lar extended an extractor from his index finger. With a quick thrust of the sharp tube, he pierced the softer scales over its bloated belly, draining its greyish water sacs into his own, like a pirate stealing CSF. He extracted every ounce he could manage, leaving the creature looking more like an emaciated version of the lizard creatures Aline thought it should be.

Glancing around as if he might find a cup sitting beside some bush, he turned to Aline. "I have nothing to put the water in, so you may drink it."

"I guess you should have made me drink the leezard guts." Aline laughed. "I'm not that dehydrated. I'll be fine."

"Saeanans can't filter the leezard fluid, but you have no water sacs to keep you going, and we must walk a great distance. This is temperate land to a Mwalgi, but to you it's a harsh desert."

"So, what do you suggest?" asked Aline.

Mela rose to her feet. "You're both pathetic. Just kiss her, Lar, and let's get on with it."

Lar shrugged to Aline. "I don't see another way, other than from my mouth to yours."

She grimaced, but nodded.

Lar stepped close to Aline, slow and calm, as if approaching a skittish laypin. She scrunched up her eyes, but tilted her face upward, opening her mouth like a thirsty child.

Despite the juvenile image, the vulnerable posture only made Aline more endearing. He could have poured the water from his sacs into her mouth without touching, but he wouldn't pass up this rare opportunity.

Holding her right shoulder with his good arm, their bodies almost touching, he leaned down so the tops of their lips met. She shuddered, but he squeezed her shoulder, holding her there. Pressing his tongue to the roof of his mouth, he released water in a slow stream.

When he'd finished, she dropped her face and swallowed. "Thank you."

He kept his hold on her shoulder, reveling in her closeness. Without her hair and covered in dust and skin cream, she no longer smelled of carpace root, but still had a unique scent that made him want to bury his face in her neck and pull her body close.

Mela interrupted the warm silence. "It's obvious you don't care, but I'm standing here near-naked, without fals-skalen, with every scratch stinging like a feukayfa swarm."

Aline stepped back and Lar released her, wishing to kick his sister back into that pit, bury her, and leave her to wait for the leezards.

"She's right," he said. "We need shelter and eventually we're going to need more supplies. From this point on, we're going to have to travel outside the main surveillance areas."

"How will we keep our direction? Do you have access to a GPS program?"

Lar shook his head. "We don't dare use any kind of comm link." He dug into the backpack, pulling out an archaic black compass. "This used to be my father's, but he had Jeraud and me carry it with us whenever we went away from camp."

"That's older than Firster tech," Aline's voice held a touch of awe.

He contemplated the weed that had stood between his feet while they hid. By studying its shadow and the sun he found north, then turned a few centimeters to the right, and adjusted the dials. "My father gave it to me. Every planet has magnetic poles, and using simple survival techniques was something my father taught us from the time we could walk."

"Even I know how to use a compass," said Mela, "and I hardly remember our time at the camp."

Lar straightened, but a muscle spasm across his shoulder forced him to pause, pain shooting down his injured arm.

"We need to do something about that bone," said Aline, rushing to his side.

The gentle touch brought a new flash of pain, but Lar didn't move. "We must get away from here, set up shelter from the sun, and then I will brace it. We have time for nothing else."

The concern in her expression eased the ache he'd felt the last few days. She may not love him, but at least she cared for him. It was something.

Following the guide of the compass, they headed toward the descending sun. It would still be many hours into sleep-time before it began to set. They needed to find shelter soon or none of them would have enough water to survive.

The leezards saved them. Though they never saw more than the large ears of one laypin, the numerous holes in the ground attested to the rodents' higher-than-usual population, which accounted for the number of fat, sluggish leezards they caught as they traveled. Recognizing their need to hunt, Lar decided to untie Mela, keeping her ahead of them, a little easier to watch. That put her in the position to catch most of the little monsters, though Aline pinned quite a few despite her constricting clothing and lack of practice.

Lar didn't try. With each kilometer, the pain in his arm grew, becoming a never-ending fire, blending with the blaze running across his Saeanan skin where the manufactured cream didn't suffice for the amount of atmosphere exposure he'd endured. He could only imagine what Aline must be feeling, though she hadn't uttered a word.

Mela complained enough to make up for anyone else. "Can we stop already? My feet are starting to burn."

"Your scales will adjust," said Lar. "I'm sure they can't hurt worse than mine or Aline's. She has only Tsefuur boots and I've been on a space vessel for the last year."

"My skin burns. Stupid, weak Saeanans. Why did I have to be born with such a horrible deformity?"

Lar's talons peeked from their sheaths. "I would mark most

men for making such a comment, sister. You walk on hot ground."

"I know it's hot. That was my point."

"That is not what I meant, and you know it. Quiet yourself."

"Make me."

"Don't tempt fate any sooner than you must."

"By the five systems," said Aline. "Now I remember what it was like to have siblings. Can both of you just shut up?"

By the time they reached a small outcropping of rock, the base worn down long ago by vulfbaeors seeking shelter from the sun and shaping the rock into a perfect canopy, everyone had dropped into a sullen silence.

Mela curled up in the shade, refusing to help Lar with the leezards they'd caught.

Aline appeared ready to pass out, wavering on her feet.

"Though small," said Lar. "Leezard meat is edible, even to Saeanans. Rest while I prepare them."

"I don't think I can eat," said Aline. "But I'll help."

With one arm, Lar toppled her over and caught her at the same time, shoving Mela aside and leaning Aline against the least-warm portion of rock. Though Aline's protests mixed with Mela's complaints, Aline didn't attempt to rise. Either she'd admitted he was right or her muscles refused to respond.

Skinning as many of the leezards as he could fit into the pot he pulled from their pack, Lar squeezed water from his sacs over them. Using the sparse dry brush around them, he lit a small fire inside a circle of sun-hot rocks. He rested the pot over the fire, covering it and the stones, not caring if the flame went out. The stones, having sat in the sun for at least 24 hours of prontom season's 30 hour days, would almost be warm enough to cook the leezards without the fire. To be sure, he placed a few more stones over the mixture then made sure the moisture containment lid held tight.

It only took a few minutes for the aroma of cooked meat to leak from the release valve on the pot. Lar stirred the mixture, placed new rocks over it, and waited, turning back to check on Aline.

Exhausted, she leaned against the rock, eyes closed, appearing to slumber. Sitting up, Mela glared, her talons twitching.

"I suggest you don't try what you are considering," he told his sister.

"You're too far away to stop me," she said with a sneer.

"Though I will kill you if you harm her," said Lar, "I will most likely be disposing of your body, not hers. Perhaps your consecration will come early."

"She's sleeping."

Lar shrugged. "I am only warning you. She is not asleep, not really."

With narrowed eyes, Mela shifted, but did not attack. Aline's eyes shot open, the hilt of her knife swinging out, in search of a target.

"That would have met your skull," said Lar.

"Maybe," replied Mela, but she scooted farther away.

The meal finished, Lar used his scaled fingertips and palms to carry it beneath their shelter.

"Good," exclaimed Mela. "I'm starving."

Lar threw the remaining dead leezards into her lap. "Then you can skin those. When we are finished with the pot, you may put in your palate-water and make yourself a meal."

"You made food, but you're going to refuse to share because I was too tired to help? What about her?"

"She is my wife," said Lar, noticing Aline's flinch at the word. "She needs the moisture. You share none of yours, so you receive none."

Mela jumped to her feet, clenching her fists as her claws pulsed in and out of their sheaths. "We're all walking through this desert. We're going to all need water. Not just your precious livestock."

Letting his arm talons peek from their sheaths, Lar went to stand. Aline put a hand on his arm, above the sheath. "Who cares what she calls me. It's not worth it."

It took a moment, but Lar bridled his anger and faced Mela with some semblance of calm. "We get what we need from the leezards. Remember, sister, one of the benefits of your Saeanan 'deformity', as you like to call it, is that you store water not only in your palate-sacs, but in your CSF sacs. In some ways, we are better suited to the desert than any pure Mwalgi could hope for."

That only infuriated her more. She stormed out into the sunlight, dragging the leezards to a large rock, skinning them with a ferocity that told Lar she probably imagined him as the little creatures in her angry hands. After only a few seconds, she cursed and sucked at a tear along her arm. She worked a little more slowly after that.

With one glance at the pot, Aline paled. "I can't eat. I feel like I'm going to throw up."

Lar shook his head. "Eat only a little, rest, then eat a little more. You will find your hunger."

It took some coaxing, but eventually Aline found her appetite. They ate in companionable silence, Lar picking out the drier pieces of meat, until Mela interrupted.

Holding up a flat rock, she pointed to the strips of raw meat making a small pile in the center. "There's not enough leezard here to tempt a nyarhoond."

"Feel free to hunt for more," said Lar. "You have no compass and there is no one around for kilometers. If you are not back in an hour, I will assume you're dead and leave you."

"I can't just leave the meat sitting here. It might cook, but it might go bad."

Aline appeared finished, so Lar cleaned out the last few bites from the pot then held it out to Mela. "You can have the pot now."

She stalked forward, yanked it from his hand, and threw the meat in, stomping to an area well away from them to cook her meager fare.

Lar dug into the pack for Aline's bone vitamin. "Mela is only going to cause more trouble."

"I know," said Aline. "I want to say slit her throat and be done."

She paused, and Lar wondered if she was suggesting he do it. The idea caused dread, but it also brought a sense of relief.

"But she's your family," said Aline with a sigh. "Even if she is as bad as Betette. We can't give up on her yet."

"She almost killed you, more than once."

Aline took the vitamin strip Lar offered, waiting for it to dissolve before speaking. "She's been brainwashed. If you remember, I almost killed you when we first met. I would have, if you hadn't saved me from that Mwalgi that pinned me to the deck."

The memory brought fresh pain, though Lar wasn't sure why. He'd saved Aline and she'd determined to repay the debt by keeping him alive until they reached Saeana. They'd never made it.

"What are you thinking?" she asked.

"I saved you from the collections soldiers, only to bring you to this. Maybe I should have let you die in combat rather than allow the Mwalgi desert to torture you."

Aline shifted the hood back so he could see her face. The skin was red, slightly blistered beneath the thick cream. "You saved me, I saved you, and I'd do it all again. We're in this desolate desert because I let Meladise set me off."

"What did my sister say?" he asked. "On the train."

"She'd given up on the insults." Aline shook her head in self-disgust. "Started talking to herself and I don't think she expected anything about what she said to bother me. Off in her own little world, she talked about how she wanted to be a collections soldier, and all she'd learned about finding Saeanans and extracting CSF. Her scenario hit a little too close to home and all the fear, frustrations, and anger of the past few weeks just seemed to explode."

Lar gave a half-smile. "I don't blame you. If there is anything we understand about one another, it is our tempers. I probably would have marked her if I'd heard. Either way, we end up wandering through the desert."

A spasm jerked Lar's hand. He winced, letting it rest on his thigh until the twitching stopped. Aline leaned close, studying the circleh doy encompassing his eye. Lar blanched, but short of closing his eyes he couldn't hide it from her.

"The black hasn't changed at all," said Aline. "Not since we arrived at your brother's house. We've been together almost constantly. What's wrong?"

"My severance is more advanced than it appears, because both episodes of our separation happened so close together." How could he tell her the truth without making her feel guilty? "Perhaps, in time."

Aline's lenses kept Lar from seeing her eyes well, but he sensed her shift in weight, the severe expression that came across her face. "Don't you lie to me," she said in Saeanan. "And omitting the truth is the same as a lie, so spill."

Did Lar want to let her know the whole truth? There was no point in making her feel guilty over emotions she couldn't control. But part of his covenants as a member of the Diseep d'All was his oath of honesty. It was one thing to omit details when talking to Mistar Peltay, but it was a deceit to do so with his bonded, even if she didn't return the feelings.

Before he could answer, Mela joined them under the rock, eating her steaming food in the shelter of the outcropping. Lar couldn't blame her, but her presence put Aline and Lar both on edge. Aline gave him a glare, as if he'd planned the interruption as a means of avoidance. But no, he needed to be out with this.

"The whole truth," he said in Saeanan, ignoring Mela's suspicious glance. "My healing depends on my emotions, not only physical proximity."

Aline leaned back, her expression surprised, but otherwise unreadable. "So, you don't love me anymore?"

Lar shook his head. "Remember, Aline, Mwalgi bond for life. I love you as much or more than I did when we left the Noble Ark. That will never change."

"Then...?"

Mela set down her pot with a bang. "I'm still hungry." She reached out her hand to Lar. "Give me the compass so I can search for food and find my way back."

About to swat Mela's hand away, Lar held back for the sake of peace. "I'm sure that if you mark your trail and don't go too far, you'll find your way back without problem."

"And if I don't?"

"I'm sorry Mela, but I can't risk you going off on your own so you can find the authorities. You might not survive the trip, but I don't want you dead nor do I want them to find us. It's best if you don't go too far."

"What if I promised?"

Lar gave a half-smile. "I wish that would mean something, but it's obvious you never made your covenants as a Diseep d'All."

Mela pursed her lips together before answering. "I did, actually. Then you came home and I realized the promises don't mean anything. They were words for feeble civilians and cowards."

With that, she stalked into the desert, killing a leezard before she'd gone ten meters.

Lar shrugged and turned back to Aline. She hadn't lost track of their conversation.

"Then why aren't you getting better?" she asked.

With a deep breath, Lar finally released the words. "Because you don't love me. That is why I'm improving little."

Aline sat for a moment in stunned silence. "I didn't realize. I mean, I knew my hesitance might make it more difficult, but I'm killing you?"

"You cannot be blamed for the changing of your feelings. You are doing nothing wrong."

After a long pause, Aline reached out a hand, gripping his left arm. "I care about you. A lot. With all that has happened, I'm just confused. I'm angry about our situation, being treated like a tsefuur, but that's just circumstances. It's not like you planned any of this."

Lar hesitated. Should he tell her that he knew, that he'd been aware of everything when he'd lain gasping in the arena with her and Cloud? He couldn't say it, but she read something in his expression.

"Why don't you believe me? What is it you think you know?"

"I was awake," said Lar. "I heard everything in the arena."

"I know," said Aline. "The pill we gave you cleared out your lungs so you could breathe. What's your point?"

"So, I know how you really feel. There's no purpose in lying to me."

Aline cocked her head, confusion scrunching up her blistered forehead. "Oh," she shook her head, almost laughing but not with real humor. "You mean my telling Cloud that I loved him."

Lar dropped his head, trying to hide his pain.

Aline put her fingers under his chin, lifting it. "I try to be honest, you know that, right?"

"Yes," said Lar. "It is one of the points about you that I admire."

She nodded. "But I can, and sometimes do, lie."

It was Lar's turn to show confusion.

The red in Aline's cheeks darkened a tad, like the dulling of scales on an embarrassed Mwalgi. "Cloud was about to die. And there was only one thing I could do for him, which was to say the words he'd wanted to hear for so long. I wanted him to leave this world thinking that I returned his feelings."

"But you cared not for him?" said Lar, unable to hide the hope swelling in his chest.

"I cared about him. He'd saved my life, and in his own way, he was kind and truly loved me. I was sometimes attracted to him, and I guess I loved him in a way, but not enough to live on this planet with him."

Lar's hope burst. "So you cared for him as you care for me."

"No," Aline's denial was instant and emphatic. "I'm confused, but I'm not that confused. The whole time I was with him, I kept wishing, praying, that you could be alive and come for me. I knew it was impossible, that you were dead, but I could never let go of that hope. In the end, I declared myself your wife to the council, insisting they make me your brother's charge rather than Cloud's tsefuur. Not that they listened to me. The point is, if I'd loved him as much as I love you, I wouldn't have done that."

Hope returned, though something in Aline's words told him that all was not right. With tentative expectation, he leaned his mouth to hers, tasting the sour salve that coated them both, but not caring. Perhaps Aline did, because she quickly pulled away.

Hands on her lap, she scooted back a few centimeters. "I want to give you what you need, to tell you I love you and force the severance away. I can only ask that you don't give up on me while

I try to figure everything out. I want to be close to you but every time I try, it's like I have to get away. You kiss me, and I like it, but yet it takes all my willpower not to go off into the desert and keep running until Lenfay's sun burns me to a raisin and the leezards suck away what little is left behind."

Lar dismayed, hoped, and laughed at the mixture of Mwalgi and Saeanan words. She might love him, in time. He must be patient, hope, and pray. These were all things he'd done before. He could do them again.

"You said you prayed?" Lar asked.

Aline laughed. "I tried. You know that hands on knees thing, where you chant or sing or whatever?"

Lar cocked his head. "I've never heard you sing."

"There's good reason. The guard always complained and turned off the sound on my surveillance."

They both laughed and Lar felt a sliver of hope that all might be right with the world in time.

Unfortunately, Mela returned much too soon, her sullen anger infecting the group with a strained silence. Aline had urged Lar to have patience with his sister, to give her time to understand why he'd made the choices he had, but Lar could see no ending to their situation that didn't involve Aline or Mela winding up dead. And if he chose, Mela's corpse would be the one left to feed the hungry desert.

Why wouldn't the livestock close her yapping jaw already?
Meladise tried putting more distance between her and Aline, but
could still hear the Saeanan. She was yappier than Meladise's nyarhoond, Sari.

"So what happened to you, that you hate humans so much?"
Aline asked.

Meladise rolled her eyes, but of course, the half-blind Saeanan
couldn't see it on a dark-day. Wasn't it bad enough that Meladise
had to hear the woman's sob story about her family. Everyone had
lost someone. Meladise had lost her mother because the woman
was weak, like Aline and her family, a breed of individuals destined
to be subservient to the Mwalgi race. Life was sad, but Meladise
would survive. If she could ever get the woman to shut up.

"You don't have to roll your eyes," said Aline. "It was a simple
question."

Meladise stared hard at her, the sliver of red moon on the horizon making Aline's features as easily visible as the bushes and
scurrying animals in their path. "You're being led by my brother
like some consecration offering and you claim you can see me roll
my eyes?"

"I can't see details like you and Lar can, but there's enough of
an outline for me to read your body language. And you have a lot
of human gestures. You roll your eyes, shrug, and I've seen you

do a dozen other things that don't come naturally to a full Mwalgi. I have yet to see you smile, but I wonder if your lips wouldn't turn up. Whether you like it or not, your mother influenced who you are. Personally, I'm grateful, because she helped make Lar the good man that he is."

Meladise spat into the dirt, wasting a portion of water to emphasize her disgust. "My mother was weak. Unable to fend off a single Mwalgi attacker."

Lar growled, a soft version of a Mwalgi challenge. "Aside from Aline, Mother was the strongest woman I've ever known. Do you think that crazed renegot, Leutsimmer, was the first Mwalgi she had to defend against? She was forced to live her entire life inside that house because of it."

Meladise's eyes narrowed. "I've heard Jeraud say that she refused to wear proper Saeanan clothing. That's why she wasn't allowed to leave. She didn't know her place."

"She knew her place. It was with her family, doing all she could to care for us, be a good mother, and keep herself and us alive, including Father."

Despite Lar's numerous threats, Meladise unsheathed her talons. "Father was a full Mwalgi. If anyone kept us alive, it was him."

Lar nodded. "Many times, yes, but I remember Mother saving his life, and ours, shortly after we moved into Trovgarshtot."

That couldn't be true. Meladise had never heard Jeraud talk of it.

"Jeraud wasn't there," Lar continued as if reading her mind. "He was in school, but I had stayed home that day and went with Father and Mother to the registration office. The government you claim to believe in so much threatened to execute our mother unless she was registered as a tsefuur, with all the resulting restrictions."

"But she couldn't even follow those," mumbled Meladise.

Then Aline had to butt her snout in where it didn't belong. "Because they're wrong. No sentient being should have their rights violated in such ways. You Mwalgi call us livestock, but treat us worse than you would a barnal or nyarhoond. At least your mother had decent principles."

"And yet she died, didn't she?"

"I didn't finish my story," said Lar. "We were ambushed. Three Mwalgi who thought they could take out our whole family with one attack. Father held his own, but the man was a scientist, not a fighter."

Meladise chuckled. "Sounds like Jeraud."

"He's much like Father. You and I are more like our mother."

"I'm nothing like her," Meladise almost spat again, but the leezards of the last day hadn't had much fluid. Her dry palate-sac convinced her to restraint.

"Father managed one of the three, marking him and threatening to kill," said Lar. "Mother pushed me in a corner with you. I swiped at the men when they came close, but my talons didn't reach far. Mother killed one and left the other with a permanent limp. Want to guess his name?"

"How should I know?" Meladise let her contempt drip into every word, but she did know. The renegot that killed her mother hadn't picked her out at random.

"Darton Leutsimmer," said Lar, confirming what she didn't want to believe. "Father always suspected that someone in the government, someone concerned about the spread of our 'Saeanan disease' had orchestrated the whole plan, but Leutsimmer was a willing participant, letting his CSF levels get low enough that he wouldn't be blamed for the attack."

Meladise shook her head, sidestepping another bush. A leezard scurried from beneath its branches, but Meladise's attempt to skewer it missed and the animal darted beneath a rock. "So why didn't Mother finish him off, like she should have before?"

"Two reasons," said Lar. "She had been very sick. I almost stayed home that day to help, but she insisted I go to school. Every moment of my life I wish I could do that day over."

"So she wasn't feeling well," said Meladise. "That wouldn't have stopped me."

"True," said Lar. "But the region officials had told her that if she killed another Mwalgi, even in self-defense, our entire family would be offerings at the next Consecration Festival. The Manifesto Party killed our mother."

Aline opened her mouth as if to ask something, then seemed to think better of it, closing it again.

"So, you're claiming Mother let herself die in order to save us."

Lar paused, his voice solemn. "It would be the honorable thing to do, to sacrifice one's life for the people you love. And Mother's honor surpassed any notion any Mwalgi has ever had of the concept, whether Diseep d'All, another religion, or especially some fascist political faction."

Meladise couldn't believe this. She wouldn't. Why should she believe her cracking brother anyway? He was trying to get her on his side so he wouldn't have to worry about Meladise harming his precious Aline, a woman whose rightful place was to be a tsefuur, as the Mwalgi Manifesto declared.

"I don't believe you," she said, but knew she couldn't call Lar a liar. He took his covenants as a Diseep d'All more seriously than anyone she had ever known. He might skirt the truth, but he never lied. "It doesn't matter anyway. She was a Saeanan, a weak tsefuur by birth who should have never tried to be more than that. She got what she deserved."

The pain that ripped across Meladise's shoulder took her by surprise. She smacked a hand across it, feeling the warm release of skalwass. As if she could afford to lose more moisture!

"Oh great, the Mwalgi cutting ritual again," said Aline to Lar. "As much as she deserves to have her throat slit, none of us can afford to be losing water."

"She should not talk of our mother in that way," said Lar, but he bowed his head, obviously abashed. "I'm sorry." The apology was directed at his precious Aline, not Meladise.

Aline glared, but then chuckled. "I guess our tempers do get us into far too much trouble. Can we get rid of the Mwalgi cutting-each other habit, though? It doesn't seem like the best way to handle a problem."

"We learn marking very young" said Lar, still not apologizing to Meladise. "Even before our talons are strong enough to do much damage. It allows us to vent our anger without permanent harm, but I will try to unlearn it."

Though he continued to lead Aline as he had before, Meladise sensed a difference. Aline walked a little bit closer, their hands clasped more like a bonded couple than just a man leading a woman. Somehow Lar's attempt to destroy Meladise with his ridiculous stories had brought him and Aline closer together. Meladise again resisted the urge to spit.

"I understand how hard it can be to let go of your prejudice," said Aline.

Meladise groaned. The Saeanan was starting up again. The woman would not shut up! Aline paused and Meladise hoped for silence. The hope was in vain.

"If you give it time," said Aline. "Eventually, you can forgive your mother for leaving you alone, let go of the bitterness, and it's like finding a new life, a new you."

This woman, a Saeanan livestock Meladise hardly knew, was not going to tell her how to live her life or what to feel. Meladise stopped in her tracks, turned and stalked up to Aline. Lar's talons unsheathed, but Meladise ignored him.

"What I feel toward my mother is disdain, contempt, and gratitude. I'm glad she died so I could get away from her weak influence and become a decent Mwalgi in spite of the deformities she strapped me with. And if you don't shut up, I will kill you, even if it means Lar's claws across my neck." Meladise laughed, making sure her lips did not turn up at the edges. "Keep talking to me, and all three of us can die out here. Up to you."

"I should mark her," said Lar.

"No," Aline said with an exaggerated sigh. "The little brat needs time, like I did."

Meladise wanted to scream, but she took a deep breath and walked away, putting more distance between herself and them, though she knew Lar wouldn't allow her to get too far ahead.

"You don't bark much when you laugh," Aline called after her. "It sounds very human."

When Meladise didn't respond, but only walked faster, Aline

finally stopped her harassment. Meladise could still hear her quiet conversation with Lar. It was the same combination of insult and hopefulness that Meladise would "come around." The first chance Meladise found, she'd either slit the woman's throat or find a Mwalgi guard to do it for her. Then the woman could gargle to death on her good intentions.

Aline sat in the sweltering heat next to Lar, hardly able to stay upright, but grateful for the rest. As Lar shifted her hood to get a better look at her face, Aline couldn't help but flinch.

"We need more supplies," he said, rising.

"Kch," Meladise mocked. "Where is your Saeanan warrior now, brother?"

Lar turned his glare on Meladise, and for a moment, Aline wondered if he might attack. Both of them had been on the verge with Meladise the last day or so. Instead, his anger turned to contempt.

"Do you know what made our mother strong? It was not her ability to fight the Mwalgi and defend herself. Any bully with training and experience might do that. What made her strong was her heart. A Saeanan without the ability to bond, yet she loved Father and us to the point that she sacrificed her life. Living in our atmosphere caused her never-ending pain, she had to suffer CSF extractions to keep Father alive, and yet she never complained. As a people, we took everything from her, and yet she made excuses for those who most hated her."

"Well you took everything away from me!" Meladise yelled, finally releasing a few of the tears Aline had long suspected she held back. "You killed Bernad and now I have nothing to live for. At least Mother found someone and was able to keep him."

The distress in the girl's voice struck Aline. She'd been so caught up in herself, so worried about Lar, she hadn't thought about what Meladise must be going through. "I'm so sorry," Aline said.

"You're the reason Lar killed him." Meladise's eyes, dotted with black now instead of gold, stayed riveted on her brother. "But he's the one who did it."

"You had only breeyaed," said Lar. "You will heal. And if you were a stronger woman, like our mother, you would see the truth of what happened instead of laying blame on everyone else."

"The truth is that you murdered the man I love, and that's something our mother never had to deal with. If you had seen Father the last year of his life, you would know that true love is not such an easy thing to just let go."

Aline took hold of Lar's hand, trying to pull him away. "Don't let her set off your sensors."

Lar seemed to take a closer look at Meladise, and his anger faded to a look of profound sadness. "If you truly loved this boy then I am sorry. I know what it is to be separated from one you love, and to believe you will never see them again."

He kissed Aline's gloved hand, and she stiffened despite herself. Even in the darkness of the day, Aline caught the look of contempt on Meladise's face as Lar released his hold.

"As for Mother," he continued, "she lost her fiancé when the Mwalgi boarded that vessel. You blame me for killing the boy you breeyaed for in defense of my wife, yet you champion the type of murder that stole the life of a man our mother loved."

Aline's mouth gaped in surprise. His mother had been in love with another man, before Lar's father?

Meladise squirmed under his gaze. "Our need for CSF justifies—"

Lar held up a hand. "They didn't take his CSF. Their collection sacs were full and they didn't need it. They murdered him while our mother watched, and I was a part of Collections Forces long enough to know such incidents aren't isolated. I would call you a hypocrite if I thought you had the slightest idea of what you speak, but I will only call you naive."

Aline closed her mouth, considering the ramifications of Lar's words. For some reason, Aline had assumed that since the Mwalgi only bonded once and it was for life that they wouldn't be okay with a spouse who had a previous lover. Aline felt a weight release from her chest that she hadn't known was there. All this time she'd been pushing Lar away, was it because she feared his rejection? In part, maybe, but it was more than that. Aline was too tired to analyze further, but something had changed.

He turned to her. "I took the lenses Meladise discarded, colored them brown. I think the rest of my disguise will hold up, even if I look a bit bedraggled."

Aline shook away her muddled thoughts. "I'll keep an eye on her." She held the thick-handled knife in her lap. Sick as she was, she could barely lift the object let alone pummel Meladise with it, but she'd do whatever she had to do.

Lar must have agreed with her self-evaluation. He shook his head. "We'll tie her so she can't escape without causing significant damage to herself." He pulled the last of his and Meladise's clothes remnants from their bag. "Talons toward your body," he told her.

With Lar's splinted arm, Aline had to help him make the ties. She wavered in the warm darkness, sweat dripping from her forehead to Meladise's back, but with gritted teeth, Aline managed to stay upright and tighten the knots.

"And what happens when a leezard comes sniffing at me?" asked Meladise from the boulder Lar had placed her on.

"The rock is still hot," he said. "It will be many hours before the leezards choose to walk on it. I will be back by then." He lifted Aline to the other side of the boulder, where it rose to a peak. She leaned against it, barely able to stand. Using his good arm, Lar's talon carved into the rock, creating a makeshift bed in the growing shade.

"That is not good for your talons, brother." Meladise's tone suggested that she didn't care, only wanted to point out his stupidity.

"I've done worse," he said. "The talons still cut flesh and bone just fine."

The smile he gave Meladise chilled Aline's blood.

Lar folded the tarp as a barrier between Aline and the hot surface then placed their pack as a pillow.

"Don't you need the pack?" asked Aline.

He held out his left hand, showing a small metal box. "I have mobile credits to buy a new pack and fill it with supplies."

Aline nodded, glancing at the carved out rock. Tears tried to moisten her eyes, but none would come. She kept turning him away, yet Lar continued to care for her as if she was the only woman in the world who mattered. Before Cloud, she might have attributed this solely to his bonding, a genetic response locked in place and forcing him to act the gentleman. But Cloud was never this thoughtful, never this kind. There was more to Lar's response than the bonding. He truly loved her in a way that Cloud hadn't been capable of.

He must have misunderstood her reaction. "I am sorry," he apologized "This will still be uncomfortable, but not as warm as the rest of the rock. I will give you water before I leave. There is a small amount in the pack. Use it up while I am gone. I will bring back more."

He came close. Despite the brown lenses masking his black-and-gold circleh doy, Aline sensed his worry in the wrinkles at his eyes, the tightness of his dimple. As he'd done many times before, he poured water from his own mouth to hers, their lips barely touching. The trembling in Aline's legs wasn't solely from exhaustion. Their lives in danger, Aline on the verge of collapse, how did his touch still make her want him, and fear him?

"Ahem," Meladise coughed. "And what happens to us if you don't come back?"

"I will," said Lar.

"And if you don't?"

"Then we all die." With that, he gave Aline a look of apology then his lips descended with such force, such longing, that it brought her back to their time spent in each other's arms on the cot aboard the Desolashon. Cloud had interrupted that kiss, and then Lar had supposedly died just a few days later. She pulled away as her legs buckled.

He caught her, wincing and adjusting his hold to his left arm. "I will come back for you," he said. "No matter what."

Aline stared at him for a long time, realizing the truth went beyond words. Even death hadn't kept Lar from coming back to her.

"I know," she said, smiling wide, blinking back more nonexistent tears. "I know."

He helped her onto the rock, making sure she was comfortable. Against all reason, Aline believed his promise. Another weight lifted from her mind and soul as exhaustion dragged her to an uncomfortable, sweat-ridden sleep while Lar checked his sister's bonds. She felt a final kiss to her forehead before he walked away.

An hour later, the hum of engines pressed into her subconscious and turned into a nightmare.

Her rock pillow's reverberating thrum woke Meladise from her uneasy sleep. An ohfertsoog, out here? No, something bigger, and with escorts. She scanned the horizon, but even Mwalgi vision couldn't penetrate midnight on a dark-day at such a distance. She listened a moment longer, figuring the distance at less than a kilometer from her position. Opportunity had finally arrived.

Meladise raised her head and screamed a full-throated Mwalgi challenge. There were some aspects of their heritage that Lar had right. Jeraud squeaked like a nyarhoond, but Meladise and Lar had learned how to project like true Mwalgi.

With a glance over her shoulder, she confirmed that Aline hadn't come to slit Meladise's throat. The Saeanan stirred, but didn't wake. The smooth hum of a smaller engine shifted its direction, the sound coming closer. Meladise gave a satisfied smile. Another minute and Meladise risked another scream, guiding the skimmer ever closer. This time Aline's eyelids opened, heavy with slumber and dehydration. With gritted teeth and a determined focus, the woman rose to her hands and knees.

Meladise pushed back thoughts of admiration or sympathy. This woman was her captor, and a stinking tsefuur. Meladise must not let Aline and Lar's moments of kindness negate the fact that she lay strapped up like leezard bait because of them.

Aline shook her head, "Why?" she rasped.

"You ask that?" Meladise shifted on the rock so she could face her enemy. "I'm tied up like a common offering ready to be thrown into a communal pot. You kidnapped me."

Head hung low, as if too heavy for her body, Aline rasped out the words Meladise would have least expected. "Only because he loves you. We didn't want you to die, and I didn't want Lar to have to choose."

They'd told her this a dozen times, but they didn't really mean it. It had all been their fault, hadn't it? Lar was an outlaw, a traitor, his bonded wife a tsefuur. Whatever guilt Meladise felt was just the sadness of making her brother accountable. Still, when Aline went to jump off the rock, Meladise felt compelled to give her warning.

"You took off your boots," said Meladise. "The tsefuur stockings won't be enough to keep back the leezards. You're better off to stay where you are."

Aline glanced at the skimmer, only a few dozen yards away. "I'll take my chances with the little bloodsuckers. Can't be worse than the big ones."

Boots in one hand, she vaulted off the rock, fell, rolled across the dirt, managed to find her feet, then took off in a stumbling run. Unable to contain her respect for Aline's tenacity, despite her Saeanan weakness, a part of Meladise hoped she would make it. But as the skimmer pilot and his military wingman vaulted their ship over the rock, the former giving Meladise a brusque turn of her arm in salute, Meladise knew the Saeanan didn't stand a chance.

With a sadness Meladise hadn't expected, she realized her duty here was done. Aline would go to a collections camp, and Lar would die, as he should have in the first place.

Resting her head against the rock, listening to the nearby scuffle, Meladise shut her eyes and tried to block out Aline's screams.

The odors emanating from the town of Bielfelt assaulted Lar first, the scent of putrid refuse and defecation saturating the alleyways. Bielfelt made Lenfay's desert appear inviting. Having grown up in the nether reaches of habitable Mwalgi terrain, bordering the belt of desert so forsaken his people named it Desolation, Lar had accompanied his father to Colfo Pluurs many times. He was familiar with untamed territories, and the types of men and women who lived in them. But even Colfo Pluurs had more civilization than Bielfelt.

He put away his surveillance scrambler as he stepped farther into the old town. Though every street corner had the required surveillance equipment, Lar could see that those not smashed to pieces, dangling a bundle of wires and rusted metal, had been disabled by less obvious means. Some of them had simply been severed from their power source. Leaning against the closest storefront, one of three Lar could see with operational solar panels lining the roofs and with repaired windows, a Mwalgi woman held a flight-capable surveillance disk in her hands. As Lar drew closer, he saw she was hacking the flight plan and transmission destination, but she was having trouble with it.

Lar stepped onto the raised metal walkway that fronted the establishments on both sides of the street, pausing near her shoulder. "If you route the transmission through a government-approved line before sending it to your earbuds, it will accept your code."

A quick glance from her confirmed his suspicions. He shouldn't be here. Her red-laced circleh doy gazed at him with more hunger than gratitude. The scales lining Lar's back would make taking his CSF difficult, but if the woman grabbed some friends, it could be done.

With a nod, Lar slipped into the store. Making it quick, he grabbed what they needed most off the rust-encrusted shelves: a pack, food and liquid, the Saeanan salve cream the store carried was nearly expired but Lar took two large tubes, and he even found a bone repair kit, the last one.

As he approached the counter, Lar saw that the woman had found friends—three men in clothing almost as ragged as his own. They came into the store as Lar brought his purchases to the counter. His check-out clerk appeared to be in slightly better shape than the four Mwalgi waiting for him, his dark brown eyes visible through the smattering of pink in his expanded circleh-doy. Still, the man's nostrils flared as Lar came close, a sign that all of them had smelled out his relative abundance of healthy CSF.

Lar extended his arm talons, resting his fists on the counter next to the merchandise. "I don't want any trouble. I have credits, so just ring up my order."

With a glance at Lar's black-and-white marbled claws, and a look into his stern face, the man gulped and nodded. Touching the metal molding on his right index finger to each item, the scanner rang up Lar's purchases, showing the amount in the air between them. They were expensive, as Lar had expected, but the large sum that Jeraud had made available to him would easily cover it. Lar searched for a finger scanner, ready with his false fingerprint.

"Our print-payment went down years ago. You have to tell me the code."

With a chuckle, Lar grabbed the man's input keyboard. "Nice try." After disabling the copycat software that would have drained his bank account, Lar entered the code, made his payment, then wiped all memory of the code from the computer's databanks. "You have your payment. Nothing more."

With another gulp, the man nodded and moved to put Lar's items in his pack.

"I've got it," said Lar, loading the pack himself as he watched the three men and woman from his periphery. Finished, he turned to them. "Should I deal with you first, to avoid my merchandise getting damaged, or are you going to let me walk out of here without any problems."

"Please," said the man at the checkout, talking to Lar as much as the others. "Not another fight in here. It took months to get power back after the last one."

"Why do you need tsefuur cream?" asked the woman, her eyes hungrier than before.

Lar released his leg talons to match those still stretched out from his forearms, facing her square on and looking down his nose with contempt. "I received a few injuries while in the Collections Corp. I need the cream for my fals-skalen." Lar knew that the edges of the fals-skalen covering his human skin had turned up. He only hoped they gave the appearance of ragged scars more than revealed his identity.

One of the men stepped forward. "What's a collections officer doing out here?"

"The same thing you're doing out here," said Lar. "Running. Trying to survive. A man in my squad made me angry. I lost my temper and killed the whole group." He didn't mention that half his squad had been sick and not present, nor that Aline had killed almost half of those soldiers. He needed these people impressed and intimidated.

The man barked a laugh. "You can't have more than forty years."

"People often mistake my age," said Lar. "While captured aboard a Saeanan ship, they found it hard to believe I was a morten-rank officer. They kept saying I had twenty years, like some child." Lar barked a laugh, making sure it sounded pure

Mwalgi, without a hint of the human lilt he'd learned from Aline. "Most of them died as the ship exploded, but I escaped. I'm a survivor, and if you want to test the truth of what I've said, you'll try to take my CSF. If you do, I can promise that none of you will leave this building alive."

Lar didn't waver. Even in his severance, with a muscle twitching at the back of his neck, he kept his gaze steady.

The woman put a hand on her partner's arm. "I believe him. Besides, he helped me with the surveillance disk. We have a tsefuur transporter due to go just north of here in an hour. We'll get our CSF there."

"They'll have protection skimmers."

The woman gave Lar another once-over, eyes focused on his talons. "I have a feeling we'll stand a better chance. We've reached the point it's get CSF or die. One man won't be enough to supply all of us, and even if we took him down, we'd lose too many of our people who could help with the transport. It's not worth it."

The man nodded and stepped back, putting a hand to his ear-bud. "I'll tell the others to stand down, but I can't make promises."

Lar gathered his pack over his shoulder. "Good choice."

On his way out of town, Lar heard the sounds he'd expected and dreaded. He turned, facing three men with eyes so red Lar wondered how they had kept their sanity. "I thought your boss told you to stand down."

"He's not our boss, and we're not waiting for any stupid transport. You're here, now, and if you don't give us any trouble, we'll make it quick."

Lar sighed, his arm twitching as the pack dropped in the dirt. He let the dust billow up around him, releasing his talons, though he wondered if he'd get more than one good swipe from his broken arm. He gestured them forward with his fingers. "Let's get this over with."

Fangs extended, as if they could pierce through his scales, they rushed him. Lar slit the two front-runners' necks as they lunged. Screaming with the pain to his right arm, he slid between their falling forms, kicked out a leg, and swiped his leg talon through the last one's midriff. The man spun away, falling to his knees with wide eyes, skalwass and blood pooling onto the parched dirt. Careful to stay out of the mess, Lar gripped the man's shoulder.

"I will fulfill your promise and make it quick," said Lar. "I am sorry it came to this." And he slit the man's neck, jumping back as blood sprayed the dirt.

Leezards and desert rats converged on the corpses as Lar took his pack and jogged across the warm sand between him and Aline. If he hurried, he would be gone no more than the two hours he'd promised. As the rock came into sight, Lar burst into a sprint. There were no Saeanan or Mwalgi silhouettes resting atop the rock, their pack was gone, and all that remained of Aline and Mela were a pile of shredded fabric and a lone tarp trapped between two rocks a few meters away.

Lar dropped the pack, landing next to it on his knees. "No!"

He dug his talons into the hard-packed dirt and bellowed a Mwalgi scream. This had to be Mela's work. He should have killed her.

After a few deep breaths and a painful muscle spasm across his chest, Lar followed the nearby dirt furrows of a skimmer to where it had hovered for a fair amount of time. He almost stepped into a damp patch, moistened by someone's blood. By the appearance of the area, the scuffle of multiple feet, and Aline's discarded knife spattered with drying blood, the damp patches probably represented hers and her attackers' fluids.

A skimmer meant a military escort, but for what? Could it be the tsefuur transport he'd heard about while in Bielfelt? He wasn't sure. Out here, it could just as easily be related to the collections training base to the north. Lar covered the area a few more times, looking for the tracks he knew he'd find. A government transport wouldn't have authorization to transport a civilian without orders and Lar's scrambler would have left them unable to verify Mela's identity. They'd have given her supplies, if they were nice, and pointed her in the direction of the most hospitable town or transportation depot. Not Bielfelt. Lar racked his memory for what it might be. Of course, the military town just east of the training facilities. It would have a hovertrain stop and plenty of places Mela could get a bite to eat, sleep, and transmit information. Depending on what his sister did first, Lar might still be able to salvage the situation. He had to find her, find Aline, and take care of both before word of their existence hit main military channels.

After he slowed down and focused on the slightest stone or scuff of sand that might be out of place, he found it. A slight mark in the dirt, a partial Mwalgi footprint headed in a different direction than all the others.

Lar sat on the rock where he'd left Aline, pulling out his broken-limb kit. He wrapped the insta-cast around the arm, screaming out in pain as the nanobots inside the fabric recognized the break's location a few inches above his talon, tightened to reset it, and then hardened, forcing his arm to an angle that would accommodate the old-fashioned sling Lar pulled from the box. It took him a few tries, a muscle spasm in his finger making him drop the bright red contraption, and the resulting stiffness making it hard to retrieve.

He'd need to find Aline soon, or he'd again be too far into severance to save her. And it would be his own fault, for leaving her here, and for leaving his sister alive. He wouldn't make that mistake again.

After a few more tries, he slipped on the sling, took one of the four accompanying pills, and pocketed the rest. Already feeling a healing tingle in his arm, he resisted the urge to flex his fingers or slit a hole in the cast for his talon.

No, he'd take care of his arm so that once he found where they'd taken Aline, he would have both hands fully capable of throttling Mela's hateful neck.

The laser shots outside the transport didn't rouse Aline, but she stirred and opened her eyes when an explosion rocked the ship. A human at the far end, the only male prisoner on board as far as Aline could see, clenched a fist and appeared ready to strain against his bonds. He didn't make it that far, one of the Mwalgi guards backhanding him.

"Stay still, livestock. You're not going anywhere."

Aline kept her eyes to slits, feigning unconsciousness. She didn't finger the dried blood and sweat that coated her fuzz-covered head, nor wipe away the fresh drops that fell onto her patched-up jumpsuit. One of the Mwalgi still lay on a cot at the back of the transfer, insta-casts over a wrist, knee, and wrapped around his ribs. By the way his face-scales continued to scrunch and twist, the man was in obvious pain. After what they'd done to haul her into this contraption, she hoped he died, even if it meant her execution.

No, she couldn't think that way. If she died, so would Lar. She had to stay alive.

More shots fired. Aline tensed, though she didn't let it be seen by the guards. If someone opened any of the doors, the man at the end of the transport wouldn't be the only one ready. A guard leaned to one side of the transport, looking through a window too high for prisoners to see through.

"Will we need to fight?" asked the guard who'd backhanded the human.

"No," said the woman scanning out the window. "They took out one of our skimmers, and it looks like they had a close fight, but our escorts beat them off. They're getting braver, though. If those crazy renegots had a couple more to their number, I think they'd have had us."

"They're really killing their own kind?"

The woman barked a sarcastic laugh. "You've never been CSF deprived have you? It reaches levels where you'd kill your own bonded to get what you need. I don't know why law enforcement hasn't bothered to come out here and get rid of these people. At the rate their numbers are expanding, next time they'll have enough people to kill us, the escorts, and drain all the livestock."

The man sighed, looking at the man he'd beaten with a mix of resignation and regret. "Then thank the All this is my last month at camp duty. I can't wait to be away from the whole stinking business."

"You hoping to get into Collections Corp?"

"Desolation, no. I'd rather join the war forces and kill the poor livestock than have to suck them dry like we do in the camps."

"You turning into a sympathizer, Reyden?"

"Can't do that, either," said the man, Reyden. "My family depends on me to do my duty or they'll be the ones running around with bandits trying to kill people and steal CSF."

The woman nodded. "It's been hard since they cut rations again. Hard for everyone."

The man leaned against one of the poles in the middle of the transport, grunting his assent.

Aline tried to stay awake for the rest of the conversation, seeing if they might talk about something useful to her escape, but she had all the symptoms of a mild concussion. Despite her throbbing head and heaving stomach, she couldn't keep her eyes open. The Mwalgis' strange dark-day, and the darkness in her mind, pulled her to oblivion.

A strange light pulsed behind Aline's eyes, sending pain to a spot at the back of her head, one of many places she'd been hit by the Mwalgi. Forcing her eyes open, she blinked against the brightness, surprised at her ability to produce tears from the blinding pain.

"It's best if you can get yourself up and eat and drink. You've missed two meals already, and I doubt they'll inject you with another water solution."

Aline turned her head, groaning at the pain. She wasn't in the transport. They must be inside the collections camp. Touching her fingers to her neck, she identified the pain that throbbed almost as much as her skull. They'd branded her like a ranch cow.

In the cell next to her own, separated by a clear wall with a few small holes drilled in, allowing the passage of sound, sat a girl in a sleeveless gray dress reaching to mid-thigh with a simple velzip down the front, the outfit as plain and stark as the white cell walls. Her brand had a symbol Aline didn't recognize, with the numbers 423 over the top. The girl shoveled some kind of slop into her mouth with her hands. She turned her head, bright-orange braids slapping against her shoulders as she gestured toward a tray of food sitting inside Aline's cell.

"If you can get to it soon, it should still be warm. Tastes weird, but you get used to it. Some of the other things happening..." The girl paled. "I don't think any of us will ever get used to."

By the girl's manner of speaking, Aline would have guessed her sixteen or seventeen years old, but the braids and the way she shoveled her food made her seem much younger.

Aline forced back the pain in her head, dropping from the cot to her hands and knees. She knew she couldn't eat much, but she at least needed the fluids. Crawling over to the door, a solid one instead of a doorfield, Aline leaned against it and sipped at the water on her tray.

"I don't plan on being here long. It's a collections camp, right?"

At Aline's words, the girl's eyes lifted with hope. "You have a way out?"

"Not exactly," said Aline. "But I have someone coming for me."

The girl deflated. "I thought I knew someone who would help me. I saw him, before they loaded me onto the transport. He looked straight at me and then turned away. There's nobody on this planet but Saeanan prisoners and Mwalgi monsters. Nobody's coming for us."

It was irrational. Aline knew it, but a fear like she hadn't experienced since her time on the Desolashon, learning of Lar's death from Cloud, gripped Aline.

Despite her best efforts, she couldn't keep her hands from shaking, or sweat from breaking out on her forehead. Her fingers tingled and her heart raced. She gasped, dropping her water packet to her tray, nearly toppling it over.

What if Lar died? What if he left her again and never came back? She was in a collections camp now, and he was still suffering from severance. He'd never find her in time, never get through the guards. She was lost.

"Are you okay?" The girl's voice finally registered with Aline.

Remembering her therapy sessions as a child, Aline crawled across the space to her cot, stroked the rough cotton of the mattress, and took steady breaths until her racing pulse finally settled.

"I'm okay," Aline tried to reassure the poor girl. "I used to wake up in a panic on a regular basis, but I haven't had an anxiety attack in a very long time. I hope I didn't scare you."

"No," said the girl. "I think I've had some of those, too. I feel like I'm going to die."

Aline gave her a half-smile as she returned to her tray. "I think can help you learn how to cope. I'm guessing your capture must have been quite traumatic."

The girl set aside her cleared tray. "They killed my father, but he was kind of dead already, addicted to brittle beetles. It's my memories from Chaerli that keep me up at night. That's where I lost my mom."

Aline finished her water, but the unappetizing food, though familiar from her days aboard the Desolashon, didn't tempt her roiling stomach.

The girl heaved another sigh. "Do you really think someone might save us?"

Her mind calming, Aline evaluated the question and evaluated her fear. Lar had practically come back from the dead, why didn't she believe in him now? And then it hit her. Fear was what had kept her from Lar, not the relationship she'd had with Cloud. After her family's deaths, she'd had trouble getting close to people, afraid they would leave her, but she thought she had gotten over that. I guess, some things you never completely get over. After thinking Lar dead, she hadn't trusted that they could ever be together. She'd believed he would die and leave her again, like he'd done before, like her family and Ark and all of her friends aboard the Noble Ark. And now, because she hadn't done all she could to reverse his severance, if he didn't come it would be because Aline had let him die.

"If my stupidity hasn't killed him already," Aline told the girl. "He's come back from the grave once. I believe he can do it again."

"What do you mean?"

"He's a unique man who has survived some impossible odds and saved my life more times than I can count."

The girl gave the wistful smile of someone who believed in romance. "What's his name?"

"Lar. Larkin Trovgar. If anyone can save us, he can."

The girl's smile disappeared. "Larkin Trovgar is a selfish, conniving, son of a Gi who only cares about one thing."

"What?" Aline said more out of surprise than as a question.

"You. You must be Aline, the girl I helped him escape for."

"Andi?" Aline couldn't believe this. Of all the places to end up, maybe Lar's All did have a hand in the universe. "Calianda...um, O'Keene, right?"

"Even after everything I did," said Andi. "Lar looked straight at me as they were loading me on that transport. They hit me to the ground and he didn't even blink. Just stepped back into his fancy car and drove away. I hope his severance eats him up and leaves him to die on his own horrible planet."

Aline shook her head. "For both our sakes, let's hope you don't get your wish."

Signal jammer in one hand, Lar paid close attention to the movements of every Mwalgi and every camera around him. The holovids he'd seen coming into town, issuing an alert on him, Mela, and Aline, held images composed from long-distance cameras at the train station. With his brown lenses and fals-skalen still appearing as scars, especially in the dim light of a dark-day, he hoped nobody would connect him with the vids. Except one of the holovids also showed him as a half-Mwalgi. If people recognized the placement of his scars as the joints between fals-skalen and real, they might start to ask questions. He flexed the fist of his injured arm, stiff but functioning. He had one pill left, and the treatment would be complete. Thank the All for one positive in this nightmare.

Lar skirted the train station first, more of a depot than a station, but there was no sign of Mela. Either she'd already left, been captured, or she was still somewhere in the town. Lar racked his brain for where his sister might go, but they hadn't been together for more than a day or two at a time in the last three years, and those had been when he was on-planet, in training. He had no idea what her interests or habits might be now. He made his way up and down the streets, strolling into stores, thinking she might have tried to purchase or steal food, but he found nothing. He eavesdropped on conversations, knowing that if she'd been taken by the authorities there would be talk of it somewhere, but the town seemed as quiet as the worn-out people who lived in it. At least the eyes he met in lighted places only held a smattering of pink, not the red, blood-shot look of the people of Bielfelt. These people didn't have much, but they weren't starving.

At the last store, Lar knew he was going in the wrong direction. He'd heard no talk of a capture or police presence, and she didn't seem to be in any of the food establishments, which meant she'd gone somewhere to think or to escape. He and his sister had opposing views, but they were alike in many ways. Where would Lar go if he were in the same situation? He almost headed off to a secluded little park on the outskirts of town, but stopped himself. No, where would he have gone when he was her age, and held her type of anger?

He'd passed it ten minutes ago. An arena.

Retracing his steps, Lar found himself fronting a worn, metal-faced building with an eclectic smattering of solar tiles on its roof. Three of its four solar windows appeared to be functioning, or near-functioning, the last covered with heat-reducing tape. Walking through the powered-down doorfield, the air felt cool if stale, but as he made his way through the press of bodies the temperature increased to the uncomfortable swelter of a tight crowd.

In the center of the arena, a translucent blue force field formed the rectangular perimeter of an arena. Inside, three ellgots, varying in height from half a meter to almost a full meter, faced one another, hissing from between their sharp beaks. The smallest of the three seemed the most aggressive, dancing back and forth on four of its legs, its sharp claws clanging against the metal floor, with its front two legs stretched forward, as if prepared to rip into one of its opponents. The other two ellgots kept a wary eye on the smaller one, almost ignoring one another, their reptilian backs arched and the long spines of their underbellies tucked in.

As Lar spotted Mela, the smaller ellgot came too close to one of the larger ones. The big one raised its front feet and stretched out its long neck, the hiss turning to a hoarse cough as acid sprayed from the back of its mouth. The small ellgot ducked and moved out of the way, running between the other two, the acid singeing the end of its stubby tail. The medium-sized ellgot saw its chance, taking a stab at the small one's side with a sharp beak. He missed, most of his attack diverted by the back-scales, but the little ellgot's underbelly started seeping small droplets of blood.

Mela yelled along with many others, raising a fist and screaming at the little ellgot to get its revenge. It was the perfect diversion that allowed Lar to pop out his brown lenses, letting his gold-and-black circleh-doy dominate his appearance, then come in from behind and get a good grip on her arm.

Before she could even realize what had happened, he started dragging her backward through the crowd.

Regaining her balance and getting a good look at Lar, Mela's scales dulled, making the contrast to fals-skalen noticeable. Lar only hoped the dim lighting would hide it, but as fast as he had the thought, Mela extended her talons and her natural armor brightened as much as it had dulled.

"Not here," Lar said. "People will get hurt."

She struggled against his grip. "I won't let you take me back."

"Hey, what's going on?" A big brute stepped in behind them, a few centimeters taller than Lar and twice as bulky. Lar couldn't tell how much was fat and how much muscle. "This man bothering you, Tenya?"

Great. She'd already made friends.

With an angry turn of his eyes, Lar faced the man, making sure he could see the full extent of his severance. "Tenya and I are bonded, as you can see by my eyes and hers. It's even legal, but she's having second thoughts. We're going to go outside and talk and then I'll let her make her decision to let me die, or find a way to get along."

The man paused. "This true? I thought you said the man you'd breeyaed for died."

A vengeful expression on her face, Mela opened her mouth and Lar knew he'd be in for a fight.

He yanked her arm, pulling her close, and whispered in her ear. "I will kill him if I have to. I'll kill you and as many people in this room that fight me. Let us work this out between the two of us instead of involving innocent people."

Mela turned to the man with an apologetic smile. "I didn't want you to know. I'll go explain some things and then I'll be back."

The man clamped a hand on her shoulder as she moved to leave. "You sure he's going to let you come back?"

"He loves me," she said, looking at Lar as if she'd like to gut him. "He has to let me leave if it's really what I want."

The man grunted his understanding as if still not sure, but released his hold. "I'll come looking for you if you're not back in ten minutes."

Lar raised his eyebrows, though the fals-skalen made them feel like stiff ridges, and tightened his grip on her arm.

"Give us half an hour," she said to the man, meeting Lar's warning look then accompanying him almost voluntarily out the door.

As soon as they'd stepped a few feet away Mela pulled her arm from his grip. "I'm not going any farther. You're not dragging me back into that desert, and to what point? She's gone. They nearly killed her and they took her. There's no getting her back now. You might as well die and have some dignity about it."

"And where are you going to go?" Lar asked. "If you believed you were safe, you'd be gone already. You're trying to figure out what to do, because there's nowhere to run."

"Because of you," she spat.

Lar shrugged. "We did what we had to do to stay alive, and I'll do what I have to do to get Aline back. Where is she?"

"You think you can waltz into a collections camp and say, 'Please give me my bonded,' and they'll just hand her over?"

Lar sighed in relief. He couldn't waltz in or ask anything, but he knew his way around a collections camp. "Looking at your new fals-skalen and healthy complexion, I'm guessing you used undisguised credits here. It won't take long for the authorities to track you down."

With a smirk, Mela put her hands on her hips. "And I'll tell them everything I know."

"By the skimmer markings," said Lar, "I know they wouldn't have spotted either of you if you hadn't somehow alerted them. You're lucky I've had time to calm down, because if I'd found you at the rock where I left you, I would have slit your throat."

Mela opened her arms. "Try it." She extended her claws. "My friend will be out soon, but it's not like I need his help."

This wasn't getting Lar anywhere. "Say we fight and you kill me," said Lar. "Where are you going to go? The authorities may believe you, but I doubt it, and they're going to want someone to blame. No matter which direction you take, this doesn't end well for you. At least with me, you have a chance to live."

She sheathed her talons, and barked a laugh. Aline was right, even with all her practice Mela's laugh had a human lilt to it. "So you expect me to come along willingly now? I don't need you, so go save your little Tsefuur and leave me out of it."

Lar held up both hands. "If that's what you want, go back into the fight-bar and see how long it takes for the enforcement officials to make you wish you'd died in the desert."

"My choice," said Mela, turning away.

Lar moved as if to continue down the road, walking behind her, but at the last minute he lunged sideways, grabbed her face and swung his fist into the back of her head. He felt a twinge of pain through his injured forearm, but nothing more severe than a severance cramp.

Mela slumped into his arms and he pulled her into an alleyway. Taking the lenses from his pocket, Lar scratched a portion of them to black and popped them into her eye sockets. She looked as deep into severance as he was.

He hoisted her over his shoulder. "Sorry, little sister. As much as I want to kill you, I can't do it. And I can't have you telling the authorities our plans."

Lar turned off the main road as Mela's friend emerged from the fight-bar. A couple more turns and the man would never find them. At the edge of town, a land enforcement agent waited for them. She had force fields set up and a perimeter. Nobody was going in or out without going through her.

With a sigh, Lar settled Mela more firmly on his shoulder and reset the scrambler in his hand, letting surveillance see him, but not identify his or Mela's bio-signature.

"I really don't want to kill anyone today," he muttered under his breath, approaching the check-point with a smile.

Meladise lashed out instinctively, only half-conscious. When the blood and skalwass splattered, she knew she'd made a mistake.

Before she could register what had happened, Lar was running, Meladise bumping across his hard shoulder. Opening her eyes, Meladise squinted at the blockaded town but it was hard to get a good view. Something obscured her vision. She blinked a few times, recognized the uncomfortable film of protective lenses, and pulled one off. Clear vision in one eye was enough to reveal the entire truth of the situation. A land enforcement officer lay on the sidewalk, a pool of blood and skalwass running from the pathway to the rocks. Meladise's right arm talon dripped a few more drops of blood onto the thirsty dirt and sand. A crowd was gathering and pointing in her and Lar's direction.

"Bloody fluids," Meladise whispered.

Lar turned off the roadway, headed for the open desert, "That's an understatement. Can you run on—?"

He went down, dropping Meladise into the rocks and managing to twist his body so he landed and rolled on her other side instead of landing his shoulder into her stomach. He lay there, beating his fist against his calf, cursing. Meladise could slit his throat right now, explain what had happened to the authorities.

She came to her feet, talons extended. It would be so easy. Lar looked up at her, expression accusing but resigned. All the times he could have killed her, probably should have for Aline's safety, and he hadn't. His eyes asked if she would turn around and slit his throat, while he was down and weak, an unworthy adversary. When she was young, about to do something crazy or wrong, Lar had given her that look. It had always quelled her, made her behave, because his opinion had always meant so much. Now, it only served to fuel her anger. How dare he judge her, after all he'd done?

She glanced back at the crowd gathering on the street, and retracted her claws. She wouldn't spare Lar because she cared about her brother. In her eyes, the Lar she'd known was dead. He deserved to die, but she'd go along because he was right about one thing, the authorities would use her as their scapegoat, especially now that she had an enforcer's blood on her hands. She'd let him live, because right now, it was her best chance to survive.

Plucking away the other lens so she could see clearly, she pulled him to her feet. "I'll kill you later. Right now, let's get out of here. I assume you have supplies stashed somewhere?"

"Yes, but I still don't trust you."

Meladise smiled, "You shouldn't."

They took off at top speed. Despite Lar's severance, as long as he didn't have major muscles tripping him up, he not only kept up with Meladise, she had to admit he was faster.

As the hum of another skimmer reached their ears, the fourth in so many hours, they threw their packs under a carpace bush; Lar pushed Meladise in next to them then huddled in close, pulling their brown tarp around them. From a distance, they must appear to be just another mound of dirt. Meladise had always thought her brother's obsession with computers and electronics strange, but as the skimmer passed by them, a surge of gratitude for that scrambling device he'd cooked up replaced any previous judgments.

The skimmer retreated and he pulled away the tarp, rolling away. Meladise tried to follow, but the branches snagged an edge of falsskalen and she had to pause to extract it from the bush's sharp grip.

She sat in the dirt a moment, trying to repair the damage. "Do you think we could hide by rocks next time? I'm going to look as hideous as you if I keep getting shoved under the bushes."

Lar's returning gaze held the same unwavering contempt she'd seen since Meladise had mistook his wife for a tsefuur. "If there had been a rock, I would have used it. If I remember the terrain at all, we should have more mountains and hills in the next hour or so. It will be much easier to hide."

"You think the enforcement skimmers will keep coming?"

"We didn't just kill a renegot civilian this time," said Lar. "We got one of their own. They won't easily forget that. I think we'll start seeing less of them soon, though. You noticed that one veered north as it passed? They're going to assume that we're finding civilization north or headed to the Col de Pluurs pass into the western provinces. Either way, they won't be looking for us near a collections camp."

"I don't know what you think you're going to do. Prisoners don't escape from places like that."

Lar smirked, a challenge in his eyes. "Mother did."

Finished with her scales, Meladise jumped to her feet. "If I have the story right, Father got her out."

"Then I'll have to find a way to do the same thing," said Lar.

"You're not on the inside, with a knowledge of the compound," Meladise pointed out.

"Then I'll have to find a way to get on the inside."

"Right. And how are you going to manage that?"

Pulling five scrambling devices from a pocket in his pack, he dropped them back in again. "That's the easy part. The rest may prove to be a bit of a challenge, though."

With a shake of her head, Meladise shouldered their other pack. "Let's get your suicide finished with so I can end up caught by the authorities and made to pay for all your crimes."

Meladise knew that was the likely result, but the slim chance that she might come out alive kept her moving.

Shouldering the other pack, Lar waited for a spasm in his biceps to pass. "The enforcer was your fault."

"I thought she was you," said Meladise, taking the opportunity to make sure Lar still knew how much she hated him.

"I know," he said.

No anger, no resentment, just disappointed resignation. Come to think of it, was there ever a time when he hadn't sounded disappointed in her?

She sneered back at him and took off at a run, not noticing or caring if he followed.

"It's daylight, Aline." Andi's voice woke her from an uneasy sleep. "Time for breakfast, if you can call it that."

Aline darted up from the cot, ready for battle, then realized where she was, and that Lar hadn't come yet.

"This is weird," said Aline, rubbing sleep from her eyes. "I'd gotten used to the Mwalgi light-days and dark-days, but this place is run on a Saeanan clock. My body isn't adjusting as well as it should."

"How can you tell the difference?" asked Andi.

"The cooling units. They don't have to run as hard on the dark-days as they do the light. I don't know what time of the day it is outside, but it's a dark-day. I'm guessing I've been in the facility for three days now, four days since they captured me."

"Then I've been here for two weeks. I wonder how much longer until they do to me what they're doing to the others."

Aline had heard the screams. At first, she'd assumed torture, but torture wasn't a regular part of a collections facility, aside from the extraction of CSF. These screams were different and they were all by women. The sobbing that followed is what finally put the pieces together for Aline.

On board the Vengeance, as the Mwalgi forces were ransacking the ship, the Mwalgi soldier who'd tried to take her from Cloud had said they had orders to bring in good "breeding stock." At the time it had seemed strange, but she was too focused on getting out of the room before someone realized the man they'd left lying on the floor, Cochran, wasn't dead.

There had only been one man, among probably twenty women or more, on the transport that had brought them here. Aline wasn't in a collections camp. She was in a breeding facility. When her menstrual cycle had started a couple of days ago she'd known for sure. They'd removed her med-inject while she was passed out. Aline rubbed at the spot on the back of her arm where she'd always felt the little bump, the med packet that kept her sterile and gave her a daily vitamin dose. This place was a worse hell than Aline was ready for. Lar had better come soon.

Halfway through breakfast a woman screamed.

"Why are they doing this?" Andi asked Aline, fear in her voice.

"I don't know," Aline said. "I understood from Lar that it was too expensive to have many collections facilities on-planet. It costs too much to maintain the prisoners. I know there are illegal ones on Chaerli and Vargal, which is why you never walk around those planets by yourself, but I don't see the purpose in this."

"Not just that," said Andi. "They could put us under and use artificial insemination, but they're breeding us like animals in a pen."

Aline did have an answer for that, but she didn't like explaining it. "Despite their intelligence and technological advances, the Mwalgi are a violent people and they hold tradition in high esteem. One of their traditions is the value of fighting to prove one's worth. Even on an intellectual level, from what Lar has told me, they receive raises and promotions based on competitions of knowledge and invention."

"So we have to compete with the men in order to be left alone?"

"Not exactly. On Saeana, many people go to bars and restaurants in order to socialize. We drink, eat, and share stories. There are restaurants here, but only for the very rich. Food and drink are too expensive and valuable to be consumed in such a casual way. Instead, they gather for competitions. Often, those are fights between creatures. Most Mwalgi, especially those in the military, consider us creatures."

Andi paled, glancing up at the camera in the high corner of her room. "So they watch us for enjoyment."

"Yes," said Aline. "And to determine which of us will make the best breeding stock. If I were to guess, I'd say this is an experiment in creating the type of Saeanans who don't fight back, and if that's the case, I have a feeling you and I aren't going to pass."

"Sludge, no," said Andi. "But why include me? I'm only thirteen."

Aline paused, not sure how to explain, so she gave it to the girl straight. "It's a breeding program. To them, you're old enough."

Andi dropped her tray to the ground, the food half-eaten. She left it by the door, scooting to the corner, wrapping the edge of her tunic up under her thighs to cover her buttocks, and embracing her knees.

As if on cue, the door to her cell slid open, Andi's food tray was removed, and a man was shoved into the room, the same Saeanan who'd been on the transport with Aline. His tunic appeared identical to the one Aline and Andi wore.

He looked at Andi, huddled in the corner, and swore. "Please, somebody just kill me now."

Andi began to cry, hugging her knees tighter. Aline pressed her face to the glass, screaming for the man to leave her alone. With an expression of sorrow and determination, he moved forward.

Aline banged a fist against the glass, but the man ignored her.

"My name is Gervin, and I'm so sorry."

"Please, no," she begged, looking into his eyes with tears streaming down her face.

He paused, looking Andi up and down. "How old are you?"

Andi's voice shook, her eyes riveted to the hand holding her arm. "Thir...thirteen."

Gervin released her, stood up, and stared at the camera, face in a snarl. He put his hand on his head, as if measuring his own height, and then held his palm halfway to the floor, as if measuring a child.

"No," He shook his head. "I won't do it. You sick monsters!"

The Mwalgi didn't even need cuffs. From small dots of metal on the ceiling, electricity sparked down, coursing over Gervin's body. He stayed on his feet until it finished then slumped to his knees, twitching.

"No!" Gervin screamed from his prostate position. He gripped the edge of the little cot Andi slept on, knuckles turning white as another surge of electricity hit.

"Okay!" Andi screamed, leaving the corner and reaching toward Gervin. "Just stop!"

The flashes of electricity ceased. Gervin had spots of reddened flesh all over his body. Electro-torture, electro-stimulation, or both?

Andi grabbed onto Gervin, but then screeched and yanked her hands back, shocked by residual current.

With a shove, Gervin shocked her again, dumping her back in the corner.

Aline slapped the wall, knowing there was nothing she could do, but still determined to try.

Gervin turned his burnt, twisted features back toward the camera. "You can roast me like a pork on a barbecue, but I will not hurt this child!"

They amped up the voltage again, Gervin's hands clamping onto the bed in a fixed grip. When they finally turned it off, he slumped to the floor in his own urine, his tan face almost as pale as the cell walls.

Sobbing, Andi crawled to his side. "They killed him. They killed him!"

In seconds, her cell door opened and a pair of Mwalgi guards, a man and a woman, started dragging Gervin out, wiping up most of the mess with his tunic as they pulled.

"You monsters!" Andi yelled. "You filthy, horrible, Gi!"

She attacked the woman, nails out, clawing at the tough Mwalgi skin, making her fingers bleed.

Aline called to Andi through the holes between cells. "Stop. Attacking them won't help."

The girl didn't stop or even slow down. Despite her advice, Aline would have joined her if she could. The female soldier had to leave Gervin to her male comrade to fend Andi off.

When the door closed, the electrocution nodules changed out, their whirring mechanics giving Aline a clue that something was about to happen. More torture? The familiar scent of cleansing spray, similar to what the Mwalgi used on their scales, clued her in before she saw the yellow mist. It didn't spray exactly, descending to the floor more like a fine powder than a liquid. As soon as it penetrated her scalp, Aline knew this was going to hurt. Andi whimpered with the burning pain, but Aline's skin still hadn't healed from her days in the desert. It was all she could do to whimper alongside her friend rather than scream. But Andi had been through enough today. Aline determined to hold herself together, for the girl and her own pride.

The mist settled, coating the floor, and the nodules above them whirred again. A fierce wind sucked Andi's ragged pigtails upward, forcing both girls to hold down their tunics as the yellow mist swirled upward and back into the vents, presumably to retrieve any unabsorbed water content. Yellow powder coated the floor, bunks, and toilets.

As soon as Aline could manage the pain well enough to speak, she turned to Andi. "Are you all right?"

"They killed him because of me."

Aline remembered something Trent Kleins, the psychiatrist aboard the Noble Ark, had said to her during one of her therapy sessions.

"He made the right choice," Aline told Andi. "And he knew the consequences. Don't diminish his sacrifice by blaming yourself."

And yet, Aline had done the same thing for so many years. She'd tried to take the blame for her family's death, still felt that blame in her heart. But her father had stayed behind, willingly died, in an effort to save his family. Another weight released from Aline's heart, small tears running unheeded down her blistered cheeks to cleanse spots off her yellow-stained tunic.

"Thank you, Dad," she whispered, believing for the first time that there might be some entity beyond this life that would let him hear.

"Aline?" Andi broke Aline's silent communion, fear in her voice. "Will they send someone else, like Gervin said?"

Considering the question, Aline paused. "Yes, but they'll send someone to me first." Aline didn't know how she knew that, but she was sure of it. "Did you ever see Lar pray?" she asked Andi.

Andi shook her head. "He said he believed in an All or something like that, and sometimes he chanted, but most of his time aboard the Future was spent strapped to a medical bed."

Aline faced the clear wall between them, crossed her legs, ignoring the way her tunic slid up her thighs, and rested her palms on her knees. Andi followed suit, both of them facing one another.

"I have to warn you," said Aline. "I couldn't hold a tune if I needed it to save my life."

Andi chuckled. "I'll make up for it then. Singing is one of the only things I'm good at. I won an award in the junior competition for my district last year."

Aline taught her the chants she'd heard from Lar. Andi adapted them into song, similar to what Lar had done, but unique to the girl's own style. In the chanting melody Aline heard Andi's fear, hope, and supplication for a guidance beyond their own. After a time, Aline stopped trying to join in, content to let Andi speak for them both. Aline still didn't know if she believed in an All or in God, but she believed in Lar. If he was out there, he would come. Aline glanced at the cell door, hoping his rescue wouldn't come too late.

"This isn't going to be easy."

Lar slumped back behind the rock from which he'd been watching the compound.

Scooting farther into the shade, Mela flinched away from the warm rock at her back. "I'm thirsty. I know we both had our water sacs full when we left, but we hardly had anything to eat or drink the entire three days we were running and now we've been sitting here for two days."

"The sun will start setting soon." Lar gestured to their packs while still staring at the rock they hid behind, studying the stark collections camp in his mind. "There's still a water packet left, near the bottom."

Mela pulled the pack to her lap, rummaging through it. "I thought you said getting in would be easy."

"This isn't an ordinary collections camp. I don't see CSF-transports, and no one has gone in or out of the compound since we arrived."

With a grin of triumph, Mela retrieved the water. "They don't transport CSF that often do they?"

"Often enough that they should have a small refrigerated transport in the side yard. The stranger part is that they usually have shifts going in and out. One of the reasons that recruits to any branch of military service, even local land enforcement, has to serve time at a camp is the ease in which Mwalgi bond with Saeanans. They have to change out the people monitoring the camp on a regular basis, and many of the lower ranks have to do multiple tours."

Mela nodded, her distaste of the concept evident in the sour twist of her lips. "I know. The ease of bonding from Mwalgi to Saeanan was a basis for their father's crazy theory that Saeanans and Mwalgi had to share species origin." She drank half the packet, not offering Lar a drop. "So they usually have more people coming in and out?"

Taking the packet from her hands, he took a couple of swallows before handing it back, ignoring her glare. "Yes, but it's not just that. Even watching from the outside, none of the movement around the compound is normal. Nobody comes out for anything, even to get some fresh air or play a game of ball."

"So do you still think you'll be able to get her out or are you finally going to admit it can't be done?"

"I can get her out," said Lar. "It just might take more time."

Lar thought of his time on the Desolashon. In the past, time hadn't always seemed to work in their favor.

Shifting his focus from the rock and the water Mela had already finished, he took a good look at his little sister. Her fals-skalen looked like his had a few days ago, a collection of scars that with a little imagination, outlined the lines between real scales versus Saeanan skin. Lar could only imagine what he must look like. There were patches of fals-skalen that had completely fallen off, leaving his skin bare to the elements. The cream he'd bought kept most discomfort at bay, and he had to wonder again why the stuff worked so well on him and yet barely sufficed for Aline. They both had human skin, so what was the difference?

Mela scooted away from the rock. "It'll be sundown soon. I'm going to do some late nakmeeta hunting before the dark-day starts."

"It's called nakmeeta for a reason. We're well past the middle of the day. It's sleep-time now. You should get some rest."

"I've slept half the day while you sat and stared at that dead compound. Sure it's not deserted? What if you have the wrong place?"

The imposing cement walls rose up on every side, only a single transport truck visible through bars at the far corner, suggesting Mela might be right.

"No," said Lar, trying to convince himself as much as her. "The walls are new, and this is the location Jeraud told me to avoid, the new collections facility."

"Maybe we should listen to him," Mela muttered. "I don't care whether it's the right place or not, but I'm hungry and I'm still thirsty."

Lar spread out in the shade she'd deserted. "Fine, but don't go far and keep a watch out for guards."

"I thought collections camps don't put any guards around the facility?"

"They don't, but they have sensors to detect large groups approaching, and like I said, this place is different."

Lar didn't wake when a group of guards left the compound. If he had, he might have found his opportunity. But he heard the scuffle, the laser-gun discharge, and he made it down the hill as they dragged Mela's still body inside the metal door, locked it, and then sealed it with a high-energy doorfield.

"Great," Lar muttered, heading back up the rocky hill for their supplies and searching the horizon for another look-out post.

If Mela was alive, and she talked, there would be guards combing the area and enforcers on their way. If she didn't talk, they'd still ID her and know exactly who she was, which meant enforcers. Or she could be dead.

Despite his intentions to be rid of his little sister, the ache in his chest at her possible death gave him pause. He had to lean against a rock and take a deep breath, gaining control of his emotions. Knowing the fight in Mela, the guards had probably been forced to kill her. Lar took a calming breath and looked at the situation logically. If Mela was dead, they might have thrown her into a temporary refrigerator, leaving the task of ID-ing the body for later. That might give him some time to figure out a plan, but without someone going in, time might not be enough. Still, he hoped they hadn't killed her.

Aline had known her turn would come, just as Andi's had, but if they were charting ovulation, it seemed a bit early.

Gervin stood inside her door, the surprise on his face mirroring Aline's. Darkened skin spotted his arms and legs, either from the effects of his strange electrocution or perhaps the treatment for his wounds.

"You're alive?" said Andi from the other room.

"We thought they'd killed you," said Aline. "Thank you for doing the right thing."

The dark circles under Gervin's eyes attested to his own horrors. "This place is a nightmare. They're turning me into a monster, but I'll make them kill me before they turn me into a child molester."

"I know. You're still a decent human being."

Gervin moved closer. "You're not a child."

Aline knew what was coming, and she was sorry for it. "No, but I'm not going to let you touch me."

The metal dots above them whirred.

Gervin's eyes darted upward. "I can't live through that torture again."

"Why are they doing this? I've kept track of the days and there's no way I could be fertile. If this is a breeding program—"

"The food," Gervin interrupted. "I think they're putting drugs in our food, making the women ovulate sooner, and making the men..." he paused, taking a deep breath, already noticeably aroused. "...making us into monsters."

He put a hand on Aline's shoulder, stroking her leathery skin. Aline allowed it, for now. "You didn't come straight from a Saeanan ship's capture. You've spent time on Lenfay. Escape and get recaptured, or were you one of their...tsefuurs, I think they call them?"

Aline sidestepped away, getting into the corner, her heel against the crevice. "I don't do well with being touched. I have enough nightmares."

Gervin moved forward, a cat stalking skittish prey. "They'll torture us both if we don't cooperate. It's better if you just let yourself enjoy it rather than fight."

"Is that the Mwalgis' test of the day, or the training they're trying to put us through? How to make the Saeanans docile about rape?"

"I'm sorry," said Gervin. "I have no..." He darted forward, hand outstretched. "...choice."

Aline used the wall to spring her body up as well as forward, landing a firm blow to his sternum. Gervin flew into the door, hitting it hard enough to make it rattle. He shook his head, clearing it from the impact.

Aline caught the whir of the electrocution nodules above. She leaped across the room, grabbing Gervin in a standing half-nelson as the currents hit. If they incapacitated her, they'd have to incapacitate him as well.

The pain only lasted a few seconds, the Mwalgi observers obviously realizing that neither one of their lab rats would mate if they were both knocked out on the floor.

Struggling to breathe, Gervin tried to turn his head in her grasp. "This is all very exciting, S and M and all that, but what now? You can't hold onto me like this forever, and when you let go, they'll shock one of us until we comply."

Aline shoved Gervin to his knees, pressing the man's belly into the edge of the cot. "Even better," he said. "You know that with the drugs they've got me on, this is only making me want you more. And not just out of duty or survival."

"Well, this is going to change your mind," said Aline, knee pressed to his back, her hands taking a firm hold on his left arm.

"Don't hurt him," Andi cried from the other room. "It's not his fault."

"How long have you been on the bone vitamins the Mwalgi give us?" asked Aline, ignoring the girl.

"What vitamins?" said Gervin.

Aline couldn't resist a small sadistic smile. "So, only since you arrived here, the same time I did."

"I guess—"

Gervin's answer cut off into a scream as Aline propped his wrist to the edge of the cot, brought her knee off his back, and slammed it across his elbow while pulling back his shoulder. The resounding crack, his agonized cry, and the sound of electrical current filling the room joined together in a cacophony of pain.

As the currents jolted her body, Aline managed to focus on the camera, raising her arms to the ceiling in defiant acceptance of the punishment.

When the voltage finally stopped and armed guards, four of them, dragged a whimpering Gervin away, he shook his sweat-ridden head. "Did you have to break it?"

Aline barely managed an answer from where she sat slumped on the cot. "You'll have at least four days free from being a monster. And I have at least one more day as a virgin. Maybe it will be enough."

Probably not understanding the English words, but obviously confused by Aline's behavior, one of the guards scrunched his eyescales in her direction.

For the first time since she'd arrived, Aline spoke Mwalgi. "I've been through a kind of desolation that you could never understand, even though you live in a place that deserves the name. I will die before I submit."

"How do you know Mwalgi?" the man asked.

"Because I am sentient, intelligent, and of value, just like you.

Saeanans are not livestock. We have families; we're just like your mother, your sister, or your daughter. When you commit these atrocities, it is the same as if you did it to them. When you stand before the judgment of the All, or whatever deity you believe in, you will be held accountable. There will be no Mwalgi Manifest in the hereafter."

The guard's eyes widened. Aline saw fear, regret, and something else she couldn't place cross his face. Maybe he would have second thoughts about what they were doing in this place.

The female guards pulled him from the room, telling him not to listen to the crazy Saeanan, but Aline could tell she'd rattled them a bit, too. They weren't used to prisoners who could communicate in their language, not without a translator. It made Aline too similar to them.

"Be ready for tomorrow," said one of the female guards with a sneer. "You will not fight off Fedrek so easily."

Aline had no idea who Fedrek must be, but by the screams she'd heard the last few days, she knew some of the Mwalgis' "studs" weren't nice about their job.

The door shut, and Andi whispered through the wall. "Did she mean a Saeanan day or Mwalgi day?"

"Saeanan, I hope. Our days are twenty-six hours. If I understood Lar correctly, during Prontom season their days are only about sixteen."

"It changes?"

"Their twin suns make for vast differences in seasons and rotations."

Andi paused. "So, somewhere between sixteen and twenty-six hours and you're going to have to do that again with Fedrek."

"Do you know him?" Aline asked.

"Yes," said Andi, hesitating.

"The more I know about the man, the better prepared I can be," said Aline. "I didn't want to hurt Gervin, but he'll heal and it buys us both time."

"Fedrek isn't like Gervin," said Andi. "He's huge, almost as big as a Mwalgi, and he's mean. As they brought me in, I saw him being subdued by guards, but it took three of them to do it."

Aline tried to waylay Andi's fears. "Sometimes the big, mean guys are gentle with women. Maybe I can try some manipulation."

Andi frowned. "Maybe, but he was leering at all the women on the transport as we got off, and making crude jokes as we passed."

Aline pushed her tired, sore body off the cot and into prone position, ignoring whatever view she might be presenting to the cameras in her skimpy dress. "I guess I'd best get prepared then."

As she exercised, she scanned the room, looking for anything she might use as a weapon. The cots were welded to the floor, the sanitizer sink that dropped yellow powder was all one piece, and the plastic toilet didn't even have a lid or removable parts.

This didn't look good.

Meladise noticed the crick in her neck first. When she raised her head, she felt the bruises along her face and jaw. In her attempt to touch them, she realized her hands were tied behind her back, to the chair she sat on. It wasn't until she shifted her weight in the chair, pulling at the restraints that tied her ankles to each side, that she experienced true pain. It shot up from her right calf, making her scream out, though she'd been determined to remain silent and assess her situation before she let anyone know she'd come awake.

A man in civilian clothing, bearing an air of authority, stepped into the room, staying in the shadows. "You broke your tibia bone, fractured the fibula. It didn't require surgery so I placed an insta-cast on it. I placed a heal-patch on your skin, something I can only do for the Saeanans in our facility. What are you?"

"Who are you?" Meladise asked with a sneer.

"Doctor Kreshev Trovgar."

A distant relative then. Trovgar was a pretty common name, usually associated with those of higher ranks, or doctors, like this man and her father.

Meladise considered refusing to talk, but saw no point. "Mwalgi father, Saeanan mother. I'm a half-breed."

"Impossible."

With a smile, followed by a wince, Meladise decided against trying to shake her head. "I get that a lot."

"You should be deformed. At best, mentally slow, but you show no signs of mental incapacity and my scans suggest you're a perfectly healthy Saeanan."

"Saeanan?" Meladise did whip her head around at that, despite the pain. "I'm Mwalgi. If I've been stuck with Saeanan skin on my body, that doesn't make me Saeanan."

"Huh," said Kreshev, leaning in closer and exposing himself to the bright light shining above Meladise. "You don't even know what you are? Mwalgi and Saeanans are extremely similar. Identical, other than a single chromosome and certain DNA markers, like Saeanans to apes only closer. But if you don't know what you are, then you must not have been in on the experiment. I'd assumed the Saeanans must have created you, so you could live on our planet as a spy, but if you were born here, as you claim, what was the point?"

"You had to have run my DNA through the system by now. You know who and what I am."

The doctor shook his head. "I know you are wanted by land enforcement and we're to hold you until they arrive, probably sometime in the morning. Other than that, they refuse to tell us anything."

Meladise considered telling the doctor they wouldn't be happy with his examination of her. Since her father died, no doctors hadn't been allowed to do examinations or treat Meladise, Jeraud, or Jeraud's children, other than the director of medicine in the collections military. But that was this man's problem. Her problem was how to get out of there.

"My name is Meladise Trovgar. I've done nothing wrong. Is there a reason I'm strapped to a chair?"

The doctor came closer, squatting close and looking up into her face. Under different circumstances, Meladise would have toppled the chair on top of him and attacked. She needed to bide her time.

"I don't believe it," said Kreshev. "You're one of Segvalt Trovgar's offspring. I'd heard he did some kind of experiment in the mountains, but I never imagined.... This is amazing. Illegal, but amazing."

Now this was getting insulting. "How am I illegal?"

Kreshev rose up again, blending partway into shadow as he leaned against the wall. "Part of the edicts of the first interplanetary council. After the cyber-wars on Earth, the first thing the Saeanan ambassadors insisted on was the non-alteration clause. No species may tamper with DNA or the basic composition of their species to make themselves more capable in warfare. That's the gist of it anyway. Same one their ancestors adopted on Earth except they insisted the five systems' edict be applicable to all species."

"My father wasn't tampering with anything other than to let my mother have children." Meladise was getting frustrated with this man's line of thought. He couldn't be saying what she thought he was. "Having Saeanan skin and hair makes me weak, not more capable."

Kreshev stared at her, incredulous. "Do you not see this? Did you believe your father did you a disservice? Your Mwalgi scales cover you like armor, yet your skin makes almost any life-saving surgery possible. If I'd needed to surgically set the bone in your leg, I could have done so. A Mwalgi would have been crippled for life, assuming other complications didn't kill her. Also, attractiveness is part of survival, and having sexual anatomy more prominent, in any species, makes them not only better able to reproduce, but it makes members of their own species less likely to commit irreparable harm. You, my dear, are very attractive by both Mwalgi and Saeanan standards. Your hair isn't as convenient on Lenfay, so thick and dark. Still, it's easier to cut and keep short and humans release heat from their heads, something Mwalgi can't do. Our scales make us able to survive here, but you have the advantage of scales and skin. And though you have to treat that skin, it has trace amounts of Lethorin-D, the strengthening agent in Mwalgi scales, making you able to withstand our atmosphere with only a small amount of intervention. A Saeanan exposed outside to the elements would have constant blisters. Believe me, we got one in last week, and her skin is barely starting to recover."

Meladise stared at him, but Lar's words came back to her and she repeated them to the doctor. "We store water in our CSF sacs, and don't need extra CSF."

"Exactly!" Kreshev's face lit up and he gestured at her with enthusiasm. "Don't you see? You're the perfect specimen to survive well on either Mwalgi or Saeana. You're a genetic marvel, though still illegal."

Cocking her head to the side, Meladise studied the doctor. "I still don't see that. Better at survival, maybe. Combat? The skin's too soft."

"Which means the Saeanan's acid antidote would work on you." Kreshev came close again, poking at the skin swirled with the scales on her arm. "With time, we could probably develop drugs that would make you immune to the acid entirely."

"If I'm such a medical wonder then why does the government hate us so much?"

"The Trovgars?" Kreshev barked a laugh. "Think about it, dear girl. The entire Trovgar Empire, their power in the government and the economy, is based on the people's need for CSF. Even water purification, imports and recycling don't compare to the money and power involved with CSF and the collections military. If they encouraged a change in our species that made us more like the 'livestock,' they would lose everything. I suspect the only reason you're alive is that you're a Trovgar and your father's reappearance after so many years put him too much in the public eye when he returned. The Saeanan conservation groups were starting to gain momentum at the time and officials didn't want to lose their votes. Of course, now that the Manifesto Party is in power, I doubt they'll let such a thing continue."

Leaning her head back, letting her circleh doy dim the light above her head, Meladise took deep breaths. Could everything she'd believed in, everything she'd fought for, have been a sham? The government officials wanted her to fight and kill Saeanans so they would have wealth and power? Her world didn't need her to fight for them so the masses would have CSF?

She returned her gaze to Kreshev. "Is this why we went to war with the Saeanans rather than negotiate CSF trade?"

"Most likely," said Kreshev. "I'm sure the Saeanan government has their own position of power and greed, but if our world became dependent on them for something we needed, the Saeanans would hold all power in the Intersystem Council and eventually the Trovgars' power would diminish and the Voserhabs would take over. That's my guess anyway."

"Why haven't I ever heard this before?" said Meladise.

Kreshev glanced up at the camera in the wall. "Because I'm not keen to be executed. That camera isn't on, and as soon as I leave this room and turn it back on then we never had this conversation. We live in the semblance of a democratic republic, but we're kept at the mercy of the government for our sustenance, for CSF and water, and the Manifestos know how to play their own system so resisting factions never threaten them again."

She hadn't thought she and Kreshev were in a contest of will, but Meladise felt beaten. Perhaps it was only a contest within herself, but Kreshev's participation lent him the victory.

"What do you want to know?" she asked.

"I'd like to know how your father made you, but I can tell that you don't have that knowledge. The guys on the other side of that door want to know if someone came with you." Kreshev glanced at the door and back. "If there's anyone out there you care about, I suggest you keep your mouth shut."

"What will they do to me if I don't talk?"

Kreshev glanced at her healing leg. "The question is whether they do it anyway. Most of the guards here are a brutal lot. I try to keep the Saeanans alive and steer clear of everyone else."

With a shrug, Meladise turned her head to the door. "Lar will be expecting them, maybe even hoping for them. It won't matter if they know he's out there. Might as well send them in and get this over with."

With a curt nod, Kreshev passed his hand over the doorfield lock-system. "Good luck to you."

Thinking of her brother, waiting out there for his opportunity to get into the facility, Meladise whispered back. "I think you'll need the luck more than I will."

With his dark Saeanan skin, and dark cloth wrapped over the armor of his chest and back, Lar blended into the compound shadows better than the guards. As he'd expected, Mela must have told them about his presence. It was the opportunity he needed, but he wasn't sure if he should be grateful Mela was alive or disappointed at his sister's expected betrayal. He kept close enough to the guards to catch their conversations, masking his presence in the dark shadows near the compound walls and bushes.

"Reyden," said a Howtman in the group, one of the seven women in the group of eight. "Where is he?"

Reyden manipulated the image projected in front of him, mentally directing his map of the area into different viewpoints. "Something is wrong with the signal. There's someone out here, but the program is only showing the locations of leezards, lapin, and a distant Vulfbaeor."

"Vulfbaeors?" the Howtman asked, her voice nervous. "I thought they were extinct."

All of the soldiers shifted, feet grating on sand and rock, staring into the darkness as if they expected something to pounce. But Vulfbaeors had no such subtlety. They didn't need it. If one was close enough to attack, all of them would hear it barreling toward them.

"They're not extinct," said Reyden. "They don't usually come this far north, but they're still around."

"For a collections recruit in the top of his class, you're not worth much, are you? Can't even find a single man hiding in the open wilderness."

"Howtman Terkis," Reyden's words were clipped and offended. "This wilderness is far from open, and it wouldn't matter if it were. If the sensors aren't functioning properly, then I'm as blind in this darkness as you. I need to go back to the compound and recalibrate my systems, see what's going on."

"Fine. It will start getting light soon. We'll keep looking. You go back to the compound and do whatever you do with the stupid equipment. Let's hope your replacement is better at the job than you are, and let's hope they send a woman."

Reyden waited.

"Dismissed," said Howtman Terkis.

Reyden gave a quick salute, an arm-sheath to his chest, then stalked away. Lar heard a final mumbled insult from the Howtman officer.

"Desolate, golden-eyed, Saeanan-lover."

Lar followed Reyden to the compound. As soon as the door-scan gave Reyden access, Lar shoved the man's back against the wall and put a talon to his neck.

"Look at my eyes, Reyden. My bonded is a Saeanan in there. You know I'm desperate, and you know I'll kill you if I have to."

"Who?" said Reyden, more concerned for the woman he'd started to bond with than for his own life. That was a good sign. "Is it Loren?"

Lar retracted his talon. "No. Her name is Aline. I believe you also have my sister in there somewhere."

Reyden's face flashed relief then disappointment. "I don't know many of the women's names. I had to stop learning them so I could do my job. I know we caught someone outside the compound in the dark-day sleep hours."

"Aline is more important," said Lar. "She has fire-red hair, like a double-sunset over the Heptsam Mountains."

"We have two with red hair that arrived recently. A very young one from about two weeks ago." His face scrunched with distaste. "Too young for the program. And another with military hair. She's aggressive and broke her intended mate's arm."

"Intended mate?" Lar's talon burst from its sheath. "What is this place?"

Reyden flinched from the claw, glancing at the closed door behind him and the camera above their heads. "It's an experimental breeding program. They say they'll eventually go full scale with multiple camps and unlimited participants."

Without meaning to, Lar shoved Reynard's back harder into the wall. "How?"

Reyden's scales paled to the point they almost appeared white. "I don't know. I'm a litund-rank new recruit. Do you think they tell me anything?"

It took a little while, but after some deep breaths, Lar retracted his talon, releasing the man. "You're going to get me in there, and you're going to help me get Aline and my sister out."

There was no reason to save Mela. She'd already told the authorities everything Lar didn't want them to know, and he was sure it was recorded. But if he could, he'd at least get her out of the facility. She might still have a chance to save herself and she could do nothing more to endanger them. The damage was done.

Reyden glanced again at the camera. "I don't know if I can do that."

Following his gaze, Lar gave his best human laugh then pulled the scrambler from his pocket. "All they're seeing or hearing is the blank desert they recorded for the ten minutes before you reached the door."

Reyden's scales perked up a bit, a light gray instead of ash-white. "I'll help you on one condition."

"You think you're in a position to insist on terms?" Lar asked. Maybe the kid had tougher scales than he appeared.

Pointing to his golden-specked eyes, Reyden's scales brightened further, a natural silver. "I'm in a position to let myself die if I don't get what I want."

Lar had to admire the young man's determination. "What do

you want?"

"You save Loren. I know I can't go with her. She wouldn't have me. But you get her out of this place and find her someplace safe."

"I'd have to create a mass breakout, but I can't lead all those Saeanans. Look at me. With my Mwalgi armor, they wouldn't trust me, and neither will your Loren."

After considering Lar's words for a moment, Reyden gave a curt nod. "You get them a chance, and I'll make sure she leaves with what she needs to survive."

"If I do this," Lar warned. "I may be forced to kill some of our own people."

"Most of the doctors and the medical staff aren't so bad." Reyden glanced at the camera again, seeming nervous about the time. "They don't like what we're doing, but they do their best to keep the Saeanans comfortable and alive. The rest of us deserve to die. We've followed the director's orders, jeered and watched what goes on here as if viewing a sporting event, and most of us don't seem to feel a particle of remorse."

"But you do," said Lar.

Reyden shook his head. "I do now, but I did some horrible things when I first arrived."

"In the universe of the All, wrongs against peace, love, and order, can be balanced by standing for what is fair and good. You will make up for what you've done by helping me release these prisoners, giving them a chance at survival."

The Saeanans Lar helped would most likely die or be recaptured, but most of them would likely prefer death in a Mwalgi desert to life in a collections camp, or worse, a breeding facility. Whether a gift or a curse, he'd give Reyden his request.

As the sun peeked over the horizon, they would have a few hours before the wake-hours crew would start shift. Reyden helped Lar attach Mela's discarded and ripped scales to the remainder of his fals-skalen, giving Lar a haggard and scarred appearance rather than half-Saeanan. They entered the facility, both of them knowing full-well the impossibility that everything would go the way they planned. Still, Lar was finally in.

Their first challenge appeared seconds after they entered.

"Who's this?" said the door-guard. "I've been monitoring the perimeter surveillance for the last hour, and neither one of you showed up before you stepped through the door."

Reyden's scales dulled, but his confused expression seemed natural. "There must be something going on with all the systems. I couldn't get my scanner to work properly either, which is why I came back. I ran into my replacement" he gestured at Lar with his chin, "trying to get the door monitor to acknowledge him."

"And who are you?" asked the guard.

Lar had taken a vow of honesty, but even he knew that bending the truth believably required staying close to it.

"Nigel Trovgar," he said, inwardly cringing at his hated middle name.

The man barked a laugh. "I guess your parents didn't want children and decided to take revenge."

Lar gave a bland smile, remembering to stretch his mouth to the side, not turn the corners up as he'd learned from Aline. "They swear they like it, but I'm the one who has to live with it."

"And you're the Saeanan-lover's replacement?" the door-guard asked, his brow furrowing. "I thought they were sending a woman, and she's supposed to be coming with the enforcement officer tomorrow."

Lar shrugged. "All I know is they told me to get on a transport, that I would be a temporary replacement for the tech officer here, and they dropped me off before waiting to see if I went through the door." Lar pointed to his black and gold eyes, hoping the shadows hid the full extent of his severance, evidenced across his retracted circleh doy. "They were probably in a hurry to be rid of me so they wouldn't have to deal with my severance recovery."

The guard punched a few strokes on his keyboard. "I'm sorry, but I'm going to have to clear this."

Reyden threw a panicked glance at Lar, but he didn't know the half of it. It wouldn't take much of a search to discover not only that Lar shouldn't be there, but also his identity, crimes, and probably a dead-or-alive reward.

"Shuldi, broter," said Lar, catching the guard's confused attention, watching it turn to surprise as Lar slit the man's throat.

The other guard lunged for a button on their control panel, but Reyden gave her an awkward shove. The guard struck out with a talon before Reyden had unsheathed. Scrambling back, Reyden tripped on the guard's abandoned chair. Skalwass spurted from the young litund's scales. Rather than preparing for the next attack, Reyden stared at his split scales, eyes wide.

With a triumphant gleam in her eye, the second guard raised her claw for the final blow. Silent as a solmond, Lar came beside her, slicing his talon into the woman's stomach. Holding her close, watching her eyes go wide with fear and death, Lar sliced his other talon across the woman's neck, ending her suffering.

She fell to the ground, her short-cropped white hair less than a meter from her comrade's. Skalwass and blood pooled on the floor and dripped from one of the empty seats. Reyden added to the mess, heaving the contents of his stomach into a corner.

Lar released a breath, heavy with regret. How many men and women had he killed to keep himself and Aline alive? Though many seemed worthy of death, or worse, did that really justify his actions? They were raised in a brutal world, with harsh laws and customs, trained from birth to admire the toughest and meanest in their race, and hardened to their crimes against Saeanans so they could feel justified in their use of them. But that didn't make this right.

Lar pulled Reyden upright from where he'd leaned on his knees in the corner. "We have little time. Can you work the computer and put me into the system, do everything as if the guard had accepted our story and we hadn't been forced to such violence?"

Scales white as granite, Reyden nodded. "What are you going to do?"

"Clean up." He gestured around the filthy room. "I'll have to leave the guards, but I'll manipulate the room surveillance so it appears we were admitted and left the room before any of this happened. They'll eventually put it together, but it might buy us thirty minutes."

Reyden nodded. "The search party will be coming back soon."

Placing a spider-bot on the door controls, Lar shook his head. "Nobody is stepping through that door until they cut it open. By then, they'll have more problems to deal with than a couple of renegade Mwalgi."

Reyden managed to get Lar to the main control room before the general alarm sounded.

"Does this happen often?" he asked the women at the prisoners' monitors. "I mean, I just arrived and there's already a breech."

They didn't even glance in his direction. "Shh. The perimeter guards will take care of whatever it is. We've got better entertainment right now."

Lar stiffened. "Entertainment?"

With a quick glance in his direction then back to the screen, the woman at the end snapped. "We've got a prisoner who thinks she's tougher than most. We're sending in the Vulfbaeor."

A chill settled in Lar's spine. "Vulfbaeor?"

"He's the biggest Saeanan we've ever captured, and he enjoys being breeding stock. I'd like to see her get out of this one."

The fact that Mwalgi women could watch this rape as sport, not realizing that in another culture they could be the victims of such atrocities, chilled Lar almost as much as the woman's words.

He tried to see around the guards' heads, mostly women, but they were crowded in every direction around the 3-D display.

"Who is the prisoner?" he asked, trying to sound casual instead of panicked.

"Number 321," said the woman in an off-handed manner. "Now be quiet. They're opening her cell."

Nodding his head, Reyden tugged on Lar's elbow. "That's the one. The red-haired woman."

Lar shoved his way between two women, forcing his voice to sound eager. "I want to see this."

At the sight in front of him, his talons unsheathed and fangs slipped from between his lips. Aline stood in the corner of a cell, stripped of everything but a fraying, short dress. Though less blistered, her skin had reddened beyond what it had been while they traveled the desert; the combination of atmosphere exposure and chemical cleanings. From the sleeves and bottom of her dress, her healthy arms and legs showed that at least she'd gained some weight and replenished her water. She faced the man entering her cell, shivering with a type of fear Lar had never seen from her before, creating a weight in his chest that burned hotter than a consecration pyre.

Though she was taller than most men in her species, the brute facing her had her by at least five inches. And the guards were right. The man appeared eager. Lar needed time to assess options, but he didn't have that luxury, not with that monster in Aline's cell. He slipped back from the screen, ignoring a snide comment about some new recruits not having the stomach for mating sport, ignoring the twitch that rippled across his side.

Regardless of the consequences, Lar had to do something to help Aline. He resisted the impulse to find her cell and beat the Saeanan male to ground meat.

Lar studied the equipment in the room, counted the number of technicians and soldiers gathered around the image projected in front of them. Panicked, Lar couldn't seem to settle on a plan of attack. He didn't have time for this. He needed to think!

Reyden's resignation to the inevitable spurred Lar to action. These people liked a good spar, well they were about to experience the ultimate show, but this time they would be the contestants.

"I suggest you find Loren and a weapon," he whispered to Reyden. "You have two minutes before this entire compound becomes chaos."

28

Aline waited, heel to the corner, patient for the right opportunity. The brute who entered her cell, tangled brown hair to his shoulders, narrow eyes watching her with tense expectation, studied her as he approached.

Hands to the partition between them, Andi mouthed, "Fedrek."

"Good," Fedrek growled like the mangy dog he resembled, focused on Aline. "I like it when they give me the women who will fight back."

She tensed against the corner, putting on a confident façade. "Last man who said that ended up with a cast on his arm."

"The new guy? You'll find I don't break so easily."

"That's okay," Aline forced bravado into her voice, but she found facing this massive fellow Saeanan more unnerving than a Mwalgi collections soldier. "You can still bleed."

Fedrek laughed without humor, lunging forward.

Aline faked jumping up and to the left. Instead, she rolled under Fedrek's outstretched arm. His fingers coiled in her smock, bringing her to a sudden halt. Aline pulled a shiv made from a broken piece of the toilet and a strip of her smock. The plastic bit into flesh from the inside of his elbow to his wrist. Fedrek released her, pulling back his hand and clutching at the bleeding wound. His features twisted into a furious grimace, a bear ticked off by a BB-gun.

The nodules above whirred and Aline knew she was about to receive her punishment. She jumped up, gripping Fedrek round the shoulders. But he was more experienced than Gervin. Shoving his elbow between them, he shoved her back. Aline staggered against the door. In a fair fight, she still could have taken the brute, but pulses of electricity raked across her body. The torture sent her to her knees while exciting a physical response, a lust that repulsed every reasonable thought. Her simple weapon, fashioned with hours of painstaking effort, fell from limp fingers as the electrical current faded.

Fedrek kicked her little knife to the corner. "That'll slow you down, you little Gi-lover."

"How can you—?"

"They told me you can speak their language. You're not an interrogator, which means you have to be one of their tsefuur, a Gi-lover."

Aline flushed. She did love Lar, but not like he insinuated. "I'm nobody's tsefuur, and I never will be."

"Doesn't matter." Fedrek gripped her by the arms, pulling her upright, her toes dangling a few centimeters from the ground. "You're mine now."

Did the idiot think a little electric shock was going to make her compliant? Sure, her muscles were twitching, and her fingers and toes were numb, but that didn't mean she was sprawled out on a holomat, game over.

He'd left himself wide open, so she took the opportunity. Wrapping an ankle behind his knee for leverage, she kicked her other leg high and as hard.

With a squeal that would do a school girl proud, he hunched over, face red. Feet now firmly on the ground, Aline wrapped her arms around those still gripping her shoulders. She kicked him again, even harder than before. Face going from red to white, he gasped for breath. Taking a step back, he latched his hand round her wrist, as if she'd wait for him to gain control. Aline yanked her wrist from his grasp, stepped back, and kicked him in the chest. His leg hit the edge of her cot, spinning him. His head reverberated against the translucent wall with an echoing crack followed by a faint hum as the wall reverberated with the impact. He crumpled on his side, next to Aline's discarded knife.

The nodules whirred above. This was it. One more electrical shock like the last one, and Aline would be compliant. Screaming a Mwalgi challenge at the camera, she raised her still-twitching arms.

"You are hypocrites and liars!" she yelled in Mwalgi. Aline then used the traditional form of a Mwalgi good-bye, but turned it to a curse. "May your children suffer as you make us suffer, and may you be there to witness their horror."

The whirring stopped. No electrical currents struck from above, no yellow mist burned her skin. Nothing. With a whoosh, and the bleat of a thousand alarms, the door behind Aline opened. Five guards stood in the hallway, the male obviously having just arrived. He seemed relieved at the sight of Aline. The women's paralyzers vacillated between her, a target somewhere down the corridor to the left and another in the opposite direction. The male held his firearm in limp fingers, a look of resignation on his face. Aline watched the situation with growing hope. Lar, or a general revolt?

One of the Mwalgi women focused on Aline, eyes narrowing. She lifted the paralyzer. The man in the group, a faint sparkle of gold in his eyes, knocked the paralyzer from her hands. Pointing farther down the hallway, he turned to the other guards.

"I think you'd better run," he said in Mwalgi

"And what are you going to do?" asked the one now bereft of her weapon. She peered into his eyes, sneering at the golden signs of his betrayal. "Try to mate with them?"

He dropped his weapon with hers, raising his hands. "I'll take my punishment, as I deserve." Glancing in Aline's direction, he bowed his head. "The Saeanan woman is right. They are people, as good as or better than any of us, and what we've done here is wrong."

The Mwalgi guard scoffed, but the fear in her eyes told another story—she was scared she might get what she deserved. The other guards fired off a few shots, only making the approaching mob's angered cries grow louder. The female guards ran, leaving the man still standing there.

Andi appeared, yanking Aline's arm, pulling her into the corridor. "Maybe if we join with the women, we can find a way out of here."

Looking up and down the hallway of open cell doors, Aline shook her head. "This is Lar's work. We have to stay where we are until he finds us."

The women reached them, and Aline was dismayed to discover at least half of them were visibly pregnant. How would these people survive long enough to escape, let alone survive Lenfay's deserts?

The Mwalgi guard in front of them went to his knees, bowing his head and waiting for the women to take their revenge. By the looks of them, they were more than willing to comply.

Aline debated. She didn't want to get into the middle of this, but this Mwalgi had saved her life. He'd committed horrible sins in this place, but he was repentant. And didn't they all have a fair share of blood on their hands.

"Wait!" yelled Aline, standing in front of the man, pointing at his eyes. "This one just saved my life. Like you, he was put here through no fault of his own and he doesn't deserve to be murdered."

Fedrek staggered through the door, Aline's knife in hand. "You filthy Gi-lover!"

He plunged the knife forward. Aline side-stepped as she shoved Andi out of the way. The knife jammed against the Mwalgi guard's side, snapping like a twig hitting a wall, leaving Fedrek with the fabric-wrapped stump.

Pointing to Fedrek, Aline yelled louder. "This is a man who would deserve it. He enjoyed what the Mwalgi asked him to do, even talked with them enough to know details about the women he raped. He's more a monster than the most deluded Gi."

"I have a simple solution," said the woman at the front, the bulge in her stomach suggesting she was at least six months pregnant. She held a paralyzer gun like a club. "We kill them both."

They surged forward, but Aline yanked the young guard to his feet. "It's okay," he said. "I deserve this."

"Oh, no," said Aline, thinking of Cloud. "Not another one."

But the guard's gaze turned to the pregnant woman at the forefront. "If I am to die, I would have it be at her hands."

"The way some of you bond is plain sick," said Aline.

Andi agreed. "And not at all romantic."

Shoving the guard through the door of her cell, Aline hoped to try again at convincing the women to spare him.

He staggered into the room, but before Aline could block the doorway, it closed, locking him inside.

Aline turned back to the women only to find Fedrek slumped to the ground, paralyzed, the women giving him a last kick.

"Is he dead?" Aline asked.

With an angry shake of her head, the lead woman dropped the paralyzer in her hand. "He forced this child on me." She rested a hand on her bulging abdomen. "But I won't commit murder."

Aline considered taking the decision from their hands, for the sake of justice, but they had more of a right to play jury than she did.

The woman reached out a hand. "My name is Loren." She gestured with her gun toward the end of the hallway. "Now let's find our way out of here."

Aline considered telling the women to come with her, but she hadn't convinced them to spare the guard, so what chance would she have to convince them to spare Lar?

"I'm going to find my own way," Aline said. "I'm sorry, but good luck to you."

Loren gripped Aline's arm. "Are you sure? I think our chances are better together."

Aline wasn't sure, but she didn't want to risk Lar's safety at these prisoners' hands or vice versa. "I'll be fine, but you need to hurry. Get out of here. But remember, some of the guards are sorry for what they've done. You don't need a massacre."

With a nod, Loren moved the group forward. "We'll put those who will cooperate into cells if we can figure out how to make them close like yours did."

Aline glanced at her former cell. "I have a feeling that whoever opened these, programmed them to respond to Mwalgi genetics. You get them in the room, the door will lock."

Loren waved everyone forward, taking the group down the corridor.

"Andi?" Aline gripped the girl's thin arm. "I don't know who has a better chance at survival, but Lar has a plan. You could still catch up with the women. Who do you want to go with?"

"I'll stay with you, but Lar better have a good explanation for leaving me at the loading docks."

"Aline!" Lar's voice echoed down the corridor.

Talons extended, ready for combat, Lar stalked toward them as if he owned the facility, his guard's uniform stained with blood and skalwass. He stumbled, another spasm somewhere in his leg, but it said something for how common they had become, because he only shifted his gait and continued on.

For once, Aline didn't hesitate. She ran to him without reservation, pushing back the twinge of panic that tried to resurface, tried to remind her of all the losses she'd suffered. It was time to start living in the moment, let go of past fears.

As a surprised Lar retracted his talons, Aline threw her arms around him, kissing him like she had aboard the Noble Ark, when she'd first realized she had feelings for him.

"I love you," she whispered in his ear. "I've been so blind and stupid."

Gripping her forearms, he pulled her back, searching her eyes as if hoping to find them dusted with gold. "Love, as in grateful to see me, or love, as in you're in love with me."

"I'm in love with you. I've been in love with you since before you kissed me aboard the Noble Ark. I'm sorry it's taken me so long to admit it."

Lar embraced her again, but only for a moment. "We must go. Your foolish risk, saving that Mwalgi, cost us time. I didn't dare approach until you were away from the mob."

Together two seconds and he'd already said the one thing that could overload her reactors more than anything else. "You, of all people, can't remotely lecture me about taking risks. You—"

Lar glanced behind Aline. "Andi?"

Aline pulled Andi forward, wrapping an arm around her thin shoulders, speaking in Saeanan. "I found an old friend of yours. Surprise."

"How?" asked Lar in Mwalgi, an odd mixture of dismay and warm welcome on his face, "Later. There's an interrogator on the way, and I don't think we will have an easy time getting out of here once a Mwalgi skimmer and its guns arrive."

Andi opened her mouth to say something, but Aline gave a curt shake of her head. Andi's issues with Lar would have to wait.

"Meladise?" Aline asked.

Lar shrugged. "They captured her outside the compound walls. She's already talked to the authorities, told them everything. I released her door, like I did for the Saeanans, but now she's on her own to survive."

Even after all they'd been through with his sister, all the times he'd threatened to kill her if she posed a danger to Aline, Lar's voice still held more sorrow than condemnation.

"We'll figure something out," Aline promised him.

"Can you at least speak English?" said Andi. "I have no idea what either of you are saying." Her glare for Aline vied with the one she'd directed at Lar.

Lar ushered them back the way he'd come, switching to his somewhat halted English. "I saw not any refrigerated transports in the vehicle yard, but I believe there's a small ohfertsoog."

Lar took them through the twists and turns of the compound without hesitation.

"How long have you been here?" Andi asked, anger rising in her voice. "You seem to know your way around pretty well."

If Lar noticed the tone, he didn't respond in kind. "An hour, maybe a little more, but I found the compound map. It's simple to remember."

Though Aline doubted it would be simple for most people, Lar had proved his intelligence time and again. He probably had an eidetic memory.

They arrived at what should have been a solid door, replacing the doorfield once the alarms went off. Instead, the wall had been torn open and the wiring shredded. The scarred door, obviously torn by a Mwalgi's talon, had been bent back far enough to allow a full-sized Mwalgi to squirm through the opening.

"How?" muttered Lar. "None of the Mwalgi should have been able to arrive here before us."

"Are we stuck?" asked Andi.

Lar shook his head. "I don't know."

He squirmed through then stopped, blocking the way. Aline had to give him a shove so she and Andi could follow. If he was in some kind of trouble, he'd have to share the fight.

When she stepped through the hole, Aline's jaw dropped alongside his.

Meladise, her fals-skalen gone, a number of dark bruises and deep cuts along her Saeanan skin, sat in the driver's seat of a transport vehicle that would easily carry twelve people or more. The boarding ramp extended toward them like a hand of friendship, or the tongue of a hungry monster. The expression on Meladise's face gave no indication whether she would whisk them away to safety, or take them to the authorities.

The ohfertsoog hovered next to them, the engine humming like a happy nyarhoond. But even domesticated nyarhoonds could have sharp teeth, Lar reminded himself. And Meladise was anything but domesticated.

"Are you coming, or do you want to wait for the consecration festival?" Meladise yelled in their native tongue from her place at the controls.

Aline squeezed Lar's hand. "Do we dare trust her?"

Eyes running over Aline's and then Andi's bare skin, Lar shook his head. "I don't have enough skin cream for all of us. We don't have a choice."

"Who is she?" asked Andi.

Lar switched to English. "A traitor, a Saeanan-hater, and a believer of the Mwalgi Manifest. That's my sister."

"Mwalgi Manifest?"

"A document," said Aline, "stating that Saeanans exist as tools and slaves for Mwalgi, to be used like cattle."

Eyes wide, Andi stepped back. "Then I'm voting this is not a good idea. Maybe we should take our chances with the pregnant women."

Lar stepped up the ramp, talons extended. "This is the only safe way from the compound."

Aline took Andi's hand in hers and followed. As soon as they'd stepped inside, the door whizzed to a close behind them and Mela powered up the thrusters.

"Strap in," said Lar to Andi and Aline, taking the seat beside his sister at the front.

Eight seats lined each side of the ohfertsoog, what Aline called a hoverbus. In the back were some storage compartments that were part of the vehicle. Lar didn't study it any longer than it took to make sure Andi and Aline were strapping themselves in.

Engaging his harness, Lar spoke to the on-board system. "Initiate pilot status."

"Pilot already engaged," said the computer.

"I've got this," said Mela. "We did training in school."

"That training is incomplete." Lar's left fist gripped the seat-arm, the muscles around his talon sheaths twitching. "The vehicle yard gate is still shut, which means you must mount the transfer vehicle and jump the wall. That's not something for a novice."

"I'm not a novice!" Mela yelled. "They said I was one of the best soldiers they'd ever trained. Just as good as you."

Any further arguments were cut off as Mela pushed the thrusters, jerking the soog forward, bouncing its gravitonics so it propelled upward, like a frightened frog, on top of the transfer ship. She actually hit it pretty well, for someone with her experience, but Lar sensed an imbalance.

"The front right—"

Mela wasn't listening to him, her face red from more than atmosphere exposure. "I can do this," she growled.

The soog bounced again, soaring over the compound wall, except for the front right side of the vehicle. It hadn't gained as much traction on the transport. Lar could only watch as his corner aimed at the top of the wall. At their current trajectory, they'd flip, thrown on their back.

Mela screamed at the computer. "Control to co-pilot. Control to co-pilot!"

Before she'd finished the phrase, Lar took the curved bar in front of him that served for manual control. He couldn't completely avoid the collision, but he might at least be able to keep them upright. Teasing the horizontal brake, he forced the ohfertsoog into a spin, the back side clearing the wall. At the same time, he pushed the front gravitonics to maximum. The ground was too far away from the thrusters to do much good, but as the vehicle soared butt first over the wall, the front right section managed to follow, scraping a two-foot chunk of mortar along with it. They went into an uncontrolled spin, but they landed belly down.

It took a few rotations before Lar managed to get the soog under control. In the distance, he could see the far away speck of an approaching skimmer.

Without a word to his overconfident idiot of a sister, he aligned the thrusters and gravitonics, taking off into the open desert toward rockier terrain. The far the right side of the soog kept drifting downward; having to be popped up in order to keep from catching in the sand and stone, it wouldn't be long until they started digging into the passing terrain, leading any half-brained enforcer straight to them.

"Can you keep it afloat?" Lar asked Mela, unable to keep the censure from his voice.

"I should have been able to do it," she said, reaching for the controls and re-initiating pilot status.

"But you didn't need to, especially with a more experienced pilot available. The difference between bravery and unnecessary risk, Mela, is wisdom."

"Don't start with your stupid Diseep d'All pellets. I don't need one of your stupid lectures. I messed up. Leave it."

"That wasn't Diseep d'All doctrine." Lar shrugged. "It's common sense, and I hope it sounded profound enough that you might remember it next time you think about getting us all killed."

Mela jerked the soog upward, barely keeping it from carving a line in the sandy dirt. "I just saved you and your Saeanan's pathetic tails. A little more gratitude and a little less big brother told-you-so might be nice."

Gripping the seat as he released his harness and stood, Lar glared down at her. "You got yourself caught, gave away all of our secrets, nearly got me killed, and I released your door on that interrogation chamber. If there is any gratitude to be given, it should be that I haven't slit your throat by now."

Mela's eyes narrowed, glancing away from their barren trek long enough to accuse Lar with spiteful vehemence. "Like you slit the throats of those innocent guards in the compound. I saw what happened, and I know it was you."

Her well-placed condemnation sucked away all his anger, leaving only grief. "Though many of the Mwalgi in that compound were compelled by law and duty, none of them could be considered innocent. The atrocities happening around them tainted everyone." He stared out at the red dirt and stone passing beneath them. "Our entire race is culpable."

As the skimmer approached the compound, a familiar voice hailed them. "Ohfertsoog 69T5M, we've detected irregularities at the Saeanan breeding facility. You are ordered to stop and wait for instruction."

It couldn't be.

"Don't stop," Lar told Mela.

"Ohfertsoog. Identify yourself or we will assume you are hostile and engage weapons."

Lar turned on the speakers and connected communications. "That's so like you, Peltay. Running in blind, lasers firing, with no idea what's really happening."

"Larkin Trovgar, you sick little mutt. It's because of you I was sent out to this desolate pit of a post. I heard your sister was in custody and I'm on my way to the best interrogation of my life. After I blast you to pieces, you filthy—"

"You might want to reconsider that, Peltay. For one, my sister is with me. For another, in the time you've taken to hail me, and the few seconds we've talked, I've moved out of range, and though you might catch us, you currently have bigger problems. There's been a prison break in that compound and I imagine the Saeanans would like your vehicle. You might want to consider surviving."

In that moment, laser fire exploded from the compound's top

turrets, shredding Peltay's aft guns and a third of the rear propulsion nodules. The skimmer started to veer sideways, headed for the compound wall.

"There is no place you can run in that bulky can where I can't find you," said Peltay. "This is personal."

"I count on it," said Lar. "And I'll enjoy the look on your face when I cut your throat. Assuming you don't die in the next ten seconds."

Another blast took out the right gun mount and part of the skimmer's gravitonics. Peltay was too busy with evasion tactics to continue his threats. Lar had no doubts, however, that if Peltay did somehow survive, he would take on the assignment of finding Lar, and the man would move mountains and sky to get his revenge.

"Who was that?" asked Mela.

"My former mistar." Could Lar never be rid of the man?

"Wow. I'm guessing you didn't part on good terms after you murdered part of his crew."

"That's not really the problem," said Lar. "He cares more that I ruined his career."

Lar left Mela to think about the kind of man who would care more about his job than the people under his command, the same kind of man she could have served under in a CSF collections ship. He staggered to Aline and Andi, waiting out a spasm in his arm before kneeling before them both, hugging Aline for a long desperate moment then staring at Andi in confused awe.

"How?" He asked in English, but didn't know how to finish the question. How had she ended up on Lenfay, in the compound, with Aline, and how had she turned so angry toward him?

"You stared straight at me," accused Andi. "On the loading grounds, I yelled for your help, and you stared directly at me, then turned and left."

"The loading grounds?"

Lar knew what she must be referring to, but he couldn't even remember what it had looked like other than a mass of Saeanans, too many of them to see, to look at, all being carted off to a type of desolation worse than any of them could know.

"You stepped out of some fancy car," said Andi. "With a Mwalgi and Aline, but you left me there to die. You left me to something worse than death."

Lar shook his head. "I didn't see you."

"But you looked straight at me!"

Lar dropped his gaze. He couldn't promise that he would have gone after her even if he had seen her. He'd just found Aline. Would he have been willing to risk her life to save Andi? In all honesty, probably not.

Though he didn't deserve it, Aline came to his defense. "He was barely alive. We both were."

Aline explained what they'd gone through, Lar interjecting when Aline needed more details for his part of the story. By the time they'd ended, Andi seemed pacified, if still a bit distrustful. Then she asked the question Lar had dreaded.

"But you would have come for me, if you'd seen me?"

She deserved honesty. Lar could see the lie on Aline's tongue, but he stopped her. "No, I wouldn't have. It would have put Aline's life at risk, and though it would have haunted me all my life, I wouldn't have come."

Andi's silence condemned him. After a few uncomfortable moments, she spoke with the voice of one betrayed. "It makes sense, because of how much you love Aline, but I risked everything for you on board the Future. You should have seen me, and you should have been willing to help."

Aline seemed unfazed by the condemnation. "How did you end up on Lenfay, Andi?"

She shrugged, the gesture still petulant with anger. "Same way anybody does. Our ship was attacked." She paused, voice choking on the next words. "They killed everyone but me and a few other women. They killed my father, sucking out his CSF while I watched."

"It is the blessing of the All that you ended up with Aline, that I was able to get you away from that place even if I didn't know you were there."

Andi unclasped her harness with shaking, angry hands. "There is no All, no God, nothing but those who survive and those who die."

Moving to the far end of the soog, she turned her back to them. "Have I destroyed her faith as well as her trust?" Lar asked.

It was a rhetorical question, but Aline answered, taking his hand in hers. "She will find her way. Pain like this takes time, sometimes a lot of time. I should know."

Lar nodded. Aline seemed to have forged a bond with Andi. Maybe she could help the girl understand.

He touched the scar at Aline's neck. "Those monsters branded you."

"It doesn't matter."

She took Lar's hand, clasping it in her lap. "I'm free and that's what counts. What about Peltay? Will we never be rid of him?"

Lar shook his head. "I'm sure he was thrilled to volunteer and get at my sister. Now, he'll come after me, which means us. If I could trust Mela to take care of you, I'd go back right now and deal with Peltay, but...."

"No," Aline's anger surprised him. "Why do you think I found it so hard to admit my feelings for you after Cloud died?"

Lar hung his head, reminded again that Aline's love could be fleeting. "I know you cared about him."

"Wrong again, leezard-brain." Aline grabbed his dust-stained face in her hands. "I've lost my family, my foster father, and almost every friend I've ever cared about. I don't want to be close to you, because I'm afraid I'll lose you too."

"But as long as I can keep you alive, you can love another man. You can—"

"I can't," she said, tears in her eyes. "If anything happened to you...again...I'd never be able to get close with anyone. You broke down those barriers I'd kept up for so long. Yes, I cared for Cloud, and I tried to convince myself that I might come to love him, but I didn't. And I never felt an emotional connection with him, because I can't let anyone else get that close. Only you."

"You don't know that."

"It took ten years for me to find someone who could touch me and leave me wanting more, instead of flinching and wishing I could hide. Don't you dare play the selfish hero and leave me to that again."

"I won't," said Lar, though he still wondered if she wouldn't be better off without him. Assuming they escaped Lenfay, where could they ever live in peace?

Aline stroked his face, running her finger along the base of his jaw, the line between scale and skin that aroused Lar's deepest passions.

She leaned forward, but then hesitated. "I'm still afraid you'll leave me, but if I'm to keep back that fear, you have to promise me...no more risking your life for mine. We stay together."

It went against his very nature, every protective part of him, but he leaned closer and whispered. "I promise."

Their lips touched, a fire long-denied exploding inside of him. Andi started to cry, soft but persistent in her dark corner, forcing Lar and Aline apart as if their happiness caused Andi pain. Lar sat beside Aline, keeping her hand in his, reveling at her willing touch as they exchanged the stories of what had happened since Mela caused Aline's capture.

Tempted again to cut Mela's throat, Lar had to remind himself, Mela was his sister, and she'd already told the authorities everything. It would only be revenge if he killed her now.

It was good that his anger had cooled somewhat before Mela called back to him a few minutes later. "Now that you're sure your precious Aline is okay, and you obviously don't care what the interrogators did to me, you should know I have no idea where we're supposed to be going."

The vehicle dipped, shuddered, and sand splattered against the front and side, thousands of taps sounding like the hungry clicking of beetle mandibles.

Mela's tone humbled a bit. "And I think we have a problem."

Meladise eyed Lar from her peripheral vision as he resumed his place in the co-pilot's chair. "Make me the primary pilot."

"Why?" Meladise couldn't believe he was doing this. She'd hot-wired and stolen the soog, but he was going to come in and take over everything, like she was some incompetent child. "I can drive it. Just tell me what to do and where we're going."

"Why in desolation would I tell you where we're going? So you can get yourself captured again and give the authorities more specific details? As it is, with the information you had for your interrogators, we have no way to get supplies without walking into an ambush."

Meladise narrowed her eyes at Lar. Just like him to assume the worst.

"I told them you were outside the compound. I had to tell them something or they would have tortured me with my broken leg. I figured you could handle a search team and probably take advantage of it. I was right."

Lar's sudden glance down told Meladise he was noticing the cast for the first time. So much for being a caring older brother.

"That wasn't from the interrogation?"

"They didn't ask about where we were going, and I didn't tell. I think they had orders to wait for some government official to come in, probably that ex-mistar you were talking to a few minutes ago."

The soog dipped again, carving a line in the dirt until it hit a half-buried boulder. The screech as it dragged across the porous lava stone set her teeth on edge, but trying to keep the beast of a machine from overturning was a lot worse. Concentrating, her fangs slipped between her teeth and the little brat in the back screamed, making it even harder to focus.

"Bloody fluids, you crazy livestock!" Meladise yelled back at her. "Shut up before you make me run this thing into a mountain."

Aline comforted the child, and Lar gave Meladise a look that could burn a hole through a mountain. Meladise bared her fangs farther and hissed at him.

"Mature, sister," he said with emphasized sarcasm. "I'm so very impressed with your ability to frighten a thirteen-year-old, traumatized girl. How old are you? Nine?"

Meladise thought of a response, crude enough to really anger her brother. She retracted her fangs and bit back the words on her tongue. Lar would only mock her again.

He sighed, as if regretting his comments. "You are an accomplished driver, but I have more experience and we need to leave as little a trail as possible for as long as we can before we stop. May I please take the controls?"

"Fine," she said, but she knew he'd meant everything he had said, and probably would have liked to have said more. Lar hadn't approved of her before he left for military training, and he never would.

Meladise transferred control to Lar, but then didn't know what to do with herself. She sure as desolation wasn't going to go in the back with the Saeanans. So she stayed in her seat, nothing to do but watch the scenery pass. After an hour, over a particularly dense patch of rocky terrain, Lar adjusted their heading from west-northwest to southwest.

"Where are you taking us?" Meladise asked. "There's nothing but desert or uninhabitable jungle if we go any farther south."

"We're going someplace Peltay will never think to look."

"But what about the supplies? You said supplies were in Col de

Pluurs, and there's nothing habitable south of that."

Lar turned to her, his face expressionless, which made his words only hurt more. "Even if you didn't tell the interrogator where we were going, which I'm not sure of, I don't trust you to behave yourself when we get there. You're likely to call the authorities on us again."

"That would be stupid. I'm wanted now, too."

"True," said Lar. "But I don't know if that would stop you. You're willing to sacrifice any of our lives if you think it will gain you something."

"I promise—"

"Stop." Lar couldn't hold up a hand, he needed both to control the ohfertsoog, but the blaze in his eyes held her as if he'd pinned both her arms to the chair. "You are not honest and I can't trust anything you say."

Meladise had no response to that. She could only turn away, hide the tears that tried to push their way to the surface. She would not cry, not in front of him. She stiffened in the chair, holding back the emotions, staring at the changing landscape while the embers of her anger burned behind a blank façade.

After another hour, Lar turned off fuel propulsions and the ohfertsoog slowed, dependent solely on solar energy. Meladise slept in the chair, hardly noticing as the light-day slipped to a dark-day and Lar eventually had to turn on the fuel engines again.

Aline slept in the back with the girl, Andi, but when morning came she joined Lar, sitting on the floor next to him like a proper tsefuur. They whispered together, laughing often, and Meladise knew she should give up her seat for Aline. Instead, Meladise pretended to sleep, taking satisfaction in making the woman act her place whether she knew it or not.

When Lar started showing Aline the controls, teaching her how to manage the soog and compensate for the damaged gravitonics, Meladise couldn't take it anymore. She went to the back, looking at the darkness outside from one of the windows, she and Andi keeping clear of one another.

Aline drove much of the next light-day, only carving a line in the rock once, then it passed to a dark-day. After some calculations, Meladise figured it was Deemosh, the believers' day of worship, and the first day of the season prehpay. Each day would be an hour shorter, it would start getting hotter, and as they came closer to Lenfay's second sun, the night-days would become less dark. She wished she were home.

As the soog sputtered, running low on fuel, Lar found a craggy hill where he could nestle the vehicle into a shallow canyon, unseen from almost every vantage but due south, and nothing lived south between this rocky terrain and the jungles, where even a Mwalgi didn't dare try to survive. Lar had to be crazy to take them in this direction.

The Saeanans found tsefuur jumpsuits and skin cream in a back compartment of the ohfertsoog, but Meladise wished they hadn't. She would have liked some time outside without their constant unsettling presence.

Lar pulled out a number of vehicle jacks to prop the soog up, making sure it was secure by placing a few rocks in key points, then turned it off and went to work on the damaged gravitonic unit. Meladise found a place to sit, far away from the Saeanans. Her conversation with the doctor in the breeding compound kept coming back to her. Every time she looked at Andi and Aline, Meladise heard the words, "You are Saeanan."

Though it was a dark-day, Meladise watched the gray outline of Lar's legs sticking out from under the cumbrous vehicle while he beat at the broken gravitonics with a welder. He'd better hope it didn't accidentally go off and shoot a hole through the Saeanan skin on his shoulder.

The thought brought her back to the doctor again. Did everything have to remind her of that cracked conversation? The idea that her Saeanan genetics made her stronger, not weaker, was still hard for Meladise to accept. Saeanans were livestock, made for the consumption of Mwalgi. But maybe not. So many lies.

She squirmed for a comfortable position on the small outcropping of rock she'd found near the hill's base. There was nothing to see but craggy rocks and sand for kilometers. Even the scrub brush had slowly diminished over the last three days. It seemed that everything had deserted them, including the All.

Lar peeked out from under the ohfertsoog, finding Aline and Andi. "You need to stay on the rocks," he yelled out. "Avoid dirt and sand, and stay away from any holes that appear drilled into the ground or the hill. Even out here, there are a few species of shlaka and leezard that still survive."

Meladise had never learned to speak Saeanan well, but she understood.

Aline nodded, but Andi looked ready to pass out with fear. What kind of lapin-scared pellet had Lar brought along?

"Meladise," he called, switching to Mwalgi. "Do something useful, and watch out for them. Let me see if I can trust you."

It wasn't like Meladise could betray them and call for anyone out here anyway. There was nothing and no one to be found for kilometers. As for Lar's fear of shlaka, even those wouldn't be living this far south. With sweat pooling from her Saeanan skin and her scales swollen tight to hold in moisture, Meladise wasn't sure she was surviving. Of course, the Saeanans looked worse. Their tsefuur outfits covered their sensitive skin, but every edge was soaked with the girls' sweat and it streamed from their faces into the suit's reclamation reservoirs.

Still, if Meladise was going to win Lar's trust and have any hope of surviving this nightmare, she'd best do what she could.

Coming to her feet, Meladise approached the two Saeanans, attempting to speak in their language. "You are bringing water? Out from de ohfertsoog?"

Andi started to shake, fear in every tremble as Meladise came closer, but at least the girl had enough scale in her to hold her ground and not go hiding behind Aline. Meladise could hand her that much.

Aline shook her head. "Lar said it wouldn't take long, and we don't have that much water to spare."

"You have true," said Meladise, "but your mind is broken if you are thinking Saeanan bodies be living in de south Lenfay deserts, during de season of Prehpay, and stay alive more than ten minutes without more water."

"We aren't stupid," said Andi, bristling with indignation despite the tremor in her voice. "How are we supposed to know? This isn't our ugly planet."

"Stupid enough you are caught and know not how to defend yourself," said Mela, not sure why she let the little livestock pull her into such a ridiculous argument. "When I had your age, I knew to defend myself."

Andi's face flushed, her fists clenching as if she had talons she could bring to bear. "You're a filthy, blood-sucking Gi, with claws sticking out of your arms and legs like an animal. Your kind probably have to defend yourselves from birth."

The little livestock, a weakling Saeanan, was calling the Mwalgi animals?

Mela extended her arm-claws. "Better predator than prey."

Deliberately, Mela opened her mouth and extended her fangs. As she'd expected, Andi ran for protection, going full tilt down the mountain toward the soog, stumbling around as if wearing a blindfold.

Meladise laughed at the sight until a fist slammed into her jaw, tossing her head to one side.

Aline's tsefuur hood had fallen to her shoulders, revealing the thick matte of brownish-red fuzz that covered her scalp. Despite the environment cream she'd smeared on her face and neck, Mela could already see a hint of blisters on Aline's nose and cheeks. The tsefuur-style contacts she wore gave the appearance of an angry insect. It was time Meladise squished this bug, once and for all.

The thought was interrupted by Andi's scream. She lay at the bottom of the hill where it appeared she'd fallen.

"You weak Saeanan," Meladise yelled down to her, cupping her hands around her mouth so Andi would hear. "Stop de crying. Find yourself some water."

But, of course, Aline and Lar had to make a big deal out of it, encouraging the child's pathetic display. As Lar scrambled from under the ohfertsoog, Aline followed Andi's path down the hill, coming to a sudden stop two meters before she reached the girl. Aline's scream made Andi's sound half-hearted. They probably heard her in Trovgarshtot.

Meladise made her own way down the hill. As she came alongside Andi, keeping a reasonable distance, she couldn't help but gasp. Lar had been right.

Only a few inches from Andi's leg, its bright purple stripes letting the world know they were dealing with something poisonous, a shlaka—a sand viper—faced Aline, coiled to strike.

"Don't move," Lar told Aline, back to speaking Mwalgi. "I'll come up behind it, and get it to strike me. If I'm not too rusty, I can catch it."

Even as he spoke, Lar's forearm spasmed. Mela's dear brother might have reunited with his beloved Saeanan, but his severance had probably gone too far to ever reverse. The likelihood that he'd be able to catch hold of a viper in mid-strike seemed rather slim.

Before she could let herself think about what might happen, Meladise rushed forward. The viper's focus shifted and it uncoiled, much faster than she'd expected. Razor sharp fangs shot toward her thigh.

Meladise grabbed for it, but she was too slow. As its fangs reached her leg, her hand clamped around its body, nowhere near its head.

She yanked back, feeling the fangs touch Saeanan her skin. The head immediately coiled to one side, aiming for her hand. In a panic, Meladise dropped it.

Writhing for only a second, it sprung again. Meladise froze when dual points of pressure hit her ankle.

Lar grabbed it by the back of its head, swiping a talon across its neck.

The body fell to the rock, oozing blood and squirming ever slower until it lay still.

Lar knelt at Meladise's side, inspecting her ankle. "I don't see anything. Did it strike?"

With a gulp, Meladise nodded.

"Did you feel it?" asked Lar.

Meladise knelt down herself, touching the area where she'd felt the snake bite. Nothing. "No, but I know it did."

Lar came back to his feet, working through another spasm as if pausing in time then continuing as if nothing happened. "You're lucky. It hit your scales. You'll be fine."

Andi lay back against the ground, no longer sobbing, thank the All.

"Can the stupid Saeanans just stay in the soog while you finish what you're doing?" asked Meladise. "It's too hot out here for them anyway."

"I'd rather not have the weight on the jacks," said Lar. "I only need another couple of minutes. I was almost done."

"Lar," said Aline, kneeling at Andi's side. "Something's wrong."

Lar joined her, feeling Andi's head, checking her over. He paused, turning her jumpsuit back and forth at the calf.

He knelt back, exhaling sharply. "There are sealed holes here. She was bitten."

As if he cared for the girl like his own child, he gathered her up in his arms and raced for the soog.

"What are you going to do for her there?" asked Meladise. "She's just more weight so why drag out the inevitable?"

"There's a first aid kit," said Lar. "I'm sure it has a venom neutralizer."

"For Mwalgi," said Meladise, still unable to fully grasp Mwalgi and Saeanan similarities. "Something like that would probably kill a Saeanan."

"They transport Saeanans on this thing, too, right?" asked Aline. "They have to have something for them."

Lar shook his head, and Meladise knew why before he answered. "They're not going to care if a Saeanan gets bitten and dies. They would do as Mela suggested. Leave her."

Placing Andi on the floor between seats, Lar found the kit and the medicine strips within. "She is rather small and she's not a Mwalgi. I'm not sure what this will do."

Andi convulsed.

"We have to do something," said Aline, tears coursing down her cheeks despite her attempt to remain calm.

Meladise gaped at her, confused as to why she would care so much about a fellow prisoner, just another girl whom Aline hadn't known a week ago.

Still gaping, Meladise relayed the doctor's words from a few days ago, though they left a sour taste in her mouth. "Saeanan and Mwalgi anatomy aren't that different. If it works on us, it will probably work on her."

Convulsing again, spittle formed at the edge of Andi's mouth, running down her cheek as she continued to twitch and shiver.

Lar pulled open the girl's jaw, opening the strips and placing two, next to one another, on her tongue. They fizzled as they dissolved. Andi moaned, more spittle emerging from her mouth, now with a taint of blue.

Aline glanced around the soog, settling on the open hatch. "We need to filter the air in here so I can open up her suit, treat the human skin and try to pull out some of the poison."

Lar nodded. "Like I said, two minutes and we can go. Just try not to move around much. I don't want this thing burying me in the dirt."

He jumped out the hatch, closing it after him. The automatic filter engaged.

"Why?" Aline asked Meladise as she stripped Andi. "Lar asked you to help us and you purposely scared her into running for cover. You knew there were dangerous things out there."

"So you're blaming me?" Meladise asked. She couldn't believe this. "It's not my fault the girl ran off and didn't watch where she was going."

"You realize we can hardly see a thing during your night-days, right?"

"What's wrong with her anyway, that she's such a coward?"

"How did you feel when you thought that snake was going to put its fangs into you?"

Meladise didn't answer. She'd been terrified. She glanced at Andi, still twitching, her eyes probably glazed beneath the eye-protectors.

Aline found the twin holes in Andi's calf. "This girl watched an entire colony get destroyed by hungry, fang-bearing, Mwalgi. She had her mother ripped away from her, probably killed by Mwalgi, at about the same age you lost yours. She watched her father being tortured and drained of his CSF, right in front of her. At one point, even Lar bit her and Andi had to suffer, paralyzed, while he extracted her CSF."

The whole poor-Saeanan story was getting repetitious, but that last part got Mela's attention. "Whoa. Wait. He participated in a raid? I thought he had some sort of twisted ideal he was living up to when he killed his own people, but Lar killed Saeanans, too?"

Aline pointed to Andi. "She's still alive."

"But how?"

Aline pulled a sterilizing pad from the med-kit and used it on her knife. "Not needing the CSF, he made sure not to take more than a person could spare. He also helped those of his unit who were willing so they could do the same. The bloodlust made them kill their first victims, but no more than that. Your brother is an honorable man. What about you? You scared an innocent girl, one who has seen too much death in her life and suffered things you can't even imagine, and to what purpose?"

Again, Meladise didn't respond. Perhaps she had behaved badly, but she hadn't meant to hurt the girl. Though Meladise stared at the floor, away from Andi's twitching form, she could feel Aline's accusations like leezard teeth.

Aline cut at the viper wound, making it bleed. "You've learned some things the last few weeks, Meladise."

The woman's words didn't hold the condemning tone Lar's usually did. She spoke matter-of-factly, not as friends but as equals. Meladise wished she could mark her with a talon.

"You don't know me," said Meladise.

"No," said Aline. "Didn't claim I did."

She attached a scale cleaner to Andi, turning off the cleanser and initiating a mild suction. It pulled blood from the girl's leg, tinged with yellowish venom. The slosh and pull of poison made Aline's words hit home.

"I can see it in your eyes," Aline continued as she turned off the machine and dressed the wound. "In the way you hold onto your defenses, as if changing your mind or seeing the world a different way will somehow mean you've been defeated, but thinking that way means you're only defeating yourself."

"Your point?" asked Meladise.

"Mwalgi talk about the Mwalgi Manifest, their superiority, and dying with honor as if that's all that matters. What's the point of dying with honor, if you haven't lived with it?"

Just as Aline redressed Andi, Lar hopped back into the ohfertsoog with the jacks in hand, closed the hatch door, and then the air filtration sequence renewed.

"It'll still pull a little bit," Lar said to Meladise, his tone bland but his eyes accusing. "Take the pilot's seat and you can drive while Aline and I try to help Andi. Stay on the same trajectory until we hit the sand deserts."

"Then what?" asked Meladise

"Then I'll tell you."

In a huff, Meladise sat down at the controls, initiating gravitonics then propulsions. They wouldn't get much farther on the fuel they had left, but they might be able to make it to the next lightday and then she could switch to solar.

As she passed over the rocky terrain, searching out valleys and low hills rather than wasting energy on trying to traverse more mountainous areas, Meladise couldn't get Aline's words out of her head. To live with honor. What did a presumptuous Saeanan know about honor? Like Meladise was going to throw away her culture, all her traditions, just because Aline thought she had changed. She hadn't changed, and she wouldn't.

But as Meladise reflected on her time in the breeding camp, she had to admit that maybe Lar was right. He'd always claimed to be a part of both worlds, while Meladise had insisted they must choose. Maybe those worlds were closer than she had realized. And if that were true, it changed everything.

As the terrain turned to ever-increasing amounts of dirt and sand mixed among the rocky hills, Lar considered taking Mela's place on the controls. The girl needed some rest.

Across from him, Aline shifted from the view window to face him. "We're running out of food."

Lar already knew that, but he understood why she felt the need to state the obvious. He'd thought about it, he'd considered their options, but he wasn't sure getting supplies was in their best interest. If they could make it to the hideout, Lar would make sure they survived.

Mela glanced back in their direction, probably hoping to hear their conversation, but her concentration was pulled back to the soog as it dipped and dug another line in the dirt. That was happening more often.

It had been almost three days, and Andi still lay pale and listless on the floor. Though Aline had done all she could to pull the poison from Andi's system, the girl's condition continued to deteriorate.

Andi's wound glared a strange blue-purple at the edges. The sound of her rapid breathing made Lar's breath come faster, trying to keep up, but he knew the sensation stemmed from the anxiety of their situation. He owed Andi his life, but was saving her worth risking everyone else? Glancing at Aline's worried brow, he knew what her answer would be. The woman had more honor than most Mwalgi could contemplate.

"I haven't wanted to do this," said Lar, "but I think we must do something. If I inject my paralyzing fluids near the wound maybe it will slow down the poison, give her more time."

He knelt beside Andi, pushing the girl's orange-red hair from her face. "But you are right. Mela and I could survive the rest of the trip without more food and water. You might. Andi definitely will not. She needs more fluids and we need a better medical kit."

"Why didn't the venom neutralizer work?" asked Aline.

Lar shook his head. "I don't know. Perhaps it is the differences between Mwalgi and Saeanan physiology. She's still alive, which means it did something, but obviously not enough."

He leaned in close to the snake bite, closed his eyes and scrunched up his face, calling up deep emotions—his anger at Peltay—until his fangs protruded from between open lips. Like a double set of old-fashioned medical needles, he pushed them into the flesh of Andi's calf. Andi gasped and her body jerked then she lay still. Too still.

Aline dropped to Lar's side, feeling Andi's neck for a pulse. "I'm not feeling a heartbeat."

"Paralysis slows down a Saeanan's heart rate and breathing," said Lar. "That's to be expected." Nudging Aline aside, he put an ear to Andi's chest. Nothing. He couldn't have.... Lar suddenly felt cold.

"What?" asked Aline. "Your scales are so dull, I would almost believe they'd turned to stone."

He closed his gaping mouth. "I think you're right. I...I killed her."

"No," said Aline. "This happens sometimes. We can bring her back then get her to...." Likely, she was going to say they could get her to an infirmary, but they had no such resources available. "Tilt her head up, check that her tongue isn't in the way, then I want you to hold her nose closed and breathe air into her mouth."

It had been many years, but his mother had trained him as a youth in emergency CPR. He followed Aline's directions before she'd finished the explanation.

As Lar tried to bring back Andi's respiration, Aline knelt above her and did chest compressions.

Aline spoke to the girl as if she shared Lar's beliefs that a person's essence could hear even when the body had gone deaf.

"You can do this. You've gone through too much to give up now. We are not going to let this desolate planet beat us. We're survivors."

Andi didn't respond.

"Come on, Andi!" she yelled. "Live!"

Tears formed in Aline's eyes, but nothing was changing. She did another set of compressions, but Andi didn't respond.

The soog came to a silent stop, as if reverencing the girl's passing.

Aline sat back.

"Keep going," said Lar. He didn't know why; only a few minutes before, he'd considered letting Andi die, but he was now determined to make the girl live.

"Let it go," Mela spoke from where she'd come behind Lar. "Even if you bring her back, she won't survive long enough for it to matter."

"It always matters, "said Aline, renewing the compressions.

"Andi!" Lar yelled, pausing between breaths.

The girl shuddered, the smallest of gasps escaping between her lips. Lar leaned back on his heels, whispering a prayer of thanks to the All.

"I don't see how you've helped her," said Mela. "You and Aline were right. Without food and water, there's no chance for the girl."

Lar hadn't wanted to do this. The risks were too great and it would let Peltay know exactly where to find them. But they'd saved Andi's life, and now they needed to commit to their decision.

"Change our course," Lar told Mela. "Thirty degrees north. There's a mining town near here, on the outskirts of an oil field. We'll get some food there."

"How?" asked Mela. "Last I saw, we didn't have any of our gear, which means no credit chips, fake or otherwise. And I doubt a legitimate mining town will take your access codes, either."

"We will get food," said Lar. "One way or another."

"Yeah, to desolation with honor," Mela grumbled as she made her way back to the pilot seat. "Let's go kill some more innocent citizens so we can keep the good-as-dead Saeanan alive."

"She's right," Aline whispered to Lar. "Can we really go in and kill innocent workers to feed ourselves? Let's stop and hunt leezards or something."

"We might find a viper or something worse this far south, but we won't find leezards. It's that mining community or nothing. And I don't want to kill anyone. We'll figure out another way to sneak in and steal what we need."

Aline paused. "And if we can't? What then? It will become a bloodbath."

She was right. How far was he willing to go in order to keep Aline alive? As much as he hated the truth, he'd killed so much, he hardly blinked at the thought anymore. For her? Anything. And what did it matter? In the judgment of the All, he was most likely condemned by this point anyway.

"If it becomes necessary, I will do it," said Lar, the weight of his decision a gargantuan vulfbaeor across his shoulders. "The sin will be mine."

"You can't."

Lar cut her off. "No, Mela was right. After what happened in the breeding compound, I am already a murderer."

"That was different. You didn't have a choice with the guards. It was self-defense, and you were saving all those people."

"For what? So they could die in the desert? Besides," Lar paused, unwilling to admit this to himself, let alone her. "I'm not sure it was entirely self-defense. I was furious when I discovered they'd put you in a breeding compound. I wanted to kill them. Is that not murder? Killing for selfish reasons?"

"You didn't walk into that room intending to hurt anyone. You can't be held responsible for—"

Lar held up a hand. "It matters not. What's done is done, and what must be done can't be helped."

Refusing to further listen to her justifications, Lar left his seat and stalked to the front of the soog.

"Let me take over for a while," he told Mela, more a demand than a request.

"You'll need your rest," Mela argued, a sneer in her voice. "For your upcoming murders."

Lar didn't let her goad him. "I won't be able to sleep. So you might as well."

Mela shrugged and went back to the passenger seats. To his surprise, Aline immediately started whispering with her, and Mela actually listened.

<hr/>

They arrived on the outskirts of the town, but it was nothing like Aline had expected. Encompassed by a near-translucent dome, the shops and dwellings seemed to crowd on top of one another, their garish colors standing out amid their bland sur-roundings. A huge pipe funneled into one side of the structure, and even from a distance, hiding behind one of the few hills they'd found, Aline could see the fountain rising in the town's center, an oasis that made her dry mouth salivate.

She wore the jumpsuit that allowed her to survive Lenfay's at-mosphere, though she hadn't yet convinced Lar her plan could work. Meladise was willing to go along, but that only made it harder to convince her distrusting brother.

"I found a collections compound officer badge, like I told you I would," she held it up to him, letting it glint in the sunlight. She wasn't noticing the reddish tint to the planet as much anymore, her eyes finally adjusting and giving her mind a somewhat normal representation of her surroundings. "This will work."

Lar dropped from his vantage near the top of a barren dirt hill into the sandy valley by the ohfertsoog. "Bloody fluids, Aline." He put out a hand to steady her as she scrambled down after him. "You still have to have an ID number to commandeer supplies—"

Aline flipped the badge over, showing where the officer had etched his ID number so he wouldn't forget it. No wonder he'd been in such a tizzy to find it.

"—And no one is going to give me anything when they see my gold and black eyes."

"Which is why you're not coming," said Aline.

"What? Then how—"

Meladise stepped from the soog, the collections officer uniform they'd found fitting better than Aline had expected. She had her short black hair hidden beneath the formal hat they'd found, some kind of extra floppy beret with a baseball cap brim to shield her face, which was good because her fals-skalen showed more scars than features. In her hands she held grey-blue empty sacks that suggested government issue, especially with the utilitarian shoulder straps that looked like a third-grader's backpack.

Lar shook his head. "After what she did to you, you're going to trust her to watch your back in that town?"

Aline adjusted Meladise's hat, hiding a line of skin. "Like Meladise said, she has as much to lose now as we do. And I know she won't watch my back. I'll have to watch my own."

Lar shook his head. "Even if she keeps to her word, which I don't believe, she'll have to treat you like a tsefuur, with the prejudice of a collections officer. You'll lose your temper. You can't go alone."

So he could risk his life, but he couldn't risk her losing her temper.

"I can keep my temper," she growled at him.

"You're not even keeping it now."

"I don't need to pretend now, I need to get it through your scaly brain that I can do this."

"I'm not going to sit here while you risk your life. I'm not sending you in there with my crazy sister!"

"Hey!" Meladise finally spoke up. "If anybody is crazy, my severance brother, it's you."

"Both of you, stop," said Aline. "It's just a waste of time."

Meladise stalked toward the soog, shooting them a final jibe as she ducked inside. "And what you're doing is so productive."

Aline tried a different tactic, getting close to Lar and wrapping her arms around his waist. He stiffened, probably recognizing Aline's attempt at manipulation, even as he returned the embrace.

"I can do this," she whispered.

"I don't want to lose you." Lar's deep voice cracked, though whether from emotion or the dryness they all felt Aline wasn't sure. "You promised we would do everything together. If something goes wrong, and I'm with you, I can protect you. My sins are already beyond redemption."

Aline squeezed him tighter, wishing he could understand. "We're soldiers in a war, Lar. You haven't killed anyone who wouldn't have killed you first. Those men, the ones who boarded my ship and the ones in the breeding compound, were part of that war and died in the line of duty. You are not a murderer."

Lar squeezed her tighter, as if trying to find a lifeline. "They were just men doing their job. Just like the men here."

Aline shook her head. "The men in the compound were part of a military operation designed to use and subvert Saeanans. In the war to free our people, they were the enemy. But Meladise is right about one thing. The people in this city are just workers, digging up rocks, trying to feed their families." She pulled back, tapping his chest. "If you're going to survive, in your heart, you have to understand the difference."

Lar grabbed her hands, rubbing her cream-covered knuckles across the stubble of his cheek. He didn't grow facial hair as fast as a human, but it obviously grew just as thick.

"I swore I would always be a Mwalgi and a Saeanan," he said. "I didn't want to take sides."

"Don't worry," said Aline, putting her cheek back against his smooth chest. "There will be other times to fight for the Mwalgi. In the war to enslave humans, we can be on the Saeanan side. In the war to arrange for a fair purchase agreement for CSF, we can be on the Mwalgi side. There are plenty of wars to be fought."

He exhaled, sounding like an old man. "I'm tired of wars. I never wanted to be part of any of it."

Aline didn't know what to say. As eager as she'd been for the life of a PC, the fire in her belly no longer burned. All she wanted anymore was peace, but death seemed the only probable means to find it.

In denial of her own thoughts, she pushed Lar to arm's length. "We'll survive this, we'll find a safe place, and we'll leave all of this behind. We just have to survive."

He smirked, an expression Aline hadn't seen in a long time that brought instant tears. She choked back a sob as he pulled her back into his embrace. Aline could survive this, she knew she could, but she had to know Lar would be waiting for her when it was finished.

"Do what you have to do," he grumbled. "But if something happens to you, I'll mete out justice on my sister and every person in that town, and to desolation with the consequences."

Meladise played her part much too well. They rounded a narrow walkway between a derelict parts store with purple paint peeling along its bottom half, and a bright green multi-level apartment. The buildings' colors had seemed more vibrant from a distance. Up close, Aline saw that most were faded, with pockmarks and missing chunks of plaster.

An acrid smell of boiled meat permeated the town, making Aline's nostrils burn despite the skin cream.

"What is that?" Aline whispered to Meladise.

Cuffing Aline, Meladise pointed to the parts shop. "That way, you stinking tsefuur. And don't get any ideas about slipping away again or you'll be in the community pot. You can be part of our consecration festival, mixed in with all the old and convicted Mwalgi. Maybe human flesh will add another spice to the flavor."

Aline stumbled and gagged. "You're cannibals?"

Meladise cuffed her again, glancing around. As far as Aline could tell, there wasn't anybody close enough to merit the act. Either Meladise wasn't taking any chances or she was enjoying herself. Probably both.

She grabbed Aline by the neck, bringing her ear close. "Now is not the time for your stupid questions."

She shoved Aline away, almost sending her to the beige rubber-like sidewalk, similar to the flooring Aline had seen in the arena in

Trovgarshtot. Aline caught herself. Biting her lower lip, she ducked her head and let Meladise herd her forward.

The parts shop ran along the town's main sidewalk. A metallic-crusted roadway divided one side of the street from the other. It stretched to the end of their community in one direction, diverting to one side to miss a glistening fountain in the middle of town. The sight made Aline's parched mouth go even drier. In a world so devoid of clean water, how could they afford such a luxury? In the far distance, a faint glimmer in the air reminded Aline that the town existed under a dome, lessening the suns' heat to bearable levels, diminishing the toxicity of the air, and retaining evaporation.

In the other direction, the metallic roadway seemed to go on forever, probably extending to the oil company's field office. At intervals along the road, narrow walkways allowed Mwalgi on foot to cross back and forth without having to touch the street. The same material served as sidewalks along the street's storefronts. Aline studied the set-up until Meladise shoved her forward again. With the tough scales on their feet, why would a Mwalgi care if they had to cross a metallic road versus pressed rubber?

They entered the shop, triggering a soft chime and alerting the owner of their presence. By the sudden stillness of Aline's breathing device, the shop air must be filtered.

"Can I help—" the golden-eyed shopkeeper stuttered on the automatic statement, staring at Meladise and Aline as if they'd entered with guns drawn. "Excuse me. Other than field inspectors we don't get visitors here, and certainly not someone who can afford a tsefuur. Um, what can I do for you?"

Meladise appeared taken aback, unsure what to say. Aline wished she could kick her in the shins, but Meladise needed a reminder that was more in character. Sidling to a shelf, Aline swiped the sharpest object she could find, a round cylindrical piece with spiked edges along one side.

The fierce fist to Aline's face took her more by surprise than it should have. Aline's shoulder crashed into the shelf as she went to her knees, her cheek stinging and her hood thrown back. Automatically, Aline shifted to a fighting crouch, fury warring with self-control. She'd promised Lar she could keep her temper. She'd even set this up so Meladise could exhibit her authority. With gritted teeth, Aline lowered her head, releasing the chunk of metal she'd stolen at Meladise's feet.

Meladise grabbed Aline by the arm, yanking her up so they stood face to face. "One more attempt at escape, Saeanan, and I'll slit your throat and be done."

Though Meladise still didn't sound like an enforcer, at least she sounded in control.

She turned to the shopkeeper, a middle-aged Mwalgi by the look of his slight paunch and thinning mohawk. "I'm Berat Deekshon. I apprehended this escaped prisoner and I need to commandeer some repair parts for my vehicle."

Aline wanted to run a hand over her face. If Meladise sounded any more rehearsed the man would assume he'd paid tickets for a play—a bad one.

The man cocked his head to one side. "You need a military code for that."

"5X-2499432 CT3R," quoted Meladise, obviously very proud of herself.

At least Meladise had memorized the code. Aline was sure if the man had seen her refer to the back of the nametag then their deception would have been over.

Standing with more confidence, Meladise continued, "I need a gravitonic stabilizer." She paused, remembering. "Part number WO-4325."

The man's brow furrowed. "For a T-class ohfertsoog? Why would you run down an escaped tsefuur in a transport vehicle?"

The scales at Meladise's neck paled, not matching the falsskalen of her face. "It was what I had on hand, from the collections facility."

"There isn't a collections facility around these parts for hundreds of kilometers."

"You think you know where all the collection compounds are?"

she stammered. "The government has dozens we don't know about."

The man's talons unsheathed. "If that were the case, I'd have seen other officers here before. I know military, and our little mining town has the only ellgot fighting rings in the district.

Meladise backed toward the door, extending her gray-marbled talons. "That's not true."

This was going to turn into a bloodbath soon, and the commotion would probably rouse others to investigate.

Wrapping her hand around something akin to an exhaust pipe, and trying to stay silent despite the bulky folds of the jumpsuit, Aline brought the pipe down. Between the Mwalgi gravity, her exhaustion, and inconsistent bone vitamins, she lacked her usual strength. The pipe ricocheted off the man's scaly skull, forcing Aline back a step. He stumbled to one side, shook his head, and turned from Meladise to face Aline.

"Stinking tsefuur!"

She did stink, Aline could smell herself, but that didn't mean she merited the talon swipe he aimed at her.

Aline jumped back, too slow. If the man had been a trained soldier, Aline would have died. Instead, he caught the edge of her gray suit, puncturing it and leaving behind a ten centimeter hole. The suit tried to heal itself, bubbling at the edges and closing wherever the bubbles touched to one another.

He swiped again. She blocked with the pipe, watching it slice in two, the end clanging to the floor as she sidestepped. Not sparing any effort, she slammed the remaining pipe across the man's skull, in the same spot as before.

This time he slumped to the floor.

Meladise stalked across the room, jumping over the man and behind the counter, rifling through boxes on backroom shelves. "I thought we weren't going to kill people?"

Aline stared at the man's still body. What was the point of Aline's plan if she was going to commit the murders she'd kept Lar from?

"I didn't have much choice," Aline said. "I had to stop him."

Meladise didn't respond, but a couple of seconds later she dropped a box with WO-4325 printed across the side into the pack they'd taken from the ohfertsoog.

She leaned over the shopkeeper. "He's breathing," she said with relief. "He'll be fine."

Aline still wasn't sure. "You don't think I caused permanent damage?"

"Mwalgi might not be able to have surgery because of our scales, but we heal well. Unless you did some pretty severe brain damage, he'll wake up after a while and come looking for us."

"We should tie him up," said Aline.

Meladise dropped the backpack, picking up the man's feet. "Nah, we'll just drag him behind the counter. By the time he starts looking, we'll be well gone from here."

Aline wasn't sure she agreed, but she helped Meladise slide the man into hiding. He lay there, his scales a pale gray. Perhaps Meladise's confidence was a little over-eager. This guy didn't look like he'd be up and moving for a long time, if ever.

They made their way back through the store. Aline had to re-mind herself, as she left the building, to hunch over, look defeated. Not that her act would help them much if Meladise continued to act like a child on a field trip, oblivious to her prisoner other than an occasional smack to the head. It only took a few seconds for Aline to recognize that her jumpsuit hadn't completely repaired itself when the too-familiar pain of Lenfay's atmosphere burned across skin.

She clenched Meladise's arm. "Hole in my suit," she whispered.

The action brought immediate stares from the three people sharing their section of street. Aline cursed to herself. How could she have let pain, a great deal of searing pain, make her lose her composure like that? She'd get them killed.

Good thing Meladise's horrible acting skills didn't translate to how much she was enjoying playing the Mwalgi master. She knocked Aline's hand aside then backhanded her across the face. Already in pain, Aline cried out, landing at Meladise's feet, just missing the metallic-crusted road and understanding why the

Mwalgi didn't want to walk on it, even with their scales. Heat emanated from the thing like a dark matter engine without shielding. Aline scrambled away from it, fearful her clothing might catch fire. Conscious of the heat outside and inside her suit, it didn't take any acting for Aline to cower at Meladise's side.

Staring down her nose with a satisfied smile, Meladise looked exactly like a collections officer. "That's better. You'll learn how to behave, yet, tsefuur."

Aline bit back her retort, fighting every urge to punch Meladise in the face.

"Our other stop is just a few stores down," Meladise said. "You'll have to suffer until we get there, but don't you dare touch me."

Aline came to her feet and stood, pulling her hood over the red fuzz that now covered her scalp, securing it at her brow and around her chin. She needed all the protection she could get as the rest of her skin slowly blistered.

Meladise took her time, sightseeing more than she watched Aline. Maybe she could pass as an overconfident Mwalgi, but Aline could have taken the girl down and thrown her into the street a dozen times before they reached the grocery store. They walked in and the first item Aline scanned the shelves for, water, she couldn't find. As the atmosphere in her suit slowly dissipated with the store's clean air, she started to physically relax even as she started to fret.

"There's no water," Aline whispered to Meladise as she pretended to cough.

"Let's get the tsefuur kit for your weak skin," said Meladise a little too loud. "We'll get some water containers and take you to the fountain."

"Tsefuurs aren't allowed near the fountains," said a squat woman near the door. "In fact, only registered town citizens are allowed access without a permit. You can purchase one on your way out."

"And who are you?" Meladise asked, sounding normal. She couldn't act, but questioning authority came naturally.

"I'm the mayor of Erdlshtat. And you?" She looked Meladise up and down. "You're dressed like a collections compound officer, but you're too young and you're in the wrong place."

"I'm older than I look," said Meladise, seeming to get her back up. At least her words didn't sound as scripted as they had before. "And I recognize that I'm far from the nearest collections compound, but I've been on this Saeanan's trail for weeks, and she took me farther south than I expected."

The mayor narrowed her eyes. "There's no way she could have stayed alive that long without help."

Aline wanted to scream at Meladise. There's your reason. Take it!

No longer challenging authority, and having to explain herself, the scripted tone returned, but Meladise said the right words. "That's the only reason she's still alive. I'm going to find out who helped her."

The mayor didn't seem appeased. "And your name?"

"Berat Deekshon," Meladise replied without hesitation.

"Berat is your rank, but what's your first name?"

Meladise's eyes widened in alarm. Aline kicked herself. She'd heard the man's first name, but even Aline knew the name was distinctly male. Meladise would be better off making one up.

She did, but it took her way too long. "Clarisse," she said. "Now if you'll excuse me, I have a long distance to travel."

"We don't have regular train service here," said the mayor, as if Meladise had asked about it.

"I have my own transportation," said Meladise, shoving Aline forward and walking away from the woman. "Just outside of town."

"Then why didn't you drive into town?"

Meladise turned, clearly exasperated and, to Aline's eyes, panicked. "It barely made it to the outskirts. I had to pick up a part, which I will install when I'm done here."

Grabbing a basket from a pile of them and placing it above a reverse magnetization strip running along the aisles, keeping the basket at hip-height, Meladise ended the conversation by going about her task. Aline watched her hands shake as she filled the basket with multiple fillable water pouches, probably more than a Mwalgi and a Saeanan would need for a short trip to the closest major city.

The mayor watched for a moment then slid out the door to the street.

Careful to remain unobserved, Aline knocked one of the clear pouches from Meladise's hands, bending down to pick it up and hand it back, whispering as she did.

"We need to hurry."

"Like I don't know that," Meladise hissed.

They rushed through the store, Aline helping load the basket with food and medical supplies when there was no one to observe. She was sure there were cameras installed somewhere, and when they went back to review the footage, they'd know everything. Right now, they just needed to get their stuff and get out.

At the register, Meladise gave the cashier her officer number, her voice as stilted as before, but the cashier didn't seem to notice or care.

"You're going to carry two of those packs," said Meladise as she stuffed supplies into the backpacks they'd bought. "Maybe that will help you learn your proper place."

Aline sighed, not at carrying the packs but at Meladise's continued stiff speech. She hauled the packs over her shoulders as the mayor walked in.

"Berat Clarisse Deekshon," the woman said, and Aline knew the mayor had figured out that Meladise, at least, wasn't who she pretended to be. But she didn't know about Aline.

Aline spoke in her best Mwalgi. "They call me solmond."

As the mayor's jaw went slack, Aline raised a leg, kicking the woman square on the sternum, sending her up and out the front door. By the scream that followed, Aline guessed she'd tumbled onto the street.

"Come on," Aline said to Meladise, grabbing their last two packs, one empty and the other still open and bulging with empty water packets.

"Don't you dare—"

"They know who you are," yelled Aline. "And soon they'll know who we all are and that we're together. Run!"

Mayor screaming, the rumble of a siren in the distance, the entire town was going to converge on them. The Saeanan's plan had gone wrong in the worst way, and now they were both going to boil.

Meladise followed Aline from the store, but the crazy woman turned toward the fountain instead of heading back the way they'd come.

Meladise grabbed her arm, trying to orient her in the right direction. "It's this way!"

Aline wrenched her arm away, and Meladise heard the tsefuur fabric tear. Couldn't be worse than the one she'd already sustained, but Aline's grimace suggested otherwise.

Whether in blind pain or some idiotic sense of misdirection, Aline ran at full speed toward the middle of town. Meladise considered leaving her, but coming back to Lar without his Saeanan would be as certain a death sentence as turning herself over to the mayor. Maybe she could still salvage the situation.

Meladise's scaled feet slapped the rubberized sidewalk as she followed. "What in desolation...you're going to get us killed! Worse. Captured!"

Vaulting over a section of bending road to one of the narrow walkways, Aline kept going. She ran a few steps then vaulted the other side of the road, landing less than a meter from the town fountain. At the pool's edge, Aline stopped, seeming to revel in the fountain's spray wastefully streaming across her face.

"What do you think you're doing?" Meladise screamed.

From far down the street, just past the auto store, Mwalgi with black armbands—local enforcers—jogged toward them, laser guns in hand. A blast from those could take out part of a building, but it would also take out a Mwalgi, scales or no.

"We—"

Meladise felt a shove, lost her balance, and found herself swimming in the fountain's pool. A lifetime of warnings and careful survival overrode her brain's attempts at logic. Meladise screamed, jumping to her feet and hopping in the water, as if she could somehow escape by staying above it.

"No!" the mayor shrieked, her voice clear despite the distance. "The tsefuur is contaminating our water supply. Kill it," she screeched. "Kill it!"

The stupid Saeanan had followed Meladise to her death? The thought brought back some sanity. A town fountain was an expensive luxury, which meant it was fully enclosed, fully filtered. There could be no salmond lurking in the depths, no hidden dangers.

Taking a deep breath, Meladise realized their water packets were floating around her knees, along with a jumpsuit repair kit and a package of fruit bars. What did that stupid Saeanan think she was doing, releasing all of their packets without activating them?

"You idiot!" yelled Meladise, hitting the yellow buttons on top of the packets as fast as she could.

Aline followed her example, activating packets and dumping full ones into their empty satchels, along with the repair kit, as fast as she could. They'd regained about half when the guards started firing. Unlike other desert towns, an oil town would have a well-trained defense presence to guard the mines and oil tanks.

The top of the fountain, a beautiful replica of a pernais flower, its petals wide and water shooting upward from the center, shattered. Water shot into the air. Raining much farther than the pool's boundaries, it sizzled across the magnetic road. Steam swirled upward, obscuring their attackers, which meant it might provide some cover. They might have a chance after all.

With two packs across each of their backs, and only half of their water, they dove from the fountain's pool as more laser blasts decimated the structure. Water shot higher into the air, splattering farther across the cooling street. On the other side of the road, a few meters away, the water splashed in the consecration pot. Hot liquids splattered in every direction. A few enforcers screamed. The steam filling the air intensified the scent of cooked meat. Meladise didn't have time to think about her stomach. One side of the retaining pool blasted apart, the water emptied in a minor flood, becoming a boiling river in both directions. Savory smelling steam obscured everything.

Grabbing Meladise's hand, Aline ran toward the safety of the sidewalk, the only direction where they wouldn't have to cross the hot street. Meladise yanked toward the way they'd come, back by the parts store. If the steam held up, they could slip around and make their way back to Lar.

Aline refused, dragging Meladise in the opposite direction. "They'll expect us to try to sneak around. If we can see the street down there, they'll see us, and I doubt they'll miss."

Meladise pulled her hand free. "But there's no way out on that side."

"There has to be an emergency exit," Aline insisted, as if she knew what she was talking about. "We have a better chance there than we will going back the way we came."

"But Lar—"

Aline took off, yelling over her shoulder. "We'll find him, or he'll find us, but we have to stay alive first."

"Desolate Saeanan!" Meladise yelled at her, but she had no choice but to follow.

The enforcers emerged from the steam as Meladise and Aline reached the force field wall surrounding the town. A tall fence, the rods made of imported allim metal, stood four meters from the glittering force field, protecting ignorant citizens and children from getting themselves vaporized.

This is how I'm going to die. Not in worthy battle, but either disintegrated for being a thief, or for being stupid enough to try going through that wall.

Aline searched the perimeter, as if expecting to find something.

"I told you," said Meladise, pointing from one direction to the other. "There are no alternate exits."

"What kind of a stupid design—"

Meladise shook her head. Could the woman really be this dense? "This is Lenfay. What would the people be escaping their town to? A barren desert in the middle of nowhere? They may have other contingencies in case of an emergency, but extra exits are not our way."

The enforcers spanned both sides of the street, closing in on them. There was nowhere left to run.

"Die fighting or get captured?" Aline asked Meladise.

That was a ridiculous question. Meladise sneered. "I'd rather get shot than be tortured to death, even by my own people."

"See," said Aline. "We do have some things in common."

"Like stupidity," said Meladise, not wanting this bantering camaraderie before she died, but it was hard not to get sucked in by the Saeanan's bravery. "You were stupid enough to run in this direction, and I was stupid enough to follow."

Aline watched the oncoming enforcers, raising her hands in a gesture of surrender. "Outcome would have been the same."

"Don't raise your hands," Meladise told her, crouching to fight. "I'm not going to pretend I surrender then attack. That's a coward's way."

"And what's to stop them from shooting us rather than getting close enough to grab hold of us?"

"Honor," said Meladise. "Shooting rather than fighting would be a sign of weakness."

Aline lowered her hands, and set her feet for combat. "Not that I believe any of those monsters have honor, but I guess I can die your way as well as my own."

Side by side, facing their attackers, Aline finally felt like she might understand Meladise somewhat. She estimated their new-found camaraderie might last ten minutes, if they were lucky.

Meladise smirked at Aline, as if their imminent death was just a new joke. The similarity to Lar's expression the first time he'd spoken to Aline, right after he'd stepped onto the Noble Ark, made Aline's breath catch. For all the horrible things Meladise had done and said, she was his sister, and it was Aline's fault that she was about to die. And Lar would either seek revenge or die of sever-ance. Maybe both.

As dread and guilt overcame fear, an explosion boomed like planet-to-space cannons. The ground beneath them shook. Meladise and Aline put out their hands like surfers on a monster wave, trying to keep their balance. Forty meters or more away, far-ther along the force field's perimeter, a plume of fire and smoke shot into the air. The glittering shine of the force field disap-peared.

Aline had thought the burning along her skin inside the dome had hurt, but she'd forgotten the excruciating burn she'd experi-enced when she and Lar had jumped from the train. The force field must have had some kind of rudimentary air-pump, because once it was gone, Aline's pain reasserted itself with vengeance. For once, such terrible luck proved their salvation.

Clenching in pain, Aline didn't jump for the fence like Meladise had, but she did hear the whine of the surrounding laser pistols.

"Wait!" Aline yelled.

Meladise had reached the top of the fence, about to swing over a leg.

Aline jumped, grabbing Meladise's pant leg, yanking her down as the pistols discharged. Falling on top of Aline, Meladise cried out. There was no time to see what had happened. Aline lay with her face in the dirt, Meladise's chest squishing it down. The girl's body pressed against the backpacks, her elbow Aline's only view.

The high-pitched release of lasers combined with the smell of metal vapor. If Aline thought the ground hot, and the atmosphere like burning acid, she had a feeling the molten metal that used to be the perimeter fence was about to give her a new perspective.

Meladise screamed again, scrambling off as Aline sensed a new source of heat near her thigh, moving closer.

Another round of laser fire released, higher-pitched and of longer duration, but it came from above.

As soon as Meladise's weight freed Aline, she rolled away from the twisted remnants of the fence and the line of liquid metal reaching for her leg. She pushed herself up into a crouch, her hood falling to her shoulders, as chunks of dirt and plaster flew through the air.

It was hard to say who felt more pain, Meladise from the liquid metal's touch, or Aline from the burning chemicals in Lenfay's atmosphere.

"Come on!" Meladise grabbed Aline's hand, as Aline had grabbed hers only minutes before.

Using her other arm to shield herself from falling debris, Meladise tightened her grip on Aline and jumped what was left of the fence—short metal teeth extending up from the steaming dirt and molten pools of iron.

As soon as they cleared the city, Lar opened fire with the ohfertsoog's laser guns. Aline hadn't even known they existed. The ground behind her and Meladise, including what was left of the fence, erupted like a violent earthquake. They ran faster, Aline trusting to Meladise's sense of direction. Despite her breather, and despite Meladise's help, Aline's legs started to drag. Her lungs burned with something more than strain, and the pain across her skin made her worst sunburn seem like a cooling balm in comparison.

When she thought she couldn't take another step, the soog suddenly materialized in front of them. Aline didn't know if they'd rounded a hill or if it had landed and she'd been too delirious to notice.

The hatch opened. Lar jumped out, scooped up Aline, and ran for the vehicle. Meladise ran beside him then past, having only her backpacks to carry.

Laser fire sounded from behind. Dirt shot up on their left side. The enforcers had caught up. Lar veered right, right again, then left. They reached the hatch.

A shot hit above them as they tumbled into the soog. Lar hit the automatic close. The soog rumbled, the hatch door straining to lower, but nothing happened.

"Of all the desolate machinery scrap," Lar cursed. "Manual override!"

The computer disengaged the automatic hatch and the whine of uncooperative machinery stopped. As Lar reached for the handle, another blast rocked the vehicle. He missed, teetering on the open edge. Meladise, now in the pilot's seat, revved their sputtering engines, and took off. The extra momentum sent Lar over. Andi slammed into a pile of equipment from the far corner, groaned, but didn't stir.

"Lar!" Aline screamed.

Scrambling for some way to hold onto him, Aline's fingers slid off the scales along his chest and arms, finally hooking in the waistband of his torn-up trousers. With a yank, the trousers ripped, but Aline pulled him far enough to land his torso across the hatch's open edge. Feet dangling in the dirt, Lar extended a talon into the soog's floor. It did almost nothing, the indestructible claw carving through the metal as the terrain caught at Lar's feet, pulling him down. Tufts of red dirt flew into the air, clogging

Aline's already-strained breather and clouding the air. She could see Lar slipping away, but she couldn't see his arms well enough to differentiate hand from claw. If she grasped hold of him in the wrong place, the talon would slice through bone and tissue, cutting off her fingers.

She didn't have time to find the right spot. If she did, Lar would be gone. She threw out a hand, hoping.

Lar grasped it, yanking her toward the hole with him. Aline twisted, managing to go feet first. Finding the wall next to the open gap, she braced her foot, but started to twist to the side. Pulling one hand from Lar's, she grabbed a seat's leg, welded to the soog.

Lar's weight and momentum wrenched her shoulder, extracting another cry of pain, but she held strong. With a couple more bumps along the terrain, Lar hauled himself into the soog, making it tip dangerously close to the ground before Meladise managed to pull it upright. The laser fire had stopped.

Meladise took a look over her shoulder. "Lar?" she asked with obvious relief. "I was afraid we were going to lose you."

"Aline saved me," he said with admiration, reminding her of the many times they'd saved one another's lives aboard the Noble Ark.

"One of these days we need to start keeping score," Aline rasped through the defective breather.

Lar laughed, though he sounded more concerned than amused.

Meladise scowled and turned back to the controls. It seemed their survival moment hadn't meant as much to Meladise as it had to Aline. Aline shouldn't have been surprised, but she didn't take the time to give their relationship much thought. The pain across her skin was growing increasingly difficult to bear. She curled up in a ball next to the seats, careful not to jostle Andi who lay in a jumble beneath her. Had they gone through all of that for nothing? Was the girl dead?

In an instant, Lar knelt at Aline's side, prodding her for injury. "What happened?"

"Fine," Aline forced between a pain-tightened jaw. "Just my skin. The jumpsuit. Holes."

Lar searched their bags for medical supplies. One of their packs had fallen out with Lar, but he found the tsefuur medical kit. It included patches and an air purifier for the suit. Once Aline's pain subsided to just dealing with the blisters left behind, Lar worked on closing their hatch while Aline gritted her teeth and cared for Andi. Lar had been thoughtful enough to put the girl in their other tsefuur outfit, so she had no blistering, but Aline couldn't get her to swallow the water they'd brought. Lar fixed the hatch, the gouge in the floor, and reinstated their air filtration system to about ninety percent effectiveness. It meant the tsefuur outfits had to stay on, but Aline could work her arms inside and put balm on her blisters.

As Aline treated her wounds, Lar found some tubing in the soog's cooling system and created a makeshift IV for Andi, using supplies from the medical kits. For a man who didn't know medicine, he sure knew how to do some unusually complicated medical procedures. He claimed his father had insisted that he and his siblings knew how to care for their mother, but Aline suspected that Lar had paid more attention than Jeraud. Despite being a hardcore warrior, he seemed to also be a natural protector and had probably learned everything his father taught with the same intensity that he watched over Aline, worried for his mother's safety.

His gaze wandered often to Aline, and she wasn't sure if she saw lust in his gold and black eyes, or curiosity, or concern; probably all three. The black of his circleh doy hadn't gone down in the last week, nor had the frequency of his muscle spasms. Aline's fears about losing him had possibly cost him his life. She didn't know how to fix it, but it wasn't like she'd had much of a chance to try.

As she finished with the tsefuur cream, Lar came behind her, checking the suit, her face, and spreading more cream along her neckline.

A deep sound, something between a feline purr and the idle of an earth-era engine, rose from Lar's chest, almost whispered in her ear. Aline turned to face him, brought her lips to his. It wasn't good timing, but neither cared anymore. He met her passion with his own, as if the floodgates had suddenly torn lose and he could no longer restrain the torrential waters. His rough tongue explored hers, demanding more. Their bodies crushed together, the uncomfortable folds of her jumpsuit an unacceptable barrier neither of them could surmount.

With each fist wrapped into a handful of cloth, Aline thought he might rip the fabric from her body. Though she knew the atmosphere leaking into the soog would further burn and blister her bare skin, part of her still wanted him to do it. Instead, he held on as if gripping the railing above a cliff.

Meladise brought Aline back to reality with her abrasive whine. "I don't care if it would save your life, Lar, I am not going to watch you two mate."

Lar released Aline. "Then don't watch.

He pulled down a black cloth from the soog's roof, separating the control center from the rest of the vehicle. He pulled Aline close again, nibbling down her cream-covered neck.

"I can still hear you," Meladise yelled.

Lar groaned in frustration. Aline was tempted to tell the girl to put her fingers in her ears. Instead, she took a step back, putting space between them that Lar quickly closed again. He bent down, kissing her long and hard. Aline wanted more, but with Meladise less than a meter away, too much clothing between them, and her stupid breather not doing a very good job of helping her breathe, there was only so much they could do.

She took Lar's face in her hands, pulling away. "We're only going to drive ourselves crazy. Your sister shouldn't have to listen to that."

"Agreed," Meladise yelled back through the cloth.

Lar nodded, but Aline could see what it cost him by the tenseness in his muscles, the fact that his fangs peeked from between his lips, loose with desire. He lifted the fabric curtain between them and Meladise.

"Oh, thank the All," she said. She glanced from him to Aline, wrinkling up her nose.

Not wanting Lar to think her decision came from a lack of passion, she pulled him to the back of the soog where she proceeded to talk with him, kiss him, and let him know in every way she could that she wanted him.

The ohfertsoog rumbled along, sounding like a water deprived Altherivan, but it was the most excruciating and most wonderful day of Aline's life. She was with Lar, finally really with him. Once safe, she would marry him in a ceremony as close to his customs as she could manage, with or without some stupid priest. She wasn't going to let him die of severance, because she would never let herself be separated from him again. Never.

She did have to ask one question, though. "Consecration Festival? I've heard bits and pieces, and I don't want to believe what I think, but tell me. Are the Mwalgi cannibals?"

Lar looked away, stared at his feet a moment, then took a deep breath. "You have to know, food and clean fluids are difficult to obtain in sufficient quantities on our planet."

"So you eat each other?" She couldn't disguise her disgust, and Lar winced.

"Some do. Whenever my father did, my mother wouldn't go near him for a week or more. I tried it once, out of curiosity."

Aline shuddered again. "Why is it called a Consecration Festival when it's just the murder of all your convicts?"

"Only convicts who are sentenced to consecration are part of the festival. The rest are men and women who have reached old age, add little value to the community, and so they consecrate themselves to the good of the community."

Aline's stomach pulsed with nausea. "You eat people when they get too old?"

Lar shrugged. "Obviously, my mother never agreed with it. And other than that one time, I never ate the Consecration Meal, which many Mwalgi consider to be an affront to the memories of those who sacrificed themselves."

Putting her disgust to one side, Aline decided she'd rather talk of other things and changed the subject.

They talked and slept, using what little fuel they'd managed to hold onto to get through the next dark-day, a rather short one. At the next light-day, as Lar took over as pilot, Meladise said it was Prehpay eighth but Aline only knew it was a lot hotter, the terrain changed from dirt, barren rocks, and canyons of sand, to rising dunes with sand so fine that it swirled around them like powder.

As the day progressed, Aline thought they might really make it. According to Lar, they only had a few days left, but the next dune the ohfertsoog hit was its last. An explosion sounded to port, a sputtering, like a dying man coughing up blood. Lar eased the ohfertsoog between two mountains of red powder, and their only means of transportation died.

"We're going to die," Meladise said. "This time, there's no place to go."

Lar appeared angry at her blunt statement, but Meladise didn't see any reason to hide the truth. The only question now, was how would they die? Trying to run, like cowards, or face down the oncoming force that would come from the town they'd just blown apart. At least they could die with some dignity.

"We're Mwalgi," Lar said. "We can survive this." He gave his precious Aline a loving gaze and glanced at Andi. "And we can help them survive. The gravitonics still work well enough to lift the ohfertsoog a few centimeters or more."

"Not well enough to go anywhere," Meladise argued. "Our fuel is gone and that last explosion was our solar converter. No propulsion."

As if she hadn't said anything, Lar pulled a roll of metal cording from the supply box at the back of the soog.

"What are you going to do with that?" Meladise asked. "Lasso the enforcers that show up?"

He continued to ignore Meladise, standing toe to toe with Aline instead, running his fingers through her short hair. "The filter will go soon. Make sure you and Andi have an extra layer of skin cream.

Aline's blistered face scrunched up with worry. "The breathers are going to be the bigger problem. Ever since the oil town, mine has felt like it's clogging up."

"There are ways to clean them, but I don't have what I need here. We have to make it to the hideout. I think we're close, by soog, but I don't know how long it will take to walk."

"Walk?" yelled Meladise. "Through this desert, during Prehpay? Are you boiling insane?"

Turning a grim face to Meladise, he went to the hatch. As he wrestled it open, its protests seemed to agree with Meladise.

"Not only will the enforcers catch up with us anyway," she said. "But we'll be so weak when they do that they won't even have to extend a claw."

"Peltay will come for us. He won't let us live anyway."

"But we could at least fight. Die with some honor."

Lar sighed, as if talking with a mentally challenged Gi, which is what most expected of the few half-breeds like them. "Honor doesn't come from violence. It comes from living with integrity and purpose." He looked again to his Saeanan. Had they planned this little speech? "Aline was right to keep me from the oil town, where I might have hurt innocent people. And there's no purpose in killing those who will come for us unless we might win, and we can't win. Our only chance is to run."

"Like cowards."

Lar shrugged. "If that's how you choose to see it."

He jumped down, red sand swirling up in a cloud, but Meladise wasn't letting him ignore the facts. She grabbed his arm, yanking him to a stop. The old Lar would have extended his talons in warning, but his sheaths merely twitched, as if too tired to bother.

Joining him outside the ohfertsoog, he pulled her out into the oppressive afternoon heat, shutting the hatch behind them. Nothing but fine sand could be seen for miles, some mounds so high they could be buildings

"You killed an entire squad of collection soldiers," accused Meladise.

"Part of a squad," Lar corrected.

Meladise brushed that aside. "Whatever. And you killed those guards in the collections compound."

"Breeding compound," he said with bitter anger. "Your point?"

"Why not stand and fight now? Like you said before the oil town, where I'm sure you added a few to your death tally, you're a murderer anyway, so why not stand and fight? Let's end this."

"Your twisted honor again, sister?" Lar challenged back.

"I'm not—"

"I have killed and I haven't felt good about that. I believe what I've had to do was justified, but it will be for the All to judge. Rather than point fingers, why don't you assess your own honor?"

"I haven't done anything wrong, other than letting myself get dragged around by you."

Lar started ticking off points on his fingers. "This mess started because you snuck around spying on Jeraud and me rather than confront us and talk out your issues. Your friend died because you convinced him to attack us. We ended up stranded in the desert because you purposely provoked Aline. In an effort to kill me you murdered an innocent enforcer—"

Panic welled inside of Meladise. "I didn't know." This wasn't all her fault. It wasn't!

Lar continued. "You are the reason Andi is in there half-dead, and your actions are what put us in the position of having to go to the oil town."

"I don't have to listen to this," said Meladise, turning toward the hatch.

As she had done to him earlier, he grabbed her arm and spun her to face him. "You started this, and I've lost patience with your accusations and your protestations of honor. Honor is doing the right thing, and you have shown nothing but deceit and selfishness since I stepped foot on this planet. I expected more from you."

"You always expect more!" Meladise exploded with long-building anger. "You and Jeraud both, but no matter what I do, I'm never good enough."

"Grow up, Meladise," said Lar. "We've loved you and done our best. You don't need to meet our expectations, but I think it's time you tried meeting your own. In the end, you're the person you have to live with."

Meladise felt like she'd been hit by a speeder. Bowled over and left lifeless on the side of the road. But she wasn't dead yet.

"So you're saying this is all my fault."

"No," said Lar. "I'm saying you had a part in it. Accept that and move on. Now get in the soog. I'm going to rig up a harness and pull us through this desolate sand. I need you to initiate the gravitonics. Put them on the lowest setting."

"If I'm such a horrible person, how can you trust me in there with your precious bonded and dying friend?"

He stared at her, as if considering another murder.

Meladise pushed her luck. "You going to threaten to kill me again?"

"No," said Lar with a sad smirk. "Too tired. If I have to, I'll just leave you. But you won't hurt them. You've changed since that girl who snuck around basements and spouted Mwalgi Destiny. Not a lot, but enough."

Why did people keep saying that? Meladise didn't want to change. Life had been simple, black and white, without so many confusing complications.

She yanked the hatch open, storming inside then yanked it closed behind her.

"What—" Aline started.

Meladise put up a hand, not realizing she'd extended a claw until she saw Aline's concerned expression turn to defensive anger.

"Stupid," muttered Meladise, turning away and going to the controls.

Not wanting conversation, she pulled down the cloth barrier Lar had found when he'd wanted to mate with Aline. Meladise shuddered. So disgusting. Through the front window, she saw Lar making ties in the end of his cable, the other end trailing behind him to the soog.

"Gravitonics to 10%," Meladise told the computer. "Engage."

Nothing happened.

"Stupid!"

Meladise flipped on the manual control switches, found the toggle for the gravitonics, pulling it down to around 10%, then pushed the buttons for it to engage. With a high-pitched whine, the soog shuddered, presumably coming off the ground though the view through the front window didn't change much.

Lar had finished his harness, a simple contraption that went over both shoulders and around his ribs. He strained, the cord going taut, his feet digging into the soft sand, making it swirl around his feet and legs. With barely a jerk, the soog moved after him. It appeared that once he got it going, he didn't have to pull hard, but he had to maintain a consistent pace.

Their bright red sun, Hontselle, shone in front of them, reflecting off the sweat pouring down Lar's face. The light seemed to be coming from both directions and Meladise wondered if a more-distant Kraitselle might be on the opposite horizon. She hated Prehpay, but she knew it would get worse before it got better. Lar was going to kill himself trying to save his bonded. Even a Mwalgi couldn't withstand this desert. That's why the Mwalgi had named it Desolation. Nothing could survive this place, not even them.

A lump formed in Meladise's throat. Would Bernad have been willing to do something like this for her? He'd attacked Lar at her request, but he would have been willing to do that anyway. Bonding made people do almost anything for their mate, but there were still variances of how far that would really go.

The truth hit Meladise with a force that even Lar's words hadn't managed. Bernad would have fought, killing whomever he could in the name of honor, but no, he wouldn't have trudged day in and day out through Lenfay's worst deserts. He wouldn't have cared about her killing the enforcer, by accident or on purpose, and the breeding compound wouldn't have bothered him. He'd probably have been excited for a chance to work there so he could tease the Saeanans, make them suffer for his entertainment.

The thought made Meladise sick to her stomach. A few weeks ago, she would have felt the same way. Hunching over, she gripped the side of the control panel. Unbidden tears slid down her face, landing on the panel's smooth surface.

She sat back, trying to gain control of herself. She couldn't afford to lose moisture. But the more she tried to stop crying, the more forceful the tirade grew. She positioned herself such that the tears fell onto the scales of her chest, but they continued, wrenching sobs from deep in her gut.

"Meladise, are you okay?" Aline asked from the other side of the partition.

"Go away!" Meladise yelled at her. The last thing she needed was a Saeanan psychologist.

The thought brought more tears, deeper sobs. Lar and Aline were right. Meladise had acted like a spoiled child, not a responsible soldier. She'd thought Bernad's ideas of honor to be the only sensible way. But Bernad had never defended anyone, only ridiculed the weak. He'd helped Meladise disguise her Saeanan side, increasing Meladise's hatred for it. Yet Aline, a Saeanan with real reason for hating the Mwalgi, almost reveled in Lar's duality. They stood up for one another, and together they also cared for Andi, a weakling girl who had nothing to recommend her but a bit of spunk. If Meladise was honest, Andi was a lot like Meladise had been at that age, especially right after she'd lost her mother.

By the All, they were right.

It took Meladise another ten minutes before she could compose herself and stop the tears. She sat for another twenty minutes, watching Lar trudge through sand past his ankles. Good thing Desolation lived up to its name and nothing lived here. Otherwise, Lar would be a welcome meal for leezards.

Taking a steadying breath, Meladise lifted the screen between her and the rest of the soog. She'd rather face a vulfbaeor than Aline right now, but honor demanded Meladise act. And this time she would act with honor, not misplaced pride.

Aline glanced up from where she sat on the floor, fanning Andi with a chunk of broken metal, turning her sincere concern to Meladise. "Are you okay?"

The breather made her words sound a bit wheezy, a sure sign the filter was going out. After all Meladise had done, she didn't deserve Aline's kindness.

Swallowing hard, Meladise took one of the seats near Andi's legs, facing Aline. "I'm sorry." Meladise felt like she would choke on the words but she forced them out. "I've ruined everything for you and Lar." Tears welled at the corners of her eyes, but Meladise blinked them back. "And I was wrong. I know that now. I was wrong about everything. I should have just left the two of you alone and let you escape the way Lar had planned. It would have worked."

Aline dropped her makeshift fan, letting it thud against the thin carpet. She joined Meladise on the seats, stretching out her arms.

"It took a lot of courage to say that. I'm impressed."

She wrapped an arm awkwardly around Meladise, giving her shoulders a little squeeze. Meladise was trying to apologize, but that didn't mean she had to suffer Aline's creepy affection. She pushed the woman off.

"Look, I'm sorry, but that doesn't make you my sister."

Aline smirked, something Meladise had never seen her do before. "If I marry your brother then I will be."

A barking laugh escaped from Meladise before she could help herself. "He's bonded to you. Only the Diseeps are that bent on a formal ceremony, so by Mwalgi custom, I guess you're already my sister." Aline put out her arms and raised her eyebrows, but Meladise slapped them away. "Keep your hands to yourself."

Aline dropped her arms with a laugh, extending her hand instead. "Still as prickly as a carpace bush, aren't you?"

Taking the hand, Meladise gave it a firm, short, shake. "You've been spending too much time with my brother. You're starting to talk like a Mwalgi."

"If you haven't noticed," said Aline. "We're speaking Mwalgi."

"Yes, but—"

Aline laughed. "I know what you meant. And Meladise?"

"Yes."

"If we survive this then it will all be worth it. Maybe the trip is harder, but we found Andi. Even if she dies, it's better than what would have happened to her in that compound. That's true for all the prisoners. And you've gained a new perspective on the world.

I think having our eyes opened is worth a little pain. I know it was for me."

"You're a good person," Meladise admitted, surprised that the words came easily.

"Thanks to your brother, I'm better than I used to be," Aline said. "With all that's happened, it's almost enough to make me believe in his All. Maybe someone is watching over us."

"Are you crazy? Our soog died in the middle of the planet's worst desert. We're all going to die."

Aline returned to Andi's side and picked up the fan. "I said maybe. I'll think about it again if we survive."

It had been a long time since Meladise had thought about the All and her former beliefs, but if they survived, Aline might have a point. Maybe it was time to think about the girl Meladise had been a few years ago, and maybe it wasn't too late to go back, or to at least try.

She rose from her seat, taking a water packet from their limited supply and heading for the hatch. "I'll be back."

Meladise had some heavy debts to repay, and it was time to get started.

Walking in the heat of the day was stupid, but Lar knew they needed to get a little farther into the desert before he could start resting. Peltay would have reached the oil town they'd escaped and he would have followed after them, assuming he could catch them before they went too deep into the desert. A little farther, then Lar could be assured that Peltay would decide to turn around and either give up or at least gather adequate supplies before he resumed his search. Their chances were slim, but not yet nonexistent.

When Mela jumped from the soog, his burden lightened, forcing him to catch himself as the gravitonics lifted the vehicle another couple of centimeters. His sister didn't weigh a lot, but certainly more than Aline or Andi, and the slight difference altered his rhythm.

She walked beside him for several moments before she spoke. "I apologized to Aline."

Lar jerked his head to one side. He almost stopped the soog. "Why? What did you do to her?"

Mela laughed, sounding more like the sister he remembered than she had since he and Aline had arrived on Lenfay. "Nothing. At least nothing new. I thought about what you said, and I realized some things. I'm sorry. I—"

Determined to manage some sign of affection, even if it was somewhat stilted with the soog lugging behind them, Lar put an arm around her shoulders. "You don't have to say any more. You've apologized to her, and to me. It is forgotten."

Mela's gaze dropped. "I should apologize to Andi."

Lar gave her a squeeze then let go. "When she wakes up."

They both knew Andi's survival was even less likely than their own, but Mela went along with it. "Yes. I'll say something to her then."

Sweat dripped from Lar's forehead to the scales of his chest and back.

"You should probably lose the pants," said Mela. "It will help your scales do their job. Maybe they can absorb the moisture in the air."

"I don't think there is any moisture here."

But he did as she suggested, not bothering to untie them, slashing through the waistband instead, completing the tear Aline had made when she'd pulled him onto the soog and saved his life. Lar kept hold with one hand until he'd shredded the fabric enough that it would drop without impairing his steps.

Mela picked it up after him. They both knew they didn't want to leave a trail.

"It's still the middle of the day," said Mela. "You should rest now and we'll start up when it gets closer to dark-day."

"Can't," said Lar. "Peltay will be after us."

"Your former mistar?" She sounded surprised, but then, she didn't know Frond Peltay as Lar did. "You think he followed you from the compound?"

"Sure of it," said Lar. "His vendetta is personal. So much so that as soon as he heard about the incident at the oil town, I'm sure he headed after us without waiting for reinforcements or supplies."

"That's stupid."

Lar shook his head. "Not if something happens to us or the soog, which it has."

"Then why are we still going? Maybe I was right and we should stand and fight."

"If we can just get a little bit farther, I think it will be enough that Peltay will have to turn back to gather supplies rather than risk getting stuck out here himself."

Mela nodded and to Lar's surprise she reached for the harness. "Then let me take it for a while. You've hardly slept, it's the middle of the day, and you're already getting skin-burnt."

"I'm okay."

"No, you're not," said Mela. "Get some sleep. Spend some time with Aline and let her know what's going on. When you've rested, then you can take a turn."

Lar wasn't sure what to make of Mela's offer. She'd been generous and helpful as a child, but he hadn't seen that side of her lately.

"It's time I did something to help instead of making things worse," she added.

"You don't need—"

She started undoing Lar's harness. "Yes, I do. Now quit being stubborn."

Lar conceded. He was so tired the dunes seemed like one massive blur, but he thought that might have something to do with the twin suns, one almost directly above and the other having just risen in the east. Either way, she was right, he'd be of more use if he had a little sleep.

Having taken off the collection camp uniform as soon as they'd escaped the town, Mela was already dressed for the desert, wearing only her beyesh. Lar helped her adjust the harness, gave her his compass, and made his way to the hatch.

Maybe his sister had changed more than he thought. She still seemed angry and on edge, but there was hope.

Lar woke with a start, his arms still around Aline despite the heat, alert to whatever sound had jerked him awake. Nothing. The dim light from the windows suggested they'd slept clear into the next night day. Andi lay on her cot, so quiet Lar wondered if she still lived.

The quiet! Aline's breather had rasped like an antique fuel-engine as they'd fallen asleep. Now, she was completely quiet.

"Lights," Lar yelled at the ohfertsoog.

There was just enough solar conversion for the overhead lights to gleam on at about twenty percent capacity. It was still dim, but enough to see Aline's pale face. She wasn't breathing.

Lar dove for the Saeanan medical kit. If Aline and Mela had grabbed a good one, it should have a portable oxygen converter. He rifled through it, not finding anything. POCs could be small, but not that—

Something clanked at the bottom of the bag, crammed into the far corner. Lar got his fingers around the slick metallic surface, shuffling the bag's contents as he pulled the small blue cylinder free.

He ran to Aline's side as Mela jumped into the soog. Lar hadn't even noticed it had stopped moving.

Lar dug out Aline's breather. It had to have hurt, but she didn't react.

She can't be dead. Not now, after all we've survived.

Hands shaking, Lar unfolded the portable face mask attached to the cylinder's side. He spread it over Aline's blue unmoving lips and up over her nose, where it attached as if the edges were coated with glue. It looked like he'd shoved a squished up wad of plastic to her face.

Pressing a small green button on the canister's side, the POC started to whoosh and wheeze, filtering the air and making the mask over Aline's face expand. Lar held her hand, which felt much too cold. Letting it drop, he put his ear to her chest. By some miracle of the All, her heart still beat. Her chest expanded, seemed to stutter, then she shot upright, eyes wide beneath their coverings. Clawing at the mask on her face, Aline ripped it loose, convulsed, and then hurled onto the soog's stained carpet like an ellgot coughing up dirtballs. A mass of green slime, speckled with dots of blood, streamed onto the floor. Aline gasped, screamed in pain, then pressed the decompressed mask to her face and lay back to the floor again.

Mela rushed to her other side. Together, she and Lar moved Aline's shaking hands away and reattached the mask. Only then did Lar see Mela's blistered skin.

"How long were you out there?" he asked.

"It's almost Prehpay 14th. Hontselle is rising."

No. "We slept through an entire day? Why didn't you wake me?"

Mela rolled her eyes. "You obviously needed the sleep, and I'm fine. Just take care of your Saeanan. Aline," she amended.

Lar checked Aline's rising and falling chest. Thank the All he'd awoken in time. He scooted away to give Aline quiet, and Mela followed him, sitting on the floor a few chairs away.

"I'm so stupid," she said. "I heard you moving around and I came in to yell at you. I thought you woke up but decided to leave me out there as punishment."

"Even if you deserved some punishment beyond a guilty conscience, I have no right to mete it out. I've done many things I'm not proud of, Mela. I'm in no position to judge anyone else."

"No," she said, her tone bitter. "That's more along my lines."

"Will you watch over Aline for me?" Lar asked, grabbing a tube of protection cream and spreading it over his exposed skin. "I don't know how long that POC will work before its filter clogs as well. I don't think we have any more breathers, not even in the Saeanan kit."

Mela nodded, helping him put cream on his back and then turning her blistered one to him. "I'll take everything out of it. They're small, so it could be hidden."

She stifled a whimper, the warm cream painful against her blisters.

"I should have searched for one earlier," said Lar. "Then this wouldn't have happened."

"Don't be cracked," said Mela. "You're trying to conserve water, food, and I'm sure the Saeanan survival resources, so we can all survive as long as possible. I imagine you wanted to wait until the last possible moment to replace it."

Mela understood more than Lar had thought. Yes, he'd put it off to conserve, but he'd also put it off because he'd been tired.

He'd figured they would get a few hours of sleep and then he would go in search of a new one. His laziness had nearly cost Aline her life.

"I'll go and pull the soog now."

"Wear some clothing," said Mela, pointing to her burnt face. "I should have thought. Less clothing works great for running around in the city, but if subjected to the suns all day, especially as Prehpay season changes to Zomeh, then we're better with some cover for our Saeanan skin."

She said the words with the same disdain she always had for their Saeanan heritage, but the edge of hatred was missing.

Lar didn't want to cover his scales because they did help him handle the heat and lack of water. Besides, the few extra uniforms in the back were too small. He searched the cabin, finally alighting on the dark curtain separating the back of the soog from the near useless control panel. With a forceful tug, he yanked it out of its moorings. Rather than take the heavy fabric, he ripped out the lining, making a lightweight sheet that would cover his back, shoulders, and drape over his head.

He checked Andi—she still had a pulse, though weak—and kissed Aline on the cheek, grateful she was alert enough to groan. True to her promise, Mela started sifting through the Saeanan first aid kit as Lar went out the screeching hatch.

They should be far enough away by now that Peltay would have turned back for reinforcements, but Lar still wasn't sure they'd survive long enough to reach the hideout.

Another trick on the horizon. Another pool of water turned the deep color of blood. As they'd done every day they'd been walking, both suns beat Lar with their never-ending heat. But in the last four days, as the twin stars started their spin around one another, Kraitselle had come closer, joining Hontselle in her light-day tortures. Soon, they would become like one blazing sun, Kraitselle hidden by her sister, but her added heat felt nonetheless. Lar's eyes had re-accustomed to Lenfay's red sun soon after arriving on the planet, but every Mwalgi suffered during this time of the year, when the planet truly seemed to be washed in blood, the light-days longer and hotter, the shorter dark-days their only relief.

Shouldn't it be closing on a dark-day by now? Lar wasn't sure, wasn't sure he was even going in the right direction anymore. A part of him knew the two suns were confusing him, but he also knew he had to keep moving.

As the suns raced after one another over the mid-day sky, Lar struggled from the harness and into the soog for a few hours of sleep. The place smelled stale, dirty, and of surface-cleaned excrement. Some of the smells had hidden below the surface from the beginning, remnants of abused Saeanans transported to their deaths in collections camps, but the last few days of stale heat had brought the smells to the forefront.

Andi slumped in the corner of the soog, near the storage compartments, but Lar didn't have the heart to check if she was still alive. They'd discontinued her IV a couple of days ago, right before they ran out of water. Was that two days or three? Mela had cared for her and cleaned her up the last couple of days, but now she and Aline lay on the floor together. Mela shivered with fever, while Aline lay still as death.

With blistered hands, Lar squeezed what he could from the spent tube of protection cream over the skin of her face. He would have put some on her hands, but there just wasn't enough. She didn't move this time, not even to groan. Lar pressed his ear to her chest, the sound of her regular heartbeat a soothing melody.

"What's wrong?" he asked, though he knew she wouldn't answer.

It could be dehydration, exhaustion, a reaction to the environment, infection, or any number of things. Mela had found a breather, so it wasn't that, but Lar had no idea what to do for her.

He curled up next to them, though not close enough to add his body heat to theirs.

Mela cried out, as if trying to make up for Aline's silence. "I'll kill...all!" She groaned, writhing, her dry scales rasping against the carpet like a shlaka slithering up from its hole. "Can't," she moaned.

Holding Aline's hand in his, he fell asleep listening to Mela's nightmares.

———

Lar woke in soothing darkness, both of Lenfay's suns finally leaving them in peace for a few hours, but he couldn't afford the time he'd spent sleeping. They needed to reach the hideout.

He checked Aline's pulse, still steady but faint, as if her heart struggled to beat as much as Lar's muscles struggled to make him rise. Mela had calmed, but her breathing was still ragged.

Despite his body's protests, Lar again wrapped the white fabric over his head and shoulders and harnessed himself to the soog.

The dark-day dragged like a never-ending space flight, yet Lar seemed to blink and found the darkness gone. He stood, his blank face staring at the long shadows the twin suns spread before him. Nothing stirred in the desert's desolate silence. How long had he been standing there, dazed? Red powder piled around his ankles. The suns sent what sweat his body could muster from his face to be absorbed by his scales or lost in the sand.

He took a step forward. His knee buckled, his groan breaking the eerie silence. Lar clenched the muscles in his other leg, forcing his body to rise. The muscle spasmed, followed immediately by the clenching of his abdomen. Eyes glazing, both knees dropped with a whoosh of swirling sand and a gritty crunch from the under layer. Lar's body followed, his head settling into the burning grit. The desert's continued silence was all Lar registered before his eyes closed and his mind went blank.

Water! Lar felt it on his tongue, recognized the slow trickle across his cracked lips. His eyes opened, but he couldn't get them wider than a crack, as if they'd crusted together and become stiff as sokra branches. Through that slit, the lack of light suggested a dark-day, but it was off. Lar couldn't quite grasp why until he turned his head and saw bright light shining through a craggy hole.

"Where," he tried to speak, but it came out more like a catch in his throat than words.

"So you are coming awake, you crazy leezard." The man's voice sounded like nothing Lar had heard before, as if he gargled sand, spitting it with his words. "I was starting to wonder if my water was just making a useless pool in your mouth, or if that jiggle in your throat meant you could still swallow."

The water flow increased, and Lar gulped it down until it suddenly stopped.

"Little at a time, boy. Too much at once and you'll be hurling it at my feet before it can do you any good."

Lar touched a finger to his tongue, wiping at the crust across his eyes until they opened fully.

He gasped, though it came out as a coughing fit. Trying to scramble away from the thing leaning over him, he didn't get far before another muscle spasm dropped him back to the hard floor, his back against a wall.

"What are you?" he managed to ask as the spasm passed.

The man barked a laugh, Mwalgi in every way, though the light reflecting off his scales did nothing to convince Lar they were of similar species.

"My name is Beyani Jadad," said the man from thin lips with cracks wider than the surface of a long-abandoned field. "I, my boy, am a miracle." He pointed to Lar, taking in his bare skin-and-armor chest. "As, it appears, are you."

"I'm half-Saeanan," said Lar. "You're...something else."

"I am old."

"Impossible."

"I could say the same about you."

Lar didn't have time for this. Old people didn't exist on Lenfay, not past the age of consecration. Lar had never seen a Mwalgi with withered brown scales, showing copious amounts of black pontreer beneath. Nor had he seen one with yellow teeth, many of which were missing, and only a few limp strands to its scalp. Beyani had braided the few strands into a tail that draped down the back side of his neck, only a centimeter thick, the ends like a stripped power cord whose exposed wires had been shoved re-peatedly against a hard surface until they kinked and frayed.

Lar searched the underground cavern for Aline. Light shone from various holes in the ground, illuminating much of the space, leaving other parts in shadow. Mela lay on a mat not far from where Lar had been, but there was no sign of anyone else.

"Where's Aline?" demanded Lar. "The Saeanan woman in the ohfertsoog."

"Dead," said Beyani, as if surprised by the question. "Or as good as. Same with the younger one, though she's even worse off."

Lar struggled to rise, but his muscles betrayed him again, send-ing him back to the floor. It was some kind of rock, though he was sure the area of desert they'd been traveling through had con-sisted of powdery sand dunes, no rock for miles. How had they gotten here?

"The soog is still outside," offered Beyani, "until I can salvage it for parts. I can bring them in, but it'll be cramped, and we'll just have to haul them out again after they die."

"We can't let them die!" Lar knew he had no right to yell at the man, but Beyani's lack of emotion toward Aline made Lar's all the more severe. "I promised I'd save her."

Beyani tapped his heel on the ground, stepping warily back. "I have medicine that helps Mwalgi, but I know nothing of Saeanans."

Lar's talons had started shifting in and out of his sheaths, so he pulled them back and forced himself to remain calm. "Do you have any diab corbay? I need the leaves."

"Yes, but the leaves aren't edible."

"I don't want to eat it!" Lar took a deep breath. He was losing his temper again. "If you have the leaves, I can make a salve for Aline and Andi's skin. Maybe that will help."

"The girl—"

"Andi," said Lar, wanting Beyani to see them as people.

"Sure, boy. Andi. She's suffering from an infection due to the shlaka bite. I'd know what to do for her if she were Mwalgi, but Saeanans..."

"We are the same," said Lar, his eyes lighting up. Maybe this freak of nature could help after all. "Do with them as you would a Mwalgi. There are some foods they can't eat, but I know what they are. Otherwise, their anatomy is almost identical to our own."

"You're not exactly Mwalgi, either."

"I'm both," said Lar. "And because of it, I can save them, if you'll bring them here and do what I ask."

Beyani barked another laugh, chortling as he left the cavern. "Why not? I'll go get us a couple of Saeanans to play with. This might be fun."

He half-jogged, half-shuffled, from the room, raising dust and making Lar cough. He heard Beyani's distant curse then the soog hatch screeched.

The old Mwalgi was crazy. Lar was sure of that. But maybe the All had sent them this insane Mwalgi so they could survive. Lar shivered at the thought of Beyani's half-desiccated body, like someone thrown in the offering pot come back to life. As soon as possible, they'd be away from this place.

～～～～

It took three days before Aline opened her eyes, and a solid week for Andi. The healer knew his medicine and because of his advanced age, he even had bone vitamins. The poultice he'd placed on Andi's leg left a nasty rash, but the infection finally cleared. Mela, whose fever had left the morning of the next dark-day, assumed care of the young girl. Her actions seemed like an effort at penance, but there was a change in Mela, She seemed to actually enjoy her time with Andi, practicing her broken English, despite the girl's obvious distrust.

"So you dug a hole in the middle of nowhere?" Aline asked Beyani. "You were just hoping you'd find a way to survive?"

Aline's fascination with the old Mwalgi unnerved Lar. She continued to ask him questions, help him with the work, and act like she'd found some long lost relative.

"Remember, little Saeanan," Beyani's pet name for Aline made Lar bristle, but didn't bother her in the slightest. "I spent years before my intended consecration planning for this. I learned from the sharbo miners how to shore up the sand and I learned how to make it look natural. I studied the water patterns and estimated the most likely spot for an underground water supply."

"But you're old!" Lar couldn't help but blurt out. "You shuffle around in pain, and your scales are weak, and your hair has fallen out. Why would you rather live this way than give yourself over to the good of the community?"

"Good of the community? What good did they ever do me that I should sacrifice my flesh for their dinner?"

"That's disgusting," said Aline.

"I know, I never participated in the feast," said Lar, "but I always admired the sacrifice of the old to benefit those still living. Isn't it good if the elderly give their lives to provide food for the poor and weak?"

He'd watched Beyani over the last week, as the man struggled to drag his old bones from his well, deep in the caverns, to their dwelling. Lar had listened to the man's night-time wheezing, sometimes wondering if Beyani would stop breathing altogether and turn into a still, pale corpse. Lar didn't entirely believe in the consecration, but if it saved the old from weakness and suffering while removing the burden of caring for them from their families then it wasn't entirely bad.

Beyani came close, so close Lar could smell his putrid breath. "I've still got some slice in these old bones." He extended his claws, yellowing almost as badly as his teeth. "They may not look as pretty as they once were, but don't doubt they still work."

Lar extended his own claws, quickly retracting them as Aline came between them.

"That's enough male stupidity," she said. "You're not going to threaten Lar," she told Beyani. "Even with his severance issues, he'll cut you fit to be boiled."

Lar grinned at the way she used the Mwalgi figure of speech, but then she turned on him. "And you are a gerontophobe, and you need to get over it. Beyani has experience, wisdom, and knowledge that he might just share with us if you quit treating him like a lurking disease."

Still weak, Aline's muscles quivered with her effort to stand. Her condition humbled him more than her words. "I'll behave myself," Lar promised. "Sit down and rest. I won't say anything more."

As if grateful for the permission, which wasn't like Aline at all, she sank to the floor next to him.

"What's a gertiphobe?" Lar asked.

"Gerontophobe," she corrected, but Beyani leaned forward, touching his aged hand to her forehead, cutting her off.

"She needs more tengle leaves."

Lar couldn't help a shudder at the man's hunched-over body as he left to the back of his little cave and a small store of supplies.

"It means you're afraid of old people," Aline finished, watching Beyani leave without a trace of discomfort.

"I'm not afraid—"

"Usually, it's because people are afraid of ever becoming old."

She kissed him, cutting off his protests for good. "And I want to be with you for a very long time, so you need to get over it."

Her argument was convincing enough that Lar determined to try.

The bleak landscape told Lar what he couldn't get that old leezard, Beyani, to reveal. Lar had taken them too far north, which was why this section of desert had a limited amount of life and the occasional shrinking shrub.

They survived on Desolation's northwestern outskirts, pulling in their leaves and appearing as a dead bush during the day, releasing their bright purple leaves from the set of one light-day until the beginning of another, using them to absorb sunlight in the cooler hours and to gather what moisture they could during the dark-days.

Amazing plants. Right now, shrouded in the dirt-encrusted curtain Lar had used to drag them here, and Beyani had used to roll Lar up and hoist him into the soog, Lar wished he could wither up like the plants and avoid the beating of the suns. They'd entered Zomeh, Lenfay's hottest season as the twin suns, Hontselle and Kraitselle, took hands and circled, preparing to swing each other to their opposite elliptical orbits. Lar glanced up at the suns again, Kraitselle largely obscured by Hontselle's looming face.

Lar longed to take Aline and Andi away from Beyani's cave, but as he suffered in the evening heat he realized he'd have to wait the twenty-one to twenty-three days until the season changed to Secur, and the weather began to temper.

A buzzing, not unlike an advancing swarm of stomressers,

though they usually only alighted on land in the cooler regions of Lenfay, filled Lar's ears. He scanned the far horizon and his heart dropped. A scout drone, only a pinprick in the distance, moved in Lar's direction. But a single drone couldn't make so much noise.

Lar raised the far-viewer he'd stolen from Beyani's supplies.

"Desolate, bloody fluids," he whispered.

Despite Frond Peltay's disgrace at Lar's hands, he must still have had some connections. A half-squad of land enforcement vehicles, seven that Lar could count, followed the drone. Plus, there were five ohfertsoogs, certainly filled with twenty land officers each, and they were following Beyani's trail to the cave. His camouflage might have fooled the occasional security flight, but a tracker would find them in a heartbeat if it came too close.

Lar scrambled from his vantage atop a crusty hill devoid of even the shrinking shrubs, hoping his curtain hid him well enough to not draw the drone-scout's attention.

Intercepting the faint trail Beyani had left another two kilometers up the path, Lar created a false lead, heading north—a more logical direction than to continue toward the central desert—and then he circled back toward Aline.

It was the middle of the next dark-day by the time he burst into the cave, wrinkling his nose momentarily at the putrid odor of boiled diab-corbay leaves used for skin protectant. Everyone lay on the mats Beyani had woven from shrub roots, including old Beyani himself, asleep and snoring. At least they were all well enough to make noise, a miracle Lar thanked the All for, though if they didn't move quickly, the miracle would be short-lived.

"Up!" Lar shouted. "We've got to get out of here. Peltay is on our trail and I doubt it will take him more than another light-day to find us."

Aline shot up from her blanket, trained by her time in the honor corps and with Captain Trenoble to jump to alert at a moment's notice. Mela was up quickly as well, doing her best to help a still-weak Andi.

Beyani raised bleary eyes, groaning as his old bones creaked in protest. "What are you going on about? Nobody has ever found my hideout. Never."

"You've never dragged a soog full of fugitives to your cave before," said Lar. "This isn't your random security fly-by. They've got heat-detecting scout droids and Peltay won't give up until he finds us. "

The old man finally seemed to find his energy, jumping to his feet and flailing his arms as he punctuated his words. "This is what I get for saving a man's life. Saeanans to care for and now a pack of government vulfbaeors breathing down my neck. What have you brought on me, you stupid half-breed?"

The points of Lar's talons twitched in and out of their sheaths. He'd had enough species slurs in his life. He wasn't going to take it from an old man without enough courage to consecrate himself for the good of his people.

Aline placed herself between them, as had become common, putting her hands out as if to keep them apart. "We don't have time for this. We've got to pack up and get out of here. Lar, do you have anywhere for us to go?"

He nodded, but he'd sworn not to keep things from Aline anymore. He had to tell her the whole truth. "If we could get a good enough head start, we might make it to the hideout, but I'm not sure I can obscure our trail enough that Peltay won't still find us. And without our supplies from Col de Pluurs, I'm not sure how long we'll survive once we get there."

"You think the Saeanans will survive walking through Desolation in the middle of Zomeh, anyway?" asked Mela from where she spread the nasty green skin cream over Andi's exposed skin.

Lar's shoulders slumped. "Without a functioning ohfertsoog? I don't know. Probably not. But I'm sure Peltay has no intention of letting any of us live when he gets here. Leaving is the only chance we have."

With multiple cracks and groans, Beyani stretched his back, touched his toes, and unsheathed his urine-colored claws. "I won't make it. Besides, I've lived fifteen years in this cave, and no stinking government hoond meat is going to take it from me. If I leave, it will be my decision, not theirs."

Lar's claws completely unsheathed. "If you think I'm talking about a renegade squad here, some motley band of enforcers thrown together to track someone unwilling to consecrate, then you're wrong. Peltay's got a force big enough to take down a border skirmish, and I'm sure he's got laser blasters and a contained chemical bomb or two."

With a grin, Beyani gestured toward the back of his cave. "Well, then it's a good thing I have my own collection."

Mela helped Andi back down to her mat where she leaned against the wall, then followed Lar and Aline as Beyani took them to the very rear of the cave. Neatly disguised beneath his stack of old allim crates full of dried food and other supplies, Beyani dusted the ground until the edges of a trapdoor became visible.

Lar helped him move the crates then Beyani pulled an attachable handle from a crevice high in the rock, fitted it to the door, and raised it. A well-carved staircase extended into blackness. Grabbing a lightstick from a supply crate, he led them down into a man-made cave. The faint trickle of water echoing against the walls explained where Beyani's well gained its supply. Such freshwater sources were rare on Lenfay, especially so far south of civilization.

Even more amazing were the boxes and piles of weapons filling the entire cavern.

"Bloody fluids," exhaled Mela.

Lar fingered a pack of bomb timers. "This is the kind of arsenal a man sets aside to participate in a coup. Who in desolation are you?"

"Just a man," said Beyani in a cold voice. "A man who won't let those double-bonded fools take whatever they want without consequence."

That was as much of an answer as Lar was going to get.

"I'm not sure we should do this," he said. "Those are enforcers with Peltay, not collection soldiers. I'm tired..."

Aline laid a hand on Lar's chest, looking up at him. "Tired of running? Tired of killing? Tired of just trying to survive?"

He nodded, wrapping his arms around her, ignoring the tremor along his hand.

Aline rested her forehead to his biceps. "We don't have much choice. We can lie down and die, but that means we condemn Mela, Andi, and Beyani to the same fate."

"I know," he said. "I wish we could just hide."

Lar looked to Beyani, but the old man shook his head. "Those military blokes have everything they need to survive a mid-Zomeh heat for a long while, but we won't have anything by the time they leave. You Saeanans require a lot of water, as does that skin cream you make. We might last two or three more weeks. "

"If we have the right weapons," said Lar, "I think we can incapacitate some of the soldiers rather than kill them. We have the rest of this dark-day to work, and probably a good share of tomorrow's light-day as well. It's worth a try." He looked at the tired faces around him. "There are only five of us, if we include Andi, and I'm not sure what she is capable of. This could become a very bad idea fast. And Peltay will do his best to make sure we die with as much pain as possible."

"You know me," Mela said from above them on the stairs. "I don't want to hurt my own kind. But I'd rather go out fighting than waiting."

Aline nodded against Lar's chest, pulling away and straightening her back in grim determination. "Me, too."

"Well yihee for us!" cried Beyani, grabbing a TK-23 laser rifle. "Let's boil us some government hoond meat."

Aline grabbed another grenade, careful to set it to remote activation, then wrapped it in soaked cloth and tied the ends. It was almost a quarter of the way through the light-day, the sunlight illuminating Aline's project from the cave's opening, and the increasing heat making her sweat. The cloth she used would dry within seconds, but Lar, Meladise, and Beyani agreed that the foul-smelling substance they'd soaked the rags in would turn the grenade from a mass-killing agent into a severely debilitating one. At least, they thought it likely.

The three of them, with Mwalgi scales to help them handle the heat, were on the surface keeping a watch and preparing their defenses.

At Aline's side, Andi wrapped grenades Aline had already activated. Hands still shaky and weak from sickness, it took Andi twice as long as Aline, but the help was appreciated.

"I still don't understand," said Andi. "If these things will kill the Mwalgi soldiers without the rags then why are we doing this?"

"These aren't collection soldiers sent out to murder us for our spinal fluid," said Aline, though she knew from experience that reasoning with Andi wouldn't make any difference; not after what the girl had been through.

Andi's pains and humiliations at Mwalgi hands were too new for her to understand their forbearance. A year ago, Aline would have felt the same way.

Aline continued anyway, hoping the girl could someday look back on the conversation and gain something from it. "Lar's former mistar, Peltay, has gathered these officers together. Killing them would be like two countries at war, but one country's soldiers infiltrate the enemy side and takes out its police officers rather than enemy soldiers. Most of the men Peltay has under his command are peace keepers, not Mwalgi trained to kill Saeanans."

"They're still Mwalgi," spat Andi, as Aline had expected. "And all Mwalgi hate us and treat Saeanans like worthless cattle."

"Most," agreed Aline. "Not all. There were a couple of soldiers aboard the Desolashon who were kind and respectful toward me, including Cloud, though he definitely had some misconceptions that would have taken years to get straightened out. One of Lar's friends helped him to find me when they reached Lenfay because the friend has a Saeanan uncle. Beyani seems to find us more intriguing than anything else, and he's come to see us as people, like himself."

"Not at first," grumbled Andi.

Aline rested a light hand on her shoulder. "Change takes time, for all of us. We can blame all Mwalgi for ideologies and stereotypes that have been ingrained into their culture by their ancestors, or we can change their minds, one Mwalgi at a time, and eventually we may find peace."

Andi shrugged off Aline's hand. "I'm not sure I want peace. Sometimes, I don't even care if they die or I do. I just want it to be over."

A spike of fear shot through Aline. "What are you saying?"

"Nothing." Andi shrugged off Aline's hand and stood, unsteady at first. "I'm thirsty."

"I can get that—"

"No," said Andi, with a glare. "I'll get it myself. And you don't need to remind me that there isn't much left. I'll only take a swallow."

She shuffled to the back of the cavern. Aline paused in her work until Andi's back disappeared into the darkness.

"Cloud," she whispered, thinking back on him with fondness. He may have tricked her, but he'd kept her alive, and his intentions—if not completely honorable—were understandable. Without him, she wouldn't be with Lar, even if their time together might soon end.

As she started wrapping more grenades, the others burst into the cave from outside. Cloths draped their heads and shoulders, even Beyani's. Lar and Meladise's skin was wet with sweat, their scales crusty with leftover residue. Beyani's usually dim scales had reached the point where they were nearly translucent. It was as if she could see the lower layer of scales—the pontreer, they called it—like vein-riddled skin. He dropped to the ground, wheezing and struggling to breathe. The smell of dried urine and dirt emanated from the old Mwalgi. Aline didn't understand why. Mwalgi defecated pellets, like some Saeanan birds, and they didn't urinate, their bodies conserving all fluids whenever possible. But then, Beyani was unlike any Mwalgi either she or Lar had seen before. He claimed that his need for extra CSF had diminished more and more as he aged and what he bought on the black market sufficed all his needs.

Lar tossed him a water pouch, refilled from their dwindling supply. With fumbling fingers, Beyani struggled to open it.

"Somebody needs to help him with it," said Aline.

Meladise moved back, even more skittish of Beyani's old age than Lar. He grudgingly moved forward and unscrewed the cap.

Disgusted, Aline wiped her hands on her pants and knelt at Beyani's side, holding the pouch steady as the water trickled steadily down the man's throat. As he finished, he lay back on the hard cave floor.

"It's too hot for him," said Lar, the edge of one lip curling up in an obvious show of disgust. She didn't know what she would have to do to get him over his revulsion, but she felt she was definitely seeing his darker side. "We'll take what you have here, don't bother with the rest, then Meladise and I will put out a few more guns and ammo supplies at our positions and make sure they're properly camouflaged."

Beyani shook his head. "There are too many of them. All of those skimmers and even a gunship. Who brings a gunship into the middle of a desert?"

"You can see them?" yelped Aline, coming to her feet. "How far away?"

"Two hours," rasped Beyani, eyes wide.

Lar put out a calming hand. "It's okay. They've stopped to let their engines cool and they've set up sleep-tents for the soldiers to stay cool while they rest."

"Are you sure we shouldn't attack them while they sleep?" asked Meladise, clearly continuing some previous argument.

Lar's grimace was entirely human. "I'm telling you, Mela. With their droid scouts on perimeter and only the two of us able to move about in this heat, they'd be ready for us by the time we reached their location. I've left clues to let them know they're close. Let's just hope they wait until dark-day to move in."

"Why?" asked Aline. "Won't that leave Andi and me at a disadvantage?"

Lar shook his head. "I've studied Beyani's night-vision lenses. They'll fit you as well as him, and Mwalgi vision is sufficient without them."

Beyani threw up his hands. "Sure, leave me defenseless. What's it matter if I can hardly see well enough to use my own weapons."

"Aline is a crack-shot," said Lar. "We need her behind a gun more than anyone else."

Aline started shifting the wrapped grenades into a large woven bag, "I thought we were going to avoid casualties."

"Enforcers, military, not much difference," said Beyani. "Trust me, they all deserve what's coming to them."

Meladise disappeared to the back of the cave.

Lar shifted the bag, helping Aline fill it. "In order for the traps we've set to work, we're going to have to kill some of Peltay's flunkies and keep them moving in the right direction. It can't be helped, if we're going to survive."

She left the bag, skirting around it to step close to Lar. Placing her goop-covered hands on his crusty scales, she brought a single finger to his chin, tracing the line along his jaw where scale met skin. Despite all their time in the wilderness, the stubble along his cheek was still short and coarse.

"I fell in love with a Mwalgi," she said.

He frowned, his scales going noticeably dull, even in the dim light from the cave entrance.

"Not Cloud, you idiot," said Aline. "You. And I know killing the enforcers bothers you, so it bothers me."

"Even with her expressionless, Saeanan eyes," interjected Beyani, "anyone can tell that girl is practically bonded. Why she'd like you is beyond reason, but if you're not interested then I wouldn't mind seeing if my eyes can still golden in my old age."

Lar grabbed Aline around the bulky fabric at her waist, pulling her to one side so he could bare his fangs and release the talon of his free arm.

Beyani chuckled. "Now that's more like I'd expect. I've got a separate room down there in the cellar, if you'd like to take some time to see if you can turn those eyes a pure gold, boy."

Sensing the sudden tightness in Lar's muscles, his desire to finally consummate their feelings for one another warring with his belief that they should have some kind of formal ceremony first, Aline pushed herself out of his grasp.

"I doubt you have an air filter in your little room, Beyani, and I'm not too fond of Lenfay's atmosphere on my bare skin."

Beyani shrugged, and Lar swallowed hard, releasing Aline.

"You should probably get those grenades wherever they need to go," she told him. "I'll check on our supply of skin cream, just in case Peltay doesn't wait until the dark-day and we need an extra layer to help us survive the light-day."

Lar nodded, a muscle in his arm clenching and releasing before he could lift the bag up and drag it outside. "Tell Meladise to come and help me when she comes back."

Aline watched him go, wondering if she was doing the right thing.

"That doesn't make any sense," said Beyani. "There's enough of that disgusting skin cream back there that it doesn't matter if the room is filtered. What's the fool waiting for?"

"I gave him my excuse to tip the scales. Not only do we not have time, he's Diseep d'All and he wants a formal ceremony before we consummate our relationship."

"Humph," Beyani smiled, wide and flat. "I didn't think anybody adhered to that anymore, even in Diseep d'All. You should have said something sooner. I'm not a formal minister, but I'm legally certified to perform the ceremony. Have been since I started performing death ceremonies in the outskirts. Same paperwork for both. And you? You're Diseep d'All, too?"

Aline managed a "No," as she dealt with her surprise, happiness, and frustration. They actually had someone to perform the ceremony, but it was too late. "It's important to him, so I agreed to wait."

"Now, that's love," said Beyani. "That kind of consideration goes beyond bonding. Now it makes sense. He would have gone with you if you'd asked, but you chose not to ask." He leaned his head against the wall and closed his eyes. "Too bad we're not going to survive the day. I know enforcers, and the ones willing to go into this desert after a nobody fugitive are as ruthless as any decorated collections officer. Those men aren't going to wait for dark-day, not when they can smell their prey so close."

The entrance to Beyani's little cave wasn't the only way out, and Meladise was pretty sure she'd found an alternative exit. Lar and Aline were spending too much time disabling the incoming soldiers, which only increased the likelihood of her getting captured. Meladise wouldn't have the guts to kill herself, so she wanted a way out in case it came down to surrender or cowardice. She'd rather be dead than a coward, but she'd rather be a coward than a prisoner.

She left Beyani, Lar and Aline to their boring conversation and made her way to the back of the cave, through a fissure in the darkest recess, and down into a man-made tunnel that wouldn't be there unless it had a purpose. The darkness pressed upon Meladise more than a moonless dark-day. The tight space and her gradual descent affirmed that an entire mountain loomed above.

After what seemed like forever, she emerged into an open cavern. Light was coming in from somewhere ahead. Even Mwalgi eyes needed some amount of light in order to make out shapes in the darkness. There was just enough for Meladise to take in a dark pit on one side of the room, a ledge running around it on the other, a continuation of the man-made tunnel from the safe side. She almost missed the figure sitting at the pit's edge.

"How'd you find me?" asked Andi, scattering some rocks as she swung her feet back and forth, the sound echoing like the skitter of lizard feet across a stone floor.

The girl touched her forehead, a bright headlamp coming to life, forcing Meladise to shield her eyes.

"Turn that off," said Meladise, a bit more comfortable with the Saeanan language. "Are you trying to make me blind or make that I fall in that hole?"

Andi tapped the light off. "What's it matter? We're all going to die anyway."

Meladise waited for the spot of light in her vision to fade and her eyes to readjust. Taking a seat next to the girl, she scattered more dirt and pebbles into the hole, listening to them clatter a good five seconds before they settled. A fall down there wouldn't merely break a leg or an arm. Meladise swung her feet like Andi had, acting like the distance didn't bother her, controlling her fear as she'd learned in training.

"You know not we are going to die," said Meladise.

With a snort, Andi threw a rock against the far wall. She was still weak, and it didn't hit stone until it had gone quite a way down the hole. "I'm not stupid. I've heard you all talking. If everything goes right, we might survive. Everything never goes right."

The words came out before Meladise could consider where they'd come from. "As long as we live, there is hope."

She paused, reflecting on the memory of her mother talking to her dad about some situation with the government. She'd died shortly after that. Hope had died with her. Lar had been recruited into the military, and somehow Father had survived long enough to see Jeraud married, Velga pregnant, and Meladise entrusted to their custody.

Yet, somehow her mother's words had stuck with Meladise.

"Hope is a fairy tale adults tell frightened children." Andi scooted her legs a little farther over the edge. "I'm not afraid. Not anymore."

Clenching the back of Andi's jumpsuit, Meladise yanked the girl back, making her legs dangle straight out, the ridge at her calf. "There was no hope for Aline and Lar to escape the city once I had broken their plans, but they stayed alive and they found a way.

Going inside a Saeanan holding camp of any kind is insanity, but we all stayed alive, and escaped. Two Saeanans surviving a walk through Desolation is not possible. Yet, here you sit, becoming ready to throw life away. Why?"

"If I'm going to die," Andi choked on the word, restraining tears, "I'd rather get it over with than have a Mwalgi extractor stuck into my back."

"So you will follow the way of the coward?"

"I'm not a coward!" Andi's shrill voice echoed in the chamber.

"I am," said Meladise, "but I am less coward than you."

Curiosity blended with the girl's anger. "What do you mean?"

"I can die in battle. If it appears we are to be captured, I will sneak to this cave and hide in the desert."

"Won't you die?"

"I think so, but a more natural dying."

"So how does that make you less a coward than me? At least I'm not running away."

"You think killing yourself is not running?" asked Meladise, only then realizing the truth. "Living is the courage. Life is hard, survival becomes hard, and we make mistakes that stay with us. It is the easy way to shut our minds in death. But the easy way is the way of the coward."

Andi stared into the dark pit. "It's not easy."

"But right now, you are thinking it is more easy. Have I right?"

Andi waited a full ten seconds before she answered. "Maybe."

"The Diseep d'All say we take problems from this life to the next. We must make them right before we can fully join the universe. I will not leave this world knowing I left people who had need of me and who will be sad for me."

"Nobody will mourn me," Andi whispered. "Everyone would have been better off if I'd died in the soog and you hadn't gone to the oil town to get supplies for me. Then that man, Peltay, wouldn't have found us."

"You have wrong again," said Meladise without pity. "Peltay was following us from the breeding compound. He would be finding us sooner." Meladise wasn't sure that was completely true, but it was a worthwhile half-truth.

Andi was stubborn, though, if nothing else. "I'm a responsibility, but nobody really cares. Lar told me he would have left me for dead even if he had seen me boarding the transport ship, and I'm just another cellmate to Aline, a kid she's been stuck with. Beyani doesn't know I exist, and you would have left me for dead after the snake bit me."

"Wow." Meladise let her full sarcasm seep into the Saeanan word she'd picked up from Andi and Aline. "So you can hear our souls and minds? Maybe I should let you keep your wrong knowledge and die with it. I could tell you what we are thinking, but I think you want not the truth." Meladise moved to leave, her eyesight good enough in the dim light to just catch Andi's stiffening frame. The girl was miserable, but she didn't really want to throw herself into that pit.

Turning back, Meladise sat down a few meters away. "Do you want to know, before you throw yourself to a death of pain?"

Andi scooted from the edge, crossing her legs and sitting across from Meladise. "I guess, but I don't know if it will really change anything."

"I know it will. It has made changes to me."

Sitting in that dark cavern, Meladise told Andi about her own transformation, about how much imperfect people can love others, and how there are even amazing people like Lar and Aline who care about people when they least deserve it.

"Even if you had not people here who care for you, the only way to be finding people is to stay alive until they are coming...or until you know they were there but you did not see. That is what my mother did, and I knew it not until now."

"I can't shoot a gun," said Andi. "I'm only going to get in the way."

"Can I teach you to load one?" Meladise asked. "If you keep guns loaded, I will shoot more fast. That could help much."

After a moment, Andi nodded. Meladise rose to her feet and lifted Andi by the hand.

"Do you think we're going to die?" asked Andi as Meladise led her back through the cave.

"I try to have honesty," said Meladise. "I cannot say no. But I think I can die better helping my friends and family than falling into a dark hole. Maybe the All will give us the more difficult challenge. Maybe we will live."

"If it looks like we're going to be captured, will you take me with you?" Andi asked.

"Yes," promised Meladise. "Stay by my side."

Meladise hoped it wouldn't come to that, but the alternative was as bleak as Andi's black hole.

Aline couldn't help but notice the way Lar stared at her as she sat against the cave's entrance in a patch of shade. He acted like he could soak her in, memorize her features to the point that they would somehow become one.

"What are you staring at?" she asked.

From his vantage point behind a rise in sand outside the cave's opening, Lar raised an eyebrow. "You. What else?"

"You're supposed to be watching for Peltay."

"That drone of theirs will see me before we ever see him. That's why I'm here, in the open, so he'll think it's only me." Despite his words, Lar scanned the horizon before turning again to face her. "We should have taken Beyani's offer...gone to the cave below."

Aline didn't tell him she'd been thinking the same thing. "Your beliefs are important to you. I understand that."

"I'm not sure I understand it."

Lar rarely sounded so bitter. To her knowledge, he'd never questioned his faith.

"What do you believe happens to us after we die?" Aline asked.

"Our essence, the spirit some call it, joins the consciousness that is the driving force of the universe. If we have lived with honesty and integrity, we become part of the All, guiding the universe and its living beings." He had started to regain some semblance of hope to his voice, but then lost it again with his next words. "If we have not, then we must remain separate from the All, without purpose, only to observe but never to participate unless we can find a way to right our wrongs."

Aline left the safety of the cave, striding to Lar's side and taking hold of his chin. She stared through her strange lenses into his black and gold circleh doy, covering his entire socket. "That's not where you'll go."

He pulled away. "I've murdered people, Aline."

"No, you've defended people and saved people. That is not the same thing. If your All knows any justice then he will know the difference. He'll know what's in your heart and he'll know that you never wanted to hurt anyone."

Lar turned back toward her, holding her grease-covered face in his scaly hands. "It is hard to hold to faith. I can see no point in what the All has put us through if we are just to die brutal deaths in the desert."

"Maybe we won't die."

Lar released her face to hold her hands. "I try to be optimistic, but even with the traps and the weapons, we are weak and outnumbered. There is no chance."

More than guns and strategy, right now Lar needed hope. "You've said that the All orchestrates the universe, right?"

"To some extent," said Lar. "We still have free choice."

"So, would the All have found us a preacher without a chance at getting married?"

Lar's brow scrunched into deep lines, the expression somewhere between Mwalgi and human. "What do you mean?"

"Old Beyani is certified by your government to perform death rites and wedding rites."

"Why didn't he say? When did you—"

"I only found out a couple of hours ago, right after you left the cave."

That flicker of hope, along with a deep longing, illuminated his eyes. Aline couldn't help but smile back.

"So, we're going to somehow live through this," she said. "All of us. And when this is over, we will be officially married and find

some version of a honeymoon suite in this All-forsaken land."
She ran a finger along the line where scale met skin, outlining his
left pectoral muscle. "And we're going to stay there a long time."

Finally, Aline saw the Lar she'd known on the Noble Ark. The
same man who had saved her life, beaten the hologames against
all odds, and found his way back to her from the dead. Lar's chin
stiffened with determination. Peltay had better enjoy what little
time in life he had left, because Lar would find a way. He always
did.

He pulled her close, touching his parched lips tenderly yet pas-
sionately to hers, the heat making them taste sweat as much as
each other. A drone shot into view then buzzed away again, like
some giant horsefly.

They pulled apart and Aline blushed. "Sorry, I guess they'll
know there are two of us."

Lar shrugged. "Two, but not five. Call the others. It's time."

Lar watched in horrified satisfaction as the first group of enforcers fell through the camouflaged hole he and Mela had prepared for them. The screams testified that some had broken
bones. The tufts of dirt that continued to rise form the hole told
him that many of the trained "peacekeepers" had extended their
claws and started climbing the sides. Eventually, they'd manage to
get above the layers of sand and make their way out again. He
pressed the remote ignition labeled "1".

Smoke billowed up from the pit, reflecting the twin suns to become sickly pink. The screams intensified. Bodies fell back to the
pit's bottom with grunts and punctuated yells.

Aline had insisted the two of them stay together. "We've stood
back to back in almost every fight we've had," she'd said. "That's
not going to change."

She called to him now, her voice low. "Will they live? They don't
sound like it."

Guilt burdened Lar more than the weaponry across his back.

"Yes, the enforcers will live," but right now they probably wished they could die.

He took in the men and women lying prostrate in the sand southeast of the pit, coloring it a reddish black. That had been the means to encourage the larger group to take cover and skirt the thin edge of rock rising up from the northern line. But they hadn't all taken that direction.

An equally large group held laser shields and continued straight forward. Another group, thinking they hadn't been seen, were skirting around the southern line with the intent of flanking Lar and Aline.

The whine of a planetary laser cannon split the receding screams of the men and women in the pit.

"Time to move," said Lar.

The smell of a lightning storm accompanied the rising of the hairs on Lar's head and arms. As he and Aline came together and moved as one under a camouflage tarp, making their way to a sand hill fifteen meters away, sand and rock shot into the air about eighty meters to the south. Again, enforcer screams filled the air, a third of the southern skirting unit pulverized or irreparably injured by their own gunfire.

"Re-routing Peltay's location signal on his remote grenades will only work once," said Lar. "Let's hurry."

As he'd suspected would happen, a few seconds later the rocky outcropping where he and Aline had hidden only moments before, exploded in its own shower of sand and rock.

They took their places behind the dune, waiting for the telltale sound of the scout drone. Instead, they heard the angry whine of multiple land enforcement vehicles, LEV's.

Lar almost laughed, but kept absolutely quiet. "They're making this too easy."

Three fully armed LEV's flew above their position. Side by side, Lar and Aline raised their laser rifles. Lar took out the engine on the southernmost one, Aline killed the engine on the middle LEV and blew out the port controls on the other. The engineless vehicles did an emergency landing in the distance. The LEV without port controls started to spin. The pilot should have been able to bounce the vehicle across the sand to a reasonable stop, but panicked. It bounced once, overcompensated, then rolled end over end until the bow slammed into a small uprising of rock. It exploded with such force, Aline and Lar steadied one another as a wave of heat and sand washed over them. Rock and metal shrapnel flew in every direction, littering the sandy landscape with chunks of black.

Lar and Aline turned away from the magnificent explosion to see two more LEVs hovering above them, laser cannons trained on their position.

"Why don't they shoot?" asked Aline.

Lar dropped his gun. "Because Peltay likes to gloat."

Aline kept a tight hold on her rifle. "I won't be a prisoner again."

"Don't worry," said Lar. "Peltay won't let us live. He just wants to humiliate us before he kills us."

As the cannon on one of the LEVs powered up, Aline still wouldn't drop the gun. "Then why not make them shoot us now?"

"Because," said Lar, "I might find a chance to kill Peltay."

Aline dropped her weapon and put her hands in the air.

From a distance, Mela heard the enforcers' screams and watched as grenade smoke rose into the air like londarb pollen then drifted back into the pit she and Lar had prepared earlier in the day.

"Ready?" she asked Andi.

The girl nodded, eyes scared but hand firm on the rifle she held.

"You need not shoot," Mela reminded her. "Keep the gun charged. Give me yours when mine has more heat."

Andi nodded, sweat running over the skin cream covering her face. The jumpsuit she wore couldn't wick the moisture away fast enough, darkening at the armpits. A Saeanan shouldn't be out during a light-day in Zomeh, but they hadn't had much choice.

Pressing another water packet into the girl's free hand, Mela silently urged Andi to drink as they crouched behind their outcropping of rock, waiting. Lar had felt sure a contingent of soldiers would try to go around their southern side so they could flank them from behind. Mela and Andi would be waiting for them. Seconds later, as they'd hoped, one of the LEVs targeted Lar's false signal, obliterating a portion of the enforcers' own troops. The remaining soldiers gave up on any pretense at secrecy, their stealthy jog turning into a purposeful advance, heading Mela and Andi's way.

Remote trigger in hand, Mela waited for the lead forces to make their way to the shadows beneath their position. At exactly the right moment, she pressed the button. A spark fizzled in the distance, but nothing else happened. Soldiers yelled an alarm. Smoke made a thin trail from a burnt fuse, exposed wire, or whatever had made the electric netting inert.

Raising her rifle, Mela targeted what she hoped was the net's closest corner. She fired.

Sand and dirt shot into the air, enforcers scrambling around it. "Bloody fluids!"

Firing again, the pulse hit its target. A three-hundred square meter net lit up beneath the enforcers' feet. Mela fired again and again, ramping up the charge in the net's coils, immobilizing a small portion of the force. Nowhere near the number they had hoped.

The gun in her hands started to steam against her scales, making the areas that held skin sweat. Andi handed her a new rifle, but Mela left off ramping up the net. Enforcers lay in clustered groups across its surface, some twitching, others still.

Mela aimed her rifle on those coming up the ridge. Dirt shot up in front of her face, a laser blast that had missed her by centimeters.

Andi screamed, though she muffled it immediately. It wouldn't matter. The enforcers knew their location, and there were too many for Mela to fight off.

She pressed a hand to Andi's back. "Down."

Angling the gun over the edge, Mela shot laser pulses in a wide arc below. The whine of the charger melded with the curses of the men and women below. Plumes of dust and sand shot into the air all around them, turning the area into a cyclone of debris.

Unimaginable pain seared Mela's forearm. With a cry, she dropped the rifle, hearing it tumble through dirt and sand until its sound melded with the approaching enforcers. It was time to run for the cave.

To Mela's surprise, Andi lifted the other rifle. The fool girl edged over the ridge, firing like a madwoman, hitting targets by blind luck. But luck could only last so far.

Without warning, Andi's scream made Mela's pain a mere whimper in comparison. The girl clutched the flesh below her shoulder as Mela used her good hand to yank her down. Rolling to her back, Andi writhed back and forth, screaming, tears streaming through the goop covering her face.

Where her arm had been was now a stump no longer than Mela's hand. Part of Andi's bone protruded from the blackened flesh, like a clump of melted plastic. The stench turned Mela's stomach. Moving fast, she threw water over the wound. It sizzled as if skittering across a hot rock. Shadows fell across both of them, as Mela squeezed skin cream over the wound while Andi continued to scream. She didn't know if the application hurt worse than the wound's exposure to the atmosphere, but it was all Mela knew to do.

When she finished and looked up, five enforcers circled them, rifles charged. Another ten gathered around as Mela held Andi's writhing body.

Beyani was already kneeling in the sand near the pit when Lar and Aline joined him. To Lar's mind, the old man already looked dead, his scales such a muted grey that he might have been a corpse on the verge of falling to its side, though his raspy breathing and the nervous clenching of his arm sheaths told them he was still very much alive. The blood and skalwass that moistened the dirt on his right side suggested he might not stay that way for long.

Aline immediately knelt at Beyani's side, inspecting a gash along his right thigh. It wasn't too deep. If cleaned and kept that way, especially with some fals-skalen to cover the deeper section of the wound, it probably wouldn't even interfere with day to day life. Except, Lar felt sure they only had a few minutes or hours left to live.

"Are you all right?" Aline asked.

"My pride's wounded more than my leg. If I could aim worth a renegade's biscuit they might not have had me so quick." He gave them a lopsided grin. "I did take down one of those fancy LEVs, though. Not bad for an old man, eh mutant boy?"

Lar might as well humor Beyani at this point. "You did all right, old man. They may be dragging our bodies behind them, but they'll limp all the way home."

"Ha!" The old man barked a laugh. "You got that right. I'll bet that sister of yours did some damage to them, too."

As the remaining four LEVs joined the empty ohfertsoogs on the other side of the pit, Lar knew they hadn't done as much damage as they'd received. Peltay wouldn't be bringing the LEVs back if Mela and Andi were still fighting. Confirming his worst fears, Mela appeared on the southwest horizon, stumbling to stay upright in front of a squad of enforcers holding laser rifles to her back. One of the men held what appeared to be a lank child, charred along one side, arms and head drooping as if dead. Only one arm hung, Lar realized as they came closer. Andi had lost the other.

Aline came to her feet. "Andi!"

Before she could try to run to the girl, the guard behind shoved the butt of her rifle in the small of Aline's back, forcing her back to her knees with a groan and an uprising of dust.

"You move again and I'll use the other end of the gun," said the woman.

Lar flashed his claws. "We're going to die anyway, enforcer. Don't make me take you with us."

The woman sneered, but she backed up a step, her grip tighter on her weapon.

His attention on Mela, Aline, and the enforcer, Lar didn't notice the heavy step of a man coming from behind until Peltay was upon them. Lar looked up as a fist knocked him to one side, sending him into Aline and knocking them both to the dirt.

Peltay snickered. "I've waited too long for that."

Springing to his feet, Lar unsheathed his claws. Ten rifles charged, aimed at him and Aline. He almost rounded on Peltay anyway, but Aline placed a hand on his arm.

"You wouldn't reach him," she said. Her eyes gave a different message. Wait for a better opportunity. Sitting down on her heels, she rested a hand on the edge of her boot, the boot with a serrated hunting knife hidden inside.

Yes, Lar would wait for his chance, but Peltay might be expecting that. He wouldn't expect Aline to be able to make an attack. Even if the knife couldn't cut the man's scales, Lar knew what

Aline could accomplish with the solid handle.

Lar eyed his former mistar, the man who had kept Aline from him on the Desolashon. "You must feel mighty proud of yourself right now, Peltay. Though you outnumbered us fifty to one, you've managed to capture us while we only killed at least twenty enforcers, debilitated more than half, and destroyed three regulation LEVs. I'm sure your supervisor will be quite proud. If you're lucky, you might be demoted to water plant guard down south when this is all done. Of course, more likely you'll find yourself guarding some All-forsaken place like this one."

Peltay's scales dulled in fearful realization then turned bright in anger. "Doesn't matter anymore. You're going to watch everyone you care about suffer and die and then you can follow. Whatever happens to me, I'll think of this moment and it will bring a smile to my face every single day."

"No, it won't." Lar rested on his heels, preparing for the opportunity he hoped Peltay's growing anger would bring. "You'll try to convince yourself, but in your heart you'll know the truth."

"There is no truth!" Peltay spat precious water that sizzled on the sand and disappeared. "You will die and I will have won."

"Won?" Lar mocked. "Like this is some game? If so, then you are a pathetic contestant. Every day you think of your supposed victory, it will gnaw at the back of your mind that not only did I cause your demotion from a mistar in the collections military to an obscure unit in land enforcement, but in my demise I will have managed to dismantle your entire career."

Mela stumbled forward, shoved to the dirt with the rest of their little group. The enforcer at her side dropped Andi. Mela tried to catch her, but only managed to soften the girl's descent. Though still as death, Lar saw the rise and fall of Andi's chest and heard the faint whistle from her breather. Thankfully, she remained unconscious. One less person for Peltay to torture, though lying on the scorching sands, even in a jumpsuit, would be torture enough. He didn't know how Aline was able to continue kneeling there. Even with his scales, Lar felt like his skin might char off and stick to the clothing supposedly protecting it.

Rather than move forward as Lar had hoped, Peltay took a step backward. The way his remaining troops gathered around him, hoping for a gruesome show, Lar thought him much like an announcer in an ellgot fighting ring. The entertainment Peltay would provide would make ellgot ferocity pale in comparison.

Peltay reached out a hand to an enforcer. "Give me one of your projectile weapons. I'm curious if I can guess the location of the mutant woman's scales based on what I've seen of the Trovgar brother. They appear identical."

With a smile, the woman handed Peltay a pistol, the barrel longer than that of a paralyzer by about ten centimeters. As he aimed, Lar prepared himself to jump. If he timed it right, Peltay would hit him in the face and Lar would be dead. There would be no point in further torture with Lar already dead.

The strange gun clicked. Peltay touched his finger to the trigger. With a sudden whine, one of the LEVs rose up from the desert, hovering behind Lar. Strange. Lar thought all of Peltay's band had cut their engines and joined their leader for the promised show.

Peltay appeared as surprised as Lar, staring back at the rising ship. With a high-pitched whine, Lar realized what Peltay, the idiot, should have recognized at once. This wasn't a LEV, or at least not a government-issued one. The silhouette stretching across the sand and through the enforcers' ranks suggested something more mundane. It was Peltay's skimmer, but someone had managed to strap a couple of collection-compound laser cannons to its front.

Horror erupted in Peltay's face, his scales as dull as stone, and then he exploded. Lar, Aline and Mela huddled over Andi's still body, getting as low to the ground as they could manage as Lar's former adversary scattered across their backs in burnt chunks of flesh and scale. Unseen lasers ripped across the gathered ranks of enforcers. Some of the Mwalgi enforcers raced for the LEVs, but those not caught by sweeping arcs of the cannons went down with less explosive results. The sheer volume of gunfire suggested there were a lot more people in that skimmer than it was designed for.

With all the enforcers gathered together, it only took a few minutes for the charred desert to become a body-littered battle-field. A few groans and wails rose from the wounded, becoming more pronounced as the skimmer landed and cut its engines.

"Is it possible?" Lar asked Aline.

She looked up from where her face had practically buried itself in the sand, eyes wide with shock and relief. "None of this seems possible."

Lar pointed to the ship that had not only saved their lives, but saved them from grisly torture. "That was Peltay's ship—"

"Mwalgi," spoke a man through the ship's external speakers, us-ing a horrible accent that was even worse than Aline's during her first days aboard the Desolashon. "You are in stepping from the livestock or we are in making you dead."

Confused, Lar cocked his head to one side.

As Aline had understood Lar's broken Saeanan when he'd boarded her ship, she seemed to also understand the man's horri-ble Mwalgi. "He wants you to step away from us, probably you and Mela."

Lar moved to comply, but Aline wrapped a hand around his wrist. "No, they've killed every Mwalgi here except the ones in the pit. I'm sure they want us separated so they can kill you, too."

Mela turned, but stayed in the hot sand, clutching Andi's body to her chest, face staring at the strange ship with a confused won-der that probably matched Lar's. Beyani just sat back in the sand, like a toddler who had lost his balance.

Bracing herself against Lar, Aline struggled to her feet, wincing. Sweat poured down her blistered face, her stance unsteady, but she managed to extend an arm across Lar's chest while positioning half of her body in front of Mela and Andi.

"These are not Mwalgi enforcers," Aline spoke in Saeanan Eng-lish. "I don't know who you are, but if the Mwalgi were an enemy then these are friends."

The speaker from the ship switched to English, which Lar un-derstood far better than the man's Mwalgi. "You can move or you can die with them."

Aline pushed back her hood, gasping either from the direct sun exposure, the touch of the atmosphere at some missed line of skin, or both. "It's not like I wasn't about to do that ten minutes ago. Murdered by the Mwalgi or my own people, I don't really care."

With that she slumped to the ground, kneeling before the cruel Saeanan's voice as she had Peltay's guns only moments before.

Lar could step away from her, perhaps save her life by giving up his own. Instead, he knelt by her side, cradling her head against his chest, careful not to touch her blistered flesh. He'd promised to fight by her side. She didn't want a martyr. It went against every instinct, but Lar would keep his promise.

The cannons' whine raised in pitch. Lar closed his eyes.

Clutching Andi to her breast, Mela watched as Lar chose to sacrifice all their lives rather than let Aline return to her people. Was he brave, selfish, or stupid? Mela didn't understand, but if she was going to die anyway, she wasn't taking Aline and Andi with her.

As tenderly as she could manage, Mela dropped Andi into Aline's lap. Aline almost let her slide to the sand, but managed to get a hand around her thighs and keep one arm under the small girl's shoulders.

Andi gasped, crying out with a pitiful wail.

Tears absorbed by her scales as fast as she could produce them, Mela wrapped her hands around Beyani's arm and dragged him a good three meters from the others.

She gestured at Lar, Aline and Andi, speaking the Saeanan she'd had to improve upon since Andi had joined them. "They live." She gestured to herself and Beyani. "Kill us."

One cannon whirred, moving to line up Mela in its sight. Both emitted the high-pitched whine that suggested imminent fire.

With an agonizing scream, Andi wrenched herself from Aline's grasp. Landing face-first in the sand, Andi screamed again. She turned onto her good side, pushing herself up with one arm, scrambling forward like a leezard missing half its legs. Was the girl deranged? She pushed through the sand, raising up tufts of dirt that made her choke, but scrambled forward until she lay in front of Beyani. With a pain-filled whimper, she used her good arm to push herself up at a slant. She couldn't quite manage to sit.

Mela knelt down beside her, grabbing under the good arm and around her waist, determined to drag her back to Aline. Andi used Mela's hold to get to her feet.

All the better. She'll be easier to move.

But as soon as Andi stood, the small girl shoved Mela away. Taken off-guard, Mela's grip loosened.

Andi took a wide stance, raising her fist at the cannons. "How dare you?" she screamed. "After everything we've gone through together, you're going to kill us without even asking who we are? You don't know why we're here, why these soldiers were after us. You're no better than them!"

Mela took a more secure hold around Andi's waist, careful not to touch the injured arm. "They just want the Mwalgi. Go with Aline and maybe they'll let you live."

Andi turned her baleful glare to Mela. "In that cave I decided to live, but you don't get to decide how. We're in this together, with honor."

She sounded like a Mwalgi, like a Diseep d'All. Mela almost dragged her away anyway, but she couldn't force herself to move under Andi's painful gaze. The girl was being stupid, but she was being brave.

The cannons continued their high-pitched whir. They'd better use them soon or the coils might explode. Tendrils of smoke leaked from the joints at the rear casing then the whine lowered in pitch, raised again, then lowered, as if a child played with the ignition switch.

"Stay exactly where you are," the man yelled through the speakers in Saeanan, but another man spoke in the background.

"I mean it. You shoot them and I quit. I'll walk into this desert and you can figure out how to keep this bucket running without me."

A muffled response, a woman, in the background.

"I don't know why they're with Mwalgi, but like the girl said, why don't we ask?"

"It's a trick," the first man said. Mela guessed he didn't realize he'd left the speaker on. "We go out—"

The second man yelled at him. "Are you an idiot? No, don't answer. You've already proved that. They're outgunned and have no back-up."

"They still have their guns."

As one, Mela, Lar, and everyone else tossed their guns.

A chuckle sounded over the speaker. "You left the speaker on, idiot, but I think you've proved my point."

The speaker shut off. A minute later, the ship's ramp descended, clanking like their ohfertsoog door after Lar's temporary fix. The ensuing cloud of dust cloaked the figures tromping in heavy boots toward them. As it cleared, Mela gasped. A hugely pregnant woman in a tsefuur jumpsuit held an assault laser rifle aimed at Lar's chest. Behind her, their legs obscured by puffs of dirt, two men carried more rifles, and another three women took up the rear line.

"My name is Loren Kett" said the pregnant woman. "Release your prisoners and we can talk."

Tough as scales, Aline rose to her feet, holding onto Lar's arm until she'd gained her balance. "We're not prisoners. Lar is my husband and he's the one who opened our doors in the breeding compound so we could escape."

"I knew it had to be someone on the inside, but a Mwalgi?"

"Half-Mwalgi" Lar and Mela said together.

"We are half-Saeanan," finished Mela, feeling a touch of pride she'd never associated with her heritage before.

The large man behind Kett guffawed as she shook her head. "That's impossible."

Aline took Lar's hand, lending one another strength as much as affection. "I said the same thing, once. They're rare, but not only are Lar and his entire family half-human, they're mentally competent. Actually, they're brilliant."

"You can't believe they're trustworthy, Loren," said the large man behind her.

The woman turned her gun on him. "The only reason you're here is because you can communicate with the Mwalgi. Don't for one second think that I value you or your opinion."

Aline relaxed, but her sneer remained. "So, Fedrek-the-rapist isn't in charge? I guess that's one good thing, but I should have broken his neck when I had the chance."

Loren dropped her gun and shrugged. "Good thing you didn't. As much as we hate him, he got us this far and we just saved your lives."

The smaller man, lean and somber, spoke up, revealing himself to be the voice of reason they'd heard over the speaker. "I think Fedrek is keen to be rid of them, because he knows that with them we won't need him anymore."

"Shut up, Gervin. You're a—"

Andi took a step forward, almost managing a smile. "Gervin? You survived. I wish...I wish—"

Her eyes rolled up in her head. Mela jumped forward to catch her the same time Gervin dropped his weapon and rushed forward. Fedrek's weapon, trained on Mela, whined then fired.

The heat of the laser blast warmed the scales along Mela's shoulder, but didn't hit. As she and Gervin took hold of Andi's limp body and Mela helped him get a secure hold, Mela watched Loren yank Fedrek's rifle from his hands. She must have knocked the rifle off target or else the man was a very bad shot.

"Get him out of here," Loren told the women standing behind.

"What about the other Mwalgi?" one of them asked.

"The old one?" asked Loren. "I guess one of you should stay here, but the rest of you get Fedrek in the ship and under lockdown. Keep him away from the weapons."

She turned back to Aline, obviously the only one she really trusted. "So, you fell in love with him after he saved you?"

Aline laughed, leaning into him as he put an arm around her shoulder. "Our story is much longer than that. Get us out of this heat and I'll tell you."

Loren pointed to Mela. "And her?"

"Lar's sister."

Mela tensed, wondering what Aline might say about her, after all she'd put them through.

With a look of honest affection, she told Loren, "She's a lot like her brother. You can trust her."

"And the old Mwalgi?"

Lar shuddered and Mela suppressed a chuckle. He still hadn't come to terms with Beyani any better than she had.

"Beyani Jadad," said Aline, making the old man's head jerk upward. The poor man didn't understand a word being spoken around him. "He's a doctor and he saved our lives when this desert would have had us."

"He's full Mwalgi," said Loren. "You sure he can be trusted?"

Aline nodded again. "Absolutely, but I'm not sure he wants to go with us. This is his home."

"We need a doctor," said Loren. "He stays with us or he dies. His choice."

"You can't just—"

"Right now, I have the guns," said Loren. "The survival of all the people in that skimmer is my responsibility and I will do everything I can to keep them safe. If that means ultimatums, then that's what I'll do."

She turned to the men and women groaning inside the pit. "How long until they become mobile. They're obviously not dead."

"Another hour," said Lar.

"I can't have them following us." She ushered another group of gun-toting tsefuurs from the edge of the ramp, where Mela hadn't seen them. "Kill them."

"What?" said Aline. "No!"

But she couldn't stop them. Within seconds the area filled with the high-pitched hum of laser rifles and the stench of burned flesh and scales. The odor reminded Mela of a pit barbecue she'd had with Jeraud and their friends a few months back. Her stomach grumbled with hunger even as it churned. She turned away, vomiting into the sand.

"Was that really necessary?" asked Aline. "It seems like soldiers killing a Saeanan police force."

Loren's eye twitched, but she kept a steady gaze. "How do you think we found you? When that pig we blasted into pieces showed up at the compound, he almost had us all killed. We finally took the upper hand, but he took guards with him and vowed to be back for us. Half the women in that pit, and those gathered around ready to kill you, are the same Mwalgi who tortured us day in and day out in that breeding compound. They deserved to die, and we need to make sure there are no witnesses. If the government knows they have slaves on the loose with enough firearms to do damage, they'll come after us with everything they've got."

Lar had bided his time through all of this, and Mela should have known her brother would be calculating. "You say you have the guns," he said. "That gives you power now, but it's obvious you're only able to fly that ship you have because you have a man who speaks some Mwalgi and a few people who can make repairs. Aline, myself, and Mela could take three more ships with us."

"With us where?"

"I know a place where the authorities won't be able to track or find us."

"Why should I believe you?"

Aline clenched a fist, but Lar kept complete calm, not even so much as a twitch of his claws. "Because I didn't come out in this desert to let the one I love die. I have a plan to get us off this planet, and if you're willing to cooperate then I might be able to get all of you off as well. The old one," he pointed to Beyani "has a stash of firearms. His cave also has food, water purifiers, and enough water to get us all there in one piece." He paused for effect. "Because without me and what I know, you won't survive our planet or our atmosphere for more than a few months at best. More likely, you'll all be dead within a couple of weeks."

"Are you threatening me?"

Mela didn't have Lar's self-control. Her talons peeked from within their sheaths. "He's offering to save you, stupid woman. If you don't like it, please leave us here with one of these soogs and he'll save us instead."

Loren squinted an eye. "Why would you do this?"

When Lar smirked, Mela knew he had them. "Because it's the right thing to do, because I could use your manpower, and because the parts off these fighters could make all the difference in our success. And, maybe, because you're holding the guns."

"Okay," Loren conceded. "But I'm in charge."

"No," said Lar, without hesitation. "Aline's in charge. I don't trust you and you don't trust me, but I have the knowledge and you have the manpower. Aline is Saeanan which allows you to trust her, and she's my bonded, which allows me to trust her. She's in charge and we have a deal."

Loren finally gave in, and Mela learned something about her brother. Not only was he honest and occasionally harsh, he could also do tough negotiations. Mela was glad she had joined his side.

She was even more grateful when they stepped out of the setting suns and started the new day, a blessedly cool dark-day, in a fully-functional, air-conditioned ohfertsoog.

Lar pushed the detonator. Three ohfertsoogs blew along with two of the fighters, their blackened shells spread across the landscape in battle formations. As the ground shook, black smoke disappearing into the dark-day, Lar held tight to Aline's side. He hoped that, at first appearances anyway, any investigators on the scene would assume they'd exploded in battle. Beyani had enough civilian clothing they were able to make some of the soldiers appear to be renegades. It would take time before anyone pieced together that Peltay had found his targets, or that the slaughter of the Mwalgi enforcers and prison guards had come from the former prisoners themselves.

He gazed over the carnage, a lump in his throat.

Aline hugged him tighter, resting her hooded face against his chest. "It's not your fault."

Lar swallowed and took a deep breath. "I know. And maybe the Loren woman is right. Many of those who attacked us were from the breeding compound and maybe they deserved to die. But I'm tired of it. This is Mwalgi justice, this kind of retribution: maiming for slights, killing when people don't go along with our ways. I never wanted to be a part of this, but it's never made me as sick as it does now." He tilted his face to Aline's as she lifted her eyes to meet his. "When does it end?"

Aline put a hand to his cheek, the cream there blending with the matching green goop covering his face. "It will end when we're free. We can't give up. We stand together until we can't stand anymore. Promise?"

He leaned his face into her hand, not caring at the nasty taste as he kissed her fingers. "Promise."

Did she realize what a strength she was to him? He'd have given up long ago if it hadn't been for her determination. Interlacing their fingers, they walked to the ohfertsoogs and the remaining LEV.

"You sure you know how to drive that thing?" Aline asked.

He waved his hand in dismissal. "Basic military training. You okay with the soog on your own?"

"If I can get past all that junk you threw inside and reach the pilot seat then I'll be fine."

Lar chuckled. "You'll be grateful for all that junk when it helps get us off this planet."

"You get me off this planet, scale-boy, and we'll celebrate a second honeymoon."

"We're not even married."

Aline hit the switch to open the soog's hatch, catching a loop of wires before it could fall out and throwing it on top of a pile of propulsion engines. "Well then, what are we waiting around for? Let's get to this hideout you keep bragging about."

Closing the few meters between them, Lar scooped her up in his arms, planting a firm kiss on her lips. She responded, her hands coursing up his back while pulling him closer, prolonging the kiss.

Lar pulled away, "Now who is making us wait around?"

She slapped him low on his buttocks and laughed, a strange show of affection that made him want to kiss her again. Without a second glance, she jumped into the soog and Lar made his way to the LEV. In the other soog, Mela had Andi, Beyani, and a few other Saeanans. Beyani was seeing to Andi's arm, putting on medicines to stave off infection. He claimed she would live, but she still looked so pale, Lar wasn't sure.

The best thing he could do for her now was to get them all away from here. With fresh vehicles, a stash of firearms, and a supply of mechanical parts, they might just stand a chance.

He jumped into the LEV, fired her up, and led his little convoy south, across the desert, to one of the last places on Lenfay that any Mwalgi would ever want to live.

No white dress, no cake, and no presents; this wasn't how Aline had imagined her wedding day...or wedding dark-day as was the case. The lanterns set around the dank cave gave the proceedings a certain ambiance that could almost be considered romantic. Lar looked fine, shirtless and with drawstring pants that almost fit his large frame. Aline felt a little self-conscious in her altered jumpsuit, battle-worn and mended, but she wasn't willing to wait one more hour let alone one more day. Who knew? Beyani could suddenly croak of old age and then where would they be? Lar had told her they could wait, but Aline had insisted.

The cavern was large enough to fit everyone, even the two men and nineteen women who had survived the breeding camp. They kept a wide berth from the water near the wall's edge that Lar had called a pond, though Aline considered it more a puddle. When he'd described the parasites that likely lived within, the salmond that collection soldiers had named Aline after, everyone was sure to keep their distance. The trickle of water Lar termed a waterfall echoed through the cavern giving the ceremony natural background music. Unfortunately, Fedrek's poor translation from Beyani's Mwalgi to English gave a less soothing backdrop that made Aline's skin crawl. Blocking out Fedrek, she turned her focus to the people here who made the moment, despite the circumstances, special.

Andi stood to one side of Aline, her stump wrapped and tied-off inside the arms of a new jumpsuit. Considering all she'd gone through, it was a miracle she could sit upright and almost smile.

Meladise stood to Lar's side, like a best man in the form of a curvaceous sister. Though she stood with the same soldier-like rigidity that Aline would have used to describe her character, Meladise's eyes had softened. They might even be watering a bit, though Aline doubted the girl would allow herself to cry in public, even at a wedding.

As she and Lar held right hands, the thumbs locked around one another as if ready to wrestle, Beyani was prattling on. "Lar, having bonded to Aline, you're going to want to be with her and protect her from outside threats. But a marriage relationship can go beyond this. Take the time to listen to your wife, consider her wants and dreams, and be involved in those things that are most important to her."

Had the man been blind the last week? That was a main difference between Lar and Cloud. Cloud had bonded with her, but Lar had fallen in love.

Beyani turned to her. What kind of Mwalgi advice would the man come up with for a human he'd only known for a little over a week?

"Aline, as you enter into this marriage, you must remember what a serious commitment you are making. As one unable to bond, you will likely be tempted to have relations with other men."

Are you kidding me? Aline's mouth hung open as he continued.

"Fidelity is natural among Mwalgi, and you must understand how hurtful your infidelity would be to Lar."

"I would never—!"

Beyani held up a hand. "I understand that there have been issues with this in the past, with another Mwalgi."

Whispered exclamations of surprise and disgust sounded louder in the cave's confines.

"You cheated on him?" Meladise asked, her claws slipping from their sheaths.

Andi's expression almost condemned Aline more than Meladise. "She didn't, she wouldn't! What are they talking about, Aline?"

Aline glared at Beyani, wishing she could rip his tongue from his mouth. She'd told him those things in confidence, but he obviously saw them as grounds to give her wedding-day warnings.

"Enough!" yelled Lar. "This is our bonding ceremony, not an interrogation into our past." He rounded on Beyani. "Stick to the vows, old man, and keep your opinions to yourself."

Beyani's scales paled to a duller grey, but he nodded.

"Larkin Nigel Trovgar," he said.

"Nigel?" Aline whispered to Lar, smothering a laugh when he gave a small groan.

Beyani gave them a glare and continued. "Do you take Aline Francis Taylor—?"

Lar raised his eyebrows at the Francis. It wasn't much better than Nigel, but Aline was too busy interrupting Beyani to give Lar a response.

"Trenoble," she said. "Trenoble-Taylor."

Beyani sighed. "Do you take Aline Francis Trenoble-Taylor as your forever bonded, to love and protect, always at your side, forever one in the sight of the All until death claims you as one?"

Lar gripped Aline's hands, the love in his black and gold eyes as unending as the expanse of space. "Yes."

"Do you, Aline Francis Trenoble-Taylor, take Larkin Nigel Trovgar as your forever bonded, to love and protect, always at your side, forever one in the sight of the All until death claims you as one?"

Here it was. Aline was only nineteen, no, twenty now. Was she ready to commit her whole life to Lar? Assuming they survived this planet, they could never go to Saeana. As long as she and Lar were together, they would be aberrations, looked down upon everywhere they went.

He still held her in his gaze, promising eternal devotion. She was only scared because she feared being left alone again. But Lar would never leave her, and she loved him more than she had ever imagined she could love anyone. She'd never made a decision with more confidence.

"Yes," she said, watching Lar's face light up, actually able to see a few specks of black turn gold at his renewing faith in her love.

Beyani still questioned whether or not she could save him. He'd told her numerous times that without certain medications, his severance was probably too far gone, but Aline didn't believe it. He'd been improving since her rescue from the compound, and she'd just seen evidence that he was healing. She'd stay by his side and all would be well.

"By the authority given me by the Kermeinde district, I pronounce you legally bonded before the government, these people, and the All. You may kiss."

Lar left previous restraint behind, releasing Aline's hands, wrapping one arm around her waist, his other stretched up her back. Pressing their bodies tight, he gave her a long, deep kiss that made Meladise whoop and holler. Even a few of the Saeanans joined in, though most politely clapped or remained silent. Aline could understand their unease at Lar's presence, let alone a Saeanan choosing to marry a man everyone considered to be a genetic impossibility at best, a monstrous mutation at worst.

Surprising to Aline, Gervin immediately came forward, shaking Aline and Lar's hands with enthusiasm. "Congratulations. I know some of the others aren't exactly celebrating here, but I'm happy to see love on this barren planet no matter who it's with. A few of us put the rations together into a semblance of a celebration feast. I hope you don't mind, but most of us are starving and I thought a little extra wouldn't be a bad start to things."

Aline glanced up to Lar, but he only narrowed his eyes at Gervin. Though the poor man had come out the worse during his attack on Aline in the breeding compound, his arm barely healed, she suspected Lar would hold a grudge for a while.

With an elbow to Lar's ribs, she gave Gervin a smile. "Of course we don't mind, as long as we aren't depleting the stores."

"No," Gervin reassured them. "Just some of the tastier options and slightly more than we'll probably be able to afford in the future. We're alive, we have a safe place and a plan, and we've just had a wedding. Some celebration would be good for morale."

"Thank you for putting forth the effort," said Aline, another elbow to Lar's ribs.

"Thanks," he grumbled.

After numerous hugs with Andi and Meladise, a few congratulations from Loren, Beyani, and those brave and open-minded enough to get close, Aline ate some of the food rations Gervin had set out. He was right, they'd seasoned and softened the meats, made fruit sauces with their precious clean water, and even managed some kind of cinnamon flat-bread for a dessert. It was good, but Aline couldn't eat much, her anticipation making her impatient.

"Is there any place we can go?" she asked Lar, her voice low.

"You mean to be alone?"

"No, I just wanted to roam around that half-dead sauna you call a jungle," Aline said with sarcasm. "It's our wedding night. Of course I mean to be alone. The cave is nice, but a little privacy..."

Lar chuckled, giving Aline his signature smirk. "There's my parents' old room. Why? Are you in a hurry?"

Two could play at this game. Aline placed her hands behind her, stretching languidly across the blanket they'd spread on the floor while they ate. "Nah. What's there to hurry about?"

Lar turned to the side, wrapping an arm around her waist. He kissed her, pressing his lips hard to hers, opening her mouth with his tongue, exploring with a need that made Aline burn hotter than Lenfay's twin suns. He turned his focus to her neck, nibbling his way to her collarbone.

"Get a room already!" yelled Gervin from a few meters away.

Lar pulled away and smiled. "I think that's our cue."

He stood, holding his hands out to Aline, lifting her to her feet. On their way to the back of the cave, Lar grabbed a lantern, illuminating a narrow fissure in the wall, obviously widened in places by man-made tools. Pulling Aline behind him, Lar stepped into the dark corridor.

"Are you sure there aren't wild animals or some horrible insects back here?" Aline asked.

With a comforting squeeze to her hand, Lar continued to pull her forward. "While the rest of us were unpacking and hiding the vehicles, I had Meladise clean this out. I assume she took care of any unwanted tenants."

That would explain Meladise's absence and the spot of blood that had been on her clothes. Had she killed a couple of leezards, or something larger? Aline decided she didn't want to know.

Another few meters and Lar pushed aside a dark drape, obviously taken from one of the ohfertsoogs and somehow attached to an old, rusty rod embedded into the rock.

Lar fingered the curtain before pulling Aline through. "As kids, we knew not to bother our parents when the curtain was pulled shut. Even before we knew what it meant, we understood that as the number two rule."

"What was number one?" asked Aline.

"Never go anywhere alone."

Aline would have asked more questions, but was distracted as the lantern illuminated a small cave, also enlarged by tools. Somehow, Meladise had found a store of mood-lights, the small kind about the size of a pinkie-nail, and had stuck them to the room's low ceiling. Lar had to hunch to get in and even Aline had to duck. Covering the floor were mats and cushions, also stolen from an ohfertsoog, and numerous blankets spread around for style. It certainly wasn't likely to get cool enough to need them.

Lar sat down, crossing his legs. Aline knelt facing him.

He brushed at the short hair above her ears. "Are you sure about this?"

Aline laughed. "Little late for that, don't you think?"

He dropped his hand. "I would understand if you still need more time. I know you want to help me with my severance, and that's probably why you were so willing to get married, but it's not worth rushing you into something that makes you nervous."

With a shove, Aline sent him back on the blankets, hopping on top of him to straddle his hips. She traced the line of scales from his neck, across his chest and abdomen, down to the edge of his trousers.

"Helping with your severance is an added bonus, but believe me, I wouldn't be enjoying myself this much if I was playing the martyr."

Lar grinned, but still looked unsure. "You could have had David, the handsomest guy on the Noble Ark."

Aline's hands stopped. "He was also a crazy psychopath rapist."

"Yes, but before you knew that, you thought you wanted to be with him."

Was Lar really this insecure about their relationship? "I was amazed he was interested in me, but whenever we were together I was uneasy. When things came close to this point, all I could think about was running away."

"It wasn't long ago that you felt the same about me."

"That was different. It wasn't you that made me uneasy, it was my fear that I would lose you."

"And Cloud? You slept in the same bed together. You didn't—"

Aline shifted off of him, sitting on the blankets. "I told you we never did anything. He tried, but every time we got close I thought of you and then I didn't want to be with him."

Lar leaned up on his elbows. "Are you sure?"

"Are you trying to ruin this?"

He reached a hand to her face, the gel of their skin rubbing together like it had so many times before. This time, at least, they'd found some of the manufactured stuff in the soog. It smelled almost nice compared to their homemade sludge.

His hand moved to Aline's neck, tracing the edge of her suit. "I don't want you to have any regrets."

"My only regret," said Aline, "is that I let you make me wait so long. Then we wouldn't be having this stupid conversation."

Laughing, Lar pulled Aline back on top of him, but immediately another worried frown creased his forehead. "I'm not sure how to go about this while keeping you covered and safe from our atmosphere."

Aline pulled at the adhesive fabric that held the suit tight around her neck. "You didn't think I would come prepared? I wasn't just fixing my hair in that soog." She rubbed her hand across her cream-slicked hair that was almost long enough to lie down.

Lar cocked his head, but his eyes remained fixed on Aline's finger as it moved to the velzip at the front of her outfit. She pulled a tube of cream from her pocket.

"I think I got it everywhere, but I brought some extra in case you wanted to help me out."

Lar took the cream and pulled the cloth from her shoulders. "Gladly."

"I love you," said Aline. "With all my heart, soul, and body."

Lar's gaze returned to her face. "I've loved you from the first moment I saw you."

Once, Aline had had a dream of Lar's hands in hers, before she'd known she was in love with him. Now, that dream turned to ecstasy.

They still had difficulties ahead. Like how they could possibly keep all the humans alive who now depended on them. And how they would get everyone off-planet when all they had were a couple of land vehicles. But as Lar's hands slid across her body, all their problems and questions faded from importance.

It was her and Lar, husband and wife, and for tonight, nothing else in the five-systems mattered.

Lenfay's Hell: Mankind's Redemption Book 4
Coming April 2016

Please leave honest reviews at Amazon, B&N, Kobo, Goodreads or your favorite retailer. Reviews help sales which help authors write more books.

Glossary of Terms

Allim: Alloy of various metals and Saeana-native organic matter; one of Lenfay's best trade goods and a primary source of income.

Altheria: The Saeanan pronunciation of Altherivan homeworld.

Avyon: Mwalgi grain with uses similar to wheat.

Barnal: Size of the average dog, barnals appear similar to a snail or slug but are part of the baeor family on Lenfay with similar scales to the vulfbaeor, Mwalgi, and other species with double-layered scales.

Beyesh: Upper-body clothing worn by child-bearing Mwalgi women to cover their breasts that develop in the late stages of pregnancy.

Bonding: the Mwalgi term for two people falling in love and becoming mates for life, their circleh doy changing to gold.

Brittle beetle: (1) Brown and white beetle native to Chaerli, often used in Chaerlish spiritual rituals. (2) Nicknamed bb's or bees by Saeanans, the brittle beetle can be used as an addictive narcotic in many forms, from raw to powder to viscous liquid.

Breeyae: (1) During bonding, the process by which the circleh-doy changes color. (2) Falling in love

Carpace: Large Mwalgi plant with spindly leaves and sharp tips. Roots smell and taste similar to Saeanan cinnamon.

Chaerli: The Saeanan pronunciation of the Chaerlish homeworld. The residents are often called Chaerlies.

Circleh doy: the membrane that circles a Mwalgi's iris. It changes to gold when a Mwalgi bonds and to black as they die. It can spread to encompass the entire eye socket.

Collections Camp: facilities on Lenfay where Saeanans are kept and their CSF harvested. They are expensive to maintain and difficult to keep staffed.

Desolashon (Desolation in English): The desert areas between the most habitable and populated areas of Lenfay and the uninhabitable equator region of the planet. Sometimes used as an expletive by Mwalgi. Also, the name of a Mwalgi vessel in the CSF Collections Fleet.

Diab-corbay (corbay): Devil's zucchini. Broad-leafed plant with black elongated fruit that make up a main staple in the Mwalgi diet.

Diseep d'All: Mwalgi religion based on belief in a single God who watches over the universe and creates balance. Devout followers believe in absolute honesty, fairness, defense of the oppressed, and the preservation of life.

Ellgot: native to Lenfay, Saeanans describe it as a sharp-clawed cross between a scaled ostrich and an angry cat.

Entrench: the point at which bonding becomes irreversible.

Fals-skalen: Manufactured Mwalgi scales designed by scientist, Segvalt Trovgar, used to repair damaged scales by integrating with the prontreer layer and mimicking real scales. Supposedly usable on Saeanan skin, though there is insufficient research in that area.

Feukayfa: A beetle on Lenfay that lives dormant deep underground during the hot seasons, will occasionally swarm in the cooler seasons as they scavenge for food and reproduce.

Five Systems: the Interstellar Council consists of five species living within five separate solar systems—Saeana with humans, Lenfay with Mwalgi, Vargal with the Vargaln, Chaerli with the Chaerlies, and Altheria with the Altherivans.

Holovid: Holographic 3-D video.

Hontselle: Red-dwarf sun around which Lenfay orbits. It is part of a binary star system with its sister-sun, Kraitselle, allowing Lenfay to resist being tidally locked.

Laypin: Rabbit-like animal indigenous to Lenfay with large ears, strong hindquarters, and skin similar to a snake's underbelly. They make intricate nests and their sharp front teeth can be used for forage or defense.

Lenfay: The name Mwalgi gave their homeworld.

Londarb tree: Similar to a very tall palm tree, londarb fruit can be a valuable source of food and moisture but is very difficult to obtain.

Mosemein: Also called Gevaulted or Chosen; Religion believing in the superiority of the Mwalgi race, their destiny to rule, and the subservient role Saeanans are meant to play. This is the primary religion on Lenfay.

LEV: Mwalgi words translate with the same first letters as English to

Land Enforcement Vehicle, a hovercraft armed with multiple KTR43 laser cannons that can be set to stun or kill, often used in mob situations.

Lerf: The pupae form of the feukayfa beetle on Lenfay, they feed on carpace root.

Neyell: Holiday on Lenfay celebrating the coolest day of the season with bright decorations, special foods, and an exchange of gifts.

Nyarhoond: black, pig-like animal raised as pets on Lenfay; sometimes used for food.

Ohfertsoog: Transport vehicle not dependent upon magnetic roads that uses gravitonics to hover over terrain of most types.

Pernais flower: Bright yellow annual that blooms atop the gernion cacti of northern Lenfay.

psf: Used to denote the years after a solar flare caused significant damage to Lenfay's populations. (vsf denotes the time before the solar flare.)

Potre: Mwalgi outer layer of scales. It's nearly impenetrable and heals quickly when damaged.

Pontreer: Mwalgi inner layer of scales. The pontreer does not heal and damage often leads to infection.

Renegot: Mwalgi whose need for CSF reaches extreme levels, causing an insanity that often results in mutilation of their victims.

Silyen flowers: Bright, night-blooming flowers that attract insects with their scent then closes on them, digesting them in their stalks.

Saeana: The name humans gave their homeworld upon arrival, after traveling for generations from their origin plant of Earth.

Sarzen: Similar to desert-rats in shape and size with three funneled tails that help moderate temperature and skin similar to pigs.

Severance: Mwalgi sickness caused by physical and/or emotional separation from their mate. If prolonged, the condition can be terminal.

Shlaka: A poisonous snake native to Lenfay identified by bright purple stripes, shlaka's live deep underground. They can regurgitate their body fat, leaving it near their hole's entrance to lure in prey.

Shvebon: Mwalgi word for a hovertrain terminal.

Skalwass: the translucent fluid inside Mwalgi scales.

Solmond: (1) slippery parasite that lives in mud and water on the

Mwalgi planet of Lenfay. (2) nickname given to Aline by Mwalgi collection soldiers.

Stomressers: Insects with solar-scales, they swarm in Lenfay's atmosphere, feeding off sunlight and any energy source that passes near. They rarely alight on land, and only on tall plants and in Lenfay's uninhabitable jungles.

Tengle bush: Plant that only extends its leaves under beneficial conditions and is otherwise dormant. Leaves are often used in healing poultices.

Tsefuur: (sometimes called comm-tsefies or tsefies): Saeanans owned by Mwalgi as a CSF supply. Sometimes the tsefuur may have bonded with a member of the family, giving them a higher status within the home than most tsefuurs might attain.

Vargal: The Saeanan pronunciation of the Vargaln's homeworld.

Velzip: a Velcro-style zipper. Run your finger up or down the teeth and they attach or release. Once locked at the end, the velzip remains strong until the lock is released.

Vetromlift: Space to planet elevator in geosynchronous orbit at certain locations of the planet, Lenfay.

Vulfbaeor: scale-covered predator that used to dominate Lenfay, but is now near extinction. Most scientists agree that Mwalgi evolved from vulfbaeors.

Military Ranks of Lenfay's CSF Collections Corp:
Personnen; Militarisse; Litund; Leutnant; Anvert; Howtman; Faynrik; Dankpol; Mistar; Opmistar; Morten

Main Ranks of Lenfay's Land Military: (not a comprehensive list)
Brigade; Berat; Hoptberat; Oberst; Directere; Contollair

Lenfay's Days of the Week: (LD=Light Day, DD=Dark Day)
Deesta (LD), Merkdi (DD), Donsta (LD), Fendi (DD), Somsta (LD), and Deemosh (DD).

Lenfay's Seasons:

Prehpay, Zomeh, and Secur are the hottest seasons. Erts, Vinteh, and Prontom are the cooler seasons.

Earth to Mwalgi age: (365 x (Earth age)) ÷ 192 = Mwalgi age
Earth to Saeana age: (Earth age) x .9411 = Saeanan age.

Acknowledgements

In Mwalgi Justice, everything changed. The environment, their circumstances, and Lar and Aline entered a difficult phase in their relationship. At least, difficult to write. I appreciate my family's patience as my mood swings seemed to emulate those of my characters. They put up with a lot and still manage to support my efforts. A special thanks to Samantha who cheers from a long distance, encouraging me despite her inability to participate in the process.

My cover artist, Suzanne Helmigh, fit me in despite an awesome Hobbit trip to New Zealand. Thanks, Suzanne. You're the best!

Through *Noble Ark*'s Howie Award win, I discovered editor Jen Hendricks. She's done a wonderful job with Fourteen (coming July 2015) and graciously accepted the job to edit Mwalgi Justice. She's been a delight to work with.

Hugs and more hugs to my fans/beta readers who gave me pre-publishing feedback: Quint Seymore, David and JoLynn Gould, Kaitlynn Tennant, and Donna Reed. Each one of you had great insights.

Fellow writer/reader, Sean Golden, author of *Warrior: Book 1 in the War Chronicles* found my books, enjoyed them, and agreed to do a cover quote. It's great to find new friends.

Last, but not least, a shout out to my writing group. We call ourselves *Group with No Name*, but I'm going to name a few. You guys helped me through the rough patches and made MJ 200% better than it would have been without you. John D. Payne, Ryan English, Daniel Braithwaite, Danielle Andrews, and Shelley Reddy, you make me look forward to Thursdays. Thank you for the support and the excellent feedback.

And to everyone who leaves reviews about the books you love, the entire writing community loves you back. You make our dreams possible.

About the Author

Colette Black keeps a dirty house and a clean mind (most of the time) as she types the stories swirling through her brain. Fascinated with early sci-fi horrors like *The Blob*, *Tarantula*, and *Planet of the Apes* she also grew to love great fantasy literature, such as C.S. Lewis' *Narnia* series, Terry Brooks *Shannara*, and Lloyd Alexander's *Chronicles of Prydain*. As the years passed and the pestering stories demanded they be told, it's no wonder that there's a little bit of science, fantasy, and horror in everything she writes...and romance. You must have romance.

Find out more at www. coletteblack.net